DANCE ON WILD I

There was a shaft of brightness coming out from the space in the stack; the old man ducked and waddled through the low passage. Stuart followed, his stunned surprise and disbelief more than redoubled.

The first thing he saw was a down-pointing propeller blade, long, heavy and polished, hugely powerful compared with the frail little mill of a modern trainer. There were four of them, great scythes of battle, gripped by the conical spinner. Beyond that there was no doubt at all, the unmistakable tapering shape of a legend. The skin was a dull metallic colour, all the paint long since flaked away. It sat with its elliptical wings spread in a big bunker of straw bales, the sides draped with black polythene fastened every few inches with a kind of thatching peg. Stuart made no attempt to hide his awe.

Also by Christopher Murphy

DANCE FOR A DIAMOND

and published by Corgi Books

DANCE ON WILD ICE

Christopher Murphy

CORGI BOOKS

DANCE ON WILD ICE

A CORGI BOOK 0 552 13330 2

First publication in Great Britain

PRINTING HISTORY
Corgi edition published 1989

The lyrics to 'I Will' by Chris De Burgh are reproduced
by kind permission of Chrysalis Music Ltd.

This book is set in 10pt Times

Corgi Books are published by Transworld Publishers Ltd.,
61–63 Uxbridge Road, Ealing, London W5 5SA, in Australia by
Transworld Publishers (Australia) Pty. Ltd., 15–23 Helles Avenue,
Moorebank, NSW 2170, and in New Zealand by Transworld
Publishers (N.Z.) Ltd., Cnr. Moselle and Waipareira Avenue,
Henderson, Auckland.

Reproduced, printed and bound in England by
Hazell Watson & Viney Ltd
Aylesbury, Bucks

My thanks again to all conspirators to
Dance for a Diamond and in addition:

Nora Belton
Robert Lamplough
Frederick Flower
Fernando Amat
Randolph Parker
Geoffrey Hamilton
Keith Halsey
Ken Wallis
Zuska Podolska
Adam Kolker
Jonas Kolker

Lala F
František A   } behind the Curtain
Rudi P

And again:
Dina Konečńa
Anthony Whitehead
Peter Grose

And finally my beloved Luisa for invaluable editorial aid
and re-alignment.

For Jessica

> Don't ask questions, it's a story!
> Old Jewish proverb.

. . . There can be few forms of employment more likely to guarantee disaster than a job where the husband is prohibited from telling his wife how he spends his days and nights, and that makes sudden, unannounced trips overseas frequent events.

Ted Allbeury, *Pay Any Price*

'Dance On Wild Ice'

By: Christopher Murphy

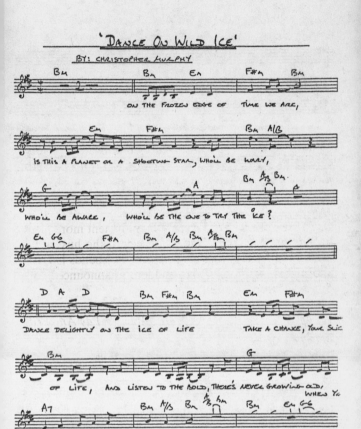

On the frozen edge of time we are,
is this a planet or a shooting star, who'll be wary,
who'll be aware, who'll be the one to try the ice?

Dance delightly on the ice of life   take a chance, your slic
of life, and listen to the bold, there's never growing old,
when yo
Keep on rolling the dice of life.

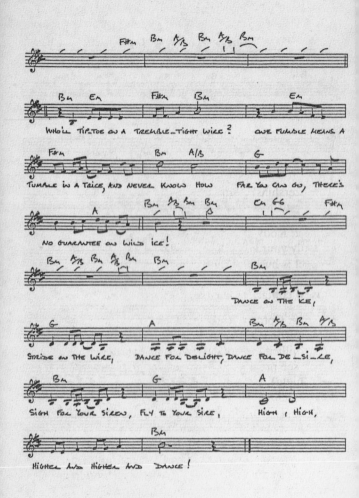

WHO'LL TIP-TOE ON A TREMBLE-TIGHT WIRE? ONE TUMBLE MEANS A

TUMBLE IN A TRICE, AND NEVER KNOW HOW FAR YOU CAN GO, THERE'S

NO GUARANTEE ON WILD ICE!

DANCE ON THE ICE,

STRIDE ON THE WIRE, DANCE FOR DELIGHT, DANCE FOR DE_SI_RE,

SIGH FOR YOUR SIREN, FLY TO YOUR SIRE, HIGH, HIGH,

HIGHER AND HIGHER AND DANCE!

PROLOGUE

CODING. NO COPY. DELETE/CONFIRM:
INITIAL SHREDDER TAG

From: RSMZ Antwerp
To: Dzershinsky Square.
   First Chief Directorate, Special Service II.

Subject: Kody S.   Ref.
In reply your last UK, strongly re-note this   UK922
contact is husband Ludmilla (Lucy) Simonova LE S.44
(my daughter). Request more delicate handling
in view contact's valuable posting.

Resumé: Contact Kody discovered/caught/freed
extra-curricular illegality (South Africa: Jo'B 85 H
carried illicit diamonds Transvaal–Swaziland
Sept., see previous: IDs concealed in fragments
windshield). Dept V, Evgeny Petrov, intercepted
this parcel Antwerp, for leverage on   VODS K267
contact. This office undertook its return in exchange
for priority info., see our memo. This   UK6818
info. since corroborated by field infiltration.   F.2232
Contact currently withholding further info. said
to be substantiating, while this office withholding
parcel. Reason given: your intransigence, real
reason: diamonds no longer in our possession.
Agent Petrov delivered parcel non-diamondiferous
window fragments, agent Petrov unable explain

discrepancy before his d. (cardiac failure,
see memo)   Petrov E. (d.)

Update: Sub your last, we to foster contact   UK922
Kody in accord scheme (my) previous
son-in-law.   Grady P. (d.)
We currently assembling parcel D and E flawless
Siberian rough whites to value U.S.$2 million,
min 2½ carat per piece.   RSMZ 98
In reply your suggest. that Kody was never in
possession, advise my memo   Grobelaar A.
corroborates recpt 3 exceptional pieces
separate main parcel, 1 E-White 45 carat cut by
Grobelaar to 26 and   de Hoek K. (d.)
sold (bribe), 1 Cape Pink approx 9 carat
cut to 6, delivered Ludmilla Kody Oct.
by G.W-Farquhar   W-Farquhar St G.
1 Cape Blue in possession diamantaire
Grobelaar awaiting instructions.
Arrest of IDB Runyan   Runyan R.
and contact Kody's altered lifestyle also
corroborates, assume based on expectations sale
of parcel, chartered execujet Dallas–Washington
(special conference Langley Va. [Stearman]) and
month's holiday Seychelles, according
CIA recds.   LaVa 86/202
Note also my previous ref SIS (Stayres)   Stayres A.
interest securing Kody after fixed W-term.

This day: await K's return and your instrs.
Owing heavy commitments (Paid bail Runyan and
sinister present interest Pte V. Cornelius,
AWOL SA Army) contact may be over-   Cornelius V.
compromised without his knowledge.
Advise ETR if known and subsequent
pressure/action directives.

A.A. Simonov.

ONE

'Courage is not measured by the issues of the battle.'
Barry Unsworth

It was an evening for quiet exhaustion, for a welcome home, not an unwelcome shock. In dark and drizzle, the minibus cruised through the long-term carpark dropping its weary travellers from Heathrow's Terminal 3. As it pulled away from him, Stuart Kody had no thought of it as a receding deterrent, an ally in the night. His immediate concern was whether the aging Datsun sports car would concede to a wintry start, so his only apprehension as he keyed the lock was for hostility of the mechanical kind.

He ducked in and swung his grip across the seat, hardly surprised that the interior light had failed but suddenly crawling with a horror that some dark reptile had fanged his hand and he had mere moments left. Whatever it was allowed him to pull away only slightly to avoid tearing his palm open but not enough for any other reaction. The pain was awful and briefly heightened with another jerk as the passenger door slammed shut. Stuart waited a long, rigid moment, all senses on emergency, desperate to assess what held him so viciously, bedded in the ball of his left thumb, the muscle tensed uselessly to resist it. Very carefully he explored with his other hand and felt a strong, taut line leading down between the seats. The nightmare quality of the trap on his travel-weary mind confused him badly, leaning

11

half into the car, bewildered, fighting panic and at the same time grateful that Lucy had waited in the baggage hall.

Over the top of the low roof a clipped, accented voice said, 'Right, hold it theer, Mister. I not keeps you. Just let go the bag, push it right across, easy does.'

The voice delved in his memory, an episode so gladly forgotten that full recall was reluctant and too slow. When he failed to respond promptly there came a sharp tug which sent violent twitches rasping up his arm as though a point was probing into bone. Still he didn't move as anger and outrage fought to dilute the pain. The passenger door was then wrenched open again, an arm snaked in to seize the bag and withdrew as quickly, Stuart's right hand failing to grip on slithery nylon. The trace tugged again, pulling his left hand down to the floor, forcing an anguished hiss through his teeth which he could feel sink numbly into the hard pressure of his jaws. The door slammed again as Stuart searched for the interior light, fumbled it on and saw the inch-long shank of the fish-hook embedded in the round of his thumb muscle, his distress worsened by certain knowledge of the damage to come: somewhere inside him was the no-retreat, the indisputable persuasion of the barb.

There was nothing in the bag worth the hold-up and only too late did he consider that equally there was nothing worth any pain of resistance. Anger overrode it; he passed a moment of brief dread, reached down and seized the hook, wrenching it out against the barb, an awful motion accompanied by a raw bass moan, but at once he was out and running, the dark attacker surprised and only yards away, fumbling with the bag's zipper, a bearded face and indistinct, nothing pale reflected except for the eyes. Aware of him the figure turned and tried to accelerate, feet slipping in a half fall, up again in a desperate lunge, swerving, finally dumping the bag at Stuart's feet. Stuart crashed headlong, cursing, wincing and furious, his left knee numbed and his assailant weaving out of sight, lost behind any number of silent dripping cars.

The whole sequence had lasted mere seconds so the bewildering information was still in process; he thought of Lucy waiting for him in the terminal and remembered he'd gone down fighting for his bag once before when it had contained little more than a change of clothes. He'd been left in an Antwerp street with just the handle, several rips in the clothes he'd been wearing, a few contusions and a later rebuke from Lucy for his pointless heroism. Still furious he got to his feet and looked around carefully before rummaging in the grip for something to wrap round his hand, feeling a steady dripping down his fingers. Inside he was mystified to discover a large hairy obstruction, instantly recognised as Lucy's *coco-de-mer*. He couldn't figure why she'd have put it in there at all, she'd been carrying it and nearly left it on the aircraft; perhaps she'd expected him to leave the bag but he'd remembered in time the parking ticket was in there somewhere, buried in a side pocket. She hadn't shown any sign of wanting to hide the libidinous-looking fruit, in fact she enjoyed flaunting its eccentric pubescence.

His jaw muscles still taut against the throbbing of his wound, he wrapped his hand in a soiled T-shirt, recovering slowly from the shock. Warily he returned to the Datsun, got in and promptly locked the doors. To his immense relief it started after some coaxing and he eased round to the pay-booth, uncaring of the sizeable cost of a month's parking and only urgent to get home. His hand pulsed wickedly inside the rough wad of cotton but being on the English shift-side it didn't hinder his driving. The wipers snickered at the drizzle spreading diamond lights on the glass and the cold London air seemed a relief after weeks of Indian Ocean sun.

At Terminal 3, Lucy waited just inside the glass door,

peering impatiently. A man stood next to her, silver-haired and suave-looking, and though wearing a three hundred dollar raincoat he still seemed an acolyte to her sunny radiance. She wore a too-long yellow oilskin top, slim legs disappearing into coloured leg warmers, one red, one green, port and starboard, and a battered sou'wester hung from her neck. When Stuart got out and stood, she turned to the man, said something and nodded, pushing her trolley towards the automatic doors, the man following casually. Stuart ducked in again to unlock the other side, wrapping his hand more tightly and keeping it out of sight. He hoped nothing streaked his face, requiring explanations when he only wanted to get going. Lucy looked suddenly chilled as a gust of drizzle whipped at her, swirling lights in her hair.

'You get in, Lu,' he called, 'I'll get the bags.' As she subsided gratefully he asked, 'Who's your friend?'

'Yours. Says he was waiting for you but you were too quick for him. Something about Washington D.C. Mean anything?'

Stuart breathed out a disgusted monosyllable and went round the car, unlocking the rear. He nodded briefly to the raincoat and put the luggage away, momentarily startled to see a second *coco-de-mer* but too preoccupied with discomfort and impatience to give it any thought.

'What is it?' he asked finally, closing the lid.

'Can we go under cover a moment?' the man replied, 'No point suffering.' The accent was mid-Atlantic, calm with authority.

Stuart blew out his cheeks impatiently and rattled the keys. 'Wait a moment. I'll start the car again, for the heater.'

'Here, gimme,' Lucy's voice came from the nearside, practical or expedient.

Stuart passed them to her and watched her wind up the

14

window, pull a face and start to worm herself across to the driver's side. He turned and accompanied the stranger back into the warmth of the building.

'Lot of folks looking out for you,' said the man, holding out his hand. 'I wanted to be the first. My name's Epiphany, Paul.'

'CIA?'

'No, but I know a few of them. I heard they dropped you right in it, and I might be able to help.'

Stuart frowned doubtfully. 'Names?'

A hand swept off in a Westerly direction. 'In Langley, Virginia, Mr Stearman.'

Stuart nodded. 'I met only him, apart from a hooligan called Randolph.'

'The man over here is called Riverson. He wants a word and—'

'Listen, I'm not interested,' Stuart said firmly, 'I'm out of it, in fact I was never in. I earned my pay-off and that's it. What do you mean, dropped me in it?'

'Did you check with your bank?'

At least there was no hint of triumph in the voice, only concern, but Stuart's midriff contracted viciously. He said nothing but watched the American's eyes, grey-blue under the muted strip-light. He saw eventual confirmation, a small repeated nod.

'I had a draft on the U.S. Treasury,' Stuart said ponderously, as if the phrase excluded any possible misfeasance.

Epiphany shrugged. 'I've said nothing. Meanwhile, in that direction, East-a-ways,' he pointed over the pale orange glow of the distant metropolis, 'Somebody you know in Belgium, wants something from you, yes? I strongly suggest you talk to me first and, in order to do so, I suggest we don't stand here. Riverson would have hauled you off to the Embassy, so the best bet is to pre-empt him.'

15

'Look, we're exhausted, we've been a day travelling, we just want to get home.'

Epiphany nodded sympathetically. 'Maybe your wife'd like to head home and I'll have you brought back tomorrow?'

Stuart shook his head. 'Come on, she's never driven that car before, and the house has been closed up for a month.'

The American's eyes watched him directly. 'Ask her if she's willing? Department business, urgent, huh?'

Stuart was suddenly aware again of the throbbing in his hand and his wish to keep it from Lucy. Without a word he breasted the automatic doors and went out to the car where she now sat behind the wheel to keep the engine above tick-over. At his tap she rolled the window down, releasing warm air, slightly scented, alluring.

'Man wants me in Town, Lu, just till tomorrow, something urgent. Do you want to come and stay in a hotel or go on home? I'm really sorry.'

After a brief look of disgust Lucy shook her hair and put a hand on his. 'It's OK, if you've got to, I'd rather go home.'

'You don't know the car.'

'I just worked it out, don't worry. Feels fun, *sportif*.'

Stuart's mouth curled again. 'All right, I'll just get my grip.' He walked round, opened the other door and reached in the back, to be intercepted with a soft kiss redolent of a month's tropical delirium. He was about to finger her hair when he remembered the bunched cotton round his hand. It felt awkward pulling away without touching her but he had little choice, fuddled in his surprise that she could be so blithe and understanding. She blipped the big engine's throttle and gave him a slight grin, forcing a similar response. He shut the door and put his lips to the glass; the high clutch-point was unfamiliar to her and the rear wheels spun slightly before gripping, then she was gone, lost among the other red swirling

16

fireflies. She hadn't even asked directions, Stuart worried, knowing it wasn't easy traversing the radials out of London.

His following thoughts were cut short by a double presence, the weighty purr of a great grey Bentley coming alongside like an admiral's launch and the American striding out from the terminal, naturally.

'Too early for a Scotch?' The man called Epiphany had left the light on in the partitioned rear of the Bentley, reaching into the walnut cabinet and then unfolding a table. The car swept them away like royalty.

Stuart looked at him anxiously, rocking his hand to show he was persuadable. The American had folded his raincoat and wore a trimly-cut sky-blue suit over a shantung silk shirt. He had a gold watchstrap that looked heavy enough to keep its owner aware of it and at his feet lay a worn but durable elk-hide briefcase. It seemed the more important for containing little. The owner seemed to radiate confidence as though he'd done all the right character-projection courses and for a grand cynical moment Stuart felt like asking him if he was going to open a new car-plant in Northern Ireland. He had the eager sheen of the soon-to-be super-rich.

Aware of Stuart's anxiety, the American poured generously and pointed to the ice-bucket. He saw Stuart nod, a deep frown creasing the younger man's face, pleasantly boyish under short curly brown hair. He'd seemed brisk and efficient and walked with gathered grace but stocky, like a good games player.

The American had also heard he'd shown remarkable self-possession in a recent crisis and wondered now if he could elicit any bravado.

'The draft on the U.S. Treasury,' he said, 'I didn't hear what it was for, exactly.'

17

'Six hundred thousand dollars,' Stuart answered, sounding as though the sum really impressed him. 'What—'

'I meant, what did you deliver? That's quite a pay-off.'

'Just an aeroplane. I wasn't working for Langley, I wasn't even pretending to.'

'Tell me.'

Stuart sighed and was about to explain when an anomaly occurred to him. 'Listen, where do you come into this if you don't know? Where exactly are we going, anyway?'

Having put this edge in the air, he felt constrained to lower his tumbler without sipping.

The answer was placid, reassuring. 'Grosvenor Square . . . I'd just like to hear your version, I'll tell you about me in a moment. Way I heard it, you were being flown from Dallas to Washington on some little business jet, something happened and you had to take over. Thing was, you demanded salvage, from the air, before landing. I don't see what else you could do, threaten *not* to land it?'

Some expensive dentistry gleamed in the amber light and Stuart responded with a diffident half-smile. The episode was also part-buried by great effort, along with all the rest he'd kept from Lucy.

'I'm very low hours, just a student pilot on small club planes. When this happened, a CIA agent went berserk and killed one of the pilots, K.O.'d the other. I had the notion I'd have more chance ditching in the Chesapeake than trying to find a runway. It would have cost them the aircraft and raised a few questions as well, I suppose, so they asked me not to. Agreed on twenty per cent of the hull value.'

Epiphany pursed his lips in restrained admiration. 'Questions yes, indeed. So you got lucky.'

'I did?' Stuart made no attempt to cover his sarcasm.

'Sure, it's a lotta cash, even if you haven't got it! Why were you in Dallas?'

'Flying school, pure and simple. There's good weather and they're cheap and efficient.'

'You were in a hurry? Why don't you enjoy your drink, I'll join you if you like. I'm a bit overloaded, on Concorde they stuff you with caviar and lobster but the damn thing's so fast you don't get enough time to enjoy it. They should do a real fancy doggy-bag . . . I've got a Peace Offering for your lady, somewhere.'

'Thanks. Are you going to tell me the rest of it, why you met me, why they're messing me about—'

Epiphany held up his hand to interrupt. 'You'll be asked to a different ball-game. They've found out you're embarrassed financially and they're about to turn the screws, get you to do something for them. I've just stolen you a little time, that's all.'

The heavy car swept down the glistening outside lane of the M4. A magic carpet on a cushion of air. The rush hour streamed mercifully in the opposite direction.

'I came into it almost by accident. Really, I'm just a teacher, you could say. I began with a seminar training scheme, you know, awareness and confrontation.'

'Encounter group, like "est"?' Stuart offered, puzzled when it was confirmed. 'Oh. They got a dubious press over here.'

'I know,' Epiphany chuckled. 'Even I can make it sound screwball: you get a few dozen people locked in a room for three days, give 'em hell and by the time you let them out they're so grateful that they love the trainer, love each other, love themselves even, and not mind all the money they've been charged. At first they didn't screen properly, got too many crazies and half-wits. I moved up the intellectual market some and suddenly it was a different bag of beans.'

He paused to sip and Stuart asked, 'Is Epiphany a given name?'

The American gleamed approvingly. 'No, I got screwed over by the "est" man. He changed *his* name to Werner Erhard. Erhard was *my* name!' He gave a short laugh and then followed Stuart's not so responsive glance as he adjusted his makeshift bandage.

'What's that on your hand?'

Stuart hesitated a moment before replying. 'I snagged it on something when I went for the car. It's a mess, actually, hurts like hell. I'm not sure what to do about it.'

'You want me to take a look?'

Stuart shook his head. 'I wouldn't want to leak on your smart leather seats.'

'OK, let's see if we can lay something on.' Epiphany lifted the car phone out of a recess and fingered buttons. As he waited he asked, 'Why did you hide it from your wife?'

Stuart shrugged. 'Recent habit . . . I was jumped, a guy was waiting in the car. I had time to work out who it was as I drove back. It's part of a whole episode I had to keep from her.'

Epiphany nodded but with surprise in his voice. 'Cornelius,' he said firmly, distracted by the telephone answering. Stuart regarded him with astonishment as he spoke into the handset, the words obscured except one which puzzled him: 'Shellshock'. He wanted to deny showing any such symptom. In some agitation he wondered who else had been expecting them at London Airport, asking the question as soon as Epiphany put the phone away.

'There was an agent I know, waiting with your photograph. I talked him up and then I had him paged just when your plane load hit the baggage hall, then I talked my way in past Customs. I missed you because you didn't hang around. I had to guess at your lady from a description. It was pretty easy, she looked as though she'd been

20

sun-and-sea-faring and she was jouncing a giant double nut, shaped like a girl's butt and underparts. She introduced me to it, called it "Pudenda".'

'The second— ' Stuart gave up on that mystery and asked with a smile, 'How did you know we were coming in?'

'Airline computers. I got the word in Washington just before I left. Langley knew you were safely out of the way and where, they were all set to contact you when you came home.'

'So who told Cornelius?'

'Ah. I was going to warn you about him but I guess he was quicker. I'm sorry. He knew when you were leaving the Seychelles, he was in Mahé, took the flight before yours.'

Stuart was baffled. 'But how— ?'

'He'd rumbled a friend of yours, someone called Runyan?' Seeing Stuart's pained surprise he added, 'You know where that was? A certain little sloop in Victoria harbour, so carefully secured and locked up by you yesterday, provisioned and sailed this afternoon, one white man limping and a local girl. Gone Fishin', all he wrote. Who owns the yacht?'

Rollo Runyan . . . Stuart thought furiously of his friend's double-dealing, lacking the guts to face him, waiting till he and Lucy had left before sneaking aboard. Epiphany watched for a moment, quizzically.

'I guess from your expression that you're not brimming with charitable thoughts.'

Stuart nodded grimly. 'He's the only one apart from me and Lucy who knows *Sailor V*'s security system.'

'"Sailor Vee", you don't say "Five"?'

'No, it was some ignorant Queenslander's way of spelling *C'est la Vie*. Runyan won her in a poker game.'

Epiphany chuckled delightedly but Stuart still simmered, the rip in his hand only the latest in a series of Rollo-based torments.

21

'This Runyan was jailed,' Epiphany said, 'In Johannesburg, suspicion of smuggling diamonds out of South Africa. Someone paid his bail, 150,000 Rand and he jumped it. I guess that was you?'

After hesitation, Stuart acknowledged. 'Yes . . . I should be double-scared here. You know all about me and you've pre-empted the CIA. What's your angle?'

'I could tell you more but it's best you get it first from them, for a natural reaction. After that I think we can work something together, maybe: if not, there's no harm done. I can tell you they want you in for the contact you made, in Antwerp, the Russian called Simonov. Remember they got that from your Foreign Office, you'd spoofed this guy that the missiles we'd just delivered were dummies, right? You confessed to your F.O. what you'd done, to cover your rear, inventing a spy-role for yourself as well as inventing the information. Just wild! What I didn't hear was why you'd done it?'

All for Lucy . . . Stuart shook his head at his own entanglement, like a spider who's missed one vital delay. 'Does it matter?'

'I dunno. What I do know is that for some reason you were to give this Simonov some more stuff and presumably he was going to do something for you. That "more stuff" is what Langley seems set to prevent.'

Irked at this mounting foolishness, Stuart protested. 'But I'd levelled with them. It's just more harmless fiction.'

Epiphany shook his head dubiously. 'I wonder . . . The first piece turned out real enough. Either there's something to the rest of it or else it's so ridiculous that you'd lose credibility with this Simonov and be no further use as a conduit.'

'A conduit? . . . Oh, for *Official* misinformation?'

'Check, you got it.' Epiphany nodded patient approval.

'I see . . . So Moscow foots the bill for whatever Langley proposes I tell them?'

The American shook his head, snorting gently. 'Too subtle. Anyway, what'd you do with the roubles, count 'em? They don't have dollars to be free with. Let me slip a little thought in your head: you take one cent from Antwerp – Moscow in other words – and they can have you chopped for treason.'

'Meanwhile, you're implying, they've stapled up my wallet?'

'I haven't told you that, remember.'

Stuart shrugged, trying to suppress his dread. 'Look, Simonov owes me. The information was just an excuse for him to cough up. His boys robbed me in Antwerp, the heist went missing and now he wants to pay me back. In kind.'

Epiphany nodded as if he'd known this and Stuart added, 'I told Stearman in Langley what else I was going to pass on to Simonov and he said "Go ahead, just let us know when you do it." He thought it was a great idea.'

'So what was it?'

Stuart smiled sceptically. 'I'm sure you already know, if you don't, you might give a thought to what it's worth. And not in roubles. It's simply the reason *why* the Americans had omitted to arm the Cruise and Pershings.'

A horn blared suddenly beside them, a smaller car balked by their impervious driver. There came a sound like an ocean-liner giving due warning and he realised it was the Bentley's horn trying to command the flow into the Cromwell Road. The driver's voice came through a loud speaker: 'Sir, that's an Embassy car, trying to cut in on us.'

Epiphany touched a button and replied, 'Just ignore him, Dudley. Lose him if you can.'

The car surged powerfully as Stuart glanced around looking for the menace. 'Did you know that Simonov

23

has a reason to favour me?' he asked, 'He's my father-in-law. My wife is Russian-born, Ludmilla. She changed it to avoid the obvious question all the time. That's one of the reasons he'd come through, another is that I have something on him, a crime he committed over here, after he'd been expelled.'

'When was that?'

'1971.'

'Ah, all those fake diplomats putsched home from the Soviet Embassy here? So how come he shows up in Antwerp?'

'He's always claimed to be just a commercial attaché, so now he's with Russalmaz, a diamond exporter.'

'That's just a front, a KGB listening post under a trade banner.'

'Whatever it is, there's nothing treasonable about giving him false information.'

'Maybe not,' Epiphany agreed, 'I see your point, unless your next invention turns out to be true, like the last one.'

'It's still not treason,' Stuart said, his protest covering a half-chuckle. 'It's a Russian secret being told to Russians.'

'You mean they don't know their own?' Epiphany's conspiratorial grin gave away no inkling of other knowledge.

'Not this one,' Stuart replied, 'It's still in my head.'

'But it'll get you dead unless it stays there, if it's untrue.'

'It's uncheckable.'

'Are you sure?' Epiphany said with quiet emphasis. 'Anyway, let's leave it for now, we're almost there. I'll take you in and get your hand fixed, then I'll have to leave you to Riverson. We can talk some more afterwards.'

The Bentley left Park Lane and swung into Grosvenor Square, 'Little America', where a line of barriers stood on the edge of the pavement, a sign of grim times, to prevent vehicles from getting within a bomb blast of the Embassy doors. The entire entrance and foyer were also a bastion of bullet-proof glass and self-locking compartments. Epiphany was waved through the checks but Stuart was scanned and his bag searched; the *coco-de-mer* excited mild suspicion and a solemn rite of passage through the scanner. Once admitted to the foyer proper, Stuart was given a visitor's tag and cautioned to wear it at all times. The elevator, he noticed, served nine floors, only six of them above ground with nothing to show the depth of excavation.

For Lucy the rain lashed in squalls and the car was unfamiliar, yet, even tired after the long flight, she had some excitement in going home alone. By this time she was sure there'd be a large crate waiting for her and she wondered deliciously how long she could keep it a secret. The driving and the rain absorbed most of her concentration but she hoped fervently that Stuart wouldn't be sent away again except for daytime jobs so she could get on with mounting her surprise – literally, she thought with a chuckle in the darkness. She was startled when the tape-player reached the end of a blank, reversed and began unbidden with a Chris De Burgh:

I'm going to an island where the sun will always shine,
Where the moon is always riding on the sea.
And when I go I'll leave behind these chains that
   hold me down,
The time has come to set my spirit free – I will!

Lucy sighed in happy memory, feeling the sensuousness of the last month and now the unusual stretching out of her legs in the low-slung machine. Sports cars were definitely sexier, she decided, but far too blatant: sensuous is subtlety.

The rain had cleared by the time she reached home and the house showed a welcoming light upstairs. She guessed it was only the time-switch as soon as she unlocked the door for inside it was cold and empty of vibrations. She turned on the heating and discarded unaccustomed shoes, flexing her feet deliciously in woollen carpeting. Glancing at her watch she toyed with the urge to hear a familiar voice and then took aim for the telephone in the corner. It was one of her zanier stunts to take a running leap at the pile of cushions, half-turning in the air as she gathered her legs up in her arms. The rump-first landing was normal but for once her mother had obeyed the house rule and hidden the television, lazily choosing the nearest cushions. Lucy knew at once what the ominous cracking signified; she closed her eyes and decided not to look, instead straightening her legs and pulling her head between them into a deep, satisfying compression. Having been without television for a month, she actually felt a certain triumph for what had happened. She rubbed at her backside and giggled ruefully. Relaxing, she picked up the phone and tried her neighbour first but he was, as expected, absent, doubtless still in the pub. She thought for a moment and then said aloud. 'Ah, hah, my beatified Baronet.' From the little book she dialled again and the call was answered at once, the voice peremptory and suspicious with affront.

'Hair?'

'St George, is it you? Look, the word is "hello"!'

'I nair . . . splendid! When did you get back? Where did you hide? Did your rotten husband find you?'

'Yes, he did, bless him. We went sailing again, second honeymoon. That's every year so far. Just got back and they grabbed him at the airport. I can't decide whether to feel important or bereft.'

'Where d'you gair?'

'Seychelles. It was perfect, like last time, we borrowed a boat.'

26

'Good-oh. How was he? Bit rattled when last I spoke to him but then so were you.'

'Yes, he was a bit tense to start with, especially refusing to go and help his friend in Durban, but later he laughed a lot and at nothing much. About normal now, I'd say. I think he'd been through the wringer but he had to keep it to himself, of course. I'm getting used to it slowly and soon I'll be ready to get my own back.'

'Ah. I'll be in Oxford tomorrow, you still want the camera?'

'Absolutely, yes please, that's a vital part of it.'

After fixing a rendezvous she hung up and went out with a flashlight into the long garden to whisper hellos to her plants and shrubs. She complained loudly about their unkempt looks but was grateful for the cold keeping random growth to a minimum. She felt spoilt in comparison, fit and tanned to deepest honey, her tawny hair streaked by the Indian Ocean's ferocious sun. After the spell of extreme heat she felt strangely refreshed by the November night wind; Russian blood, she mused, and wondered again how her mother was faring in the friendly squalor of the peace camp. Having boarded at an English ballet school and having a good musical ear Lucy had no trace of her childhood accent in spite of its marked remnant in her mother Alicia, a severe and somewhat humourless person although to Lucy eminently teasable. A long-estranged and mischievous husband had soured Alicia against mankind and heightened her protectiveness for their only child, an attitude that would have had Stuart constantly on the defensive but for Lucy's bantering support.

The house, a random stone cottage converted from a derelict barn, was clean and fairly recently dusted so she assumed that her mother was still basking in courage and defiance at the peace camp but sneaking off once a week to hitch-hike the forty-odd miles for a hot bath and a change of clothes. The fridge was stocked with

27

essentials and there was a single plate on the drainer, a kind of statement that Alicia had obeyed the injunction not to bring a troop of her new-found cronies.

There were too many things she wanted to do at once but after taking her small amount of luggage upstairs and simply upending it on the bedroom floor, she undressed and showered with great relief, pleased to see herself full-length in a mirror after four weeks almost without amenities. She had a detached gratitude for her physique, it was exactly what she would have ordered, small, neat and tautly-rounded, her fine muscle tone burnished by the sun and sea-winds. Sideways she pouted her chest for firmness, laughing to herself at Stuart's teasing compliment about her usefulness on a boat, that she couldn't hold a cigarette paper under one of her breasts, let alone something useful like a winch-handle. She did some bends and stretches distractedly but soon gave it up and dressed again in a hurry, knowing she couldn't wait any longer, even if somehow Stuart arrived and asked ruinous questions. She took the stairs in her usual two reckless leaps and ran out down the lane to their nearest neighbour's house. Humphrey Horrock's car wasn't there but through the small rear entrance to his double garage her flashlight showed the dim outline of a huge packing case. Lucy felt like a burglar and her heart pounded softly with that special excitement which comes with the realisation of a dream only half-believed-in.

From Simon's Wood an owl hooted distantly while around her the night noises seemed normal, but as she crept out again and back to the road she had a sudden strong awareness of a sinister interest, that unseen eyes had marked her passing. Although intent on walking briskly the one long field's length and exploring the hedges with the wand of light, her instinct unexpectedly overcame her spirit's elation with an urgent shiver. Clicking off the betraying light she started to run, almost involuntarily, fluid and lithe but swishing audibly in the dark, her cotton skirt pulling at her legs, an unfamiliar constraint after weeks of careless nakedness. Minutes earlier she'd been feeling in love with excitement, with the optimism of boundless possibilities; now the chill and something indefinable had put her to unreasoning flight. Curiously, with such a certainty that her dash was seen or overheard, she regathered her control and pulled herself back to a stride, refusing to heed dark precaution or any prescient inner warning.

Reaching her front door she turned and gestured defiantly into the dark but then scampered quickly inside as if in self-mockery. She felt thankful for the weight of the door as she heaved it closed, a welcome solidity.

It was gratitude too that brought a smile to her eyes on the point of sleeping, for just around eleven o'clock the telephone warbled shrilly, once, cancelling alarms. It seemed as if nothing had changed, the course was steady and the watch above calling: six bells and all's well.

Stuart closed his eyes wearily as the elevator surged upwards and he suddenly thought of the Embassy as a control tower or 'island' when he recalled a cartoon sketch in which, the British Isles were shown as an aircraft carrier steaming up the North Sea at flank speed, with angled decks and launch-catapults, cluttered with American jets, helicopters and a huge array of armaments. The first Cruise missiles had long been delivered and sparked off the Women's Peace Movement, the gate camps which had created so much admiration, scorn and even hatred. His own mother-in-law had joined them a month previously; Russian by birth and marriage but now naturalised, she stood firm against nuclear arms, international tension, espionage, adultery and anything else represented by her errant husband.

Lucy had relayed a vivid picture of the pathetic tiny tents of polythene stretched awkwardly on bent branches, opaque with moisture and protecting some ragged-clothed martyr against outside rain but not against inside condensation, earth-damp, mildew and natural griminess from extended denial of facilities.

The description of these dripping ghostly sheets of plastic and the shivering soulful bundles they contained extinguished any spark of humour born of safely distant comfort and indifference. Lucy had however leavened it with a delightful flash of eyes, that really her mother had only decided to join when she heard Stuart's primary piece of 'inside' information, that the missiles were blanks and that it was therefore technically safe to be around them.

Epiphany led him into a small bright windowless office with Swedish style furniture. One wall had a bank of keyboards, screens and printers. He looked round distastefully as if to emphasise it had nothing to do with him.

'Y'know, they've shown that people are up to 30 per cent less efficient when working under fluorescent light. Imagine what that does in schools?'

There was a sharp knock on the door and the doctor came in with an oversized case. He was sallow, bald and taciturn to absurdity; without a word he went to a cupboard, poured himself a shot of expensive malt whisky, waved the bottle interrogatively at the two men and then put it away. He sipped his drink and then balefully unwrapped Stuart's hand for him. Opening the case and brandishing a syringe, he gave him a local anaesthetic, drank some of the whisky and then cut open a prepared suture. Stuart looked away to avoid dizziness but felt as though torn flesh was being pushed back into the dome of muscle. At least it didn't hurt any more and he was too tired to care about details. When next he looked there were three minute and perfect stitches.

'Possible tetanus?' the doctor almost growled.

'Doubt it. It looked like a brand new fish-hook. Shiny.'

''Kay. These pills, pain killers. Take it easy.'

'Thanks.'

'Yeah.' He closed the case, drained his glass, nodded to Epiphany and left.

'Doc Shellshock, they call him. Don't ask why . . . A fish-hook did you say? What for?'

'I suppose it was to hold me in place while he made off with something.'

'Moses! . . . What did you do?'

'Pulled it out.'

'But you're supposed to push them right through, for the barb – oh, I see, forgive me.' Epiphany grimaced and reached into the elk-hide case, riffled and produced a photograph.

'This office belongs to the Resident Company man, Riverson. You can say I brought you right here, all right? I don't know what's holding him up, but I don't suppose he'll be too pleased with me. The Brits have issued a photograph, identikit beard added. You recognise it?'

'Cornelius.' Stuart said promptly.

'OK. What's he want from you anyway? I guess something to do with your friend Runyan and illicit diamonds?'

Stuart nodded ponderously. 'I'd almost forgotten about him. He shot a fellow soldier and would have killed me too. I made a bargain with him, with some diamonds I was supposed to be carrying.'

'You mean you weren't?'

Stuart shrugged almost dismally. 'I thought I was.'

Epiphany's mind jumped sharply, his eyes gleaming with mischief. 'So – in Antwerp, what were you robbed *of*?'

Stuart hesitated, his mouth turned down. 'Simonov doesn't know this, you understand?' When Epiphany nodded seriously, Stuart scowled and said, 'Glass . . . The diamonds never left South Africa. Rollo— '

'But Simonov doesn't know and wants to make it up to you, I get it! What was the parcel worth?'

Stuart hesitated for some moments in resentment at

being over-drawn. With a wry face he held up two fingers.

Epiphany merely nodded, his lack of surprise surprising Stuart. 'Two million . . . Dollars, I take it? And you've no idea where they ended up?'

'No, no idea. But this renegade Cornelius must think differently, on the run for murder and mad that he got nothing for it, nothing to lose.' Stuart went still, a thought snaking through entrails of fear. 'He might know where I live, be heading there now.'

Epiphany allayed him with a gesture. 'Hasn't been here long enough. Only got in this morning. The Resident, Riverson, found out too late, again, but there's a net prepared for you. They're taking you seriously, as an asset, just in case the South Africans don't catch him first. Don't worry on that score, right?' He picked up the phone and asked 'Did Mr Riverson get in yet?' He gave a mystified shrug at the answer and smiled at Stuart.

'When he does, I suggest you stick with your outrage and promise to do as he tells you. Then come and see me, I may have a different angle for you . . . Tell me, why were you in a hurry for your licence, the flying? Was it departmental urging?'

Stuart's puzzlement bordered on annoyance. 'That sounds like a trap question. I don't work for any department, for anyone. After I got stitched by Rollo, by chance I met someone with a proposition for me involving some quick cash, for which I had to be air-worthy.'

'Helicopter as well?'

Stuart shook his head. 'I did that just because I was there, a little bonus, it sounded like I'd make enough to afford it.'

'Is it still open, as an option?'

'I don't know. I hate to think. It was a desperate measure. Why do you ask?'

'I'm checking your motive status. I've got a feeling that

Riverson is going to bluster and threaten and you're not the type to listen.' He glanced at the dressing on Stuart's hand. 'Your type pulls the hook, barb and all.'

Freshly aware of the effect of pain on bravado, Stuart said, 'I hope they're right about fish, not feeling pain.'

'Baloney. A myth put about by the Catholics. Even grass screams when you mow it.' Epiphany smiled in bland acceptance. 'I've got to go now, I'll see you tomorrow or whenever. Here's my address, it's only about three blocks East. If Riverson doesn't come soon I should go and get something to eat. OK? *Hasta mañana.*'

'*Ano.*'

'What?'

Stuart grinned. 'It's Czech for "Yes". My first language, as I'm sure you know. I'll lay odds it's why they want me.'

Epiphany's expression betrayed neither confirmation nor denial and only later did Stuart realise what connivance that implied.

TWO

'Married women are kept women – and they're beginning to find it out.'

L.P. Smith

Triggered perhaps by his conversation with Epiphany and
the reference to his desperate measure, Stuart's unconscious wandered where he seldom allowed his waking
hours, a vivid dream of flight. He wondered if his father's
friend Jára had been anything like Rollo, inventive,
troublesome and fascinating in his energy for mischief.

It was surely different then, two dashing young Czechs
fighting from a foreign country and with little left to be
pillaged. They'd flown the 1940 crisis together after a
frantic dash for freedom from the Nazis, they'd both
been shot down several times, frequently separated by
postings or hospitalisation and finally accompanied the
invasion of Europe in their fighters as troop support
and as tank- and train-stoppers. Jaroslav had eight kills
in the air, his father seven. Their survival through such
times was almost miraculous considering the odds – and
then, in the final days, on a simple reconnaissance patrol
close to the Czech border with Southern Germany, Jára
hadn't been able to resist the 70 mile low-level dash to
zoom and roll over his parents' farm near Rakovnik;
the diversion there and back in a Mark IX should only
have taken 25 minutes and Karel Kody waited, circling
for a full despairing hour, his fuel-state becoming critical and forcing him down well short of his base for an

awkward enquiry. He made special efforts not to speak too sadly of Jaroslav afterwards but, in his dream, Stuart put his hand on his father's shoulder to comfort him; in reality he'd merely listened wide-eyed to tales of horror and hilarity with the underlying pang of envy which an intense reminiscence can provoke. He was in the cockpit where he'd never sat, only been held over close enough to be infected by others' awe, to marvel at the Spitfire's astonishing elegance and beauty of line, yet the cockpit and fittings were so crude and wartime stark; to gaze in wonder along the great length of cowling which obscured forward vision until a good fifty knots of airflow raised the tail. The baritone and unmistakeable growl of seventeen hundred horsepower, and he'd asked why it was horsepower in the air; instead of mocking him, his father had nodded and agreed that the mighty Merlins weren't horses but lions, great-hearted English lions all fierce, aloof and invincible. And even in the dream there was fear in unleashing them, too quick on the throttle and the massive torque would slew a rattling airframe violently to port and to probable casualty upside down in a ditch, the muted lions smoking, fuming in disgust at all the wasted roar and adrenalin.

He awoke musing nervously on the dream's significance, fumbling for a switch in a strange place, the light revealing a small spartan room with a sealed and opaque window. He recalled the long frustrating wait and eventual search for something to eat in this most expensive part of town, his gratitude at somewhere to sleep, still not yet interviewed by the Resident. He also felt surprise at remembering so easily the name of his father's friend, the village he'd gone to buzz and the airfield base in Germany. He also enjoyed the metaphor with a smile and thought of St George Wennersley-Farquhar, an ascetic-looking toffee-nosed aristocrat, a most unlikely lion-tamer with his slim, fastidious hands and the boyish eagerness which frequently betrayed an

35

air of supercilious boredom. Finally he recalled just before sleeping he'd dialled his home and given a single trill, a private code of reassurance for when he was 'working', a merest clandestine contact.

When he'd dressed and showered and checked his identity tag Stuart was given friendly directions down to the canteen. Hungry from lean pickings the night before, he was just taking advantage of the monstrous American idea of breakfast when he was interrupted in mid-mouthful, a hand on his shoulder. The Resident was a man brimming with ferocious energy, short and compact with a crew-cut under retraining, partially successful in a wet and flattened area. His eyes were cold enough for wickedness.

'Sorry I didn't catch up with you last evening, Mr Kody. My name's Charles Riverson. Tied up again right now, have to ask you to stay around, there's a library, newspapers, so forth. I'll have you paged, right?' His voice was so shaly that speech seemed like the effort of a tropic toad.

His mouth still busy with waffle and maple syrup, Stuart couldn't reply beyond a helpless and moronic shrug. Riverson merely nodded and strode out, to be occupied for three more hours, hours that didn't make him any more affable when Stuart was escorted to the same falsely-bright office.

'Clear a point before we start. How is it the Soviets didn't immediately suspect your claim, when you told Comrade Simonov you were working for MI6?'

'I didn't tell him . . . You're very abrupt, Mr Riverson. Do you push a lot of pawns?'

Riverson looked surprised. 'What's your meaning?'

'Well . . . Do you think chess is aggressive?' Stuart put the question mildly enough and Riverson considered it a moment before making up his mind.

'Yes, damn right it's aggressive.'

'Well, I hate chess.'

36

'Hate's aggressive.'

Stuart sighed. 'Dislike then, let's say indifference.'

'Never mind that now. How did he find out?'

Stuart resigned himself to Riverson's clinical approach. 'There was something I had to do, a private matter though Langley found out. Must've told you?' With no change in Riverson's expression, he went on patiently, 'I made out to my wife that I'd been offered a temporary job in some Ministry, I don't think I even said which one, just something secret. My wife told her mother, which is how it got back to her father. He couldn't check on me through any of their records and he decided I must be with the new W-section. I simply didn't deny it, in fact I made up some titbits for him. I needed a bargaining point at that stage. It seemed a huge joke at the time, you understand?'

Riverson nodded heavily, folding his hands. 'I'm trying. This isn't the jokiest of professions and it looks like you still need that bargaining point.'

'Meaning?' Stuart watched him, narrowly.

'I guess you thought you were clear away but Langley had some other ideas, afterthoughts. They got your cheque stopped, probably just to get your attention.'

Although this merely confirmed what Stuart had expected after his talk with Epiphany, his reaction was real, cold furious. 'That is plain *disgusting*,' he hissed, the restraint from obscenity seeming to add weight to the judgement. 'I'm hocked up to here, what do they expect me to do now? And that money was *earned*, because of the behaviour of one of your hoodlums.'

Riverson shook his head. 'Agent Randolph was not one of ours, he was freelance. We would hope that our people generally comport themselves with better judgement, certainly not hazard the very airplane they're flying in.'

'So that's admitted? Now do I have to sue the U.S. government? I'd have all the evidence I need, there must have been dozens of radios on that frequency all relishing a talk-down, certainly the Air Force Controller, the Memphis Controller— '

Nodding his squat head, Riverson interrupted placidly. 'Well, you know how it is, I expect they moved those guys and filed their tapes . . . Sure, you could probably prove it, cost you every cent, take about three years and they'd settle on the court-house steps. Did Paul Epiphany recruit you?'

The change of topic seemed deliberately disconcerting. 'To what?' Stuart asked with a costly effort at control.

'Group headbanging,' Riverson betrayed distaste as at something personally threatening. 'He's the kind to get the ear of any doodlebrain needing a guru.' He grinned without real humour. 'I've told him I'll get him on a Federal charge, peddling cerebral snorts, rushes to the brain.'

Wondering if Riverson simply envied Epiphany his charm, Stuart said, 'Sounds fun to me.'

'Hm, didn't think you were the type. And it's mighty costly.'

Sure he wasn't meant to miss the weight of this remark, Stuart found his resentment mounting intolerably. Riverson watched him, an interval of toying irritation until Stuart broke it, thumping his hands on his knees, flinching at his injury.

'All right, are you going to spell it out?'

The American looked neither surprised nor gratified. 'There's not a lot for me to spell at the moment. Mainly they say you're not to give the Comrade Simonov any more of your invention, I guess it's dangerous ground.'

'Can you tell me why it's dangerous?'

Riverson shook his head. 'You were in H.Q. Langley, a few weeks back. You see the inscription on the marble wall: "And ye shall know the truth and the truth shall make you free." John the Evangelist? In this case it would do that all right, permanently. Too near the bone. So, we may have something less, er, moot for you to pass on in due course. The stuff you're toying with, well, it could be misleading.'

'If it's completely false?'

'If it's only a matter of belief. Doesn't matter whose belief.' He held up a hand as Stuart protested. 'I know, cash-wise they've got your chestnuts in the roaster but there's a neat solution for that. You may not like it, of course.'

'So tell me,' Stuart said flatly, without interest.

'Adrian Stayres was looking for you. SIS can use your Czech and then,' Riverson brightened patronisingly, 'Then your lie becomes truth, you can look your little lady in the eye again. Also we'll know where to find you and you'll be nicely sewn up by the Official Secrets Act. I expect they'll be in touch.'

A private exasperation finally surfaced and Riverson asked tersely, 'What the hell happened at Heathrow last night? I was waiting for you, my man got sidetracked and the next thing I know you've been here in my office, getting stitched.'

Stuart found no hesitation in covering for Epiphany in the face of this charmless individual. 'He was being the Good Samaritan, I expect. What happened to you?'

'Traffic accident,' Riverson said sourly and Stuart hid a smile, aided by the thought of his attacker.

'What about Cornelius, are you getting on to him?'

The gravelly voice sounded disinterested. 'We're expecting the South Africans to take care of it for us. But you'll be covered, don't worry. Get on home and you'll be contacted.'

'Thanks.'

'You're welcome.' Riverson showed no reaction to the acid in Stuart's monosyllable, unless his detachment was exaggerated.

*   *   *

At almost the same time, eighty miles away, Lucy drove up in bright sunshine to the Fox and Hounds, an Oxfordshire public house held captive by Elizabethan timbers and shouldering tall chimneys. It was crowded and rowdy with pre-lunchers and had a loud-clicking door which caused heads to turn whenever it opened. The men drinking at the bar played an obvious game of double-takes for pretty girls entering, even if they were accompanied, testing their reactions for shyness, aloofness, coyness or flustered annoyance.

Lucy was wearing a very dark green silk blouse with a ragged blonde chamois skirt, low heels and no handbag. The double-takes lingered on her and some became triples, but Lucy feigned shock, turning quickly to the door to go out and come back in for more. She regretted the impulse to clown when she heard a commotion in an alcove where, on seeing the focus of their attention, Wennersley-Farquhar had stood up and banged his head solidly on a beam. Seeing his stooping plight, she hurried to him in consternation along with other well-wishers and it took several minutes to disperse the sympathetic confusion and too many offers of drinks.

In the darkened alcove near the fire, Lucy twice said she was sorry but St George shook his aloof narrow head and combed his sandy hair calmly over the bump.

He had a fine long nose with a pronounced flare to the nostrils like a keen gun-dog. His mouth was horsey and he tended to curl back his upper lip when smiling or curious, something he obviously knew about and tried to control, the effort only making it worse. He drank plain tonic water and swallowed pickled onions with a peculiar expression.

'Not your fault, m'dear. I was just startled, that's all. You look even more delectable than I remember.'

'Stop that,' Lucy teased in relief, 'You'd have stood up anyway, a man of your breeding.'

St George nodded with pretended smugness and

quickly placed a sandwich order after she'd seen the menu card. He then turned to the case he had with him and opened it to show her. It contained his unwanted camera, an immaculate OM2 with a satchel full of accessories. He'd explained before that he'd once thought to make a living as an élite photographer, using his social position and connections to provide him not so much with a profession as a sport. To his mixture of disappointment and relief he found he had no flair for it and wasn't even promiscuous. Instead he flew an aging twin-engined Piper Seneca as an air taxi and as 'Sen George' he was popular among the aristocrats as well as treasured by the unembroidered wealthy. Some called him the Blue Baron for the supposed tint in his veins and delighted in having a titled aerial chauffeur. The Saint had been added at the insistence of his mother, an intense patriot who had never heard the other side of an argument. St George had been reluctantly born to her on the last day of the war in Europe, on which day also his father, Sir Wilfred, had drunkenly stolen a fighter plane, a Mark V Spitfire, from a Norfolk aerodrome and hidden it in a barn on the estate. St George suffered terribly the affront that his old man had squandered and left him insufficient family fortunes to rebuild it to airworthiness. He himself spent every spare penny having it lovingly restored by an old, crusty aircraftsman and he brimmed with endless wiles to resolve his taunting shortage of funds.

It was on the beginnings of one such scheme that he had found the key to a fortune and persuaded Stuart Kody to renew his pilot's licence a short while before, landing him up in Texas in search of fine weather for it. Both the scheme and Stuart's flying were secret from Lucy, but St George was also under a dangerous false impression about Stuart's experience.

Lucy now took the proffered camera from him with gentle reverence. St George watched her for a moment and said, 'I was going to hold onto it until you told me what it was all about, but I suppose that's not very house-trained.'

He glanced at her for approval and delighted shyly in her smile.

'I take it you can keep a secret?' she asked, cradling the camera on her skirt.

'Serpently.'

'Duly sworn, Off'cer and gent?'

'*Çela va sans dire*,' he saluted stiffly with such an appalling French accent that a newcomer nearby gazed at him in horror. Lucy chuckled and leant forward in conspiracy, acting precautions against eavesdroppers. St George looked back into her green and gold eyes all bright with excitement and his adam's apple jerked twice in betrayal.

'Down the lane we have a chunky neighbour,' Lucy began, 'He's called Humphrey Horrocks. He's got a fairly on-its-own cottage, no wife, an extra garage and he seems to like me.'

A shadow crossed St George's face. 'Private detective?'

'No, silly! He's a brewery executive, with a gut to match.' Her tone was enough to chide him for the interruption and he realised he didn't much care what the secret was as long as he could simply watch her speaking and the diverse frames her mouth made round enticingly perfect teeth.

'Sorry,' he said, tucking in his chin like a guilty guardsman. 'What are you going to do in this garage, some sort of studio?'

A buxom girl brought them their tray of drinks and sandwiches.

'I'll get to that,' Lucy said, gasping her lips, 'Can I just have a mouthful first?' She took a swig of beer and then a deliberately huge bite of bread, cheese and chutney, her eyes wide, delighting in the pretence of not taunting him. St George's eyebrows rose in reciprocal measure to a point where she nearly burst out with laughter. Taking her time, she swallowed, wiped her mouth lengthily and said quietly as if relenting,

'Actually, it's a sort of stable for my steed so I can hide it from Stuart.'

'Gosh . . . He's anti-huntin'?'

His expression bemused her completely, not showing his own stance on the matter. She decided not to pursue it in case she got it wrong and distressed him further. The look held the most devoted flattery she'd seen in a long while and she couldn't help but find it charming nor resist squeezing it for a little more. She dropped her voice just above a whisper and St George leaned in to catch every syllable like pearl droplets.

'It's not that sort of steed. This one comes in a crate and now I have to find someone to put it together for me and find me an engine. The steed is of the genus Bensen and I shall call her Decibelle.'

'Bensen . . . Bensen . . .' He looked at her with teeth bared in a broadening smile and finally twirled his finger interrogatively. 'Gyrocopter, or autogyro?'

'Bingo.'

'Gosh . . . aerial photographs, is that it?'

'Yes.' She nodded in quick approval of the right answer and then realised with a giggle that he'd been holding his breath. St George exhaled suddenly and had to cough away his embarrassment.

'Have you ever flown one?' he managed at last, regathered.

'Certainly. I have a princely, princessly twenty-six hours. You have to have an ordinary airplane licence first. Before we went away I'd been going off to Enstone and spending the housekeeping on proper lessons, but for the Bensen they tow you behind a truck so you can't get away until you get the hang of it. It's very peculiar at first, you get jerky with tension or over-reaction. But then the real thing, untethered. Wow! It seems a tight-rope, it's a terrible feeling of exposure, just a tube and

43

pedals in front of you and over the side nothing between you and the rolling green, all under a floppy rotor.'

She put her legs out in front of her and held an imaginary control column between them, juggling it for a moment with a tense expression before hearing a burst of laughter in the hubbub from the bar. She quickly realised the attention her action must have attracted even in a pub so near an airfield. She tucked her knees in together and smoothed down the skirt deliberately before giving a prim nod to her unwanted audience. St George kept his glance under control, at least in the manner of his forebears, as if he'd noticed none of the peasantry and was intent only on the subject and his companion.

'But our Ken Wallis, remember the James Bond machine? He's got all the records and he's *British*!'

'I know, but he doesn't sell his machines, except someone does a nasty military version. He's quite happy doing exhibition work and being a genius and just inventing. Like Bensen, he says pilot error's the big problem but the poor manufacturer gets the raspberry when someone does something hasty. Anyway, I'll be very careful and spread the risk, American machine, English engine – and Igor Bensen was a Russian,' she added smugly. 'Anyway, they've had no fatalities from stress failure. Personally I think it's statistics and newsmen who do all the damage. If there were no newsmen we could all kill ourselves in peace and quiet.'

St George made a nervous adjustment to his tie and said compliantly, 'I suppose you're right. I hadn't thought of it.'

''Course,' she grinned back happily, 'But it's been fascinating, I always thought helicopters sort of hung there under their own fans. It was amazing to learn that only centrifugal force keeps the blades out stiff when they're whirring, so if you work them too hard or let them get too slow they go all floppy and crumple up. I'm going to stun poor Stuart with my mechanical knowledge.'

St George had been trying to get some attention for their empty glasses and said vaguely, 'Well, he'll know all that, won't he?'

Lucy pulled her head back in affront. 'Why? Just because he's a man? I don't think he's got a clue about aeroplanes.'

St George couldn't help the expression of horror at his near-gaffe which twitched his facial muscles alarmingly. He held up his arm as an insistent bar-signal surreptitiously to hide his face from Lucy, and when his only answer was a headshake from an overworked barman he was able to transfer his discomfort. He couldn't remember if Stuart had ever told him why his flying was a secret from Lucy and he picked at crumbs in puzzlement, muttering about service. Freshly he turned to Lucy and beamed, letting his enthusiasm come to the rescue, nodding eagerly, his upper lip curled back in toothy rapture.

'Well, actually, if the power comes through the rotor, it does behave like a down-blowing fan to start with, y'know? It changes rather awkwardly when you make the machine go forward, then you have to think of it as a wing, a disc-shaped wing . . . Gawd, what must it have been like for the chap who first tried it and discovered the awful truth! Leonardo da Vinci never knew his luck in not getting the bad news, about lag and twist and flap, did he?' St George shook his head in distant dismay but Lucy hadn't understood him. He brightened to her when she voiced it cautiously.

'I don't know what that means, St G.'

'You don't? Ah, well you have a free-spinning rotor with the blade angles fixed – surprised they don't tell you about choppers, though, must be too hard to understand.'

He grinned cautiously at this tease so Lucy feigned an elbow in his ribs. 'Try me.'

'Very well. Not many people know this but a helicopter is something almost magical . . . As each blade whizzes round it also wriggles and waves and shimmies like a demented dervish trying out a new sabre. You can't see it, of course, but each blade has to be able to flap up and down over its whole length as well as twist from the root as well as hinge back and forwards. That's why they're so costly, all that wear and tear.'

Lucy regarded him sadly. 'St G, I'm going to have to eat humble pie or flounder in technicalities. You've lost me, dear.'

He looked surprised for a moment before adopting his tone to logical rescue, holding out his arm and demonstrating. Just then the barman appeared with another beer and tonic water and when St George hardly noticed, thumped the glasses down and went off grumpily.

'Look, when the machine starts moving forward, the advancing blade meeting the wind has more airflow and therefore greater lift than the one retreating, so the machine promptly rolled over, Prang!' His arm went up over his head and he slumped against the booth like a slain stag. Lucy's laughter restored him vividly.

'Tell you the truth, I don't understand it myself, but they had to compensate, obviously. Anyway, the main difference with the autogyro is that the air passes up through the rotor as it gets pushed along whereas with the helicopter it's forced *down* through, which makes it inherently unstable, see, 'cos a helicopter sits on a column of air but the gyro is sort of suspended from the air flowing out above it. Stability.'

'I think I follow that bit, it's why I can fly hands off and hold the camera.'

'Um! Can't do that with a chopper, not for a second. Me, I'll stick to wings and two engines, unless . . .' He was about to mention his Spitfire under restoration but couldn't decide whether this would add complications. It did however lead him back to his worries and his next thought.

'Allcock!' he said with sudden brightness.

46

'What is?'

'I mean, he'll do it for you, he's my engineer, I think he's even worked for someone who'd wangled a Wallis. Shall I send him to you? He whinges a lot but he's the best around, a wizard improviser and expert parts-ferret. What sort of motor are you after, Woler?'

Lucy remembered with a smile that this was Sloanese for Rolls-Royce. She nodded and said with deliberate quaintness, 'Yes, it needs to have a hundred horses' powers.'

'Gosh. I'll ask him, leave it to me. Where?'

'Um . . . I was going to say Horrocks' garage but there's always busybodies. I don't want Stuart to find out until its been earning for a bit. Why not Enstone airfield, I'm sure I can get some hangar space.'

'Right oh. Can you pay him?'

Lucy nodded warily and St George's obvious priority evaporated, concern that she might have assumed a free favour. He hadn't paid Allcock's wages for nearly a month and was desperate not to lose him.

'Allcock's getting on a bit,' he said, 'Started as an aircraft-fitter apprentice at the end of the war. Typical zenophobe, always got some nasty phrase or sobriquet for every brand of foreigner. But you'll love him, I promise.'

'I will? What does he think of Russians?'

'Heavens, I forgot! I shouldn't tell him, if I were you. He never lets up with the pun and cliché. Mind you, I nearly gaffed myself at your house, the evening you told me. It was really confusing, you whispering about the camera and Stuart . . .'

He saw danger looming and coughed uncomfortably as Lucy watched in some puzzlement. He recalled also from the same evening jocularly describing himself as a gun-runner just because he liked the sound of the words; the false boast had brought him trouble since the Kody's house had been under sinister surveillance. He sipped thoughtfully at his drink for a moment and then made a diffident suggestion.

'Er, look here, I don't happen to be running guns nor much else this afternoon, care to come up for a spin?'

Lucy shook her head slowly and put a hand on his arm. 'Thank you, but no. I don't know even roughly what an air-taxi costs to run but I'll bet it's heaps, it's just not *on* to go joy-riding, it's your business.'

He looked disappointed as if unable to please her. 'Well . . . of course, you . . . know what it's like,' he finished lamely, realising he'd been about to blunder again by suggesting she'd been up many times with Stuart when she didn't even know he had any experience.

'Where is he, the duty Officer?' he asked for something to say.

'Stuart? St G., they picked him up at Heathrow and sent me on home, and then I got a call only this morning from the Foreign Office, none other than the P.S. to the Secretary of State, asking to speak to him and where is he? I think it's deliberate mystery, but at least I got my single buzz on the phone so I know he's OK. What am I supposed to think when his employer rings up and asks where he is? Am I supposed to cover up for him, or what?'

'Hmph,' St George shuffled his feet. 'You might ask him to get in touch with me too. It's all jolly confusing, isn't it?' He now had trouble meeting her eyes which made him doubly uncomfortable since his gaze wanted to linger. 'Getting out of hand,' he muttered to himself and Lucy seized on it.

'What is?'

He straightened his posture and looked at her. 'Secrets. Can't you and Stuart have a sort of moratorium, wipe the slate clean, keep score? Fifteen-all, um?'

'But he's bound by the Act, it's not fair. That's why I'm keeping Decibelle a secret, Lord knows how long

I can manage it. I'm not under an oath, I have to do it on self-control. It's all right for him and agony for me.'

St George clearly wanted to sympathise and take sides. 'I shouldn't worry. He'll have something not covered by the Act, surely?' He lowered his voice teasingly to say, 'I'll bet he's told you a few things he shouldn't.'

Lucy smiled back wickedly. 'Well, come to think of it, he did, yes. It was something quite amazing, to do with missiles. I can't tell *anyone* else, naturally.'

'But what have you told him in exchange?' His tone was now feigning querulousness on Stuart's behalf.

'Lots of things. I . . .' Lucy found she didn't want to tell St George about her previous brief and disastrous marriage nor the cause of her husband's suicide.

'I did tell him I was karate-ka,' she admitted shyly.

'There you are, fifteen all! Gosh, are you really, black belt and all that?'

Lucy nodded distantly. 'I gave it up, ages ago, it seemed like dangerous knowledge. Well anyway,' she dropped her voice to another confidence, 'He doesn't know about me teaching gymnastics at two local schools, I just told him I have "clients", that's all.' Her smile for this was all innocence but then the faraway look returned. 'Decibelle will be the humdinger, especially if she makes a few beans for me. I wonder if I'm being fair, really, do you think? I just don't know.'

'Of course it's fair,' he protested for her with too much enthusiasm and then clumsily tried to temper it. 'I mean he wouldn't be actually deceiving you, you haven't . . .'

'Been married long enough?' Lucy's laugh was rueful and slightly nervous. 'What a horrid, cynical thought.'

'Oh, I say,' St George protested, crestfallen to be in disfavour.

'I dare say you do,' she answered, 'I'm sorry, I wasn't sure whose side you were on.' She patted his arm to relent on his distress. 'Oh, by the way, thank you again for the silver birch you sent, it was a huge thankyou just for a home-cooked dinner. I see it's taken nicely in the garden, doesn't seem to resent my bossiness. I scare most of plants into action.' She took out one of the lenses to toy with it. 'Did you know it was the Russian national tree, St G?'

'Well, tell you the truth, I would have sent you flowers. I rang the Russian Embassy first to ask which was the national flower, a sort of peace offering in case I'd insulted the Motherland.'

'Oh, I used to know lots of the Embassy people. They'd have put you on to Leon Borisov, I expect?'

'Why?' St George's lip twitched in anticipation of voicing a silliness and he delivered it with slow relish. 'Is he the haughty-cultural attaché?'

Lucy's laughter pealed out and drew more glances from the bar while St George flushed with pleasure.

'Actually,' he said recovering, 'They didn't put me on to anybody, far as I could tell. When you call they don't even say who they are, just a very gruff male voice says *Hullo* in a threatening kind of way. When I asked my question they got all suspicious and wouldn't tell me. I had to get my answer from a friend of Tuffy's, an Oxford tutor. Why would they want to make a secret of something like that?'

'They *love* secrets, that's why. I'm surprised they even pass on information like how to reproduce. Westerners know far too many things they don't need to, it leads to decadence and unrest.'

'It's true.'

'St G., you don't have to agree with everything I say, really.'

'All right. But it is jolly confusing to be a receptacle of secrets, however exciting.'

'A receptacle?' Lucy's eyes fixed on him as she turned her head away, narrowing in suspicion. 'St George,' she said in a near-growl of warning, 'Do you *mean* he's told *you* something he hasn't told *me*?'

. St George recoiled from her rising emphasis, shaking his head despairingly. Lucy prodded him and wouldn't let it go.

'There *is*, isn't there?'

'No . . . well, not what you think. It's mine, really.' His voice sounded half-strangled. 'I told *him* something which I'm not even sure about yet, that's all. It's not an Official one.'

'But he's only got Official ones, he'd tell me everything else!'

St George struggled to regain his sangfroid. 'Calm yourself, please. We've hardly discussed it, just the out-line. It's a sort of probe into a business venture, that's all, though there's a slight diplomatic angle as well, so— '

'Diplomatic!' Lucy snorted, 'All right, tell me about the business, is he putting some money in?'

St George shook his head but still wriggled under her gaze. 'Not if he doesn't like the look of it, no, but with his background and experience, I— '

He paused and Lucy let the tension build. 'You're talk-ing about *my husband*. What do you mean, background and experience? He speaks fluent Czech which is the only reason they hired him, far as I know. His three years in the army was rag-time, drinking and ski-ing, he had this dreadful tearaway friend called Rollo Runyan. Since then he's been doing up houses, plumbing and plas-tering.'

'Is that . . .' Firm suddenly and looking away, St George said, 'Angels-fear-to-tread land. I say no more, not one word. And you're not to give me away by asking him. Women shouldn't be allowed to ask questions, in my opinion.'

Lucy bristled and then gave in. 'I'll buy my own lunch,' she said with a quick smile.

'You will not!'

51

'Don't be a pig.'

'Virago!' St George blurted in affront, surprising himself.

Lucy was taken aback and then her look softened when he apologised. 'Gosh, I'm awfully sorry.'

'A compliment, I assure you. A virago was a female warrior. I didn't mean to be beastly, I'm sorry.' She giggled lightly. 'If I'd flounced out in a huff I'd have had to leave the camera.'

'I'll waive the rent.'

'No you won't, it's business. Don't worry, I'll get to the bottom of this even without your help. I won't give you away. I'll let you buy me lunch after all. I suppose you're quite sure, that you couldn't make a decent income from it? Don't you think people would be quite happy with crummy photos, once they knew who you were?'

St George had no answer because her returning sparkle was like a sunburst for him, a massage of pleasure. Lucy shook her head, mystified at such unabashed and preposterous Englishness.

Seeing smoke from the chimney, Lucy felt a quickening that Stuart might be home but just behind the door was a pile of discarded clothes reeking of wet mud and woodsmoke. Stepping around them she called out airily and heard an answering shriek from upstairs. Her mother appeared on the landing in a towel, pink and dripping from the bath. Lucy took the stairs three at a time to embrace her joyfully.

Alicia was tiny without her shoes, her grey hair pinned up in a bun, her rather severe face looking pinched and hollow-eyed even through the bath-glow. Lucy had once been through a period of great misery and only at that time in her mirror had she seen any resemblance to her mother. The realisation had done a lot to nurture her compassion.

'Well, I timed that right,' she said, stepping back.

'What is it, Mama? You're looking apologetic or something.'

'Well, I am. I couldn't know when you are coming, nor ask. I disobeyed you, Liouba, but I want you to understand. There are the clothes of two people there, but not the whole gang, be sure.'

'O Mama! A man?' While Lucy clasped her hands in excitement, her expression held disbelief and consternation.

'Ach, no. It's Nadia from Ukraina, with us at the camp. She's ill and so sad I had to bring her. She's in the other bathroom, so glad the water was hot. And you are back, looking like one of the graces.'

Lucy looked uncertain. 'Did you smell like the clothes?'

'Please don't. We're called stinking old whores day and night at the camp, and much, much worse. I'm lucky I don't understand enough of the words of the soldiers and the hooligans. I don't think you'd believe it. The thing men say they love best in all the world, why do they use it as an insult?'

'Ignorance and deprivation thereof. Stuart says desire can addle a man's brains, literally. You're looking thin and unhealthy, Mama, don't you eat?'

'Ah, we just sit around and drink tea, then crawl into damp yurts of Polythene, they call them benders, then the bailiffs come and smash them up. They take everything you're not actually wearing, they even took my house keys. If you have a sleeping bag you have to hop around wearing it, otherwise it goes. They can do everything except strip you. Let me dress now and dry my hair. Look at yours, bleached and lovely. Child, you look a picture of health and so brown? Where did you go?'

'Sailing.' She snaked her hand up and down casually. 'Would you like some tea?'

Alicia grinned ruefully and shook her head. 'Coffee?

Tea is the British woman's answer to all the pain, rain, boredom, grief, hunger, everything. I'll come down and tell you all about it.'

'All right. Did you tell them you're Russian?'

'Why not, they understand. We have people from all over the world. Poor Nadia, though, she defected and something went wrong with the arrangements, her child got left behind. Now Nadia cannot go back.'

Lucy showed a clench of real pain. 'That must be too cruel. Who's got the child?'

'A little boy of two, he's with his father . . . Nadia has a fever, I was going to look after her. Do you mind?'

Lucy shook her head but a little warily. 'Is she nice?'

'When someone is so hurt it's hard to say.' Alicia circled a halo above her. 'I think she is a saint. Where's Stuart?'

'Don't ask!' Lucy put a finger to her mouth knowing from experience not to encourage mother-in-law censure. 'Something's going on, but it's fine, I got my little ping on the phone.'

It was an effort not to add that Stuart's supposed employer was looking for him and she was beginning to have a suspicion that he'd invented the job as a cover for something else. 'I'll go and put the kettle on. Sheets for the spare room in the cupboard, well, you know.'

Lucy poised briefly at the top of the sage-carpeted staircase, balanced and launched off, an almost slow-motion half-turn to the marked tread halfway down. Thump! facing inwards and thighs flexing for the completion, down to the hall and a deep bent absorption. Alicia hated and admired it, flinching for slender bones, but she went back into the bathroom shaking her head and smiling, feeling happier than she had for a month.

A little later down in the kitchen Lucy made coffee and asked, 'Did you meet some nice people there, Mar.a, or are they all cranks?'

'I'll tell you, just let me take a cup to Nadia.' She was gone some minutes and when she came down she said simply, 'Life lovers, they are. Ach, like everywhere there's assortment. Some freaks, orange hair or shaved patterns like Red Indians, Lesbians putting on a show. But the centre, the spine, is mothers and grandmothers who only care for the future and their children, not at all for their own comfort. One said to me, the world is so beautiful I cannot bear for it to be destroyed. If we allow these things, there is universal agreement, one day there'll be a *katastropha*, is it?'

'Catastrophe.'

'*Da*. And such courage, moral certainty, day after rainy day, always wet and freezing cold, nothing to do but knit little symbols to put on the wire and the soldiers tearing them off in fury, so full of hatred and abusing, filthy, incredible words. You know they have standing orders not to have *eye contact* with us?' She snorted derisively. 'Yesterday a soldier bus goes out of Main Gate, every window horrible white with flesh, their actual arseholes pressed to the glass.'

Lucy's eyebrows jerked up and she barely suppressed a smile at such an epithet from her mother. But then she imagined sitting dedicated, wet and frozen on behalf of a world which subsidised and tolerated such ignorant savages and she was suddenly moved almost to tears. She avoided showing emotion to Alicia because it would start a link-reaction, but she sensed a change in her, an increase of stature perhaps for a new place in the world.

Alicia spoke again, not trying to impress but factual, her eyes distant. 'The hunters came through, terrifying us with huge horses and the master cracking his whip left and right, dogs all over, barking and baying. No fox, just harassment. We thought they'd gone but then the whip-man with the red coat, I wonder how can he live with the shame of it, he came back alone and went wild crazy, galloping all about our benders, his whip slashing,

55

so mad he forgot his hounds and they were all scattered on the road, cars screeching. Then, you see, the women ran out to stop the traffic, to save the animals.'

Alicia shook her head in wonderment, then she took Lucy's hand and pressed it to her face. 'There is so much hate for them you can't believe. They think our little benders are a pain in the eye, but they've got used to the foul and ugly base, nine long miles around the awful razor wire, stealing the common land. That was against the law, did you know?'

'Are you going to stay there, Mamushka?'

'I don't know. I'll have to go back with my friend. Would you like to come up and see her?'

Nadia Feodorovna lay against the pillows like a wax model, with fine albino-blonde hair and her skin translucent. Her front teeth slanted inwards in the bow of her smile to make it meltingly piteous. She spoke English so haltingly that Lucy switched to Russian but Nadia tried to resist even in her weakened state.

'I have to apprehend,' she said.

'When you're better,' Lucy answered adamantly, smoothing the coverlet.

Nadia's story fell into place over the rest of the day as she recovered just by apparent determination. It was as poignant as it was horrifying, drawn out of her with great pain and without hope in any catharsis of sharing. Lucy was surprised that her mother hadn't blurted the whole story at once; it seemed a new restraint in her for she still suffered in her own way that there was, by definition, no armour against intimate treachery.

Nadia and her husband had been moved from Kiev to Leipzig in the DDR for his work and ambition as a power-station engineer. Under various pressures the marriage began to falter and willing to try anything to heal the rift but also with deep misgivings, she had agreed to attempt an escape with him, to start a new life in the West with their two-year-old son, Feodor.

56

Their escape was by different methods, the father to bring the child. Nadia's method worked very neatly, hidden in the deliberately ruptured spare tyre of a returning butter transporter, her small thin body arched within the huge cover for an aching four hours. For security's sake, her husband hadn't revealed his own method to her and he never appeared at the rendezvous. After weeks of waiting and frantic stolen calls she at last discovered that he had never intended to leave. That her little boy was irretrievably lost needed no statement for, as she said, there was no question of going back to face pointless imprisonment and exile, and no benefit in denouncing the father. He had since taken up with another woman and only because Nadia's parents had access to the child did she receive any news at all.

'They could even steal him away for me,' she exlained, 'But then how get him out? Can you imagine to be betrayed, by someone you gave all, body with soul? Such wickedness is outside, beyond imagining.'

Lucy found it too extreme to empathise with this distress and thought briefly of her own first marriage before her thoughts skipped in a dangerous pattern. It was so frightening that she avoided any leading questions at first yet she felt an impossible, crazy dare had sneaked in through the back door of her consciousness. There must be stretches of the wire near open ground where a tiny, below-radar and minimal-profile machine could execute a smart hop over it and be back undetected in a matter of minutes. She imagined herself perched in the precarious metal insect with enough space found for a child. She felt sure the size of the little extra burden posed no problems, particularly if sedated.

Without intimating the fluttering of her thoughts she learned that Nadia's parents, who had loudly denounced her for their own protection, had a small car and sometimes looked after the boy for whole weekends. The West German border was only 150 kilometres distant and apparently they were bright and defiant people. Nadia declared with timid certainty that her father would have killed her husband were it not for the child.

The more answers Lucy heard to make her notion feasible, the more frightened she became and she knew that if she attempted such a thing, let alone succeeded, and was found out, Department V would certainly come and exact the full price for her presumption. And she could never tell Stuart or Alicia because of the fright they would feel for her even long afterwards, even assuming she got clear away with it. It also seemed an irresistible dare but it would be weeks before she could gather her courage sufficiently to broach her idea to Nadia, from which point, out of pity, she knew there could be no retreat. Nadia insisted that she would leave the next day for the camp, determinedly tough and admitting it was all she had to live for. Alicia agreed to stay a while longer, delighting to have Lucy all to herself.

THREE

'It impresses me not, how many angels can dance on the head of a Pershing 2.'

C. Randolph Parker

Frustrated with what seemed a futile day, Stuart nearly gave up in mid-afternoon but on the third attempt Epiphany had at last returned to his apartment. An aging bull-terrier of a porter admitted him to the building, a suspicious old brawler who walked bunched, like a barrel of hard muscle.

The door was ajar as Stuart emerged from the elevator into a flat that was light and airy in spite of extensive pine panelling. There was a trace of perfume, flowers in two vases and a pair of high-heeled boots behind the door.

'Sorry for the hold-off, Ted said you'd been earlier. How did it go?' Epiphany's voice came from the kitchen with a clink of crockery. 'Have a seat, I'm bringing coffee.'

'Riverson is an ill-mannered ogre,' Stuart replied, settling himself in a deep settee, its cover a rich *poult-de-soie* of mixed pastels. On the low greenheart table in front of him stood an odd-shaped, elegant bottle, the cork caged, on a glossy blue card.

Epiphany came through with a percolator bubbling on a tray. Over shirtsleeves he wore a waistcoat and trousers in dark pin-stripe, tie-less, the shirt open.

'The bottle is for you, a *douceur* to take home. Tells about it in the card. Don't show her the menu when she's

59

hungry, she mightn't thank you.'

Stuart slid the card out, a Concorde menu from the day before. In the wine-list he read: Champagne: *Laurent Perrier Grand Siècle – presented in a bottle of unique shape used in the reign of Louis Quatorze, a classic blend of three selected vintages epitomising perfection, from the best growths of the Montaigne des Reims and the Côtes des Blancs.*

'Thank you,' Stuart said simply and Epiphany smiled as he poured coffee.

'Talking about misinformation, did you know that airplane was a classic? The Brits leaked the prototype plans to the Russians, when they realised it was badly flawed. Somehow it was made to fly anyway, the Concordski, much to the Brits' disgust, but it wasn't much good. They had to scrap it . . . Forgive me if I talk a little circuitously. You'll come to appreciate the reasons in time. I hope. Did it go as predicted?'

'I think so. They stopped the money, told me to keep quiet and get a job.'

'Did you tell him where to put it?'

Stuart shook his head. 'I just listened.'

'Good. You want to know the definition of a fall guy – just look in the back of that menu, there's a list of the most frequent fool questions the suffering crew get asked: "How do we know how fast we're going, why does the nose droop, why is the sky darker," and the answers to them. Now, the interesting one is: "Why are the windows smaller than in subsonic aircraft?" Smaller hell, they're tiny! Read the answer.'

Stuart complied, '"The design could have featured larger windows but various international regulations precluded this".'

'Delicious gobbledegook!' Epiphany said with relish. 'I'll tell you the reason, it's because if a window blows out, the decompression at eleven miles high would be stoo-pendous, but then the little window would be

60

immediately suction-blocked by the nearest soft object. Guess what that is?'

Stuart grinned palely. 'I'd hazard the nearest Mark One Human leak-stopper.'

'Right! I suppose the rest of the passengers would look sympathetic but still carry on with their caviar, maybe feed him the odd canapé . . . Metaphorically speaking, about another subject, you realise of course who is nearest to the leak?' Epiphany curled his hands together and fired both forefingers at Stuart's chest.

'You've got my attention, don't worry,' Stuart said dryly and the faint answering smile carried approval. After a weighty pause, Epiphany again seemed to digress with a planned assurance.

'Another metaphor, from William Ury, I think it was: Two small boys in a garage, four inches of gasoline on the floor. One has six large matches, the other has seven slightly smaller ones and they're arguing furiously about strategic superiority, yes? Let's call 'em Sam and Ivan . . . Here I thought to add a little colour, another boy wants to play but he's a real outsider who's not getting enough attention, let's call him Muhammar, he's kinda sneaky, he's just beyond the open window and he's got hold of just one match from somewhere and he might conceivably survive the blast. Meanwhile the two main rivals are so busy shouting and carrying on that they haven't fully understood, they're not so much enemies as that they've created a common enemy called Mutual Assured Destruction.'

Stuart began to feel irritated by this steered conversational course and the implied patronage. 'MAD could be called a common ally too,' he ventured, 'It's worked so far. But OK, the outside interest is a further problem. What's your solution?'

Epiphany pushed both his hands away firmly. 'The garage, the arsenal, has to go. Get rid of it, mop up the gasoline and hand in the matches. Quote Admiral

Gaylen: "The way to get rid of nuclear weapons is to get rid of nuclear weapons." First, you stop building them, and then you hand in fissile weapons material pound for pound to a nice Swiss arbiter, on a voluntary basis. Both the Russians and the Chinese have claimed to be willing so the real shame now lies with us. Our politicos cannot stand up against the military and big business lobbies since their jobs are so mutually dependent. See, for all its robustness and conviction about whose side God is rooting for, the greed-and-power ingredient of capitalism can yet kill us all. And is SDI a brilliant solution, a smokescreen, a bargaining chip or just another criminal lunacy?'

Stuart looked sceptical. 'Won't it at least keep them all busy and voting for each other?' He realised he was deliberately resisting Epiphany's charm while suspiciously glimpsing his fanaticism. The American merely nodded approvingly.

'Right, but only as long as it can't possibly work. All the independent studies seem to show that quite clearly, so isn't it sinister that they still press ahead? Well, there's a few other things showing some light, if only at the near end of the tunnel. Who can break the impasse?' Again the twin fingers fired at Stuart's chest, the eyes above them unblinking.

'*Me*?' Stuart pecked in astonishment.

'Uh-huh. You, with an apparently self-interested, treacherous leak. There seems to be a large official hang-up about crediting you with a unique invention. Can you see what I'm saying?'

The threat of flattery filled Stuart with disquiet, blurring the issue. With a visible effort he pushed past it.

'Do tell,' he said with a smile and then held up his hand. 'I think I see . . . Suppose one of the boys has been economising on match-heads, topping sticks with plain red paint – but the other one is going to find out, by spying on him, right?'

Epiphany nodded sagely, leaning forward. 'But a spy is a third party and he could be making it up, couldn't he? A very dangerous practice unless he's established credibility.' The fingers took aim yet again. 'Can the same spy tell both boys the same thing without being suspected and stomped?'

Stuart grinned quickly but then inflated his cheeks with growing alarm. 'Maybe . . . provided he has an impeccable source – or unprovable material . . . You see, I thought my first invention would be unprovable, a little joke, but I was wrong and apparently lucky.'

Epiphany snorted at the understatement but his gaze became more intense and penetrating. 'How about the second piece?'

'There shouldn't be any fuss, it's much more nebulous, it simply reports to the Kremlin that there's a *belief* in the Pentagon that the same situation prevails east of the Curtain, with the weapons the Soviets line up for Europe.'

'Ah, that's neater . . . See, I thought you meant to tell them a fact, that their SS20s are duds. They'd go crazy!'

Stuart nodded, but a smile played nervously. 'They'd go nuts having to check all their own warheads before they came to get me. I've no idea how it's done, have you? How many people in the world can look at an atomic warhead and tell you categorically that it will go off when you push the red button – and how can you trust them?'

With a sigh Epiphany stood and paced for a long silence, then he leaned on the back of the settee. 'OK. But both sides know how to *make* the big bangs so we have to assume that there's way, way too much of the lethal stuff lying around, the gasoline on the floor . . . Switching analogies: in Chinese medicine the active principles in a cure were called qualities, the soldierly, the magisterial and the princely qualities. Which of them describes a potion with the largest quantity of active principle?'

Stuart frowned into a sudden shaft of sunlight from the window. 'Am I supposed to say the princely?'

The light seemed to form a silver aura round Epiphany's hair. 'That's the natural answer for our blunt culture but it isn't correct. In that so subtle Chinese way of thinking, the highest quality is the one that does the job with the least force. Thus to be princely is to obtain the desired effect with the minimum quantity.'

'I'm not sure I'm with you. Are you asking what is the minimum quantity of nukes required to do so much damage as to make their use unthinkable?'

With a wry smile Epiphany sat down again and offered more coffee. 'Frankly, yes, that's the first step. There is something unusual going on at the moment, too peaceable for the hawks, too cautious for the doves and perhaps much too subtle for our guardians of Intelligence. So, put yourself, if you can, in the shoes of Riverson's chief: what's he going to do with you? Shall I spell it out, short and sweet?'

Warily Stuart saw the grey-blue eyes more clearly as cloud-shadow darkened the background. He wondered why the skin showing on the American's chest was pale while his face was so deeply tanned.

'He has to use you or get rid of you, so he'll probably do both. Remember, these kind of people are not seeking peace. They're seeking strategic advantage, constantly and exclusively, they even have to ignore our terrible reality that if these things ever have to be used, just one match struck in error or anger, then it's all over anyway, no boys and no garage. Meanwhile the growling goes on, Sam even tries to cut Muhammar's throat without upsetting Ivan too much, the spy's left his job half-finished and the threatening behaviour becomes more damaging and dangerous.'

Stuart folded his hands thoughtfully and cleared his throat. 'Hm . . . So how do you stop a syndrome? How do I get out of it, including the financial stranglehold?'

'Those were negative questions . . . I don't know yet, but let's just say I've heard a tiny rumour, coming from your patch – I mean your original patch.' He shrugged speculatively. 'One thing would make it more than that, maybe: does Riverson want you to sign up with the Brits?'

Stuart felt surprise and concern. 'How the hell did you know that?'

'Let's just say it follows. Are you going to do it?'

After a slow shake of his head, Stuart said, 'I don't like being shoved around. I'm looking for a way out. What were you going to suggest?'

Epiphany grinned. 'He's not exactly appealing, is he? I'd have encouraged it, frankly, but without pushing. If it's really "No", you could pretend it's "Yes", cautiously, see how the wind blows, but try not to spoil the effects of your holiday. Quite a tan you both got.'

'You too,' Stuart answered, expecting some evasion.

'Face only,' Epiphany admitted easily. 'I have to tell my staff a lie, that I've a sunbed for my vanity while in fact . . . I take it you can keep a secret? Huh, I guess the supreme test must be to keep something from a bride of one year, a Russian one at that!'

Stuart nodded gently, drawn by the wry humour, but confused again by the other's swift changes.

'She'd no trace of an accent, that I noticed.'

'None. She spent her teens in England, up-market ballet school.'

Epiphany raised his eyebrows. 'That right? My girl-friend did the same, I forget which one but she's a bit senior. How old is your Lucy?'

'She's twenty-four. It was Elmhurst, by courtesy of Moscow.'

'You know, I think that was it.'

Stuart showed surprise but wanted to make a point. 'She was being groomed by the Soviets but she found out in time and won't play their games at all. That's why

65

my position is touchy.' He thought of Lucy's recklessness and also her firm if naïve conviction that they couldn't be used against each other. 'We're like dolphins,' she'd said, 'We have fearless life.' He shivered at the presumption and pushed himself back to the point. 'Where's all this leading, in your scheme of things?'

Epiphany didn't answer for a moment, lost in after-thought.

'It's the real beginning of S.T.A.R.T., maybe. Instead of all the waffle of the Limitation Talks, once the actual reductions can begin, politicians can at last find popularity in something negative, it'll become "the New Thing", the backswing. The boys would rather play something else anyway, that game led nowhere because they couldn't play with the matches, it was a bust, a stand-off . . . Do you ski, by any chance?'

Amused by his feigned shiftiness, Stuart nodded cautiously.

'But ski well, I mean real hot, black runs and off-piste?'

'I got a few cups in the Army.'

'Oh, great! . . . Then you'll know. Trouble with my secret, it's kind of expensive, but maybe you'll be solvent again one day, yeah?'

Struggling for a connection, Stuart looked blank. 'I haven't ski-ed for a while, Lucy's never tried it. Have you just been?'

'Um. I've got a similar problem, as it's not for beginners. I go deep powder, up in the Canadian Buggaboos. Ever done any?'

Stuart shook his head. 'Not really deep, no. Off-piste in new falls, seldom more than a foot because it's heavy, seldom fine powder. So tell me, is it as good as they say?'

'No, it's better! One of the best things in the world. The problem is that to find and get on the deep virgin powder you need a helicopter which is kind of expensive so you do it in a group but you gotta be good because the others can't stand to wait around. Falling is pretty much unthinkable . . . The 'copter's down there at the rendezvous ready to find you another untouched mountain and you get a money-back guarantee of 100,000 vertical feet in a week but nobody settles for that, it's worse than a drug and you pay like maniacs for extra . . .' Epiphany's eyes seemed unfocused as he spoke, wistful and quiet. 'It's almost soundless, this waist-high, even chest-high floating powder, it has weird kind of flexible resilience, they call it goosefeathers . . . Silent speed, disbelief, adrenalin, a feeling of weightlessness, floating through another dimension, more, more, more! And there's fear, of course, the risk of avalanche, you're daring those killers all the way. Ever see one go, tearing out trees and boulders? You're always aware of them, like teetering on the edge . . . Some folks like to stop at the bottom and look back up their own tracks but the real hell-cat powder-hounds don't even glance, just straight into the 'copter and scream at the slow-pokes. Kind of single-minded. You go on through daylight, beyond exhaustion. There's no night-life, just a big bunk-room, a so-so meal, one drink and out cold by seven o'clock. You like to try it sometime?'

Stuart exhaled with finality. 'Nice picture . . . No, I can't have any more secrets from her. It's too much of a strain already.'

'I can imagine . . . Espionage carries a broad fascination doesn't it? All those thrillers and movies, our-guys-the-good-guys, but you notice there's never a reward angle, as if that was ignoble? Do it for patriotism but not for gain. There's far more industrial than patriotic espionage. But it's not interesting to Joe Public, he wants a real hero, a man too pure and noble to be self-seeking. This virtuous paragon, the patriot spy, is not accessible to the businessman although he's the one who could use him to immense profit. Had you thought of that? I bet you'd prefer to see yourself touching off some great global benefit than being dangled on a financial string?'

Stuart had to smile at this perspicacity, and the pale eyes repaid his scrutiny with a lively and likeable assurance. He straightened up and spoke directly to the American.

'The sums involved, whether from Washington or, say, Antwerp, would be quite enough to retire on. If they allowed me either, I wouldn't be controllable any more, so they won't do it. Therefore I'm going to ignore the whole thing. I'll find my own solution.'

'Pull the hook, in other words?'

Stuart glanced down grimly. 'I guess so.'

'Hm . . . twenty-eight is young to retire. Y'know, big business works differently, it pays for continuity. We might be able to help.'

'I keep wondering where you stand, how you know so much. The Concorde doesn't fly from Canada.'

'Check. Well, there's a certain Senator who pays me to straighten him out every now and again, a man very well connected. One might even guess he's in armaments, if untraceably. Imagine exchanging truthful eye-contact with a politician and you'll understand why I charge him five thousand dollars a half-hour, plus air-fare. Don't ask me who it is because it's a secret.'

'Sounds like one of the rich ones . . . Can you psyche him into becoming the next President?'

Epiphany stiffened in surprise. 'Very sharp of you. Yes, I believe I can, that is certainly the intention. Then you'll find out who it is, won't you?'

Stuart grinned. 'I suppose so. Will he stop the SDI – who christened it Star Wars? It annoys the hell out of me.'

'Me too. No, he couldn't, but he'll influence its direction. At the moment there's a preposterous Presidential Directive demanding certain capabilities of the system, in the face of the best scientifically informed sources which say they can never be achieved. None of our politicians has found a way to keep office and buck the Military/Industrial Complex – or Conspiracy you called it. Still, as long as they're building something outlandish and unworkable . . .'

'Provided the other side knows and therefore doesn't feel threatened by it.'

Epiphany smiled with satisfaction. 'Exactly, and they'll know. Now look, obviously you're going to have to think things over, but if you do decide to play them along and something newsworthy looks like coming out of it, I would not have a serious difficulty diverting just one of my Senator's approximately 600 millions, just for a 24 hour drop on the market. That would offer you one solution, wouldn't it?'

Without waiting for a reply, Epiphany pushed a pad across. 'Write me your address, we're going to have "a bit of a thrash", as the English say. Hever Castle, down in Kent. Black tie. In about three weeks, how does that sound? Maybe we could talk some more then, I don't suppose anything'll happen in the meantime. I won't offer to help out, they might trace it to me. Why do you smile?'

'I was just thinking, if I had six hundred dollars I could peel one off and give it to the doorman without blinking. If you add six noughts, is it the same feeling?'

'Sure,' Epiphany said as if believing it. 'The difference is the bracket each person selects for himself, it can be a conscious act, how big a slice to command. You were probably quite content with a smallholding, using your hands and keeping it simple. It varies with how it was acquired, of course.'

Stuart considered this for a moment. 'It's when it goes suddenly missing there's another difference. People get really nasty and terminal over the heavy figures. I had a friend who changed brackets and was doing the same to mine. Which is not going to help when someone finds out there's no house and garden any more.'

'Have you got a photograph of her?'

'Lucy?' Startled for a moment, Stuart reached into his wallet and slid out a snapshot, cautiously to show only Lucy's face. He'd taken it from the dinghy a year before and a little defiantly he allowed Epiphany to extract it all the way, gratified at his expression. Lucy was hand-balanced on the main boom, torso canted forward and her legs split to tiptoe along it, her arms concealing her nakedness except for the round of bare hips. She was clowning for the camera, her cheeks puffed with effort, her body taut with a corded elegance, hair dripping and bleached with sunstrokes. He had a violent longing to be home with her.

Epiphany said drily, 'I don't suppose you want to leave that . . . At school, wouldn't she have had a Russian whatchamacallit, patronymic?'

'Simonova.'

'Of course.' Epiphany scribbled it down and handed back the photograph. Thoughtfully he added, 'Carrots work better than sticks, positive motivation, capitalism as opposed to terror. The stick is fearfully limited, literally. Survival is its limit, not the sky. In the East they've always had too many people and not enough carrots . . . Now they're beginning to realise it. Think of all those new markets!' Epiphany raised his eyes as if mocking his own remark. 'My car can take you home, if you don't mind dropping me in Whitehall first, all right?'

Nodding gratefully, Stuart ventured, 'Tame Member of Parliament, too?'

Epiphany only smiled and said, 'Use the phone if you like.'

'Thanks.' Stuart dialled and was answered on the third ring, a sharp 'Yes?'

'Me,' he said and heard a soft relief. 'Oh . . . coming home?'

70

'Yes. Couple of hours.'

'Lovely. Mother's here.'

Stuart suppressed a sinking feeling and said lightly, 'Slip her a Mickey.'

Lucy chuckled and answered throatily, 'Roger.'

The driver, Dudley, was mercifully short of small-talk and the journey passed for Stuart in a semi-dozing anxiety. With his innuendo somewhat pedantic and full of metaphor, Epiphany wasn't offering any real solution unless Stuart could furnish him with some miraculous and substantial insider gossip for which no tongue-in-cheek inventions could possibly serve. Luck could never be so strained again and his position without some aid or initiative was impossibly precarious; the thought of sharing this anxiety with Lucy made him physically nauseous. In the dark of the plush interior he railed silently for some minutes at Rollo for his chicanery until, feeling his facial muscles taut with the emotion, he grinned suddenly in recognition: it was entirely in Rollo's character – a character he knew too well and was even partly responsible for encouraging. Having swallowed the blatant lure to run a South African blockade, he had to accept a share of the blame himself that things had gone wrong, if only for his naïveté; the irony lay in his belief at the time that he was risking life and freedom for contraband, in actuality 'diverted' even before he reached the border. The fact that Simonov believed *his* team responsible for a similar diversion long afterwards was no longer useful because of Riverson's embargo; he knew he'd run out of possible inventions anyway when it came to supplying his father-in-law with savouries of espionage. Similarly trapped were the proceeds from a single huge diamond that he'd carried on a key-ring and used to bribe his way to freedom, even though the recipient Police Chief had shortly met with a fatal accident, certainly arranged by the practical if ruthless Simonov.

71

One final option, a 'fancy' Cape Blue, Rollo had forbidden him to sell because it was inherently unpriceable and Stuart knew too little of the trade to argue. At this point he felt a sudden change in himself like a chill but needed breeze, the grit and excitement of independence. He saw that he could even thank the manipulators for the push into initiative and the only limiting factor was how much rope they'd allow him.

When the great car finally pulled into their drive his resolution had hardened to the extent that he saw himself centre-arena, with Riverson, Epiphany, Stayres and Simonov all waiting in an expectant circle, trying to anticipate the direction of his break-out while he scoured the shadows for fanged reptiles like Cornelius. Glowing before him in the dark was the most stiffening reason for resistance; soft light shone bloomed through the drawing-room window and then he saw Lucy's head distorted by old leaded glass, approaching and peering through hooded hands. The exhilaration of seeing her was blighted by anxiety which retreated when she gathered him in the doorway gleefully, clinging on his neck and swinging between kisses. He lifted her by the waist, wondering if there was a statutory time-limit for being newly-wed. He was about to voice the thought when Lucy looked over his shoulder at the huge Bentley backing away.

'Oooh, tell him I'll have the car instead,' she gabbled like a quiz-show winner. 'Quick!'

Stuart grinned and shook his head. 'No more mother-in-law jokes, we promised.' He opened his eyes and saw Alicia behind her.

'Hello, Stuart,' she said with a smile, not her usual reserve.

'Alicia . . . How was the camp?'

'Don't!' Lucy interposed, 'No sanctimoniums before supper. Come on, we're starving, you can have a drink at the table.'

'You shouldn't have waited . . . Lucy, tell me, last night at Heathrow when I went to get a trolley, how did I get stuck with another *coco*?'

'I didn't . . .' She stopped and stared at him. 'There wasn't room in either of the bags, that's why I was carrying it. You packed you own grip in Mahé, it was full.'

'I don't remember, half maybe. I thought you'd done it for me.'

She shook her head in some puzzlement and pointed to the sideboard where a dark brown double nut was propped coyly on lop-sided stumps. Stuart unzipped his grip and produced the second one, placing them side by side.

'They're hellish expensive,' he said almost complainingly and Lucy rose at once. 'Don't blame me! You're not allowed to take more than one, anyway. I feel awful.'

'Which one? All right where did you get that one, the one you were carrying?'

'The hotel where we changed and got a shower, just before we left. I felt such a booby, when you went to call a taxi, the manager brought it to me in the hall, saying "*N'oubliez pas*" something garbled. I suppose I looked sheepish and thanked him.'

'He wasn't giving it like a present, then?'

'Hardly, it's worth ten times the cost of the room, he'd have been ugh, loco, I was going to say nuts.'

Stuart gave a mystified shrug but Lucy rubbed her hands and said, 'Well, there we are. Getting a bit cluttered with them. Mama, would you like to take one home?'

Stuart knew her tone was bantering but Alicia often failed to catch the nuance.

'Certainly I would not! Anyway, I am not going home. And those things are too suggesting.'

'Nearly as bad as the things they imitate,' Stuart smiled easily. 'Where's your pooch?'

'Harvey Smith is at Main Gate, being very spoiled,'

she answered seriously. 'I miss him but it's not good to hitchhike, even with a tiny Yorkshire Terrier. Last time . . . well, I don't say.'

'No, don't,' Lucy said severely. 'Pass the potatoes. We have to seduce her back with luxury, Stuart, she's been living in squalor, being the conscience of us all. I must take a plate upstairs, darling, we have another guest, dare I say another Ukrainian? She's in bed, getting over some bug. I told Mama this is not a way station for dropouts but then I made the mistake of meeting the unfortunate lady. She's sublime, Stuart, ethereal. She has the most beautiful smile and it doesn't help to look at her eyes. This is Heartbreak Hostel. Well, I'll tell you later.'

She started to serve a fourth plate and then added, 'There was a call for you this morning. Someone in Century House, Czech Section. Isn't that what you work for?'

Stuart frowned but didn't answer. 'Well,' Lucy went on archly, 'They were looking for you so I suggested, politely, that as you'd been intercepted by officialdom at the airport, perhaps you were already in the cipher room or hiding in the loo. Anyway, I said I'd get you to phone them if I saw you first. A man called Stayres.' She gave the curious spelling. 'He asked where you'd been – hey, you didn't tell me that was a sneak, unofficial holiday, I'd have relished it even more. I asked this Stayres if he was the Pry Minister, ha ha! He was rather cool, I'd say. Can one ask where you were, actually?'

Stuart shrugged. 'Grosvenor Square.'

'With that American? Who is he exactly? Reminds me of an actor.'

'He, according to himself, bends the little pink ear of the next President of the United States, that is, when he's not banging his head.' Stuart smiled, deliberately not looking at Alicia's expression so that Lucy might think he said it just for effect. He could tell they were both

74

staring at him so he concentrated on his food but with little appetite. He wondered how long Lucy could stay baffled by his secret status without seriously doubting it, but at the very least, for his own safety, he had to keep Simonov convinced and in part that meant Alicia as well. She could too easily let the truth slip and he knew quite enough about the Russian's ruthlessness.

'He was just off the Concorde and sent you a little present for your co-operation.' Stuart wanted to recount at least Epiphany's tale about the Concordski plans but realised it would only incense Alicia's competitive spirit. She was unable to grasp the British attitude to sport, and thoughts of *Rodina,* the Motherland, still plucked at her heartstrings a little sombrely.

He got up to retrieve the bottle and put it down in front of Lucy; with delight she ran her hand appreciatively over its lustrous elegance. Stuart put the card down as well, saying, 'Don't look at that if you're still hungry.'

Lucy promptly did so and squealed her outrage. '*Terrine de légumes au homard,*' she read with a terrible accent, 'Vegetable paté garnished with medallions of fresh lobster and caviar pearls, Marie-Rose sauce . . . *Tournedos Rossini,* with Strasbourg *foie gras,* Vladimir Ilyich!' Her voice rose theatrically. '*Filet de Sole Florentine . . . Caille farcie,* oh yes? Roasted quail stuffed with butter-basted herb seasoning . . . Do have another hard-boiled potato. Mother did them specially.'

Alicia ignored the unjust remark. 'So now you work for Americans also?' she asked somewhat sharply.

'Not if I can help it, no.'

'What happened to your hand?'

Lucy looked up in startled concern, eyes wide as she leaned over to look, her breath held. 'Oh, I feel guilty because I didn't see it, poor love, what did you do, does it hurt?'

Stuart shook his head quickly and would have turned his hand away but Alicia leaned over and took his wrist firmly, pre-empting her daughter for a closer look. The dressing had loosened and she clucked sympathetically, holding it over for Lucy to see.

'I snagged it on a piece of metal, in a car park. It's OK, get on with your dinner.'

Alicia relented, saying, 'Good stitching. Now you have to sue the owners of the car park, like they do in America.' While the remark was typically snide, Stuart noticed she said it with a smile, looking at him slightly askance so that he too felt there was a change in her.

They lay facing in a low light, their hands clustered between them. Just above a whisper Lucy asked, 'Are you worried about something?'

Stuart nodded imperceptibly. 'A bit, I've been given a slight tangle to unravel. Shouldn't take long.'

There was a moment's pause as Lucy brushed his hand with her fingertips, carefully skirting his injury. 'Would it get up your nose if I asked you why St George knows something about you that I don't?'

'What is it?'

'Well, I don't know, do I? He didn't say. He got all cryptic and shifty on me. I've concluded it's something illegal or dangerous or both. St G just said it was business.'

'It was going to be a surprise,' Stuart tried to sound affronted. 'He's a bumbling oaf.'

'That's true, but he's so sweet . . . By the way, he said to tell you he's still in love with me, didn't want to be underhand about it, you being a splendid chap and all that . . . So it's a surprise for me?'

'Sure.'

'You don't sound as if you could be wheedled . . . It's so good to be home. I do love it here.'

Stuart held his dread at bay very carefully. 'And so good on the boat, I feel spoilt for life . . . I want to give you the delight you give me.'

76

'Oh, you do, Earthman, don't ever worry,' she slid a knee between his thighs and it seemed the sweetest gesture in creation until she capped it by smoothing the hair on his temple, forcing an indrawn gasp.

'I wish I could believe that,' he whispered.

There was a sibilant chuckle. 'You'll never know, will you? But I've been sending pheromones since during dinner, you knew that, didn't you?'

'I always know. Your eyes smoulder and then you start squirming your legs around.'

'I do not! Squirm? God, is it that obvious? Then why didn't you haul me off then and there? Oh . . . Hey, and there's my course of injections, if you miss one you have to start all over again.'

'You just completed four whole weeks . . . Anyway, you like being alone sometimes.'

'It's true, and so do you. Yes, I adore it, and mainly for the contrast. It'd be awful if I didn't know you'd be back, that's the snag with your job, the uncertainty but . . . never mind, I'm sorry. Why are we talking so much, being so restrained?'

'Who is?' he asked, still holding back.

'Well, I can wait till morning, if you like, be all fresh and tingling.'

'Sour breath and whiskers.'

Lucy clucked softly. 'I don't mind, it's earthy.' She moved against him and began exploring with her fingertips in subtle circlings. 'We could do both, if you like?'

She smiled and closed her eyes when she heard him growling a response. Lucy revelled in the clenching excitement that springs from newness and unpredictability, and she had a permanent fear that sameness, choosing the known and comfortable, was the defeat of wonder and invention. Left to itself, her body seemed to move without a programme and she loved the way it could arouse with its quicksilver suppleness and a little wickedness of improvisation. She could lead and still be elusive and in the lamp-glow see his eyes on the brink of ecstasy. He strove like a young conductor believing he could rein in a violin section exuberant with brio and bubbling with grace notes, while the violin pretended some control of itself so as not to hasten him. When the effort became too much she submitted joyfully to a new tempo and allowed a gathering respite, then from some mysterious source came that great dynamic upsurge, its power deafening them to any muted bellow or high whimpered keening. As the echoes faded they held on as if in terror of mortal seizure, receding in longing, too reluctant even for an exchange of smiles, a delirious rallentando.

After a long meditative interval Lucy whispered impishly, 'You can't ever know what it's like from anyone else, you know why?'

Stuart shook his head, mutely questioning.

She answered with assurance, almost smugly. 'It's 'cos real lovers never tell.'

Lucy woke in the grey November light while Stuart was still deeply asleep. The furrows of the evening were still etched on his face, a face too tanned and youthful for them. She watched him quietly, wishing they could bring everything out into the open except for her own harmless secrets. At the thought she felt an ominous crawling, seeing the harmlessness completely undermined by the bravado of her sketch-plan. It was something she certainly could not confide without being flatly forbidden. She wondered if there was any possibility of justifying her terrible dare against Stuart's own actions or perhaps against whatever he was planning with St George. She'd a strong feeling that there was more than officialdom to cause him worry. Some mysterious and unspecified trouble had followed him before, severe enough that she'd been forced to disappear so as not to be used against him. Although he hadn't been allowed to explain the reasons for the threat which had involved something unspeakable to do with kneecapping and a South African, it was apparently all cleared up. Somehow she'd managed not to press him for details, relying on his promise that one day . . . As if they'd chosen to live partly like two scouts checking each side of the track, it was acutely disappointing that they couldn't gossip and compare notes on each reconvergence.

She couldn't wait now to get the autogyro commissioned, nor could she suppress the hope that Stuart would find out, just so she could relish his amazement. She wondered if he himself would feel the urge to fly after seeing Decibelle in action. Her breathless and slightly fearful anticipation was protracted by Alicia's stay because Lucy had no intention of alarming her mother or worse, having to quell her protests.

Her thoughts turned to life in the peace camp and it occurred to her more forcibly that some had to be willing ascetics for her own life to be so enchanting. She felt there was some direct connection, as if their suffering and sanctity somehow procured the grace. At the same time she knew she wouldn't think of joining them, fearing the self-indulgence of martyrdom and harbouring what she thought was a healthy wariness of fanatics. Unfair thoughts, she murmured to herself, the wise only judge if they're elected to it – and the wise aren't only twenty-four years old and rampantly in love, bubbling with life and mischief . . . Cruise Missile: She felt sure it was a marketing name because it sounded almost benign, whereas Alicia had told her that its designed nuclear payload, if fitted, contained the power of sixteen Hiroshimas and should be dubbed accordingly, something like 'Exterminator', not with a whimper like 'cruising' but 'This-is-the-way-the-World-ends', Bang. Or Blast. If you mouth the word Blast, she thought, Atomic BLAST! it feels like the ultimate obscenity, boiling blood and vapourised stone. And they actually spoke of Limited or 'Theater' Nuclear War as if they were discussing a kind of pre-season warm-up, a charity match. She wondered whom she could ask, are hooligans less vicious at charity matches?

Her own personal dare, the unthinkable bid to retrieve Nadia's child, still hovered darkly. The notion felt temptingly safe – there had to be a dozen factors to make it impossible and she could be hopeful of any of them, at least until she told the bereft young mother of her plan. After that, however, there could be no change of decision. Because of her birth and bilingualism, they'd tried to single her out as an instrument of continuing conflict, an extra pip on her father's epaulette, as she saw it. She was, however, a child of a more hopeful generation and she'd rejected the rôle with neither a wink nor a clenched fist; this little venture on the other hand could be her own private gesture towards world harmony.

She smiled broadly to herself because these thoughts had blossomed in a large, comfortable and joyously shared bed. The waves of loving's euphoria returned in a swelling rhythm, spreading as if from the chakra at the base of her spine. She buried her face in the solidity of Stuart's shoulder and felt she was breathing life in unfair measure.

Stuart slept late and came down to find Lucy and Alicia getting ready to go out. While he sat, tousled, in the kitchen, sipping coffee, he watched Lucy as she teased him silently, pretending to be furtive. She wore a running suit and was clutching a list, murmuring through it as if to memorise, shielding it defiantly when, to humour her, he pretended to peer at it. Her lists consisted of children's names linked with points for exercises, flight training mnemonics or plain shopping items but they were all equally guarded. Stuart said he'd be out for lunch and Lucy answered that she'd be out all afternoon. Neither asked questions but the air between them seemed to pulse and tingle.

After her airy farewell he called and spoke to St George's secretary, arranging a meeting with him at Staverton where the Piper was due for some radio checks. They met in a little clubhouse where St George had already made such a fuss about machine coffee and plastic cups that the meek little secretary had quailed and gone shopping for the real thing. The seats were very low and St George's knees stuck out jauntily.

'Well, well,' he said once they were alone, 'What you been up to, then? Heard you'd been rind and abite.'

'What?' Stuart chewed on it for a moment and came up with 'round and about'. 'Yes, sort of. Look, your proposition, you never really filled me in. Can I assume it's still on?'

'Um?' St George's inflection could have been either caution or boredom and Stuart felt another squeeze of the pincer. It was only momentary, however, and soon replaced by a different dread. St George was still waiting so he prodded gently, 'Prague?'

'Ah . . . Certainly still on far as I know.' His tone carried a hint of resentment. 'Frankly, it was a bit cavalier of you, rushing off and then not a word. Me getting all wound up and of course this wretched Czech still bleating at me, sort of.'

'Well, I'm under a bit of pressure and I'm back, so I'm listening. Sorry if you were put out.'

'Very well. You do appreciate that I'm selling this information, don't you?'

'Yes, but on results?'

'Yes, of course, I need £44,000 to finish restoring me own machine, so that's what you owe me if we pull it off, um? Done?'

Stuart nodded and held out his hand but St George waved it away as an unnecessary embarrassment, settled himself and quickly warmed to his theme. 'Right. Tell you all I know. Place half-way out of Prague called Kbely, there's a museum where they've a Mark IX in almost flying condition, completely restored. I had to do some hush-hush hokey-pokey through diplomat friends to get parts to them, been going on for some time. I even made a few bob on the deal. But we got many repeats and then latterly requests for two of everything, it all got a bit tricky. The problem is getting stuff out this end, not getting it into theirs, embargoes on exports to commie countries and so on. Anyway, see, over the years just sitting in a hangar, old fashioned materials on things like tubes, belts, wiring, oil seals, oleo and hydraulic seals, stuff just rotted away, perspex yellowing and so on. But I know where to get bits or, if I don't, Allcock is a wizard on surpluses, he's like a rat in a biscuit barrel. Anyway, two of everything was making it difficult so I queried it. Chappie in the Foreign Office went to see the museum curator and was quickly pulled into the corner of the shed for a quiet whisper behind the daily paper, extraordinary name, what is it?'

'*Rude Pravo,*' Stuart supplied.

'Right. Sounds like a sordid bum-and-tit job. Anyway, our Rodney gets some garbled story about a crazy old man in Bohemia risking his scrawny neck to get these bits as though there was a war on. It was actually your name that triggered it for me, 'cos this old feller's obsession, apparently, is contained in the question: "When is Kody coming? I'm always waiting, tell him it's ready," – except that he wants two brake bladders or a certain kind of jubilee clip. "Tell Kody not to worry about the tyres, she's chocked by the axles . . . Can't get 150 octane any more, only rubbish . . . My heart is going . . .", stuff like that.'

'But all this only came out because you asked me my father's name. You didn't explain why.'

St George waved his hand placatingly. 'I was going to . . . I thought I'd test your gristle first, frankly. My diplomat friend scared the knickers off the poor curator but got to the bottom of it eventually. The message from this old Bohemian wallah was "Karel Kody has to come for the Spitfire, only him". Apparently it was a promise to his son when he lay dying.'

'And his name was Mišek, am I right?'

'*Is*, old boy,' St George answered with glee. 'He's still ticking over though it sounds as though he's left his choke out and got a misfire. Seems he has this letter of condolence from your old man, you pronounce it "Karl", right? Sent over forty years ago. Mišek answered it, telling him about the Spit but he heard no more. He's still waiting. There are no Kodys in the London telephone directory and I gave up after about thirty of the provincial ones, I got jumpy like you do in art galleries, had to rush off the crapper, know what I mean? Meeting you in the flesh, well, the chances are too many millions to one, don't you think?'

Stuart shook his head in shared amazement and some fear of the reality. 'My father couldn't have got the letter, he never found out what happened. As far as he knew, Jaroslav had just disappeared. That's certainly all he told me, and quite a few times. The Russians were in Czechoslovakia by then, it was late 1945. Young Mišek and my dad were patrolling the Bavarian border, very cautiously I gather because a couple of our chaps had shot down some Russian Yaks by mistake. Or vice-versa, I'm not sure.'

'Not sure?' St George sat up and almost squealed, 'Those Yaks wouldn't have stood a – sorry, do go on.'

Stuart grinned. 'Thank you. Mišek Junior went to beat up his parents' farm, it was about seventy miles inside the border. He just never came back.'

'So they weren't with the Czechs when this happened? That would explain it because the rest were more or less accounted for. There were three Czech squadrons all with Spits, there was 310, 312 and 313. One of them was

83

disbanded in France, the other two went Czecho-wards and got disbanded from the R.A.F. in February '46. We gave them away, imagine it! They had the usual wastage, all logged, then the rest were sold to Israel. Anyway, if young Mišek was with your father we can easily find out which squadron he was with.'

'It was 326, if it matters. I've got a photograph. They were stationed on the Austrian border near Passau. He'd been with the Czechs before but he didn't want to go back. He was in love with a Scottish nurse.'

'And together they begat you. Of course it matters, sort of thing is the breath of life to archivists. But listen, you still haven't checked out in a Spitfire and I can't arrange it here. That's why I sent you off to Texas and you never even got down to Harlingen to meet the Confederate Air Force, did you? My uncle the Colonel was ready to pull the chocks away for you himself.'

'I know, St G., I'm sorry. Something came up. How's your own restoration going?'

'Lurch and stagger. Allcock's whingeing like mad at the lack of readies and I was hoping you were going to bail me out. Well, never mind. I was going to say there's a two-seat Spit around, only one though and it's having a coronary at the moment – maybe when you get back, um? Otherwise the only way to get the ins-and-outs is – you're not going to believe this – they asked me to sit on the wing like some twerp of a tourist behind a plexiglass shield and watch the ace-body performing his loops and rolls in cushioned comfort *inside*. What d'you think of that? And the price for the privilege? Something like £1000 per hour! They won't let you near one any other way unless you're Neil Armstrong standard. Natch, I protested with maximum baronial vehemence, said I had a commercial licence, a saint is as good as an angel, 1500 hours *and* me own machine whereupon, predictably I suppose, they politely told me to go and fly it.'

Stuart shook his head, mystified by lack of knowledge

and experience. 'My old man told me they were regularly pushed into full battle versions with as little as 20 hours on Tiger Moths.'

'I nair! God, what a pant-wetter, eh?' St George rounded his eyes and clung with both hands to an imaginary joystick, his teeth forced out like a winded thoroughbred.

'Mind, d'you realise how many they wrote off just in training accidents? Allcock says it was more like a government-sponsored all-comers wrecking rally, all those frightful Horsey Henrys with their silver hip-flasks and dashing white scarves, reading *Dandy* and *The Beano* and *Boy's Own* for their further education, just waiting for the scramble to get up at the bloody Hun, and at the oxygen for their hangovers!'

Stuart grinned but thought of his father and added a mild protest. 'They say they saved the country in its darkest hour. Splendid chaps, um?'

'I know, old boy, can't you tell I'm just jealous . . . But you get the point, I'm sure. It's a primitive plane really, but grotesquely over-powered. Twenty-seven *litres*! The few Spitfire owners don't have that wondrous sponsorship any more, insurance is very awkward and what's the point?' His voice dropped soft and confidential. 'But listen, the thing is, this chappie told me there's not much point in having just *one* Spitfire, you can only rush about in it at hideous expense, forty-five gallons on hour, – no, he said, you have to have *two* so you can have *dog-fights*, come up for the weekend, better than croquet, the way he said it, eyes afire with rat-a-tat-tat and tally-ho, rather exciting, um?'

His hands chased each other over their heads in figure-eights, chandelles and Immelmann turns. The accompanying vocals dealt zizzling machine-guns, thump of cannon and engines snarling over limits, stopping abruptly when the dowdy little secretary returned with a packet of ground coffee. St George blew her an unabashed kiss and then asked Stuart what seemed a leading question.

'By the way, what did they put you on in Texas?'

Stuart was still privately amused about St George's assumption of his wide flying experience, wondering how it would go if the truth were known. He was forgetting how much trouble had already followed the assumption. At least he was able to answer the question truthfully to include the helicopter lessons but without describing it as student time, adding the quite accidental jet hours just for good measure.

'Various . . . Aerobat, R22, JetRanger. And I got a couple of hours free in a Citation 2.'

St George's eyebrows went up in dutiful surprise. 'Lucky bastard. A chopper and a jet would put me nicely up-market, think of all those svelte little racing driver groupies, pit-lizards. You know, I did have the idea of going with you to Prague, see if this second one really exists, maybe it's a spoof, and if not then I could sneak it out the backdoor myself, earn the restoration money the hard way, you being a bit rusty and so on. But with your jet time as well, plus you speak the lingo, anyway, you can sort of go and have a bit of chat, I mean if this Bohemian wants to just give it to us, see how he wants to play it, put him out of his misery, poor old buggah, do you suppose the Commies would ever let it out, they'd shoot him first or give him sixty-five years hard labour for keeping it in the first place – or they might even charge HMG for storage. And that's a point, it's not theirs, it's bloody well *ours*! Anyway, let me know if you need anything, and I've got a buyer for you, cash on the barrel. When can you go?'

'A few days. Your diplomat friend, did he keep all this to himself?'

'We rowed together at Henley, Steward's Cup,' St George replied archly as if it explained everything. Abruptly he stood up. 'Listen, I must go and hurry them up. I've got a little charter to Holland for some naughty playboys, all get the clap and teach 'em a lesson. Be in touch, um? Can you phone from there?'

'Czechoslovakia? Sure, but international calls are all monitored.'

'Ah. Never mind, it's all rather exciting, isn't it? I'll think up some code-words, give me a ping before you go and I'll have the contact's number for you. Dagga-dagga and love to the missus.'

He slipped through the door unseen by the secretary. Stuart had to cope with her affront and gladly drank two cups of fresh coffee in appeasement but he felt a far greater restorative in the prospect of independent action free of strings. If there was any gold in this crazy rainbow notion and it could be taken quietly, Riverson need never know how he could afford not to co-operate with Langley and his credibility with Simonov would not be at issue.

Just let it be simple, he prayed quietly, thinking he was no match for the machinators.

FOUR

'I had been afraid of Russia
ever since I could remember.'

Colin Thubron, *Among the Russians*

With Lucy's weakness for the frisson of surprises Stuart
might have taken expectant delight in filling a vault
of them but the sinister aspects steadily mounted into
bleak anxiety. Overall he supposed he could justify his
pretences by their motives but the prospect of eventual
revelation became more alarming with each tangle. He
had no idea how to tell her that he had met her father
some time before in Antwerp without revealing that it
was no chance meeting, that the KGB had found out
about his diamond run for Rollo even before he'd left
South Africa, waiting upon his arrival in Belgium to exert
the huge lever of robbing him. The pretence that he was
working for a British Special Intelligence department,
having come to Simonov through Alicia very shortly
after Stuart had invented it and gone off to South
Africa, Stuart had been impelled to play out the rôle
for the Russian in an attempt to redeem Rollo's 'lost'
fortune, discovering in the process that his father-in-law
possessed a mischievous philandering nature and a streak
of uncomplicated ruthlessness.

Not many years earlier, Alicia had also informed
Simonov that Lucy's first husband was showing repeated
violence towards her; Simonov had made a risky and
illegal visit back to the UK and summarily shot him, not

knowing at that point that a desperate Lucy had already responded to the violence and defended herself, putting her lethal training to actual use for the first time. Of the family, Simonov was the only one who knew that the silver-tongued Irishman was on Moscow's payroll and had been steered towards Lucy deliberately. Simonov had no qualms about writing off a KGB asset and, cornering him in the dark of Acton cemetery a week later, didn't see the marks of Lucy's resistance on his face, not that they would have stopped him. After the killing he slipped back to Belgium undetected and soon heard from Alicia that Lucy was a widow, verdict suicide, proving his method's efficiency. He now felt it was better for Lucy to believe in the Irishman's suicide rather than his murder by her own father, even if she felt some guilt for her contribution. Until his drunken savagery had pushed her to breaking point, the man had had no reason to suspect her of lethal skills but he'd had a mercurial character; being bested by his wife in a straight fight could well have mortified him beyond repentance.

Stuart resented being the probable sole hearer of Simonov's boast because Lucy still admitted this residual guilt, largely because she'd broken the code by losing her temper. Stuart wanted to tell her the truth to lighten her conscience but couldn't do so without revealing his acquaintance with Simonov and the multiple entanglements behind it. He had learned, after inventing his cover rôle, that she herself had refused any co-operation with her father's twilight world and her husband's duplicity so it must have been a great effort for her to be silent when Stuart apparently joined its British equivalent. The problem was exacerbated by insolvency because he'd used the invention of this enigmatic post to explain their greatly improved circumstances; in expectation of riches he'd been extravagant himself and given Lucy a slice of capital for her own enterprise. Lucy was now keeping this project secret from him as a kind of joyous riposte but the disappearance of Rollo and the hoard of stones had spelt ruin.

Lucy and Alicia were still out when Stuart returned home and Simonov telephoned him an eerie few moments later. At first Stuart had some guilty confusion because he hadn't been going to contact him, particularly after the warning issued by Riverson. The Russian's deep voice with its unmistakable accent evoked a startling and intensely frustrating interlude.

'Stuart? At last, when did you get back?' There was a merriment in the tone which seemed to belie the question, so Stuart's answer was accordingly cynical.

'I thought the KGB knew everything.'

'Yes, they do. But they don't know whom to tell it to, so it often goes wasted. I wanted – no, first how is Beloved-of-all-the-People?'

'Do you mean Lucy?'

'Yes, that is the meaning of Ludmilla in old Russian. Sounds a bit loose to you, I expect, rather keep her to yourself.'

Stuart checked the response which would surely lead to an argument about love versus sexuality. 'Well,' he said after a moment. 'She's fine and brown and up to something mysterious.'

'What? Who for?'

'For herself, I think it's a capitalist venture.'

'Do you want us to find out what it is?'

'No, Alexei, I don't. I know what you want and you know what I want.'

'Good. Then let's meet. Your parcel is coming together nicely, I could bring a sample to show you. Why don't you fly yourself to, say, Dunkirk, that's a good symbol of British phlegm and composure. I'll meet you on the beach, we can take a stroll.'

'Alexei, I can't afford it.'

'Oh, why? Aren't they paying you properly?'

'They never did. I'm getting a transfer.'

'Oh no, you mustn't! The spot is too valuable, everyone else's business at your fingertips. They don't suspect you, do they?'

Stuart suddenly saw more complications in his line of frivolity, since the Russians would drop him like a spent cartridge if he seemed to be facing any compromise. He also had to keep up the charade if he was not to dismiss Riverson and a possible last link with solvency. It would all be for nothing if Simonov discovered the one vital factor about the section employing him. So mysterious and clandestine was it that the KGB had no access to it whatever except through S. Kody who was unlisted in any Civil Service department and only responsible directly to the Foreign Secretary: this supposed section, watch-dogs section, did not exist and had only once been openly proposed by Downing Street to send certain moles tunnelling for cover.

'It's economy as well as security,' he answered vaguely, 'they want to keep us moving so we can't entrench. I can hang on for a bit, I think.'

'Good, good, longer the better. You said you had something for me, can you give me a hint now, so I have no trouble getting over to meet you?'

'It's very hot, Alexei. I've got to run another check on it, just to be absolutely sure. If I gave you what I came across and it proved unfounded, you might put something unpleasant in my cereals.' Stuart felt real nervousness in his own voice.

'Nonsense. Your previous stuff was first class, you should have seen the attention I got! I wanted to make up your losses straight away but the *Vlasti* wouldn't let me.'

'That sounds unpleasant itself.'

'Ssh . . . It means the Bosses. They wanted more, the second half. Your phone isn't bugged, by the way, we checked it.'

'Gee, thanks. Did you bug it yourselves again?'

'No, I think they learnt their lesson. We trust you

now. What they want is the source and the reason for it, the empty Tomahawks and Pershings.'

'I thought I had it, Alexei, and it's even led me on to something else. You must understand, I've simply got to verify it, you'll have to *wait*.'

'All right, all right. At least tell me the source, then I can convince them it's worth waiting. They're so hasty when they think they're being laughed at. Damn it, I've been keeping them at bay for a month now. The source, boy, point to it at least!'

Stuart scratched his head, unable to envision anything real that might also be uncheckable and thus not prove his undoing. Epiphany at first sprang to mind for his mysterious function but he was too specific and available for pressure. The extension to his unnamed senator seemed almost miraculous.

'I can only tell you this, Alexei: I got it from the next President of the US.'

After a lengthy silence the deep voice said in cold affront, 'Yes? Go on, please.'

'What?'

'Go ON! The name, who is it?'

'Oh, come off it, Alexei. If you don't know, you haven't done your homework. Look, they'll be back, I can't talk now.'

Simonov blurted in a fluster, 'They can't be, they're still at the school . . . Give me the name!'

'What do you mean? How – Alexei, have you got us under surveillance, even here?'

'Never mind that now! It's purely for your protection.'

A zoo-animal feeling surged through Stuart and he slammed down the receiver, regretting at once that he hadn't asked from whom they needed protecting. Then his sore hand reminded him that the Americans too were watching for a renegade, a South African soldier with a grievance. He looked instinctively out of the window but saw nothing unusual, turned round and jumped when his eyes went up to a slender figure at the top of the stairs, white-blonde, ultra-fine hair, translucent skin and an un-readable expression. She smiled awkwardly.

'Good morning, I am Nadia Feodorovna. Thank you for welcome to your house.'

He was about to go to her with offers of coffee and breakfast but the telephone rang again. Stuart whirled on it and then covered his haste. Simonov spoke without preamble.

'You remember the South African BOSS chief?'

'De Hoek? You owe me all his loot as well less your 10 per cent.'

'Yes, You recall he met with a fatal accident in his helicopter before he could make good any threats against you or Ludmilla. I assume you felt some gratitude, yes?'

'I suppose . . . I had intended to pay him, though. That's what you call protection, is it?'

'Yes. We now hear that an underling called Cornelius has similar extortionate ideas, he believes you have diamonds but as yet he does not know that we, ah, borrowed them. We are, therefore, keeping an eye out for him.'

'So are the – Alexei, how on earth did you find out?'

'Simple enough. We have contacts in South Africa and they have a team over your way, three SAPs looking for him. When they find him they will simply execute him, rather than ask the British for extradition and have to put up with all the red tape. The Jaapies aren't too hot on legal niceties but neither are they inter-ested in your safety, in fact you are making excellent bait. The effete Brits no longer seem to hold with this kind of rough justice because they are soft and decadent, so they are looking out for the South African team. So, you see you owe us, considerably. When can you come to France and meet me?'

Stuart didn't answer for a moment since he was think-ing of the Americans also on the look-out for Cornelius who had been able to jump him two days ago by waiting at the airport. He wondered if it were possible for anyone to arrive in a strange country with nothing but the name of an unemployed man and find him somewhere deep in the country. The assorted reception parties awaiting him seemed to make it comfortingly not worth the effort. Stuart glanced through the distortions of the little diamond-shaped panes and saw a man stroll casually past with only a nonchalant glance in his direction. He wasn't a local yet his garb didn't have the look of a stroller, perhaps a house prospector getting the feel of the village or one of those fascist building inspectors. At this thought his eyes narrowed with hostility firmly based on his experience but then he heard a car and saw Lucy's Golf sweep into the short driveway. He glanced around but saw no sign of Nadia.

'I won't be able to talk, Alexei. They've just come back.'

'All right, just listen and grunt. Is it any of the following: Bush, Dole, Barker, Cuomo, Hart? Or Biden? Or Clint Eastwood?'

Stuart barely suppressed a chuckle. 'I can't tell you anything yet.'

Simonov kept on relentlessly. 'But you will fly and meet me?'

'All right.' Stuart wondered crazily how long he could stall and how long he would have to live under the glower of Langley. 'Maybe next week sometime.'

'Will you know for sure by then?'

'Maybe.'

'Don't bait the Bear, Stuart,' the deep voice seemed to growl, 'Every maybe will cost you a three carat.'

'I have to go now.' Stuart heard the front door open and Lucy's laughter, then her arms came round him from behind in a brief renewal.

'Sorry, yes, you can't talk now. One moment.' Stuart turned to give her a distracted kiss on the nose and then

94

the voice in his ear deepened even further. 'Forgive me, I have been told to say that from this point on, misinformation from you will lead to prejudicial sanction.' The Russian coughed to cover his embarrassment. 'Right . . . so we meet next week, you'll call me – oh, one moment, I must confer again.' Simonov's inflection had returned to the formality of being monitored and Stuart could discern foreign words on the line in distant hushed conference. In a slow crawl he began to grasp what prejudicial sanction meant in Simonov's borrowed Langleyism. He looked fearfully over his shoulder only to see the women now out in the garden. Lucy's head ducked down and her legs suddenly arced in the air as if she was demonstrating, her face reappearing and laughing gaily as Alicia tried to show something with her hands. His own confusion and fear blended, swirled and came out as anger.

'Stuart?'

'Yes. Listen, Alexei, that remark you made or passed on, about sanction. What's the idea? You're trying to hold roubles in one hand and a gun in the other. It won't work.'

'That's what I tried to tell him. Barbaric, isn't it? Actually, it usually works quite well. He's gone now. He told me to tell you also that lack of information would get you turned in for treason which seems illogical, I assume it's retro-active. Meanwhile he allowed me to give you the good news I've been saving, they let me take some of the pressure off you. If you call Mr Hamish Browne, your lawyer, you'll find that we've cleared your mortgage for you.'

Stuart reeled in relief and astonishment for the sum was frighteningly large. 'Just like that, no strings?'

He thought he heard a tiny snigger. 'One little one, perhaps. The cheque was drawn on the Moscow Narodny Bank.'

'Oh great, thanks,' Stuart hissed with as much forced sarcasm as he could transmit.

'*Pas de quoi*. Mark of good faith, you'll agree.'

'Agree? Don't be ridiculous, it's just a bloody arm-lock!'

'Yes, I told them you'd see it that way. Not my fault, truly. Perhaps no one will find out. Anyway, next week, I'll have some little white stones for you, all nice and anonymous. Who's the winsome blonde lady staying with you?' The leer in his voice aroused Stuart's anger again.

'None of your bloody business, you old lecher!'

'It certainly is my business. She was heard speaking Russian and arrived with Alicia. Conspiracy smells, however prettily.'

'Oh, get off the line, damn you! She's just a harmless peace camper.'

'We'll see . . . Till next week then. *Dasvidania*.'

Stuart checked to see if the women we're still in the garden before telephoning his lawyer. He only succeeded in deepening his oppression.

'Hamish, did you get a cheque from a Moscow bank?'

'Indeed, dear boy. I was somewhat surprised, I must say.'

'Well, don't pay it in, whatever you do.'

'I'm afraid it went to your bank this morning, shall I try to retrieve it? I couldn't put it into Client's Account, it was firmly crossed to your name, I'd need your authority or more, I'm so sorry.'

'Don't worry, I'll deal with it.'

'Um. I thought it most timely. You've got a payment coming due, you know, on the house.'

'I know. I'm working on it. Thanks.'

Stuart put down the receiver in quiet fury at the Russians' heavy-handed chicanery, the cheque a blatant label for treachery or at the very least a juicy paper-chase for the harriers of the Revenue. He had no idea about how to launder such things and it was singularly painful to instruct his bank to send back such a heavy and vital amount. Mentally he sentenced Simonov,

96

Runyan and the whole of Langley to a slow and sadistic perdition.

Stuart went to Kidlington that afternoon hoping at last to take the General Flying test for his Private Licence but even that was denied him by a front coming through trailing vicious squalls and rain. Lucy and Alicia returned late, still animated about an antique shop they'd found in Cheltenham where the owner was hilariously gloomy because of an acquisitive disease.

'It's quite a big shop,' Lucy said, 'We've renamed it Catch 22. Do you want to hear why?'

Stuart smiled at the lilt in her voice and gave an exaggerated nod.

'All right then. We could only just get in the door and the man was reduced to about three square feet of space because it was so crammed with stuff, most of it out of reach. I'd seen these lovely glasses from the far window and he said, "Not for Sale, everybody wants those". "Why aren't they?" I asked and he said, "Cos I can't reach them". Mama just stood there gaping and we took some persuading that he meant it. Anyway, we went off and I found a long pole and tied a forked branch to it and tried again. I was so pleased with my invention, I thought he'd praise me for it or reduce the price but he just said gloomily, "I've got one of those, much better too".

'I nearly shrieked at him. I asked him, "Why didn't you tell me, you silly old fellow?" Darling, you'll never guess what he said.'

Stuart had to cover his own gloom and look expectant.

'He said he couldn't *reach* it!' Lucy clapped delightedly and set Alicia laughing again, then she brought the glasses to the table, four very old yellowing crystal goblets, each cut slightly different.

'Beautiful,' he said, fully praising her choice but then he had the thought of a fourth person and asked after Nadia. The question restored their feelings about the lost baby to a matching gloom, for Nadia had slipped away quietly and gone back to the camp. There was, however, some light-hearted consternation when Alicia requested hunt-the-television because of a small item she'd seen in the paper. The person who last concealed the set could not participate in this ritual.

'I'm afraid I've already found it,' Lucy announced ruefully, 'The last ogler took no trouble over her hiding place.'

She fixed her mother with a beady look but there was careless merriment in her eyes. She pulled the little set from under the cushions and held it up for Stuart to see, the casing all cracked and askew. 'Direct hit from a hundred and ten pounder,' she said, 'Shall I try it?'

Stuart grinned palely, trying to visualise which of her acrobatics had done the damage. He nodded shrinkingly, putting his fingers in his ears. Lucy plugged it in and astonishingly the set fizzled for a moment and produced a clear picture. She drummed her hands with delight at such a tiny symbol battered into intellectual snobbery, its very size a mark of disdain, as yet compromised by its still functioning. She kept chuckling at it until Alicia sternly achieved the correct channel and then 'Great Sporting Moments' gave them ten minutes to treasure in Olga Korbut, the diminutive Russian gymnast of the early '70s, gold-medal pioneer of astonishing courage and agility combined with a lyrical pixie elegance. Sadly, she was already shaded out by the new greats, ever younger and suppler and more cruelly over-trained.

Alicia sat tight-lipped and thoughtful when the feature ended. Lucy ritually switched off at once saying, 'Poor little thing, the pleasure she gave millions and millions, then the limelight cancelled. Marriage and baby. Phut!' She snapped her fingers, grinned and ruffled Stuart's hair.

Alicia said, 'If we had stayed at Leningrad, you would have been perhaps the next.'

'A star? Not me, Mama, the life's too grim.'

'That's right, Alicia,' Stuart agreed, 'Lucy would have hammed it up and been sent to Siberia for clowning. You in disgrace for not being a State-dedicated mother, and father drummed out of the KGB.'

'He's not *with* the KGB!' Alicia protested at high pitch. 'He's just a diamond expert.'

Diamond thief, Stuart said to himself with questionable accuracy.

'And indiscriminate bed-hop,' Lucy added, looking at Stuart strangely, wondering why he should have any awareness of Simonov. Her father's wayward habits were a private sore-spot for herself and her mother, so Lucy hardly ever spoke of him.

Stuart brushed her fingers in a light sympathy. He believed with almost violent certainty that he could never be unfaithful but then he became starkly aware of a sombre thought, that if he wasn't careful there might not be time anyway.

He knew his mood puzzled Lucy even after they were alone in their room and at one point she took his head in both hands to examine his expression. With real regret at having to be less than open, Stuart pleaded tiredness and Alicia's always slightly inhibiting presence in the house. Lucy promised to be very quiet and then became her most subtly inventive, seeming to pour herself like a balm all around him, a softly melting pool of sublime and intuitive rapture. Reluctant to lose not just the moment he clung to her too fiercely and she cried out against him, yet they both slept profoundly and unmoving. The sweetness of waking still entwined seemed to force his new determination.

At breakfast, just before he left for London, the postman delivered an embossed dinner invitation from Paul

Epiphany and one Giles Raintree. It was for just over three weeks away and Lucy read it out with tip-toe glee, her thoughts soaring.

'Who on earth are they, Stuart? Wait – I think I know the second name, where from, school? And Hever Castle in Kent. Look, Mama.' She put the card on the table and Alicia peered at it suspiciously. 'I'll show you, I've got pictures in a book, it's heavenly, it's got two moats and a maze, it was where that beastly Henry fell for Anne Boleyn, remember? Do you know, I read that the Pope would have given him his annulment just like that except that Catherine of Aragon was Auntie to the French king and he had more pull with the Vatican? Poor Anne made a mistake insisting on marriage before giving away her cherries, did you learn that in school, Mama?' With a huge twinkle she assumed a bored tone. 'I suppose I'll have to get a new dress. Pink, I think, yes?'

Stuart arched a querulous eyebrow and sighed theatrically. 'Not worth it, it'll only be crumpled by the time you get there. It's going to be hell, think of it, all the way from here, right across London in the rush-hour on a Friday evening, for heaven's sake!'

Lucy over-acted a great wince for his scepticism but had a sudden secret hankering that the autogiro might have two seats and a speed of 130 knots. It would dumbfound him completely and the gaiety of the imagined scene captivated her. She couldn't have any idea of what was running so parallel in his mind that he could hardly bear anticipating the day, revelling in his surprise, almost trembling to think of arriving home, tauntingly late, to see the delight on her face as the hired JetRanger whickered down onto the lawn, himself at the controls feigning a snooty, blasé expression, switching off, going in for her with a bouquet and watching her play her own rôle, laying her new gown carefully across the three rear seats and then helping her into the left front. Going expertly through the starting procedures and she'd probably watch him solemnly, going with the gag, pull, press, tap, test and turn with practised fingers, rotor spinning slowly up with ominous purpose, muttered check-list, decision-time, a surge of abundant power in a light-laden craft, airborne to high hover then a stomach-clenching transition, a swooping dip to port, Lucy's window towards the earth in squeals of delight to crack the mock-seriousness, accelerating level and on their way, climbing to the Southeast, calling London FIR for clearance down the Thames valley and the special low-level helicopter lanes across the twilit sprawl of a struggling city . . . Hever Castle in the fading light, peacocks scurrying with indignation, the casual dip into his pocket for another jewel, the blue diamond this time, he'd buy it from Rollo, however priceless . . .

When reality matches the fantasy, it's still partly spoiled by having been lived already in imagination. He tried to put it out of his mind since magic only comes unbidden and events somehow find a way of punishing presumption.

At the Czech Embassy in Holland Park he had his visa renewed without query, this time as a tourist instead of the student of ten years before. The visa clerk, a handsome young woman, was strangely wooden and lacking in warmth, suspicious even when he spoke to her in colloquial Czech. As a last attempt, after receiving his documents, he looked her frankly up and down and confessed with narrow humour that he was there to trap her. The shrug of total indifference sent him reeling out into the drizzle, aghast yet soberly recalling the grey pessimism he had found in the aftermath of the '68 occupation; it was that saddest season which became known as the Prague Spring, the year in which the spirit of springtime was officially abolished and the new hopes of millions simply wept and withered away.

*   *   *

The length of new Bond Street amazed him once again by its daunting, blatant opulence so tastefully disguised, its windows so artfully furnished with superfluous accessories. Stuart realised he'd never had much hankering for trappings and wealth, and he wished fervently he could somehow avoid his current mission even though it was only in pursuit of mere solvency. The sums involved were outside his natural parameters and he had long felt that fulfilment had nothing to do with acquisition, in fact quite the opposite, that money was simply a tool and he had enough tools for his needs.

A few doors past the end of this alley of affluence, in Old Bond Street, nestled Cedok, a non-capitalist Czech travel agency attached like a mollusc to filter hard currency. He walked gloomily inside and asked for a long week-end in Prague. A much more cheerful and matronly figure obliged him for the following Friday, at first clucking her doubts and then showing him favour when Stuart responded in kind to her occasional Czech remarks to the computer. There was a lengthy wait for endorsement and then a hiatus of embarrassment as the cashier came over, her face stern with guarded reproof, to say that the automatic link was refusing payment clearance on his card. Stuart felt little of the embarrassment because in spite of his situation he was sure he hadn't reached his credit limit. He was angry, however, and made an effort not to direct it unfairly at the agent.

'Please try it again,' he said, 'I'm quite certain it's in order.'

His tone seemed to convince her and he sat down to wait, leafing through pamphlets on the delights of Prague and Marienbad, faces showing the delirious joys to be savoured behind the protection of the Iron Curtain.

He waited a good twenty minutes, getting up to glower a couple of times and being told the line was still engaged. His vague suspicions of subterfuge were confirmed when a man came in wearing a trilby hat, a padded raincoat and galoshes, exchanged nods with one of the women and turned to Stuart. He looked pinch-faced and defeated by under-promotion.

'Could I have a word with you, Mr Kody? My name's Forbes.'

'What the hell's going on?' Stuart bristled icily.

'Mr Stayres sent me, sir. Says he'd like a word with you before you go. I'm sorry to put you out, sir.'

Stuart was about to send back a peremptory reply about what officialdom might do to itself but Forbes' apologetic manner softened him fatefully. He sighed his irritation and asked,

'What does he want, did he tell you?'

'No, sir, only that it could do more than pay for your trip.'

'Don't tell me they own Cedok? How did they pick me out?'

'Not for me to say, sir. I'm sure Mr Stayres will fill you in. It'll be no bother, sir, I've a taxi waiting.'

'Just tell me one thing: is Stayres in any position to stop me going where I want?'

Forbes shrugged uneasily. 'Well, you know how these things are, sir. Lawfully of course he can't, but let's say influentially it might be different. So many clauses they can invoke, you know?'

Stuart regarded Forbes for long moments, mulling over this distilled truth. As if clarified, he decided it was better to find out what he was up against rather than force a tangle of red tape.

He nodded abruptly. 'OK, if the cab brings me back here afterwards.'

Forbes agreed and on the journey there seemed little more to discuss than the grey threatening weather. Eventually they pulled up at No 3 Carlton Gardens where Forbes' relief glowed right through his impatience at the security clearance on the door. As they waited, Stuart remembered the surreptitious lace curtains spoiling the view of the Mall and St James's Park. Once inside, Forbes led him upstairs on worn carpets and then put his head cautiously round a forbidding door. Given a signal, he pushed it wide open and ushered Stuart inside. Behind a dark mahogany desk, Adrian Stayres hesitated before standing, giving an affable smile of recognition. Silver of hair and impeccably dressed, he held an ivory paper knife oscillating in his left hand, yet there was still something just in Class 2 about his mannered arrogance, a sense of undeserved failure perhaps. Behind him the window-sill bustled with the perennial activity of two scruffy London pigeons which looked bored enough to have been copulating solidly for a month and still waiting for a day warm enough to go exploring.

As Forbes silently withdrew, Stuart sat in an indicated chair and glanced quickly round him. The room was part-panelled and he was sure there'd been a woodland scene over the mantelpiece, now replaced with a smaller oil of a full-rigged ship leaving a two inch unfaded mark in the surrounding wall-paper.

'Well, well,' Stayres began but Stuart interrupted at once.

'My wife said you called. What did you want?'

'Foreign Sec's office asked me where you were. I thought they knew, something to do with Washington. Coming across you like this is very curious. Are you lying low or something?'

Stuart shook his head quickly. 'I've just been on holiday.'

'Ah, then they found you and didn't bother to let me know. Typical. So what's this? I suppose you off-side chaps like to keep a pale silhouette, going like a normal tourist, but I'd like to know what you're doing on my patch, should have consulted me, only good manners, don't you think?'

Stuart wished he could clear up the former misappre-

104

hension under which Stayres too laboured, his invented rôle as an unlisted watchdog, but he realised he had scant chance of being believed at this stage and it was probably better to find out what Stayres was chasing. His answer was anyway largely truthful.

'My visit is actually quite unofficial, that's to say it *was* going to be private. Father's relatives.'

Stayres didn't miss the emphasis. 'You mean it's not private any more, now that we've spotted you?'

Stuart shook his head again, determined not to rise. 'I hope you're not going to be abrasive. As far as I'm concerned, it's still private, but your man Forbes implied that you could make things tricky for me. Why don't you just give it to me straight? What do you want and why did you pick me up like that?' He tapped the desk for emphasis. 'Anyone resents being told he can't afford something.'

'Um.' Stayres' understanding nod contained no apology. 'You probably won't believe me. When you were last here I just added your name to a pitifully small list of possibles, just because of your Czech accent. I was looking for someone then, remember? I need a damn civilian, that's the trouble, someone not on a list, just to take some papers. Simple job, might mean a bit of address hunting, that's all. It's not on for my people, nor for the diplomats, they all get tagged by ferrets and can't move. We're a bit short of the right personnel, d'you see?'

'Didn't you have an agent holed up somewhere and no means of getting him out?'

'Correct, but "her". Piece of gateau for someone of your experience, the miracle is you're ex-directory, shouldn't get tagged at all. We could give you a change of passport to go with it, might help.'

'I haven't said I'll do anything yet.'

Stayres looked suddenly more affable. 'So you haven't. We do pay, you know. All expenses, good travel? Are you going to need a car?'

When Stuart nodded, Stayres gave a theatrical hiss of alarm. 'Hellish expensive, you'll find. Ergo, a little job for us and instead of being a few hundred down, you'll come back from Grandma's a few hundred up and no risk, why not?'

'That's all I'd have to do, take someone some papers?'

'More or less.' Stayres leaned towards his intercom and pushed the button. 'Sylvia? Procházka file, please.' He looked up. 'Best thing is if she comes out with you as your wife, far less noteworthy. Presume you don't mind being someone else for a weekend.'

'What? Oh, I see. But I've already got my visa and booking in my own name.'

'Oh, function!' Stayres looked annoyed and toyed with the ivory for a moment, then rather impressively snapped a decision. 'Very well, if you'll agree to do it in your own name, we'll change the paperwork for our girl, Maryša.' He gave a resigned and heavy sigh. 'If you can't find her, well, I suppose it's too bad. I'll have to trust you to try, all right?'

Stuart nodded slowly and then said, 'All right, but there's a time limit. Just keep it uncomplicated, can you?'

Stayres was plainly relieved and began to brim with co-operation and bonhomie. His secretary came in with a file and took notes of his orders. She walked heavily and seemed to be wearing a grey halo. 'Tell me,' Stayres asked when she'd gone, 'Did your section have any leads at all for our leak? A leak got Maryša blown in the first place but we still don't know which end. I asked you to look into it, remember?'

'Fraid there's nothing to report yet,' Stuart invented, 'They're still working on it, far as I know.'

'Hmph . . . Well, perhaps when you get back you can jizz them up on it.'

The secretary returned and Stayres leafed through her folder again, revealing a photograph. 'She's quite a beauty, if a trifle frosty. Don't forget to sign the cards, will you?'

Stuart couldn't really tell from the small posed photograph, a pale face framed with dark hair, the eyes penetrating. He scanned it without interest, wondering how they contained frauds with all the credit available, but didn't care in the least. He was on his way in less than an hour after practising a casual trick for the Czech immigration barrier. It worried him at first when Stayres explained that his 'wife' had to go in legitimately in order to be allowed out again but Forbes was called to join in the demonstration and they made it seem like a jolly prank, teasing away his alarm. He was primed with three addresses, memorised only, a wad of travellers cheques, three new credit cards and an undertaking for scale remuneration, low risk category.

He was also assured of continuing unlisted anonymity and was told this meant he had no support, no back-stop, no official sanction and no squawk-number to call. As soon as her visa had been processed, a courier would come with his 'wife's' documents and the two air-tickets, paid for by the department. No debriefing would be necessary unless he had to abort and curiously no mention was made of the duration of his credit. Stuart didn't bother to ask about it.

Without doubt, he thought, it would be quietly cancelled immediately on his return; he didn't enquire because Stayres had become distant by the end of this sequence as if the orders were given and he could now detach himself. Stuart became aware of a certain relief; they could have made it difficult for him to go at all if he'd refused the job but now he could justifiably think of it as a paid-for reconnaissance instead of a desperate, once-only gamble.

Stayres had made an odd, faraway remark to the North window, that it might turn out to be a long winter.

Stuart attached nothing to this chill prognosis and as he left he began to smile, realising that he had just joined some branch of the clandestine where he was supposed to have lurked for months – which pretence had got him into all his difficulties in the first place and which he so often longed to clarify with Lucy.

If a man steals an heirloom and then discovers it bequeathed to him, can the new truth bestow some retroactive absolution?

Lucy felt her own small measure of self-reproach when Stuart came home and told her he'd be away for the weekend, a slight shame because of a mixed elation. His absence would leave her free to go to Enstone where Allcock would be starting to assemble her hybrid Bensen and she'd be able to get some more flying on the trainer if the weather allowed.

A few minutes after he'd spoken, however, and she'd routinely expressed her disappointment, she had a feeling that there was an untruth in the air. In a stage where lovers linger round the paradox of their fettered freedom, she felt somehow that Stuart was hiding in the wings; thus a few drops of guilt were added to this shame when a motor-cycle courier arrived all the way from London with a sealed package marked OHMS, Private. Stuart was out in the garden sawing wood and she asked the courier casually the name of the sender. Chewing gum with an open mouth he reluctantly showed the endorsement in his book and the clear signature: Sylvia Cornwallis. He smelled dreadfully of oil and dirty leather so Lucy walked upwind around the motorcycle saying Gosh! and Wow! to its huge engine and six shiny pipes. This only earned her a curled lip presumably for uncoolness so she urged him to thumb it into life without a coffee and biscuit reward. In a softly violent hawking of Japanese horsepower he was up to sixty mph well inside three seconds of pulling down his road-knight's visor and Lucy was happily sure of the expression inside it, a sneer which took in her looks, her clothes, the quiet village, the old stone house and a suspicious abundance of fresh air.

Turning indoors she was also aware of a passer-by with a guarded walk and further down the road a car parked by the hedge, its position without evidence of purpose.

Stuart took the package casually and put it aside in the kitchen without opening it. Lucy looked at him mischievously, wanting to ask him about it although his expression seemed to say it wasn't interesting.

'Is it homework?' she asked eventually.

'Oh, kind of, needs checking over.'

'Can't you look shifty so I can be suspicious?'

He smiled and put his arms round her, feeling her suppleness arched against him. 'You can be anything you like except wicked and risky. And noisy. Hey, I thought we were really quiet last night, why do I still get reproachful looks from your mother in the morning?'

'Me too! All right, quit stalling: Who is the beautiful, nay, mysterious and delectable Sylvia Cornwallis?'

'I've no idea, why?'

'Liar! She sent you that package.'

'Oh, it's only some papers from Stayres, she signed for it, I suppose. His secretary.'

'Stayres? That's the man who was looking for you. Your boss?'

'Sort of, yes, though I'm not sure he likes the idea.' He grinned crookedly at her, arms' length.

'Is he nice?'

'Dreadful, why?'

'Give it up then. Do something else. I won't mind tightening the belt, not after last month. Please, Stuart, I so want you here, I mean out in the open as well. With me, like before. If you do, I'll even let you in on my secret.'

He nodded in slow assurance. 'All right. After this

weekend I'll start to get clear, well, it's four days really, I'm afraid.'

'Oh . . . And you won't resent me?'

Stuart shook his head with a smile and added, 'Lu, tell me, your own thing, is it dangerous?'

Lucy derided the idea with emphasis. 'No, it's a piece of cake.'

'*That* sounds like St George,' Stuart answered with heavy suspicion. 'An old RAF-ism.' He looked at her innocent eyes and added, 'It's the sort of thing they'd say after a one-wheel dead-stick landing, both feet shot off, eighty per cent burns and blinded with glycol. British sangfroid, y'know, wizard show and all that.'

'Just like your daddy, um?'

'Not exactly. He said they used to drive him mad with their childishness and unreality.'

'Don't know their luck, do they?' she mused. 'Everything's a giggle until you get invaded.'

'That's right,' he laughed. 'The Brits are so arrogant they don't even realise they're under-privileged, they haven't had a decent invasion in 900 years. That reminds me, take care and lock up properly while I'm away, won't you? You're a bit casual sometimes.'

'I certainly will. There's a funny feeling in Carsey. Restlessness, strangers about, kind of spooky. Mother noticed it too . . . I wonder if she'll stay at the camp, she's really into it. They've a true belief that their passionate feelings can somehow reach and affect the stream of world consciousness. I don't see any reason to be sceptical about it either, like prayers being answered, it's the will and feeling behind them that counts. Well, things are certainly changing, talks of disarmament, talks of summits, talks of talks, and of course the delicious secret you told us . . . Puzzles me, one thing, surely the people who fit the warheads know what they're about, so it can't be kept totally secret?'

'Sure. But the fissile parts are taken out on the way

110

over here, in the C-5s, the Galaxies, then they put them on ice somewhere.' Stuart wondered why this invention bred no new guilt.

'Oh, gosh! Where?'

'I don't know yet. I think I'm about to find out.'

'Well, if it's anywhere near here, I don't want to know. Let's hope they chuck them out in mid-Atlantic, that would keep everyone happy, wouldn't it? Hey, that's what I'll tell Mama, she'll be delighted. Prayers all answered – all except Nadia's, poor thing.'

Stuart nodded distantly, aware of her intense but hopeless sympathy with the bereaved young mother.

'What's a dead-stick landing?' Lucy asked in apparent innocence.

'What? Oh, engine cut-out. Means you don't get the lively . . . response, I think,' he finished lamely, conscious that he could at least share that secret with her in a week or two provided the weather would grant him a slot to take his ratings. He wondered for a moment why she'd asked, despite her arch and smiling interest in his answer, as if it were the kind of technical item only a man would care to hear. She savoured with real delight the moment when he'd learn that she'd known all along; a huge and thrilling surprise.

Stuart waited in the departure lounge heavy with resignation and almost too much to ponder. Believing he was working out his own solution he also realised the imposed controls remained effective not only because they'd forced his hand but also because he must continue to show himself immaculate. By leaving Stuart's affairs in ruins, the CIA had in fact over-reined him into lunging away from the snaffle, successfully, Stuart believed, though its effect still lingered.

A small remaining guilt lay in a secret pre-arrangement with St George's secretary. While he was away she'd agreed to make the daily single phone ring for him at around six pm, just in case he should have any problems doing it himself. He told her it would be just for a few days and that he would let her know the moment he returned. To himself he made a clenched and determined reminder over this since it would be a shameful give-away to be already home and have it happen. She took the request in her stride and made a playful remark about the handsome *coco-de-mer* which now graced St George's desk and absorbed much of his attention. She was convinced he had some peculiar design upon it, giggling when she asked why it was named Pudenda.

Meanwhile the prime disruptor of his peaceful domesticity, Rollo Runyan, had been allotted only a small dark space in his thinking. Far more went to the soldier, Vincent Cornelius, who had got to London ahead of them and tried to rob him in a strange and vicious way; whenever he thought of it, Stuart's hand still throbbed from the processes of deep repair. He knew that if he ever met Cornelius again it would be a merely dangerous waste of time trying to explain that they'd both come out of Africa duped and penniless. Stuart wondered again how difficult it would be for a stranger to the country to find him among 55 million without any hint of an address and with an icy catch he remembered about the telephone directories contained in any large public library. Looking for him, St George hadn't gone through them all, hadn't got as far as Oxford, but Cornelius could well do so if the idea occurred to him. It would also be very easy with such a rare spelling of his name. The thought alarmed Stuart into a deep dread swallow, although he could give himself a measure of reassurance. There were after all up to three different parties looking to intercept the renegade, all with different reasons.

His practical nature reasserted itself gradually, as it had when he'd gently asked Stayres why they didn't forward exit-papers for his missing agent via the diplomatic bag to Prague and post them from there. Stayres had given him a rheumy look and an answer that was convincing enough, that the lead address had been changed already several times and that, being on the run, she did not have a correlating entry-quadruplicate for her exit unless someone took it in for her and had it registered on arrival. That person had to be unquestionably fluent in case there was a need to search without drawing attention; they'd had some notable betrayals using 'trusted' nationals within Czechoslovakia and sending an unsuspectable courier seemed to be the only solution.

Stayres had been flippant and happily assured him he'd be home on Monday night; he hadn't flattered him with notions of an espionage coup of the decade, but he had hinted that his female agent might have come across something very valuable. Stuart knew he'd been chosen for his fluency in the language and there was no reason for him to imagine it had anything to do with his conformity to a specific physical description, the square, boyish face with Slavic cheekbones. It would be easy enough for Stayres to deny should it ever threaten embarrassment, for it was known only in few circles outside the section that he had a singularly pragmatic and ruthless approach to his work. The slowing of his progress up the Civil Service ladder had been justified by his expertise in Czech affairs; the truth was far more sinister, that too many feared him, for of the unconventional back-stab he was a whispered master.

FIVE

'A censored Press only serves to demoralise. That greatest of all vices, hypocrisy, is inseparable from it.'
Karl Marx, 1842

Stuart responded to the flight call with reluctance, wryly amused at Stayres' apology that he couldn't travel First like other operatives, but only because it was an all-tourist flight, no privileges allowed. Stuart didn't care in the slightest because he'd had enough pampering to feel it worth ashes if not shared with Lucy. Her brightness made life outshine its own reality and the empty seat beside him, paid for as if occupied, was almost an accusation of his curious temporary employment. The obscure naggings which accompanied these thoughts didn't quite penetrate a feeling of aloofness about Stayres and the mission into which penury had coerced him. He saw with a grim satisfaction that his few years of independence had rendered him almost unemployable while Stayres appeared to have a misguided triumph in securing his services. Stuart knew it was a baseless vanity but enjoyed it nonetheless, fervently hoping that if his task was impossible it would show itself early. Typically it didn't occur to him not to bother with it at all, even though he had something far more intriguing to investigate.

Cloud covered most of Germany but cleared towards the end of the flight and during the descent he could see miles of new curving freeways outside Prague although

114

dotted with very few vehicles. By the evening, he knew, the weekend private traffic would be seething for the countryside and a brief return to the semblance of freedom.

The feeling he'd had on his last visit was even more palpable as he walked into the airport, noting blank-faced officials and a general air of hostile disinterest. The queue at Passport control was his main hurdle for which he'd been specially briefed. The Czech official tore off the top copy of each visa quadruplicate and stamped the second. Stuart's practised fumble, a slip with a pass-port rubber band sending his other copies flying past the man into the booth, gave him the instant required to deposit his 'wife's' top copy with the remainder on the desk. It carried the agent's photograph and she was thus officially inside, her own passport and duplicate visa already stamped by Stayres' forgers. Finally he had to change $20 for each of them before being allowed to the next stage where he passed through without query. For import inspection he had to go into a private booth with a short, grey-haired and destroyed-looking woman who glared penetratingly at him for fully fifteen seconds and then abruptly waved him through.

He shared a taxi with two pretty English students, one dark, one fair, both on an exchange from Durham University. They declared the airport atmosphere had made them shudder. The driver spoke rough English and offered twice the official exchange rate, lapsing into sullen silence when Stuart, briefed on this point too, told them what they could get elsewhere. The day was grey under high clouds and the man drove appallingly: Stuart found he was regretting his journey already and distracted himself by answering brightly the girls' ques-tions about what to see and do. He sounded to himself like a propagandist.

'All the Old Town is fascinating, the architecture's so flamboyant in places, even zany. And go to the Old

Town clock on the hour to see the rigmarole. It's a marvellous piece of whimsy, built about 1400 and still working, far as I know.'

'Your eyes are all alight,' said the other girl, caught up and smiling. 'You sound as though you love it.'

Stuart's face lit with pleasure. 'Well, it's very special. It clanks away and these doors open and the twelve Apostles troop past and bow to you while the Death Skeleton tugs on the bell rope and rattles his hour-glass. And there's much more, a whole Zodiac and calendarium, all moving . . . And there's the whole of Prague Castle, I don't suppose I've seen a quarter of it, I've a limited capacity for sightseeing, but the cathedral up there took six hundred years to build. Dozens of fine churches and many synagogues, the oldest was new in the thirteenth century and *still* called *Stará-Nová*, the Old-New. I don't know if they look after them though, the Jewish community is tiny since the war.'

'Where did they all go?' asked the blonde in full innocence, so that Stuart had to smother his surprise.

'The Nazis murdered them. There were about 77,000,' he answered quietly, trying not to sound admonishing. 'Yet they carefully preserved the Josefov district so it could be the object of study – for the children of the New Order, the Master Race of Europe. The Jews were a vital part of Prague, they'd been here a thousand years . . . You'll see more whimsy everywhere, houses with little signs outside before the bureaucrats insisted on numbers, a key for the locksmith, three violins for the instrument-maker and so on, some with no reason at all, a toad, a swan, a feather.'

'A man on the plane said he comes here for the girls and to have a good time, because his money goes so far,' the dark-haired girl said with some disdain.

Stuart nodded. 'It's understandable. The pay is low and it's not at all easy for the locals to have a good time.'

'Is that why you've come, for the girls?' the fair one

116

asked playfully; Stuart shook his head firmly but without answering, wishing again that it was already Monday. He resolved suddenly never to go secret ski-ing in Canada with Epiphany, even if by some miracle he became wildly rich again; he wanted all of his life spent either with or for Lucy. He looked from one to the other but they were gazing out of the windows, perhaps wondering why they had come themselves, since youth shouldn't go looking for sadness.

'I'm told,' he said eventually, 'And I haven't seen many of the others myself, that Prague is the most beautiful city in Europe. You'll walk your stumps off finding it, but it's worth the effort. Observe without judging.'

'Why is there a black market for Western currency?'

'Partly because you can't take a holiday in the West without it, assuming you get permission which is very complicated and wearisome but mainly because anything of any quality is in very short supply. The shops you'll find full of stuff that's quite uninteresting, stuff that's produced without flair under state quotas. But nobody wants it, they want quality goods and Western goods which they can only buy with hard currency in the Tuzex shops. It's very much resented and it's iniquitous in a way, but it's also supply and demand at work.'

'Will you show us round?' asked the blonde, favouring him with her frank blue eyes. He demurred, saying he'd come on business. The word made him think of his brief stay in Dallas and as the taxi crossed the Vltava over the Mánesův bridge and into the Old Town with its narrow streets and wobbling tramcars, it's seething silent pedestrians, he couldn't imagine a greater contrast.

They came at last into Wenceslas square and he pointed out the 'Good King' on his horse at the upper end, a huge flamboyant bronze statue. But the trams no longer swept round it and down what was really an enormous broad avenue rather than a square, giving a new feeling of space since there was so little traffic. There were many more metro stations, however, the pedestrians dutifully using them to cross the road junctions. Stuart was a natural jay-walker and loathed being herded. In London you could take your chances, he observed, but here you got arrested for risking state property, namely yourself. In New York, jay-walkers got arrested because they might interfere with the traffic flow.

With a vague agreement to meet up later, he dropped the girls at the Ambassador and checked in to the Zlata Husa next door. The hotel was the cheapest on the Cedok list but he had already booked it before Stayres' messenger arrived. Again he didn't care but had to explain to the concierge that his wife would join him perhaps tomorrow, she was staying with her brother and they had no room for him. The problem was readily understood because of the permanent housing shortage.

In Štěpánská Street he found the car hire office and confirmation of Stayres' gloomy warning, over $70 per day, dollars only, and just for a small Skoda. Translating directly he called it *to je oskubani*, literally 'a rip-off' but the girl simply shrugged as she said, 'Nobody cares, who's to compete with us. Come back in two hours and it will be ready.'

'Does the company make a criminal profit?' he asked but she simply laughed in reply, uncomprehending or uncaring. Stuart felt a grim satisfaction that Stayres was footing the bill.

The afternoon had warmed and he strolled morosely through the Old Town, the sightseers gathering as always in front of the clock and the huge Jan Hus statue in the centre, Hus the revolutionary theologian straining forward in tremendous bronze vigour while those around him slumped or reached out for his command or assistance. One of three pretending Popes had had him murdered for his urbane yet too-advanced thinking, an

118

act which provoked sufficient reaction to bury it for centuries. To postulate freedom of thought remains dangerously counter-productive in parts of the world where they simply execute you for trying.

By this hour many of the townspeople would be setting off for their country retreats, often little more than a hardboard hut or a rough log cabin where they could talk freely and replace the grey of their lives with a contrast of autumn colours, breathing air free of the pollution which still ravaged their historic city. Stuart knew from long before that the Police had clamped down on the early leavers, the Friday morning truants, by spot-checking on the roads out of town, but the more enterprising Praguers soon got round it by leaving on Thursday instead. It was certain to be an incurable malaise as long as the weekends remained the major incentive for living.

He gazed again at the marvellous variety of roof lines, the dazzling mix of Gothic, Baroque and Renaissance façades, trying to lose himself in faraway thoughts of Prague's incredible history and fortune that it had never been seriously damaged by war, except for some absurd gestures of Nazi spite. On leaving they had tried to blow up the fabled Town Hall clock but only succeeded in demolishing the back of it. It had been left unrepaired as a mark of uttermost scorn.

The attempt led him nowhere but to find himself with Lucy, walking with hands twined or running like colts, and never anywhere but in the dancing dappled light, laughing or sighing, a constant game of hide and seek, or find and enfold, always nourished by the tumbling variety of a life undeformed by the despairing wistfulness that was here breathed all around him. His feeling of overprivilege was almost unbearable; he looked at his watch and decided to visit the serried saints who line the monumental Charles Bridge, wondering as he quickened if it would be for the last time.

*   *   *

After collecting the car, Stuart wrestled his way through the rush-hour traffic and finally got clear to the North, reaching Roudnice on the Elbe by early evening. The car rattled with abuse but at least the heater worked even if the radio did not. He had to ask for help several times in pursuit of the first of his addresses, meeting difficulty with rapid and unfamiliar country accents. Roudnice was an industrial town he'd had no cause to visit before and he wondered if it was for its very anonymity that Stayres' agent should have holed up there. During his circuit of the town he kept a constant watch on his rear-view mirror and stopped several times as if to confer with his map; he saw no evidence of a tail but felt some embarrassment at Stayres' blithe assumption that he knew all the techniques. He also grew more nervous as his search localised, being aware from before of the widespread fear which totalitarianism must foster to survive, the dark dread of the informer. He'd been nurtured in a country where they despise tale-bearing as shameful, without realising the compulsions available, the setting of traps by deliberate misdemeanours, on which failure to inform is considered as treacherous as the deed.

His given address was a house in the middle of a dingy terrace; an aging, grey woman answered the door and exclaimed 'Miloš!' before putting a hand to her mouth. She listened with suspicious shakes of her head. She even tried to shut the door but Stuart jammed it with his foot, wondering how to get round her. He had a sudden intuition.

'I must find her, I have some tragic news. A terrible thing.'

'What is it? What has happened, oh, the poor darling!'

'Tell me where she is, please.'

'No . . .' There was hesitation as if the old woman was searching for a convincing reason. 'She should not hear bad news from a stranger.'

'All right. Do you have a telephone?'

'Are you crazy? Me, here?'

'Listen,' Stuart said urgently, 'If I was from the Cheka, I would know that, wouldn't I? And I wouldn't be asking you gently, either. I'd get some big nasty men to bump you around, burn all your pictures and mementoes. Now look, may I come in?'

'No!'

'I don't want to be seen standing here . . . All right, listen. Are you in a position to betray us both, me and her, right now? Answer me that.'

'I – I'm not sure. She may have moved on.'

'But you could have done so before, yes?'

'Oh, by all that remains good, don't ask! I love her, and there could be yet another reason.' She paused for an alarmed and exaggerated breath. 'She has a friend who could wreck my life, so even if you are Cheka, then *you* better be careful. I can get protection. You know something?'

'What?'

Suddenly she released her pressure on the door and stepped back into a tiny hallway. 'You sound educated but not familiar with our language, uneasy. Did you learn it in Russia?'

Stuart shook his head but remained silent.

'What was the bad news to tell her?'

'None. I was going to make something up. I'm sorry. I've actually brought travel documents.'

'Let me look at them.'

'I can't, don't you see? God, how can they make people live in such a tangle of suspicion?'

The woman sighed and leaned against a child-size dresser. 'Because they cannot do otherwise. Heaven help me, I have only my instinct . . . I will write it down, but you can't take it. You would never have forced it from me, I swear. Maryša, bless me or forgive me.'

She wrote, printing in careful, slow capitals another

address and held it for him to see. Stuart didn't reach for it but memorised it with meticulous care.

'Be there in two days' time at seven o'clock in the evening. If anyone but you comes, they will find no one. If you bring others it will be the same, but for quite certain you will die. If there are flowers in the window, go past and never come back, do you understand?'

'Yes, but two days, can't it be sooner, I've got to— '

'Impossible. This is not a test of your patience, it simply cannot be done sooner. Please go now, quickly and pray that you are a friend. Our oppressors make life worth dying for but they make it impossible at the same time. But I, I am too old to care. Do you know I have even killed? You believe me?'

'Yes, I think I do. All right, I'll be back on Sunday.'

'Good. And who sent you?'

'Adrian. Adrian Backstairs.' Stuart was bewildered that she'd taken so long to ask for his retriever's code and his relief was almost explosive. He was under strict orders not to proffer it first and now she smiled at last and opened the door for him. Only then did his eyes catch the glinting-sharp kitchen knife in her left hand and he wondered if she had enough influence to dispose of a body. The whole encounter left him drained but somehow alert and optimistic, even in his dread of time to fritter.

'*Dobru cestu*,' he repeated grimly to her farewell from the swiftly closing door. He turned away and then heard her calling again. He went back and she spoke quietly from the shadows, tense with conspiracy.

'It's an apartment block. Telephone the concierge before you come. Ask for Lalla, then call back. If it is I and it is safe, I'll say *Nezapomón na to co jsem ti řekl!*'

Stuart wrote down the number and repeated the sentence, finding it ominous: 'Don't forget what I told you'. '*Slíbula*,' he said, 'I promise. That will be my answer.'

'Yes. Be careful.'

Driving back to Prague with an expanding nervousness, Stuart wondered why Stayres hadn't given him more cause for caution. He imagined he was at no great risk merely carrying his 'wife's' documents. The danger lay in the actual meeting, if she had already been tagged but it was too uncomfortable to dwell on it. He began to realise however that he'd involved or allied himself unwillingly to the extent that he couldn't just dump the errand or even hand over the papers to the old woman. If Maryša had already been compromised he began to picture himself in deep trouble, with no fall-back. The two days stretched ahead alarmingly and speculative fears began to multiply.

Wondering if his inspiration was merely paranoia, he bought a powerful torch and spare battery at a filling station, and once out in the country he stopped off the highway and jacked up the car on one side. He was ready to deflate a tyre if anyone stopped but he drew no apparent interest. By torchlight he examined every inch of the car, his fingers numbing in the cold but finding no foreign attachments. He'd almost reconciled to the paranoia before one anomaly struck him: the useless radio had no external aerial. Following that it was easy, for the silent receiver, a plain one-band AM set, hadn't even any connections to a loud speaker; it simply sat in isolation, mutely self-accusing. It was held in by shiny new screws and seemed too absurdly naïve. Anyone with the slightest fix-it tendencies might immediately want to know why a radio didn't function, especially if it involved getting his money's worth. The thought made him wonder again about other plants on the vehicle but he dismissed it with angry impatience, fearing the same projection to a third and a fourth. You only rate a single, he told himself firmly, putting the car back on the road and gratefully thawing out on the way back to the capital.

He forgot immediately what he had for dinner, for it was dull and cooked without care and in this space of time he was keeping no mental diary for Lucy. After-wards he tried and failed to get tickets either for a Bach concert at the Dvořak Hall or a new ballet at the National Theatre, not an unusual disappointment in a city of long-intense theatre and music lovers. Culture seems to thrive with oppression, unhappiness or boredom, he reflected sadly; the Praguers loved their music with a mystic, mel-ancholic passion, its emotions intensifying their own in a will to resist and outlive their bleakened circumstances.

The Alhambra night club was vibrant if frowzy but the two girl-students were enjoying themselves and gladly accepted a drink, understandably from the size of the tab. They'd heard about another place over the river and badgered him to take them there. Stuart agreed easily but once arrived he soon pleaded exhaustion, enjoying self-mockery and no chagrin that they didn't seem to mind him leaving. Neither of them was the type to be intrigued by reticence. In the dim-lit carpark he tried several identical Skodas until he found one with the rear door unlocked. Quickly detaching the radio from his own car he stuffed the box down behind the other rear seat and then left without hurrying. He took down the car's number in case of the remote offchance to replace the set before leaving, otherwise he would simply declare a robbery to the rental agency.

Returning to the Zlata Husa, he still had to read for several hours before sleep came. He missed the gesture of the single ring to Lucy; though it would have been done for him, he missed even that tenuous contact which had always worried him somewhat since she couldn't contact him if she needed anything. She'd assured him it didn't concern her, but now the missing weighed on him even heavier than the lugubrious atmosphere and soulless service. When he finally slept it was ragged with snatches of urgent dreams.

He awoke to early sounds of destruction in the open centre of the hotel, an affront even though he wanted to get up early and be about his primary business. St George had given him a telephone number and an extension within the Kbely museum and after a few questions his contact named a rendezvous, a café in the Republiky Square. He sat and waited for over ten minutes after the time, feeling he was being watched; somehow it wasn't disconcerting since precautions were surely justified. He ordered Turkish coffee because the standard version offered with breakfast had been depressingly watery.

Finally an oval-faced, jolly man sat down opposite him with a friendly greeting. 'Hello, are you Kody?'

'Yes, that is I'm Karel's son. I didn't say on the telephone but my father is dead now.'

The man nodded without unction. 'I won't give you my name but it was very kind of you to come. Louis is still full of passion but he has a mad despair. I think his heart . . . but anyway, to see you will mean so much to him. This is how to find the farm.'

He drew carefully on a piece of napkin. 'All this used to be his land, it's collective now, of course. He keeps his house and the old barn and a small piece to cultivate privately. He's retired on pension now, of course, and he never co-operated too much.' He gave a wrinkled smile.

'I've been waiting for you to tell me,' Stuart grinned back, 'Is he really keeping an old Spitfire on the farm?'

'Of course not,' came the answer with firm conviction. 'He's merely a crazy old man who lost everything and went into pure fantasy-land. Come out to Kbely and see the real thing if you get the chance. I'll be proud to show it to you before the museum shuts for the winter. Let me know if I can help you with anything.' He stood up, shook hands and went quickly out.

Stuart drove westwards in minimal traffic on route 6 before turning left for the town of Rakovnik. He found the farm after some extensive backroads meandering but the directions were fortunately clear. His contact had been very thorough and he wondered if this was to save

125

him asking questions. He felt confident that he wasn't followed.

There was a long, well-tended orchard of apples and pears, their leaves browning and the fruit long-since picked; beyond it a little red tractor puttered noisily. After a while the driver saw his car and came trudging towards him. Faint smoke rose from the chimney of the grey stone house which looked rough and unkempt, its garden overgrown where once there must have been order with trellises and little gravel pathways. Two big barns stood on either side of the track, the approach to one heavily marred by broad wheels, the other grassy but sere with loose straw.

A stooping, weathered old man with a deep-furrowed face shrouding bright blue eyes came towards him, treading very slowly the last few yards, appraising carefully. He had coarse-woven trousers tucked into muddy rubber boots.

'I'm looking for Louis Mišek,' Stuart said, 'I'm the son of Karel Kody, he asked for him.'

The old man took off his cap to reveal a whole head of hair, thin and very white. 'I did. Where is he, dead?'

'Yes. I don't thing he can have got your letter, he would have contacted you, I'm sure.'

'I want to ask and ask and ask, what kept you so long? Half my lifetime waiting, ignorant old peasant trying to stay alive because of a foolish promise to a foolish, beloved son.'

'Tell me. I don't know anything.'

'I will. Come inside, I feel like a strong drink . . . It will turn cold soon, I think. That's a nice, warm coat you have.' He fingered Stuart's quilted jacket but watched his eyes. After a moment, he turned and went to the door of the house, pulling off his boots against a wooden v-block. He led into a kitchen of only moderate squalor.

'Anna comes once a week,' he said apologetically, 'This must be day six, I can tell by the number of plates.'

126

He chuckled and went to a cupboard for a bottle of Slivo-vitz and two tumblers, pouring generous measures. His hands shook visibly and they clinked glasses in a strange apprehension.

'The first twenty years or so were harder,' Mišek said, coughing after his first large gulp, 'since we didn't have a tractor, there was no machinery to cover sound. I used to wait for big gales and I had to borrow batteries. What a labour! It got easier but then there was much deterio-ration. I've grumbled all the time and probably enjoyed it, though the farm is messy and untidy by comparison. I loved the precision and perfection. You are looking strange, puzzled perhaps?'

'I was waiting, that's all. You are talking in riddles but no doubt you will explain, when you are ready.'

The old man cocked his head at this, beady like an old turkey. 'Hmph. Have you got proof of identity?'

Stuart produced his passport and let him study it care-fully. Mišek handed it back after tapping it on his other hand. 'I even had to learn to read English. It may be limited, I suspect. What is *Jak se nás?*'

'How do you do?' Stuart answered with a smile.

'Ah. But I can certainly enquire as to the condition of your carburettors. Fortunately you will understand the mixture, of language, I mean.' Suddenly he gulped back the remains of his drink, made an exclamation which sounded like 'Gwah!' and jerked his head in a follow-me. He put on some ordinary leather boots and trudged out to the barn, Stuart tip-toeing and jumping mud-patches behind him. Louis hauled the big door open; inside was another tractor, very ancient, a har-row and a bailer; the rest of the building was about three-quarters full of straw, stacked to about 5 metres high. Louis grasped the twine on the end of two bottom bales and pulled them out with unexpected ease. Then he went and flicked a switch on the wall; somewhere outside a generator started up and a light came on. There was also a shaft of brightness coming out from the space in the stack; the old man ducked and waddled through the low passage. Stuart followed, almost crouching because of his greater height. His meeting with the contact that morning had fully prepared him for disappointment over St George's insane optimism so his stunned surprise and near-disbelief were more than redoubled.

The first thing he saw was a down-pointing propeller blade, long, heavy and polished, hugely powerful compared with the almost frail little mill of a modern trainer. There were four of them, great scythes of battle, centring on the conical spinner which enclosed the variable constant-speed hub. Beyond that there was no doubt at all, the unmistakable tapering shape of a legend, it's up-angle accentuated by having its wheel oleos lifted onto stout wooden blocks. The skin was a dull metallic colour, all the paint long since flaked away. It sat with its elliptical wings spread in a big bunker of straw bales, the sides draped with black polythene fastened every few inches with a kind of thatching peg. Stuart made no attempt to hide his awe.

'The first time it was chaos,' Louis said, beaming at him, 'Straw blew everywhere and blocked the supercharger intake, filled the whole place with dust. You couldn't live. The dust is still bad. The problem is that the propellor won't neutralise, I think they call it feathering, I don't think it's that kind, so it's always pulling air.'

Stuart was still only beginning to get the full implications. From the exhaust manifolds on each side of the cowling, the old man had attached, with asbestos padding and clamps, six flexible steel tubes leading to a forty gallon drum on each side, buried half in the straw. The tubes were jammed into them with more padding.

'Not pretty,' Louis said, pointing, 'But very necessary, for silence, for monoxide removal and to contain the sparks. By God, but it takes some battery to turn it

128

over. Terrible load on the starter, there's a limit on it, twenty seconds continuous, stop for thirty, but of course you'll know all about that. I can't tell if the supercharger is doing all it should, you'll find out at 18,000 feet if the rubbish gasoline will get you up that far, when the second stage comes in. On the ground you've only got the test button.'

He seemed to be muttering distantly and Stuart suddenly realised how much control he must be exercising, being almost in the grip of great emotion.

'What happened to your son? Jaroslav, wasn't it?'

The lined face turned towards him and nodded. 'Yes. He loved your father, they were like this.' He hooked his forefingers together.

'Yes, I know. He told me.'

'Ah. Jára came over the house, so low, so terrifying, such a roaring, snarling thing you never heard, Marie and I fell to the grass, we thought it was the Russians again but he came back screaming down at us and pulled up into a loop, then he rolled all over the sky just for us, such exuberance, then one last low pass, quite slowly, waving, going away westwards. He'd gone about two kilometres when František shot him with that stupid old muzzle-loader. There, look.'

Louis pointed to the hinged-down side panel on the left of the cockpit. 'See the hole, the size of it! There's a crow-bar stored in that little door, I had to read the manuals to find out its purpose, it's to smash open the canopy if you have to get under your parachute, if it's been damaged and won't slide open. The crow-bar split the ball, one half stopped, the other cut into his spine.'

He was silent and thoughtful for a moment, then pulled himself back. 'He flew round again, slowly, he put down his wheels and landed in the meadow. The grass was heavy and wet, to slow him down. He couldn't use the brakes or the rudder and finished in a great sweep round, almost going over. We got him out but he was paralysed from the waist down. I think he died from blood poisoning, though, about four days later. There was a useless doctor and no antibiotics, you see. But perhaps it was best . . .

'František was my friend, he said he thought he was shooting a Nazi. He wasn't even a good shot. When he found out what he had done, he turned the gun on himself. It was a bad day. Marie, my wife, she never got over it, just went quietly, sadly downhill and died a year later . . .

'Jaroslav told me to put the Spitfire in the barn, your father would come and get it, he said. He wrote me some translations from the manuals, what to check over to have it working properly for him, when he came. He made me promise.'

'But it's well over forty years!' Stuart exclaimed. 'Why didn't you ever give up, there must have been a point—'

Louis put a hand on his arm. 'Perhaps you don't understand. For a long time I was in a frenzy, to be certain everything was still good, I couldn't let him down with the promise. Perhaps it was all I had, yes, there was nothing else to feel. He would have been sixty years old just a few weeks ago . . . I went to Prague once when it all seemed hopeless and I read in the paper about the museum, then I learnt from them all the things which deteriorate with time, even in a perfect dry place like this, and so I began once more.'

'You mean the museum knows about this?'

'No. One man only, the one who told you.' Louis grinned at the conspiracy.

'And he told me you were just a crazy old fellow with a fantasy.'

'Good. And perhaps I am. But she feels real enough. I used to turn the engine every week by hand, it was years before I could start it again. It became a shining goal along with the fear that K.K., as Jára called him, would arrive and find me not ready.' He paused and looked at Stuart with great pride. 'I am ready,' he announced. 'See for yourself.'

Using a trestle, he unlatched the port engine cowling with a screwdriver. Underneath, the huge Merlin gleamed black and fearsome, the clips shining on new hoses and wires, not a speck of dirt or oil visible. Stuart was speechless with admiration and deliberately wiped the block with his hand. He saw the old man almost shimmer at his appreciation.

'You will find oil under the wings in places,' he said, as a kind of admission, 'I couldn't get at all the cables to wipe them so I sprayed them through a tube.' He put the cowling back and walked round behind the wing, stepped stiffly onto the roof, slid back the canopy and leaned inside. The ailerons and elevator snapped briskly in response to his churning the yoke around, showing how freely it moved. He looked back down at Stuart and grinned, stopping abruptly as his dentures came loose. He adjusted them shyly.

'There's a plug over the other side, leading from the extra battery box. Push it into the socket under the engine. They're fully charged.'

'I believe you,' Stuart said, smiling and getting a crinkle-eyed response.

'Then, come here. You can do this. I mean, I know how, but you're the expert.'

Stuart shook his head adamantly. 'Not at all. You go ahead.'

The old man looked pleased and with stiff but practised movements, lowered himself into the cockpit and took his cap off as if with respect. Stuart came round and stood on the wing to watch him.

'Fuel ON,' said Louis firmly in English, touching the fuel-cock in the centre with his right hand. 'Throttle half inch. Propeller full fine forward.' He smiled a little. 'The first time I did this, I almost died from heart failure. Such power you cannot believe. Jára said he wanted to hear it once more from the bedroom.'

He checked the settings and went on, stiffly accented. 'Prime KI-Gass up to resistance.' He pumped away fiercely at the little handle on the lower right of the panel until it slowed up. 'Ignition ON, contact.' There was a definite note of excitement in his voice as his left hand flicked on the two switches. 'Starter and booster coil together, Contact!'

He pushed two fingers of his left hand on the push-buttons and kept pumping away at the primer with his right. With a solid jerk the great paddles lashed over, once, twice, three times. There was a muffled explosion somewhere in the flexible tubes and then the huge engine was miraculously running.

The airframe shook and the slipstream tore at their hair and clothes. The polythene wall flapped and rattled and the dust swirled thickly all around them. There was some noise from small leaks in the exhaust pipes but the oil drums made very effective expansion boxes. A Merlin had probably never been so muted; Louis adjusted the throttle to give 1000 rpm, pointing at the dial. The vibration lessened slightly, increasing for a momentary rpm drop as he switched off the two magnetos in turn. One showed a slightly greater loss than the other but both were within limits. Louis see-sawed his hand in almost satisfied judgement, then he turned and looked at Stuart. His face had a beatified smile even as sparse strands of white hair whipped his face. He grasped the ringed fighter's column and moved it around, pretending to be airborne. He cycled the propeller and the engine slowed viciously against the coarsened pitch before he let it pick up again. The loudest noise came from the propeller itself. Louis pointed behind the rudder trim wheel and shouted 'Supercharger test!' He pressed the button and the red light glowed on the panel, the engine slowing slightly. He pointed at the oil and manifold pressure gauges and gave a satisfied nod, then made a big mouth-down at the fuel contents which read almost empty. Abruptly he pulled the cut-out back and switched off. The sudden quiet was broken after a few seconds by a belated gurgle from some part of the cooling system.

'The wheels go up and down as well,' Louis said, 'That's important.' He pulled up with his old gnarled hands and rather unsteadily extricated himself.

'I put a big cushion in the seat, but you will have the parachute. I didn't open it because I don't know about repacking them. Best to leave it alone. I squeezed in a couple of mothballs, but I hope you don't have to use it. It's pure silk, did you know?'

Stuart said nothing, disguising any facial reaction by bending down and unplugging the external lead. 'Will it turn over on its own battery?' he asked.

'No, and there isn't room for much of one, only 48 amps. But the starter is poor, that's the trouble, so I boost the voltage up to about 18. It's strange, isn't it, that you can describe an engine as beautiful, or even a whole war-plane. It has so much aura, even without the paint. They say it won the war, the Spitfire, but I think it was the people, their *Will*. If we only had a war now we could win, we have the will. But there's no war, they cannot fight the bosses, we cannot roar like tigers for our freedom. It makes little difference to me out here, now that I don't have my farm, except of course that I have to hide this. I'm certain to be shot if they find it. They nearly did, several times. I had this barn full of straw and I built surprise-holes everywhere. The soldiers kept falling through and having to be rescued. They gave up in the end and set fire to it but it smothered from lack of air. My hair turned white.'

Stuart shook his head in wonder. 'How did you manage to pay for the spare parts all this time, did the museum help somehow?'

'Heaven above, no! Marie had inherited some fine

133

jewellery, though she never wore it. There was no other use for it.' Louis' tone sounded almost like an apology to her.

He led out through the tunnel, replaced the bales and switched off the generator. 'We'll have to get you a lot of gasoline, you need eighty five gallons, that's nearly four hundred litres, then you can go. A quarter of that I have already in the methanol over there, I've got a friend who steals it for me litre by litre from the refinery. The Merlin won't run on 90 octane, I'm assured it would blow up right here. The methanol boosts it up to about 125 or 130 octane, I think, anyway enough to make it run. But the Kbely man said to take it easy even on that . . . You know, I've thought about it so much but I still can't imagine how I'll feel when it's gone. Cold, I expect. Lonely. Nothing. I love it in a way, it's part of me, it's kept my spirit in defiance when I've seen others bend and submit. Sometimes I soar with it in might and freedom, like pounding your chest when you're a young buck and just stolen a "Yes" from your first woman. That's something you never forget, eh? Do you have a wife?'

To Stuart's answer he added, 'Does she know what you're doing, risking?'

Almost frantically, Stuart tried to picture the old man's reaction to being told the facts, that his long-held notion was insane, that the 'pilot' was woefully short of experience, and that with modern defence weapons, the twenty minutes dash for the border was no longer remotely feasible. He imagined confusion, shatterment, even outright fury, a *raison d'être* wiped out along with forty years of virtual slavery to a promise: the Spitfire must be ready to fly.

'No, she doesn't know I'm here,' he said, feeling a sudden hollow awareness of her looking at him, wondering at his feelings, a tiny hesitant dip into his well-water of courage. He had a sudden jolting recognition that what

134

was coursing violently through him was fear, simple basic terror. His right arm developed a rapid tremor and bile rose in his throat, barely controlled. He went quickly outside and stood breathing deeply in the crisp afternoon sunlight. Ahead the meadow stretched away in short grass with a slight dip, largely safe and smooth. He heard the barn door close behind him.

'Do you have money for the gasoline?' Louis asked. When Stuart nodded dumbly he went on, 'We can collect it with the car. Will you leave me the car when you go?'

'The car's hired, Louis. But it can't happen yet, we have to think this through, make plans, I'll have to get a friend of mine, St George— '

He stopped abruptly, his confusion and dry fear impossible to explain, but Louis jumped in at once.

'Plans, what plans? Now that you've come, it's *time*, don't you see? I don't have much of it now. I've lived longer than I would have, just for this day, understand? I hated the farming too, I still do it out of habit, and God, feeding yourself is so tedious!'

'Would you rather have been an aircraft engineer?' Stuart asked with a pale covering smile, realising his tone was almost accusing the old man of boxing him into an inextricable embarrassment.

'Oh, yes!' Louis said, nodding anciently. 'The triumphs of the farmer are so delicate and slow, everything ripening, but engines like those are full of might and drama.'

'Did you manage to get hold of the full maintenance hand-books?'

'Yes, they were inside. Jára said it was very lucky, usually there's only the log but they'd just been re-posted, the first time he'd come within range of here. They're in the house. You'll want to go over everything, I suppose? The aircraft log is there and Jára's own log. The plane had only seventeen hours flight time, Jára told me he'd crashed his previous one in Germany. He laughed about

135

it. He had time on Tiger Moths, then the Hurricane, after only twenty-two hours, but he had hundreds and hundreds when he . . . This one was the best, he said, like a violin or a ballerina. Delicacy. Precision and power . . . Ah, well.' He shrugged, 'I can only imagine. I have never flown, never will, but it's an easy dream. That power though, I suppose it's ignorance that makes me say it but I quiver at the thought of how much courage it must take for the first step, the dare. Come in, I will build the fire for you, finish my work and and you can tell me all about it. Jára was not very well, he didn't say as much as we wanted. He kept on laughing at everything and it hurt him. He said Karel, your father, was much braver than he, but of course we didn't believe it.'

'My father said the same of him.'

'Did he?' Louis looked carefully for sincerity and apparently found it. 'Do you have any children?'

'No, I haven't been married very long.'

Louis pulled off his boots and led inside. He went to the ancient stove in a blackened corner of the sitting-room and fed in some wood off-cuts. 'This century, these times we live in . . . you know, for a long time I refused to believe that men had been to the moon. I told everyone they were deceived, it was all put up, even the pictures of the modern machines, the high-speed jets – the TU 144, like Concorde, did you ever see that? I felt like a child with a picture book of spacemen, I didn't believe it until I saw the war helicopters, near the Bavarian border.'

'Oh? What did you see?'

'Russian Mil 24s. Gunships, I was told. Dear God, was there ever anything so evil? Enormous things with huge eyes like gross insects, two engines and a four blade rotor but *wings* as well, not for flying, no, just to carry the terror weapons, six big lumps of deadly things, rockets and missiles and a terrible gun in front, a cannon with four barrels. By the way, your Spitfire has no machine guns now, I sold them to some, er, patriots, but I never heard if they were put to good use. I suppose not, as we are still prisoners. Four Brownings, .303. It should make her very light to handle without them. Also it should not upset the trim, they were near the centre of gravity, she might go a bit nose-heavy, if anything. All the bullets were there, boxes of running belts. What a machine, eh? But you still have the two Hispano cannons, 20 mm. I don't know if they work, I didn't want to try them.'

The stove blazed up suddenly and Louis stood back, stumbling. Stuart put a hand out in support and almost at once the old man recovered, turned and hugged him fiercely. He had plainly shrunk with age but still had a corded strength. Stuart felt him shaking but still just in control. He hugged him back in spite of the musty smell of his clothes, feeling a great compassion as Louis fought to compose himself.

Eventually he said in a quavering voice, 'I suppose I still don't believe it, this day after all those long, long years. You can imagine I don't want to entrust it now to anyone, eh? But something happened here.' He tapped his chest. 'I realised there wasn't long, my own little engine has almost had enough. So, how many hours have you got on Spitfires, my boy? Hundreds and thousands, I suppose?'

Stuart had a very mixed reaction to this query, wanting to reassure the old man yet knowing his ignorance would be obvious, and another part of him half hoped for a refusal because of it, a release from his personal challenge.

He said, 'I've got experience in more modern machines, I haven't flown this one. There are not so many left, they are antiques really, very valuable, very expensive to fly.' He did a rough calculation. 'For one hour in England you would have to pay about 24,000 crowns.'

Louis nodded his understanding until the figure penetrated. He ogled Stuart in astonishment. 'I could buy a

137

new baby tractor for less than that!' he exclaimed. 'When they get it back, they'll save a fortune with it.'

'Who will?'

'The owners of course, the British Royal Air Force. It's almost new, there's a thousand hours of good service in her, she'll outfly those overstuffed armchair gunships any day, six hundred kilometres per hour and turn on a heller, climb to 12,000 metres, 40,000 feet, Jára told me. *And* a Rolls Royce engine.'

Stuart kept away from dispute about ownership and hours of service, about Soviet 'Swatter' missiles with a 1200 mile-an-hour punch to stop a 40-ton battle tank at full bore.

'Tell them I'm sorry about the machine guns, won't you?' Louis added, pulling a box out from under a dustry cupboard. 'Here are the logs and maintenance books. Naturally I want to keep Jára's log but the rest belong with the plane . . . I ought to get workshop wages for forty years. The trouble is that Jára shouldn't have been here, he was naughty, so it was his fault really. At least he got it down safely, but they're sure to be very angry about the guns, don't you think?'

Stuart was about to mollify him when the old man's defiance broke through. 'To hell with them! What can they do to me now? A pitch-fork up their arses, I say!' He cackled mischievously and handed over the books. 'You have a look while I fetch the tractor back down. We'll have a drink and later a meal. It won't be much, some cabbage soup, bread and cheese, I'm afraid that's about all.'

'Is there somewhere we could go, could I take you to a restaurant for dinner?'

'Perhaps. Let me think about it. Rich food upsets me but *escargots* I cannot resist. Marie used to sleep downstairs for three days when I had them . . . yes, yes, why not? We won't have to walk back six kilometres belching, we can fill your car with terrible smells, eh?'

138

SIX

'Die now and avoid the rush.'

Frank Schwake

A small dark little restaurant in Rakovnik called the Apollo served them escargots with Crimean champagne followed by Wiener Schnitzel. Louis was warmly remembered, much to his pleasure since he hadn't been there for half a dozen years. Stuart sat in suspended bewilderment that Louis had automatically assumed he was a flier, and that it was far too late to deny it, while the old man talked brightly of practicalities, of jacking the wheels down, collecting gasoline and mixing methanol, finding longer cable for the starting boost and other complications. After a while Louis tired of the subject and became more reflective.

'What a century it has been, such changes of fortune . . . It's still beyond my understanding how they think they can get people to work for a faceless system. You should see how slack they are in the fields these days, and that's not just an old man moaning. A man will work till his back breaks for his woman and his children, but for a co-operative? Perhaps he should be able to work just the same, but the fact is that he is not. It's madness. Everyone has to conform so they lose their hearts, their identities and their happiness. Then you have complete inefficiency and a second- or third-rate system because there's no incentive. This country used to have such clever people, inventors, seekers, everything quivering with life. And now? When were you last here? And did you see St Vitus' cathedral this time?'

Stuart shook his head.

'I used to make the journey to go to Mass on Marie's anniversary until – you know when the Catholic Church did its up-to-date, *aggiornamento*, they put another altar in the sanctuary so the priest could turn and face the people and talk to them in Czech. Well, if you want to see a modern obscenity, it's like the authorities have done this' – he made a basic gesture – 'to the Church; in this fabulous Cathedral, a monument of ageless beauty, the new altar is a thick slab supported on six pitted pieces of iron girder with gold paint slapped on them . . . Socialism . . . I have to credit someone for a dream of a perfect community on earth and in a way it's amazing how far they have taken it. I know little about politics or philosophy but it seems they've missed one vital factor: that none of the people who make up this dream community are perfect nor ever could be, nor can they be the same in talent, energy, strength. So it cannot work, trying to make them all the same. On the radio they talk about your capitalism as though it was a disgusting perversion but it seems to me that it's just another system, but one which works and generates energy and talent. Only the use of his gifts makes a man happy and no woman can be happy with a miserable man. Is your wife happy and proud of you, as a pilot?'

Stuart hesitated for a moment and again decided that candour would only confuse the old man. He nodded understandingly instead, aware of making a tangle.

Louis' face took on a slightly cunning look, his voice still low. 'It bothers me that there is no one to ask this question: "Please, why are you trying so hard to catch up and overtake the Americans that you despise so much and to whom you say you are superior in every way? If this were true, you would let us go there and see for ourselves, and read all their decadent literature and listen to their radio. You see, Mr Soviet, we know you are lying to us but unfortunately there is nothing we can do about it without being transported or shot." The hardest thing to bear, you know what it is? When you've fought for your country, lost friends and health and fortune for her and then somebody takes away your pride in her honour and truth and energy – but WHY?, I scream, why do it?'

Stuart said quietly, 'I think I understand how you feel. It began with a man's honest if ruthless efforts to save his country. He said, "Follow me or you will die, either at the enemy's hand or mine". Then when he'd saved them he had to keep it up to save himself.'

'Stalin,' Louis nodded more calmly. 'And at the end of the war, do you know what happened to that ruthless monster Churchill, who the Nazis told us started the war and only wanted it to go on forever so he could bomb Europe flat? Jára and your father went to follow him and they said he was almost worshipped and then this terrible dictator was quietly voted out of office in 1945. Then later on the English decided to let him back for a bit longer. Amazing. Then Moscow tells us that he sold Bohemia to Hitler in 1938 but I know that's not true. If they lie to us, surely they cut their own throats? I hate them for taking away our pride and if I was young and clever I would leave, go back to Paris, I was there as a student, my mother was French. Do you speak French?'

'Oui, à point. Listen, if I sent you some money, you could apply for a holiday visa, couldn't you? Would you like that?'

'Maybe. First comes first, the Spitfire just needs gasoline, then the next good dawn you go off straight down the Berounka meadow, fast and low for the border. No one will see you or even know where you came from. After that we'll see how it goes, perhaps I will come and visit, perhaps not, I don't know. I'm getting very old and useless, I feel like getting off, no, I feel like starting again with a new body, I want to love again, to create

141

in freedom, to feel the *richesse* of pride and growing. When I was young they told us God was everywhere and I believed it. Now I think that God is only where he is believed, the rest he leaves like a fallow field. Well, I believe! God is in me, God *is* me, my breath, my heart, my love, my pride, and with that belief I cannot be wrong or even do any wrong. I don't need men's commands. The Church used to do what the Communists are doing, do you realise that? Keep the people in chains, they must be kept ignorant otherwise we cannot control them. Give them a God who is mighty and jealous and vengeful of sin, make them fear Him, put the fear of God into them, then we, His annointed, can tell them what to do and what to believe. For God read Politburo, for fear read KGB, for purgatory and hell read Siberia and the Gulag. Well, to use a Russian expression, I make *fig v karmane*, you know what it means, no? It's the finger, like this, but you do it in your pocket. That's not cowardice, it's prudence. "Screw you", it says.

'God is still here because I believe and *that* is the only thing they have to fear, that they cannot persuade me otherwise, because I *know*, I have worked the field and felt His goodness – in here!' Louis prodded his chest fiercely with his thumb and then looked defiant about his show of emotion, softening it to a smile.

'Enough of this old man's drivel. There is work to be done, I must have a clear head.' He dropped his voice and looked around but their corner was out of earshot. 'Juliet Bravo is to fly again. Is that *exciting*? Isn't that *Life*?'

Stuart nodded seriously in a seethe of confusion and misgiving, aware also of a spark of boldness fuelled by alcohol. Gradually it occurred to him that it might take more courage to tell Louis the truth and give him a flat refusal than to accept the unthinkable and succumb to his fervour. He could think of several experienced pilots who would probably say, 'Well, come on, it's only an aeroplane.' Gung ho, he muttered to himself, and his

142

milling thoughts kept him silent; Louis seemed content with his own monologue even on the way home.

At the old man's insistence he agreed to stay the night rather than risk arrest for drunken driving. The spare bedroom was damp and musty but after a stiff nightcap of some old, hoarded Cognac he was fortunately past caring.

In the morning he awoke with a surprisingly clear head and after two strong cups of coffee made by a strangely silent Louis, he was left alone for a while to assess his position. St George had assured him of a ready buyer for a machine in flying condition, a fortune that would not likely be in dispute in spite of Louis' quaint notions of correctness. Chillingly, it was an opportunity hardly to be missed in itself even without the compulsions presented by Louis' astonishing years of devotion and the unspoken, unspeakable challenge of St George's likely disdain, even if it might be softened with the truth about his inexperience. Although a meticulous professional pilot, St George had hallmarks of mad bravado about him but would justly deserve the whole of the cake if he was lured to come and make the break himself. Stuart's quandary intensified when he recalled their conversation about wartime youngsters being pressed into fighter aircraft with only student time in their logs; more compelling still was that with this prize he could escape all the pressures created by his obligatory charade and return to a normal existence.

From this train of thought he realised he had little faith in Simonov's good intentions and Langley too had shown extreme perfidy. Without his wholehearted co-operation, which would then bind him inextricably, they'd both shut the purse with a snap. He writhed against the compulsions and longed to extricate himself somehow, without leaping into the nearest furnace. His natural sense of devil-may-care, quickened during his army time with Rollo Runyan, had become manageable since Lucy

143

had enhanced every value, even though she professed to share the same attitude. Here lay the crux of his decision, he thought, and it was unfair to her. It was because he was so afraid for her that he could feel a real hesitation about being reckless with himself and he knew that if he were to ask her approval even silently, she would ask him not to do it. At this point he had the sudden inspiration that she would also say, 'I wish you hadn't asked me,' and she'd smile and turn wistfully away. He quailed from what he knew this meant to him.

He became overly conscious of hiding his fear from Louis who directed him to service stations with presumption and zest. He spent all his available cash buying gasoline in five litre cans in different places, filling and syphoning the car's tank as well, to provide for the Merlin's gargantuan thirst. Louis had to accept that he must return to Prague for more money and that there was something else he had to do, but the old face looked very crestfallen.

'When will you come, then?'

'Well, I . . . it's a little hard to say. It depends on a contact of mine . . . a few days, perhaps a week.'

'Why do you do this to me? I'm ready, as I promised!'

Stuart writhed inwardly with the guilt of his own vacillation, despite his other task. He realised he was being rather hard on himself under the duress of an ancient promise to his father's friend, and he wondered what his father would have done in his place, regretful that he hadn't known him long enough. He thought ruefully that an ace pilot who survived all those air-battles must have had that special stamp which the Irish call desperate, the calculated boldness of the high-roller. In the early afternoon he drove away feeling abject, leaving Louis pale and depressed, the mighty ransom mute among the straw bales only waiting for a warrior.

In Prague he went back to his hotel for a shave and a shower and to change some more money using his credit card. Nobody asked him why he hadn't spent the night in the hotel and he didn't appear to have attracted any curiosity. He filled the car once more and set off for Roudnice, after making the prearranged call and having Lalla return it with an all-clear. Her voice sounded strained but he couldn't draw from it anything but speculations, all of them worrisome. Even with his ominous feelings there didn't seem to be any choice about putting his head in the noose. He felt as though his preoccupations weren't allowing him to think straight and that the whole approach was ludicrously unprofessional. Surely too that had been intentional all along, in Stayres' requirement for an amateur?

He allowed a caution of time but found the new address easily enough and was early for the rendezvous. A youth lounged almost invisibly on a dark corner of the building, taking no apparent interest in anything but his watch; at seven o'clock exactly he straightened up with an abrupt movement and strode away. Stuart made an effort not to look furtive and went directly to the third floor using the staircase and casually checked the passage window of number 38 for flowers. It was empty and the same old woman answered his knock, looked him over quickly and pulled him inside.

With the door closed she turned the light on again and he saw at once, seated, a composed, black-haired, sad-looking woman of about 30, beautiful with the palest skin and very serious. Her eyes seemed to give him a too-thorough inspection.

'Maryša Kubin?' he asked.

'Show me what you have,' she said simply. 'Quickly, we should leave here.'

'Where to?' he asked, handing her the passport and visa papers.

'I'll show you. Are you armed?'

'No, of course not.'

'All right . . . So, I'm Ludmilla Kody. These look good. We'll go in your car.'

'Back to Prague? The flight's tomorrow afternoon but I have a hotel room. We—'

She shook her head. 'Not yet. There's someone for you to meet first.'

'Me? Why?'

'No questions now.' Her eyes darted to Lalla and slid away, then she gathered a few things and slipped on an old brown coat. She turned at the door and said gravely, 'Thank you, Lalla. Nothing is forgotten.'

The old woman acknowledged, showing the pain of her concern as she ushered them out. To Stuart it wasn't sinister, only that a permanent farewell was beyond embraces.

The car glistened with the beginnings of a morose drizzle. Stuart opened the passenger door for Maryša, getting no click with the key although he was certain he'd locked it from inside. That it should have triggered an early warning he was aware a half-moment late, after he'd gone round, started and begun to move off. Just as he stiffened a voice from the back said in Czech, 'Turn right at the next crossing, go very carefully and attract no attention. Disobey and you will die in that second.'

'While we're still moving?' Stuart barked, accelerating and as quietly furious with himself as with the man behind. Containing the speed for his own reasons and after some moments with no reply, he said, 'I'm not going to do anything sudden so don't get twitchy. I am not going to obey you, I am going to slow down and stop, then we can have a little chat. All right?'

Without any demur from behind he pulled up in the next hundred metres, between lamp-posts and by a huge unlit building. The lack of protest surprised and gratified him slightly, the assertion diluting his fear, though the car was brimming with tension.

'That was very daring of you,' said the voice from behind.

'Not really. There was no advantage to you to pull the trigger. You picked the wrong moment.'

'All right. Do you know my name?'

'No. What's the idea?'

'We had to be sure. There's a leak in Maryša's circuit, we think in London. London thinks it's here. That's why she's on the run and your own journey could have been a set-up.'

'Adrian Stayres was almost my only contact. I'm just a courier, with a low-key cover to bring her out. That's why they married us.'

'Married you?' The voice strained with outrage.

'Temporary, Miloš,' Maryša said quickly, 'A couple is less suspicious. Mr Kody, we need your professional advice. This is Captain Miloš Procházka, Czechoslovak Army. He has something for the West, some information and he's convinced that the Americans will treat it with more generosity than the British will. The British know about him, through me. We need some way of getting past them, we'll make it in your interest to help. Do you have any contacts with the CIA in Washington, someone absolutely trusted?'

Trust was the last thing Stuart felt for Riverson or Stearman though it could no doubt be applied to their loyalty. It certainly seemed no moment to deny his own usefulness.

'Naturally,' he answered, 'I can certainly give you a name.' To be more convincing he added, 'It depends what kind of stuff it is.'

'He won't tell me,' she said. 'If I'm caught they can't get it out of me.'

A gloved hand came over from behind and gently clasped her shoulder. Maryša placed hers on top of it and leaned her head to the junction while Stuart began to get the picture. The man's voice came over nervously.

'I don't think it's wise to stay here, Mr Kody. I have the use of a small apartment just a few minutes away. If you'll drive straight on; I apologise for our introduction, please understand, these are infernal times.'

'Of course.'

'Come then, we'll share a glass. Maryša will stay in the car while we have a word, all right?'

Stuart wasn't sure if it was right at all but could see no option. He obeyed the directions, stopped and followed the shadowy figure into a forbidding building. The flat itself was small and cold at the top of a dark stairway; except for a tiny kitchen, one room contained everything, a bed, two chairs and a side table, the lavatory only separated in an uncurtained booth. Stuart was startled when Procházka turned to shake hands, remembering the old woman's reaction to him on his first meeting her, the exclamation 'Miloš!' Like himself, the man was square of face, boyish-looking and of similar build. His hair was much fairer which would not have shown in a dark doorway. He wore green uniform with Captain's pips.

'I only made Lieutenant,' Stuart said with an attempt to be affable.

'Then you're lucky. You like a beer?' Procházka handed him a bottle of Prasdroj and a soiled glass. Stuart sipped from the bottle and the other grimaced his understanding.

'I'll give it to you quickly, I don't want to leave her long. I need you to tell me who will listen and pay the best. I've been trying for some time.'

'Wait a minute—'

Procházka held up his hand impatiently, his nervousness becoming more apparent. 'You can't tell me how to go about it if you don't know what it is. I'll share it with you, I think you are someone I can trust.'

'No thanks. You've made it sound like lethal knowledge.'

'Shut up and listen! How can you judge if you don't know?'

Stuart tried angrily to interrupt again but Procházka launched into a hoarse and lengthy cough which racked him almost double. He recovered with unconcealed and disarming effort.

'I'm sorry . . . I'll just give you the outline. I did one of those memory training programmes, with remarkable effect in my case. It's not quite photographic but using mnemonic systems I can remember lists and figures quite readily. You know the Soviets try to keep a low profile here, it's to contain the resentment, so the withdrawal of SS4s and their replacement with SS20s is most often run or assisted and guarded by Czech soldiers. I was at a field engineers' headquarters between here and Liberec on the Polish border and I have always managed to be correct with them whilst not responding at all to their speech. I admit I cannot be certain, but I believe they are sure I don't speak Russian. Some of the things they say in front of me could not be intended to trap, and mostly they are fairly discreet anyway.

'Naturally all the logistics are computerised and from time to time I've been able to take casual glances at print-outs while those goons try to sort themselves out. They're not very efficient and of course they grumble at all the wasted effort because the American satellites can see where all the carriers are anyway.'

'Does that mean mobile launchers?'

'Yes. The SS20 is a tactical weapon, not intercontinental. Some are in fixed silos but the majority are at least semi-mobile. They have naturally to be kept strictly tallied, they're not just like shells for a long-range gun, they're like individuals.'

Stuart sniffed drily. 'They give them pet names?'

149

Procházka returned a bevelled grin. 'Not exactly. But serial numbers, yes. The printouts come in columns, serial number and date, then map reference, preset target for the multiple warheads, you call them MIRVs, a feasible sector of alternate targets within the missile's range, its code for realignment, the master access code for required authority, its rota for engineers' inspection. Now the engineers' inspection list has a separate printout sent to their department and this is where my curiosity was stimulated because a further series of coded numbers is added to their list by a central command computer, a series which isn't on the main printout. I have noticed, I'm quite proud to say, there is a distinct correlation between certain engineers' codes and changes in the feasible sector of alternates, even when a particular missile has remained in the same launch site. The engineers are exclusively Russian and I could not have any contact with them, naturally. But there is no doubt in my mind that as the engineers move around doing their job, missiles ranges are adjusted. I cannot see them adding or discharging propellant, can you? Therefore they must be altering the payload. There's obviously a big and predictable difference when a vehicle is propelling say 500kg of conventional high explosive as opposed to 40kg of fissile material.'

Stuart found his interest quickened despite his resistance. He mouthed a silent whistle which did nothing to humour Procházka. 'All right, why don't they replace the HE with 500kg of nuclear material?'

Procházka shook his head impatiently. 'Stupid, that's overkill.'

Stuart shrugged off the rebuff. 'It's not expensive stuff, once you've written off the cost of the manufacturing base.'

'Listen, these are tactical weapons, their value is in their accuracy and versatility, which is in so much doubt that they have to overstock massively. Each leap means a hugely increased risk of accidental firing, something which they regard with extraordinary terror, thanks to God. And rightly, when you think of the reaction available from Western Europe and the submarines. I think they're doing everything they can to minimise the risk and still seem mightily defended.'

Stuart couldn't resist a slow smile because of the parallel with Cruise. 'Or else they don't see the point.'

Procházka didn't return the smile. 'I agree, but that is too subtle for the Russian mind, like a bluff. Chess is not poker. I think it reaches bottom on sheer manageability – and perhaps some widespread corruption. As you suggest, if they ever have to be used, it's all over for the lot of us anyway. The Americans would be delighted with this information, think of the strategic reductions they could make themselves.'

For a savoured moment, Stuart could see himself confounding Riverson with this windfall. 'Yes, I do see . . . Are you able to deduce how many are at any one time capable of their greater ranges?'

Procházka's motives were more fundamental and in spite of his still dominant impatience and nervousness, his eyes grew steely. 'That is what I have to sell, it's the big point.' His voice softened to a more confidential level. 'I've tried, naturally, but I'd need a computer to correlate the lists properly and particularly to illustrate a trend. It's a task beyond the head, beyond this one certainly.' He tapped his own temple ponderously. 'So. The only thing I could say is not reliable but I tried to cerebrate it, you know, see if my subconscious could work it out without my chewing at it. I kept waking with a very low figure, very low indeed, but naturally I cannot be sure. I have the lists hidden in high speed, behind white noise on a tape cassette of Bohemian dances. Any good computerman could tell you from that. My feeling is less than ten per cent.'

The Czech took a tight swallow from his Prasdroj,

raising his head and looking down at Stuart as if in command. 'They'll get it when Maryša and I are both safely in the West with new identities and a million dollars.'

Stuart coughed and said with feeling, 'I understand. So if I get Maryša out—'

Procházka's eyes flamed wildly and he hissed, tight and quiet, 'Not with you! I want us out together, she is carrying my child these three months, she will run out of courage and so will I if I do not go with her.'

Stuart raised his arms in a helpless shrug but then turned away to hide a sudden surge of private fear. He recognised clearly that Procházka, his hair darkened, would resemble himself among strangers sufficiently to pass everything but fingerprinting or a listed peculiarity. His eyes were not the same shade but the colour brown in his passport covered any difference.

Procházka was saying, 'Who is your man in Langley, whom do you trust?'

Stuart's thoughts weren't on the same track. 'Do you speak English?' he asked and was surprised by the bitterness in the Czech's reply.

'Why this question? Do you think I would not make a useful member of Western society?'

His pique annoyed Stuart and he didn't fully conceal it. 'The debriefing would be long and searching. For all they know you could be making it up to get yourself out.'

Procházka swore and thumped the back of a chair with his bottle. 'I am NOT making it up! There's proof of origin on the tape.'

'Also they'd have to be forewarned in case you had problems on entry. You wouldn't want to be sent straight back.'

'You are not making sense. If the Americans get us out, of course they'll be expecting me. In London I would be in transit, straight on to United States. Maryša's chief doesn't get this gem, you can be sure, even though he knows about me. Give me a name!'

Procházka . . . Stuart remembered with a chill that Stayres had asked for this file by name, that his own was going to be changed for the mission. It puzzled him but his single-mindedness obscured the reasons, that Maryša might have stated their case strongly enough for Stayres to sacrifice the first available substitute.

'I was thinking of something else.' Stuart found his left arm had started to shake, a premonition of what he was about to offer. He had a terrible sinking dread of it, knowing that to challenge himself so severely was almost evil and that calling his own bluff for his vacillation with Louis was almost too cruel to bear. The favour he was about to confer also seemed too princely, its generosity so worthy of suspicion that he was prompted to try for a bargain.

He took a deep breath and threw the first of his hand. 'I have a possible different route out,' he said shakily, 'You could adjust your face and hair to resemble my passport and visa photographs. In exchange you let me have your cassette to take with me. Maryša will be able to talk for both of you, and Stayres is fluent in Czech anyway.'

'It has to be America! You can't have the tape, it's our entire future.' Procházka's eyes narrowed. 'Besides, you know what's on it. Just give me the name in Langley.'

Stuart resisted. 'I'll give you full credit with Langley for it, don't worry.'

'No! I will not haggle with you.'

His blunt refusal lifted Stuart's dread somewhat as if it might justify cancellation of his dare. He shrugged as if to say 'take it or leave it', although Procházka had sounded particularly adamant.

He wasn't sure then how to play it because he had become so fraught with nervousness and a violent urge to be away from there. Simply talking to this man must be lethally dangerous for both of them, and he'd no idea if the apartment was secure. His nerves quivered taut at that moment because they heard a slight fumble

153

outside and then a double knock on the door. Fatally Stuart turned towards it in alarm, having already made the elementary blunder of not projecting himself into Procházka's position. Of all people he should have been aware of the power of love, of its dominion over the will so powerful that a man may desert every ingrained principle for it, however high-flown or sacred.

A single knock followed but he was not to know it was Maryša's signal. He sensed a fast movement behind him, too sudden for an intention to open the door. Instinctively he ducked away from it but the iron bedleg aimed at his head glanced off and crunched into his shoulder. The pain was instant and excruciating but from his army rough-house training he dimly remembered to aim for a joint, lashing his heel into the side of Procházka's right knee. There was an anguished and furious groan but the iron was already chopping down again, catching him just behind the right ear with such impassioned force that it cracked his skull.

He stayed unconscious for uncounted hours, coming half-awake to find himself in parched and throbbing agony, lying on the bed with an oversized gag in his mouth, his feet and hands bound together behind him. His brain fuzzed in distress at any attempt to function, or to answer why there should be a strong smell of kerosene. His skull seemed to amplify his pulse like a huge drum, his hands and feet had no feeling and he'd fouled himself which gave him an awful recollection of a child's distress.

He opened one eye minutely against the huge pain it caused him. A frail light flickered yellow shadows off the wall where some kind soul had left a candle burning. Logic faded away but kept returning to nag at him in short phases. Kerosene burns and the candle stays alight, hours and hours, a wonderful candle, a night light for comfort in his suffering, so long lasting and so generous.

154

'It's for delay,' said logic, 'it's a fuse for the getaway.' 'It's against pain and fear,' said the sufferer, 'it's for warmth and comfort.'

He struggled limply for a while, breathing with terrified difficulty through a blocked nose before passing out again, just aware that it was grey daylight outside and raining.

'Don't call, nurse is busy,' said the patient coming round again, interrupted by logic screaming, 'Bomb scare! Get the sappers!' He shook his head in a tiny excruciating arc to refute it, an accusation of murder, long-premeditated, inconceivably callous, by persons with names erased from memory. Straining his head over the side of the bed he could see only the reflected glow of the candle in the varnish of the wardrobe, dull and diffuse. The flame reflected also the shiny outside of the tin in which it nestled. For a second's miraculous clarity he saw an aura of what the candle had once been, nearly a metre high of sections melted together, to be still burning long after the killer had gone, leaving no trace of arson, the wax all vapourised once the soaked cloth in the tin of fuel was touched with fire. Screaming death flickered just out of sight, its flashpoint anywhere between one second and tortuous hours.

Twisting his racked body he could see a stout cord extending to the radiator from where his hands and feet were tethered. He wrenched at it repeatedly, effecting nothing but more pain while the thoughts of fire kept stabbing at his panic centre. He understood dimly that pain and pity would reduce him in moments to a writhing, helpless sacrifice unless he could smother it with some control but there seemed no memory of instinct left, no trained reaction.

How to kill an unseen candle flame, too far away to blow, no hands free to unzip trousers or direct a non-existent flow since he felt empty and dry as the desert? He couldn't move the bed to smother it without the risk of simply toppling the candle into the fuel.

He had one remaining option, a certain knowledge of a childhod skill, the memory erased of all the forbidden practice which had perfected it. First he had to get rid of the gag, an action impossible without a purchase point. Twisting himself he found he could just get his mouth to the rope tether, sawing it across the bundle inside and trapping tiny folds between it and the corners of his mouth. It took an age before there was even any encouragement to shift the bulk of it and once free, in his wild single-mindedness he never thought to try chewing at the rope itself nor even to call for help. He had a certainty that he was running out of time, in a completely hostile environment.

The gag had dessicated him completely. He sucked desperately on his cheeks for ammunition but nothing flowed from dehydrated glands. The thought of favourite food might have triggered it but he couldn't remember one single dish. The frustration tried to bring tears to dry eyes but then he had a vision of someone else eating and drinking, sharing joy and relish and gratitude, a face only impressionist and indistinct, alight and wholesome . . . The picture brought a surge of moisture into his cheeks. He sucked hard and greedily like squeezing dried fruit, then he straightened himself and spat with perfect compactness over the end of the mattress. The line was right but the trajectory he could only guess, a small sputtering telling him he was close but which way he couldn't predict. It was like pin-point mortar-firing without a spotter, he thought grimly, without knowing whence the notion arose.

It took several minutes to re-arm his mouth and try again and then again, the intervals growing longer, more dizzying and more desperate. It must be the longest candle in the world, he thought, unless it was

156

a gas flame set to torture him to madness. As a manic final measure he sought to draw blood from himself but in his trussed position there was no part of his body he could reach with his teeth. The next attempt took more than ten minutes to prepare, the arid sucking giving him so much distress that he simply had to ignore it. His mind moved into a super-clarity and he believed he could see the firing range from the side, a whole vista away. It looked so easy; the aimer could coldly assess the range and trajectory, turn his mind through ninety degrees and let the mechanism take over. Extraneous thoughts like hit or miss, success or failure had to be disbarred, quite simply; there was only one action, one target and one more attempt.

It seemed like blowing a kiss at the moon on a clear night: once it's gone there is no more control and only the thought creating it was perfect. His final round curved over the end of the bed in a holy slow motion, extinguishing the flame even after he'd passed out again in blessed certainty.

When next he came round it was dark but they'd left the light on in the tiny kitchen area. Turning his body and racking his arms and feet sideways, he began to gnaw at the line holding him to the radiator. It took him another eternity and when a throbbing eyetooth finally cut the last strand, his limited concentration merely switched to another area of pain. Rationing the effort carefully, he rolled off the bed onto his knees. His hands screamed at the limited circulation the movement afforded and he wondered vaguely if they had gangrene. He was able to knee-walk inch by inch through the straggle of the damaged bead curtain towards the light.

He couldn't stand or even use his teeth to open a drawer; about the only movement available was to swing his head back and forth over the top of the short counter, knocking off a stack of plates, cups and a saucepan, finally trapping a breadknife with his nose and sliding

157

it wetly over the edge, his flexed thighs on fire with the strain. Then he had to lie on his side and grasp it with almost useless fingers, millimetrically sawing at the stocking which bound his feet together, When it finally parted, everything swam away and it seemed more hours before he came round once again. Finally he jammed the breadknife in a drawer behind him, sawing away desperately and almost unfeeling of the damage he did to himself, hearing the blood dripping to the floor. He knew all the time there was something terribly wrong with his head.

Release when it came was so exquisite in its further pain that a loud, parched and cracking groan escaped his throat. He turned on the tap and drank for eternity, his head pulsing wildly like a machine out of control. Finally he lurched into the main room and fell over the bed again, semi-conscious and imagining he was trying with black-roasted hands to force open the canopy, prying with the little kit-crowbar. It was no use, all the controls had gone and this was the way it ended . . . must get her down, Jaroslav had done it with his spine shot away, move, MOVE, do something . . .

Dimly he saw the candle in the tin, just half a centimetre above the fuel-soaked cloth and it seemed to fill him with the previous fear. The next he knew he was outside and stumbling down the street, a voice commanding him, why was it speaking Czech, very roughly, telling him to halt? He tried to obey but but his legs wouldn't co-operate. He half-turned to explain the problem, still moving away in a sideways stagger when the steel-jacketed 7.62 caught him in the left side, ripped through his chest and kept going for another mile. With a gasp of shocked breath, pink mist sprayed out of his nose and mouth as his system closed off and ceased to struggle. He went down in a sodden heap, the gutter water reddening with each dying exhalation. In a final, crazy clawing to remain conscious, he saw his only motive in a golden light surrounding a face, and there was a gentleness trying sadly to touch some last deep-hidden vein of the fury of survival.

SEVEN

No, make me mistress to the man I love.
If there be yet another name more free,
More fond than mistress, make me that to thee.

Alexander Pope, Eloise

With Alicia preparing to return to the camp, Lucy had started tingling unbearably with the thought of getting her little Bensen into the air. Not knowing when Stuart would return, her feeling of mischief and furtiveness was deliciously over-exciting and for the time being her thoughts about Nadia's tragedy were safely in abeyance.

She missed fingering the platinum-set rose-jewel Stuart had given her since she'd left it with an Oxford jeweller for valuation. She'd been surprised that they'd asked to keep it for a day or two and slightly irked because with such a fine setting, she hoped they'd confound Alicia's derogatory remarks about costume jewellery. Stuart had wanted to give her a diamond and she'd told him it made no difference, the thought was perfect. His smile had seemed full of gratitude and delight.

The important thing was to have it back for Hever Castle, to go with the shrewdly wicked black dress now being altered to fit her lithe figure. Alicia's shock at the choice pleased Lucy immensely, not knowing her mother was in for an even tougher morning.

She was making her bed when Alicia came in, helping to fluff the duvet before noticing two rope-ends hanging from the oak beam in the roof.

'What are those for, child?'

'Oh . . . exercising.'

'Over the bed, what is it for?'

'It's experimental so far,' Lucy answered distractedly, forgetting her mother's inexorable curiosity.

'It's a new routine? Oh, tell me.'

'No, you wouldn't . . .' She saw from Alicia's face that she was too late. With her own distant thoughts about Stuart, she hadn't chosen her words carefully enough and her mother picked up the hedging at once. The hook was in and Lucy was furious with herself since she hadn't even been fishing.

'Tell me what it's for!' Alicia demanded eagerly.

'No, you wouldn't like it.'

'Of course I would.'

'It'll shock you.'

'Nothing shocks me any more, don't be silly.'

'This would. Anyway, it's private and this is my bedroom, don't be so bossy.'

It was rapidly becoming a contest, she realised, more than reluctant to share her new invention with anyone but Stuart. It was surely least appropriate with her mother.

'You must tell me,' Alicia pleaded, 'Don't play more secrets.'

Lucy eyed her levelly for several seconds, then she slipped off her shoes, stepped onto the bed, sloughed aside the duvet and wound the rope ends round her wrists, up through her hands. She crouched to gauge her height above the mattress then, using her legs to start the movement, spun her body slowly, twisting the ropes and thus gradually raising herself. Tucking her lower legs inwards rapidly accelerated the spin which slowed up gradually.

'Had enough, Mama?'

'No, it isn't anything clever.'

'All right, then. Stop me now. You have to help.'

161

Alicia came forward and held her tentatively by one leg. 'What do I do?'

Lucy looked down between her upraised arms. 'Now are you sure, mother?'

'Of course. Come on, child.'

Lucy sighed theatrically. 'All right. Put my feet into Lotus, one on each thigh, well, I can do one, push the other one over . . . That's it. Now you can let go.'

Alicia kept hold. 'You can't have someone helping with a proper routine.'

'For this one you have to.'

'Why, is it dangerous?'

'Golly, I've no idea. Mama, where's your imagination?'

'You mean . . . when I let go, you spin back down, like *that*?' Alicia stepped backwards, her eyes wide with astonished speculation. Freed, Lucy began to spin in suspension, accelerating with a high pitched 'Whee-eee!', reaching the end of the spiral and starting up again before unlocking her feet and standing. She thought to pull the barbs a little for good measure even though it was unlikely to cure her mother's inquisitiveness. In truth she knew the combination would never be realised because they'd be prostrate with laughter; she found kinkiness hilarious enough even without the seediness of premeditation but she saw no need to make it easier for Alicia.

'Do you think he'll like it?' she asked, her smile alight with feigned innocence.

Her mother was looking rather pale. 'I'm sure he will,' she answered stiffly, 'Let's have breakfast.'

With a sigh Lucy flipped back the duvet and followed onto the landing; in the big mirror she caught the trace of a grin on Alicia's pursed mouth. She blew softly through her nose and shrugged, waiting for her mother to clear the stairs so she could do her double

162

leap down. From there she heard a sudden snort of laughter and saw her mother looking back with a hand over her mouth, her eyes bright with amusement. Lucy felt real compassion then, and a deep gratitude for her generation's privilege.

'Well, really!' Alicia said, stressing a newly acquired Anglicism. 'Ludmilla, I think it must be almost worth to be a man to be married to you.'

Lucy was genuinely taken aback by the grace of this remark and flushed with pleasure. 'Thank you, Mama, very much. I do hope so, it's my job to make sure of it. I've called it Autogyro, that invention.'

Alicia looked puzzled but Lucy was determined to keep the Bensen secret from her so didn't elaborate, keeping her on the same tack.

'Stuart's a giver and not very good at receiving, either presents or pleasure. He's too concerned for me. I'm trying to teach him that to accept pleasing from me is to please me much more, it makes me feel needed and cherished. I think to be really nice to people, to be a real all-rounder, you have to learn to be selfish . . . Postman!'

She ran back from the front door opening a single letter while Alicia poured coffee. After a second reading, Lucy was standing tense in dumbfounded silence, her eyes far away and the letter dangling. With a look of sudden concern, Alicia came and took it out of her limp hand, fumbling for glasses.

It came from the Oxford jeweller explaining that he'd decided to take the pendant personally to Hatton Garden for a second opinion and that it was now waiting for her collection. The London jeweller's valuation, under a distinctly Hasidic letter-heading, was included together with a monstrous bill for the service, though it was their statement which had stunned Lucy into silence.

It read: *Valuation*

1 off, 6 carat (approx) pendeloque Rose-cut cerise diamond in pendant, set in 11/2 inch lozenge platinum skein.
We humbly apologise that we are unable to put a firm valuation on this unique piece. In the absence of anything comparable, we can only say that if approached for such a specimen we would be obliged to ask at minimum £250,000 subject to availability of Internally Flawless rough of this quality and colour.

They added that should she ever decide to offer the piece for sale, they would be pleased to seek a buyer at this figure, subject to their usual commission, which was unspecified.

Alicia read it three times, her tight control accentuating her astonishment. Finally she handed it back without a word, knowing what to expect if she voiced any suspicion about the absent Stuart. Her restraint was gently appreciated as Lucy came back to earth, speaking for herself as well.

'I know, Mama, we're bound to think he must have stolen it, but he doesn't steal, he can't, it upsets him even to get too much change. Everything's been mysterious since he started this business, whatever he's doing, I don't know . . . God, it's terrible, he used to let me wear it even while swimming in hundreds of fathoms, I should keep it in a vault, or live in a cage surrounded by tigers. I really want it back and now I daren't go and get it!'

Alicia smiled faintly. 'I wonder what your father would say . . . They don't find any coloured ones in Siberia, mostly they're from South Africa.'

'How apt! But listen, which would it please Stuart more, to know that I know or to think he's kept it to himself and watch me being careless and blasé with it –

or exaggeratedly careful? Then we could both pretend, over and over again!'

'Then you can't ask the truth about it.'

'Damn, you're right. But you've seen what these cryptomaniacs are like. He might tell me I've No Need to Know. Which come to think of it, I haven't.'

'Well, I am afraid that I do have,' Alicia answered, shaking her head sadly. Lucy smiled at the admission but held up a warning finger, growling. Each time she looked at the letter her pulse seemed to accelerate.

'I feel like a bulb getting too many volts,' she said and Alicia shook her head at the invention. Lucy had always made her feel doltish and slow, a bore to Simonov who had bequeathed Lucy his private sparkle. Alicia wished she wasn't jealous of Stuart because he had Lucy with him all the time, yet she found herself in heavy disapproval of his absences. Life at the Peace Camp was squalid but at least uncomplicated.

The short-bearded man in a borrowed car would have attracted little attention even doubling back through the village lane, except that the Police watch, to ease the sheer boredom of their vigil, had set up a modem and were feeding every car number into a distant computer. They were themselves unaware that the South Africans were ready for a significant reply from the computer having given a hefty bribe to the local telephone engineer, a silent man called Fogarty. When the computer flashed back that the car had been reported stolen, both teams were alerted but both powerless to intercept it. The local Police had no patrol car close enough and the South Africans' vehicle had gone to London airport to meet a replacement.

The bearded man had seen the Kody's house with the Golf parked outside but he was wary enough not to stop or be seen looking. His interest quickened on the return run when he saw a pretty young woman jouncing out to the car wearing a grey running suit. He stopped in the pub carpark for a few moments only and followed her when she passed him, although out of the village he had to stay back to avoid her attention. She drove neatly but rather fast, the corners full of verve, but after about three miles he caught up with her in another village. She'd parked outside the school and was already in the playground amidst milling children. Some of them dragged a heavy coir mat from the covered corner and others shifted an unraised four-inch balance beam alongside it. The rest clamoured or did cartwheels until the woman organised them and led through some warm-ups. Then she simply walked along the beam, stopped in the middle, spun on one foot, proved her balance and walked off the end on elegantly turned feet.

The children followed one by one, showing how deceptively simple she'd made it. Only three managed without toppling and one honey-blonde show-off did a handstand as well which earned her a mock-stern reprimand. After further exercises breath began to steam in the chill air and the teacher slipped off her track-suit pants and adjusted her shorts casually. Her figure was ballerina-neat, her legs finely toned and very brown, and the watcher felt a primal surge. He stared with narrowed eyes and nurtured his prurience, eventually leaving the car and approaching the railings. He attracted glances but didn't think it mattered this far from the target house. If Kody was not immediately forthcoming, he thought, there were further possibilities here for turning up the pressure, but first he needed the enforcement of a gun. He got back into the car and drove carefully back to London, unaware that two surveillance teams had seen but not tagged him.

For the visitors, weeks of tense waiting had at least been requited, tense because they were forcefully aware of their mission's illegality. In Pretoria, Inspector Strijdom had been unequivocal; he wasn't going to mess with extraditions and endless formalities, even assuming a foreign Police force could be bothered to put half as much effort into the hunt for his murderer. He wanted Cornelius executed and he wanted him to know, just before it happened, this being his notion of justice seen to be done.

Four days, he'd said, certainly no more than a week, then he'd be home for keeps, home for Christmas, they'd go skiing together and she could learn from an expert instructor and sleep with him every night and before that was a splendid castle dinner, certainly he couldn't miss that with her black dress tight as a sheath and split to the tops of both hips but *so* discreetly; she soon gave up the struggle not to anticipate his reaction and savoured it until her stomach fluttered deliciously.

The single trill came every evening as if with the end of office hours. She wondered if he was really quite near, may be even at GCHQ Cheltenham, or somewhere in London or somewhere highly secret. It didn't occur to her that he might be abroad and she was discomfited that they wouldn't let him have an ordinary conversation with her, to share affection and mundane matters. Nevertheless the trill gave her a satisfying warmth.

One point of his absence was acceptable, that she couldn't blurt the other reason for her state of high-wire excitement even in spite of Allcock's taciturnity. She'd had the big crate transferred to Enstone and the elderly, stocky little Cockney sent by St George had taken over the rented hangar as if it were entirely his own idea. He was ruddy-faced and sharp-eared with a cap stuck permanently on his flat-topped head; his attitude was morose and fatalistic and he did his best to discourage Lucy's visits and to ignore her when she came to peep round the hangar door. She won him eventually by clowning and fawning with a grossly exaggerated marvel of his expertise. Allcock was an all-round zenophobe, with a particular suspicion of all things American dating from his apprenticeship during the war, when Packards contracted to make Rolls-Royce engines under licence to make up shortages and losses. He told her that in the true spirit of planned obsolescence, the Yanks had generously allowed a projected life of ten hours to their version of the Merlin engine since the average war-time expectancy of a Hurricane or Spitfire was reportedly five hours. If an ace or lucky pilot managed to stay aloft for more than ten, he assured her, there'd be a white trail of vapourised coolant, the sudden death of a Packard-Merlin and likely the same for the hero. Needless to add, each Rolls version was a masterpiece of precision engineering but his over-rapt listener would turn glassy with the technicality of alloy sealing rings and micro-tolerances. It was however no trouble to tell him how wonderful he was for finding Decibelle a Rolls engine of her own in spite of Bensen's protests that this was over-powering overweight. It gleamed like a shrine even in the darkened hangar yet Allcock was so meticulous that she wondered if he was deliberately stalling, making fresh promises almost daily.

At home she had three calls from Miss Cornwallis, secretary to Adrian Stayres, asking if she'd had any word from her husband. She left a number to call in such event; Lucy called back to check it but only heard an answering machine which didn't bother to identify itself. On the third enquiry she asked the secretary why she didn't speak to Stuart's employer but was answered briskly that there were perhaps more than one.

Lucy began to feel this secrecy and mystery getting out of hand but she kept up her flight training and took full advantage of Stuart's absence. One day at last she arrived at the airfield to find Decibelle sitting out in the pale sunshine, the curving rotor tethered with red pennants. For the regulations, each side was firmly placarded 'EX-PERIMENTAL'. In a state of breathlessness she hunted vainly for Allcock but after nearly an hour she calmed herself and made to understand his attitude, that of the earthbound to the flier, the meticulous to the vivacious, and perhaps too the bathos at the end of a project. It made her think of all the craftsmen, the poignancy the carpenter/shipwright must endure as he sees his creation sliding down the ways to the questionable care of one spoilt or ruthless enough to afford her.

Lucy removed the locks and pennants herself, pre-flighted like an inch-worm in case he was watching, started the drive engine on the second flick and carefully strapped herself aboard. As the overhead rotor reached flight speed, she taxied to the holding point, did her run-up checks, scanned all round and released the brakes with a surge of purest joy. Decibelle took to the almost-still air within forty feet and Lucy drifted off-line in the merest crosswind feeling close to delirium. Two rich ploughed fields away she saw a lone figure with its arms raised against the sun; certain it was Allcock, she approached in sharp descent, seeing his features and shiny pate, shielding his sight with his permanent cap held aloft. The turned field precluded landing or at least another take-off so she circled him, waving and showing off the machine's trim and balance with her arms out sideways, holding nothing. She couldn't tell if Allcock smiled but she felt great understanding of his feelings.

She flew it from Enstone for several days afterwards while Allcock made small adjustments and a special box for camera spares. Lucy loaded the OM2 and finally began her business in earnest, preferring to begin away from home for a trial period, to prolong the secrecy.

She kept a plot on her knee-pad and started circling Warwickshire villages in widening circles, photographing individual houses after first doing a high pan with a polaroid and numbering off. She would then take an enlarged black and white print to the house and offer it to the owner for £10, or £35 for the order of a full colour version; she was undercutting the professionals considerably being a one-person operation with a slow, stable and inexpensive machine.

Her early mistake was to land in someone's paddock and offer a picture there and then but with nothing but the polaroid to show and an old man's fury at the intrusion only partly mollified when she took off her helmet, she decided not to risk it again. After that she sold them by car with great success, meeting many of the county's moneyed middle class as well as some rare eccentrics and having to go slow on the offered drinks. There was so much amusement in what she had to tell Stuart that she began to keep a diary although it wasn't easy to keep her resentment for his absence off the paper.

He'd been gone many more days when St George called and asked for him, knowing nothing about the private arrangement with his own secretary which produced the faithful calls. Lucy betrayed an emotional response when she explained the position.

''straordinary,' St George opined, knowing where Stuart had gone and hating the secrecy from Lucy mainly because it meant he himself couldn't tell her what he knew or offer any consolation. In fact he'd been more than ominously concerned since the absence of news likely meant that Stuart had tried something and failed, with a terminal result.

His own voice sounded peculiar to him when he added, 'I hope nothing's happened to him.'

'It hasn't, that's just it! I get this damn jingle every day to say "I'm all right"'.

'You do?' St George mulled, puzzled. 'Oh. Well, that's something, I suppose. How long's he bin gorn now?'

St George drawled to sound casual and hide his bewilderment, still fearful that he had instigated something which had gone off-line. He resolved to contact his diplomat friend but in the event had no success there either.

170

'Well over a fortnight . . . I'm becoming a rampant capitalist and meeting some of the others. St G., Allcock was a treasure, did he tell you all about it?'

'Sixteen times, I should say. Someone seems to have plucked at those rusty old rigging wires he calls heartstrings. Now I have to pay him again, I suppose, but thanks for a few weeks' grace.'

'Oh . . . And it's going so well! It's amazing how they love a God's-eye view of their irremoveable assets, take a picture to show *Him* . . . I'll have paid for Decibelle in another month, I've got a new dress that'll slay him dead as a post, a fabulous dinner coming up and no bloody husband.'

After St George had expressed his sympathy and rung off, Lucy called the mysterious Paul Epiphany, reminded him diffidently who she was and wailed that she might not be able to come. He listened and was then typically succinct.

'What would he want you to do? If you don't know, reverse your positions and say what you'd want for him. It wasn't supposed to be for spouses anyway, so drum up another squire. You have to come, you're going to dance for us.'

'What? Who says?'

'Giles Raintree. Three years ahead of you at Elmhurst.'

'*That's* where I remember. They called her Boy, not very aptly.'

'Boy Giles? No. Anyway, I call the tune because it's my thrash, you can do us a *pas de deux*. I was going to tell you in time so you could warm up, stretch and whatever you do.'

'What sort of dance are you talking about?'

'That's for you to work out. Just be there, OK?'

Lucy rang off with a nervous laugh and later she called St George and told him about it. He exclaimed about the setting and said he and his parents had once been guests there when the Astors owned the castle.

'The thing is, St G., you wouldn't like to escort me, would you, just supposing Stuart doesn't turn up?'

There was an affronted cough at the other end of the line. 'Really, I ought to say that a baronet doesn't play second fiddle to anyone much, let alone a damn foreigner. But since it's you, I suppose one would have to be delighted. By the way, my conscience is quite clear, I told him already that I'm in love with you, so that's all right, isn't it?'

'Is it?' she answered doubtfully. 'What did he say?'

'Um . . . He said, "Me too" as a matter of fact . . . Oh, gawd, please don't sob, I'm sure there's a very good reason. Look, you get your glad-rags on and meet me at Kidlington, say 5 pm on the day. We can pole down to Biggin Hill and get a cab from there. If he does turn up then I'll gatecrash, how's that?'

'Yes! You mean fly? Oh, wizard. God, I'm so furious!'

'Thanks,' he muttered drily, 'You can pretend to have a good time, at least. I'll make you an honorary baroness for the evening, how's that?'

'You'll be honourable?'

'If nobility obliges . . . Don't forget there's *droit de seigneur*, first leg over the peasants. I wonder if it only applies on one's own patch? I better look it up to make sure.'

Lucy managed to smile and project it in her voice. 'All right, and thank you so much. If he does turn up, I'll tell him he can't come.'

Confused, St George could only mutter 'Gosh' before a mumbling repeat of the arrangements.

Knowing herself fairly well, Lucy realised that an idea couldn't burn long in her head without bearing fruit or being dismissed. She was almost saturated with flying every day and felt the need to reorganise herself. She bought a three-drawer filing cabinet for correspondence and photographs, plastering signs on each, Top Secret, Highly Confidential, Absolutely Private. It could stand

172

there as a permanent taunt because she knew he'd never dare to look in it, however meanly tempted.

Somehow her heaviest decision seemed to make itself one unflyable morning. With the grimmest possible weather forecast on the radio, she simply took down her big Atlas, went out to the car and was soon on the road to the Peace Camp.

The main gate was in chaos since the bailiffs had also heard the forecast and struck that morning during an early downpour, creating the most awful misery. A group of bruised and dishevelled women stood silent, defiant and dispossessed, holding a sheet of plastic over a sleeping infant, the first to be born and nourished at the camp. There were several smartly dressed onlookers under umbrellas and Lucy saw a portly, middle-aged man put fingers in his mouth for a cat-call. She took two rapid paces and just as he drew breath she placed her foot across the back of his knee and pressed firmly. The whistle stopped short as the knee bent irresistibly to her pressure and the man went down slowly in the mud. The only way he could release the offending foot was by lying full length to straighten his leg, thereby crushing his umbrella. Lucy skipped away and promptly forgot about him.

There was no sign of her another or of Nadia but she was re-directed round to another gate where she found them trying to keep a fire alight, a column of smoke beneath a home-made umbrella, a tin of water perched on a makeshift stand. Their lack of proper equipment seemed to scorn the mean thoroughness of the enforcers of the so-called Law. Lucy felt sorry that she hadn't thought to bring a thermos or some chocolate but was to learn that they didn't care and when people came with gifts, nobody pounced on them but always waited quietly for someone else to make a fair distribution. There were further signs of sanctity in a detached lack of gratitude for such contributions, which filled her with amazement

173

though her own gift of a huge bag of purple beet-root elicited some melting smiles.

Although pleased to be the focus of another *borscht* feast, Alicia feigned annoyance to see Lucy, proclaiming that it was not her place and that there were other things to do, while Harvey Smith, the terrier, greeted her with a bedraggled, wet little dance. Lucy didn't argue but waited until Alicia was committed to her chore with the beets before asking Nadia to show her the other camps.

In the car, after driving a silent half-mile, Lucy crossed her Rubicon. She stopped, opened a big Atlas at Northwest Germany and asked, 'Nadia, where do your parents live, exactly?'

Her porcelain-frail blondeness marred with straggled hair and mudstreaks, Nadia looked at her suspiciously before peering and pointing.

'Here, between Leipzig and Merseburg. Piotr works in Leipzig. Why do you want to know?'

'I'll get to that, but first tell me would they co-operate, would they be happy for you to have your child back?'

'Feodor . . . oh, please, *please* don't be holding anything out to me. We have talked it all away and it only twists the knife, over and over.'

'I can imagine. Listen now. I have a little flying machine, tiny like a toy helicopter. Somewhere along here there'll be open country, no factories or towns and I could bring it up to the border in a covered trailer, say within half a mile of the wire. We make a rendezvous on the other side, I can go over in silence, sort of gliding, that would be unseen and without warning. Feodor should be ready for me, then there's just the sound of an engine, up and over and no one would ever know. You could be waiting there in the truck, perhaps three minutes. A sentry wouldn't even report it if he hadn't spotted anything certain. If your parents are willing, they should leave Feodor in a basket sedated

174

with a sleeping draught so they can be away from the scene and back home to report his disappearance as if it were a crime.'

Nadia stared rigidly out of the streaming windscreen. It's done, Lucy thought in terror, and unless the young mother refused the risk, Lucy could no more back away than glide with her arms out. She too stared ahead with her knuckles white, thinking of Stuart and the risking of life. She sensed Nadia turn and stare at her for a heavily protracted moment with no sound of breathing.

Suddenly she heard choking and unexpectedly a flow of Russian. 'I want to claw at you for suggesting this nonsense! How can you tear at my guts with such childish imaginings, such complete shit rubbish!'

Lucy turned in astonishment, seeing the pale hands flexing in an awful tension of restraint. She imagined them going for her eyes, her cheeks, and her arms flexed for the parry; she shook her head in fright and denial. Nadia began to wail.

'Stop, Nadia, listen! How does my mother speak of me? Like the sort of person who dreams and lies and has flights of fancy? Tell me.'

'No, but she's your mother. How can I—'

'Nadia, I can tell you I was secretly hoping you would refuse or that your family was back in Russia, something, but I have to tell you the whole of it. My machine is a secret, otherwise I'd have brought it to show you. If you come to our house again I'll take you to have a look, to see it's real. Only two people know of it, not my husband, nor even Alicia. I'm sure it's never been done before, not in-and-out, but there have been several escapes by light aircraft, you must know that. Very difficult to detect and stop. They can't have a gun for every metre of wire and if there's any alert it would be too late, we'd already be gone.'

'But little Feodor – what if they did shoot at you?'

175

'I'm much bigger, and I've no intention of being anyone's target. Was your father in the Services, can he read a map, go to a reference with certain accuracy?'

'Oh, I'm sure. He was a sergeant in Signals.'

'Perfect! So if I pick an area then somehow get hold of some high altitude photos we can plan it exactly. You can write to your parents safely through the diplomatic bag, I can arrange that, and put the whole thing down for them. I suppose they'll be very sorry to see him go . . . They're not against you, are they?'

Nadia shook her head. 'No. Papa would have killed Piotr for what he did but he had to pretend. That's why Piotr got them transferred to Leipzig. Piotr is a power-station engineer. I think Papa might still do it if Feodor is out of the way, kill him, I mean.'

'Wouldn't that stop you?'

'No!' The answer came with furious vehemence. 'I hope he does!' She moaned then into her hands. 'I don't, I don't, I can't stand any more of this horror. Ludmilla, Lucy, I say to you all right, if it can be done, do it. If not, I can go on as before. Just don't lie to me about anything – and don't endanger your life. How long to get everything ready?'

'Let's say Christmas or just after. Six weeks. I'll go and practise hedge-hopping in the dark. And we must keep it from Mama, you know, it would be too much for her to think about.'

'Too much for KGB, you mean. If they find out afterwards they'll come for you, even here. It's a terrible affront, terrible impudence. I say nothing of your courage which seems to be insanity, forgive me –'

'Don't think about it, Nadia. How can they possibly find out, anyway?'

Nadia shuddered and didn't reply. Her tears broke then and she sobbed for long minutes, holding Lucy's hands with reverent gentleness, the smell of leaf-smoke and mud strong in the steamed-up car. Lucy's thoughts filed away to set up difficulties and practical solutions and she realised they were in large part practical distractions. They became a habit to cultivate whenever the ghastly chills assailed her, beseeching her to invent any excuse, clutch at any small straw of pretext to cancel.

EIGHT

O body swayed to music, O brightening glance,
How can we tell the dancer from the dance?

W.B.Yeats

The wintry afternoon was wreathed in full dusk as the
sleek Bell helicopter spotlighted and settled on the grass
between the inner and outer moats. In the front seat,
Lucy was quietly thrilled to have seen Hever first from
the air, however darkly, the huge lake by the River
Eden, the Castle and its Tudor village, the maze and
the tree-lined walks, the Italian gardens leading to the
huge stone loggia. She thought Stuart would have loved
the helicopter ride though it wouldn't have happened if
he'd been there.

On the pilot's side, Tuffy Beauchamp danced and
spun the JetRanger for an all-round view before settling
on the marked 'H'. St George peered through toothily
from the rear and made bantering remarks to his
friend. As soon as they'd stepped down and the doors
were closed, Beauchamp waved languidly and with an
aristocrat's blasé refocus, hoisted his own nose and the
Bell's collective lever as if they were a unit, tilting and
dipping away over the trees.

'Bit o'luck, that,' St George said, 'I mean, he owes
me plenty but getting the hot-and-stickies on it is another
matter, um?'

Arriving at Biggin Hill in his Seneca and about to call
for a cab, he'd spotted Tuffy and cornered him for the

ten minute ride to Edenbridge. 'And I got the impression he was about to wriggle out with some lavatorial excuse and then he clapped his focals on you, rather. And I must commend your back-up, slightly wicked pretending you've never been in a helicopter before, I mean for someone who even owns one . . .'

'Decibelle's only little,' Lucy said archly, 'How does one get inside this monument to royal lust?' She shivered as the wind swirled and leaves spiralled up from the path. Through leaded windows across the moat they could see silhouettes passing in warm amber light before welcoming fires.

'Round the front and across the drawbridge,' he answered with a proprietorial gesture.

Due to stay the night, they'd arrived early to change and were still able to see in the gloom. Chains ran down to the inner half of the drawbridge and above it the spikes of portcullis hung threateningly out of a slot in the ancient stonework. Lucy felt an abrupt backpace in time, to pass from a flying machine onto a venerable wooden bridge, unchallenged but daintily greeted by a little chambermaid on the far side of the inner courtyard. Lucy gave her name and she inclined her head confidently.

'You're in the Primrose suite, Mrs Kody. And Mr Kody? Follow me, please.'

St George tagged along after them, carrying the small cases and looking slightly worried. Thick and silky red carpets stretched down long, soft-lit passages until the girl opened a door and ushered them inside.

'The reception's not till seven,' she said, 'In the Inner Hall. You can always explore in the meantime. Would you like some tea?'

They both shook their heads and she left. The room was twin-bedded and St George looked embarrassed until Lucy chuckled at him.

'I suppose I was marked down to be with husband,' she said wistfully, 'He'd have loved the chopper, I should think, or did they use them in the Army, I wonder? Anyway, don't worry about this, we'll sort out some arrangement.'

'Airce. I'll probably get pickled and pass out. I'm only a real nuisance in the mornings, given the chance.'

'Oh,' Lucy said with mock-disappointment, wary of his feelings, but sure she could find a solution in laughter if necessary. 'Isn't this heaven, dignified peace?'

'Oh, you haven't seen anything yet. One hopes a good use will get it over its dudgeon at last.'

'Meaning Anne Boleyn?'

'Um. Gather she was a happy little girl here and she inherited it. Henry had his own bed for when he came a-sniffing. It's still upstairs. After he gave her the chop, he gave the castle to Anne of Cleves. It rather fell down and Astor fixed it up in about 1900. Spent millions. Smashing place for a bun-fight, all the same. Now, where shall I . . . ?'

They took turns with the bathroom and changed with hilarity but when they were ready, Lucy struck a pose and St George gulped. The low-necked silky sheath flowed down to her feet and met with little pink leather sandals but it was the slit to mid-thigh which had caused the reaction.

'Actually, St G., it was split all the way to the hip-joint but I got them to tack it up. I don't feel too showy.'

'Can't you tack it all the way down?' he protested gamely.

'Don't be daft, I couldn't walk. Anyway, if I was wearing shorts you wouldn't look twice. It's peepability that pulls the organ-stops.'

St George shrugged and looked away. 'I'll show you round, if you like. First, I've got something for you, right colour too, I think.'

She looked at him in surprise as he passed her a soft cylindrical package and she took it with curious hesitation.

'I had this rather posh Frog charter from Toulouse to the Balearics and one of the over-indulged ladies told me that if I had a loved one I should get her a Dupin.'

Lucy opened the tissue and tumbled out an uncoiling skein of soft leather in graded pastel pinks, sixteen strands, longer below than above so as to snug over the flare of hips. She ran it through her hands in quiet appreciation, letting her pleasure show. St George brushed it over defensively.

'Eccentric titled French couple, sort of gone back to nature, do all their own dyeing as well, clear dyes to bring out the natural colours. That's the latest, it's called "*Mystique, Ibiza*".'

Lucy passed it round her waist and tried to look at it, then went wordlessly to the mirror over the dressing table. St George followed, watching her as she moved. She looked round at him, slid the belt off-centre to drape over one side and jauntily cocked her rump. He grinned and clapped silently.

'Thank you,' she said gravely after a long admiring scrutiny and turning back to him. 'Beautiful. It's the kind of thing a girl really lusts after, then buys a dress or a skirt specially to go with it. And it matches my shoes!'

St George almost simpered with delight and then Lucy dipped into her bag for her pendant. As she attached it behind her head, he peered at it curiously.

'I say, that's rather fun, splendid setting, what's the stone, tourmaline, garnet?'

Lucy raised her chin snootily. 'Oh no, it's a cerise diamond in pendeloque, can't you tell?'

St George giggled. 'Really? Heirloom, was it?'

'No,' she answered in a blasé tone, 'It's the little parcel you brought me from Antwerp. Stuart had it knocked up for me. I'm afraid I've got nothing for you.'

181

'Quite all right, thanks. Got enough bother with your last present, that damn salacious nut. My secretary Stella keeps catching me ogling it on my desk. I'm thinking of having it cut open, it can be a fruitbowl or something useful. At the moment I can never decide which way up to put her, I mean it, you know what I mean?' Flustered he added, 'Look, we could sort of take a turn, couldn't we, and you can look in all the mirrors and I can try and get my hands on some lubricant, gargle-wise. What d'you say, um?'

'Top hole. Let's amble, frankly.'

'Look, stop taking the piddle, just because I'm a touch over-bred.'

'Sorry. Everything's pink . . . I want pink champagne and to make a beast of myself.'

'Oh,' St George said doubtfully, 'I was sort of hoping you'd be co-pilot and take control.'

Lucy shook her head firmly and they went out feeling full of mischief and slightly forced laughter.

The only people they saw at first were trying not to be noticed, busy and scurrying with their final preparations while St George and Lucy wandered, enthralled by the carvings, the tiny intricacies of leaded windows and the sheer craftsmanship in plaster. In the drawing room Lucy took off her sandals and pretended to wade in the luxury of the Khotan carpet, gazing in awe at the marquetry panels, each one unique. The ancient patina of the Inner Hall's walls, columns and gallery in Italian walnut seemed to spread a reassurance of eternal continuity; the care and polish lavished on them and on the linenfold panels in the Dining Hall, overhung by the enormous Henry VIII tapestry, filled them with hushed reverence, a sense of unqualified privilege. Being largely alone as they wandered, only the preparations and the profusion of winter flowers showed the busy care behind the scenes and they had time to point things out to each other.

'I love the fireplaces stuffed with cymbidiums,' Lucy said, 'Such colour, and they last and last.'

'What are those feathery things behind?' St George asked.

She wasn't sure if his interest was feigned for her so she laughed. 'You might well not know, St G. It's schizanthus, the poor man's orchid. On the window sills are cyclamen.'

He smiled knowingly; they moved to the library to be assailed with such headiness of hyacinth that Lucy ventured, 'So this is what it's like to be canonised, um? I feel a sort of huge, quiet dignity, a self-respect I haven't earned, just caused by the surroundings.'

He nodded solemnly. 'The problem is the bills. Pinkies don't like this sort of thing, there's a sad, small-minded jealousy.'

'I don't get it. I rejoice that anyone's enjoying it. It doesn't have to be me.'

'Right-o. There's some kind of twisted satisfaction in taxing it out of existence. Then the dignity is slightly marred when your house is filled with variously odorous sightseers, squashed sandwiches, howling kids and locks on the silver. We're rather lucky to be doing this alone.'

'Oh, we are! And such flowers for November – do you notice flowers? A lot of men don't.'

'You may continue to point them out, just in case.'

Although the little stronghold was compact by castle standards, they became happily lost in the upper part on tiny spiral stone staircases; Lucy became absorbed in the Long Gallery's display of Tudor costumes while St George had later to be pried away from the instruments of torture in the Council Chamber.

'Who was it said something about preach a better sermon?' he asked, giving in to her tugging, 'you know, Make a better chastity-belt, though he build his house in the woods, the world will still beat a path to his door?'

'It was a better mousetrap, silly,' Lucy answered giggling, 'All those horrid things are bringing out your kinks. It was Ralph Waldo . . . Listen, I hear revellers and coaches, don't you?'

'Ay, marry, and the thirst is upon me, I had forgot it, such tormentous geegaws have befuddled my priorities.'

'Verily, i' sooth, lead me to 't, my pet Baronet.'

'Rather,' he answered, almost skipping with excitement.

By the time they regained the Inner Hall some two-dozen guests had already arrived. Epiphany was receiving them with a young woman at his side whom Lucy recognised immediately, a tall, auburn-haired, green-eyed dazzling beauty. She was quick-spoken and sharply attentive, assured as if nurtured in safe surroundings. Because of their age difference, they'd seldom spoken at school but she remembered the hair and the frosty beauty. In retrospect she seemed also too diverse to have pursued a career as a ballerina, in spite of a serious turn of mind. Looking at her now, Lucy suspected that she might also have grown too tall, her green eyes seemed at least three inches above her own. She dazzled in a loose and shimmering velour trouser-suit with a scooped neckline, a vivid lime green over little gold shoes. Lucy felt a curious pleasure just to look at her and sensed an enviable assurance in her caused by more than seniority, perhaps achievement. She felt St George's hand tighten on her elbow.

When it was her turn to be introduced, she touched fingers and looked at her, seeing a delight of recognition but she filled in quickly for a possible memory gap. Humble junior's built-in reaction, she thought at once, amused.

'Lucy,' she said but the other girl nodded away the prompt. 'I remember the Giles – and still Raintree?'

Giles nodded, looking gratified. 'The Rush, Lucy the tumbler. I remember they liked you for being naughty,

184

it must have been the way you did it. What happened to you, well we can talk later. The Boss's got a plan, did he tell you, an ad-lib?'

Lucy nodded looking slightly helpless and the introductions moved them on. Epiphany radiated bonhomie, taking both her hands and exclaiming, 'Ah, delighted, the mystery caller. Is this your stand-in?' he added, looking to her right.

'That's the one, my pilot/chauffeur/escort. You may decide you need an interpreter. He has a title, naturally, as well as being sainted, so he's a bit far back to understand at times, especially when he's feeling at home as in a place like this. It seems the breath-taking Giles has done me a favour, St George was in love with me until just half a minute ago.'

They both looked again and laughed. St George was talking earnestly to Giles, holding on to her hand as if for life, the line growing watchfully behind him. He noticed their attention and came off his heady cloud of imaginings, releasing her reluctantly. He saw Lucy's ironic smile and turned his mouth down, feigning disapproval.

'Must be frightfully expensive to run,' he stage-whispered to her and Epiphany overheard him.

'Not at all,' he countered easily, 'She's self-supporting, a professional shrink. She takes the winter off one year, spring the next and so on. This year it's winter. No news of the errant husband?'

Lucy shook her head and flapped her arms helplessly. 'I don't know what to do so I do nothing.'

'Right. He's lurking behind the curtain, no doubt. I'll talk to you later when all the Hoovers are in. Have a drink.'

He looked again at St George and Lucy introduced them. Epiphany shook hands and asked blandly, 'You're not hiding anything, are you?'

St George was puzzled and didn't answer, giving a

nervous, toothy grin before moving away. Lucy looked round at the other guests before voicing her thought.

'St G., have you noticed, everyone seems to be frightfully good-looking?'

'Yes, I'm afraid they rather are.'

'Heaven's above, can you re-phrase that?'

'What?' he asked her, baffled.

'Never mind.' Lucy controlled the urge for a mad giggle and made a mental note to tell Stuart. At the thought, she clutched her pendant wistfully and stopped herself from saying anything. As St George accepted drinks from a waiter, there was a sudden silence as Epiphany looked down the queue and made a quick gesture of dismissal.

His action seemed to frame a still-shot in the moving sequence, high-lighting postures and a variety of exquisite clothing. The guests seemed entirely of an age, mid-twenties to mid-thirties, many with an air of easy calm and familiarity with each other. Among the men, the standard dinner jacket seemed to fit with less assurance than the more exotic trappings of the confident; white or coloured jackets served to emphasise a carefree flamboyance. Dowdiness among the women was almost absent, the most grace attaching to the simple, classical dress, the most exuberant with the daring or frivolous. Neither seemed to be much pre-occupied with the usual narrow-eyed, languid or shrewish mutual assessment.

Overall hummed a great feeling of occasion and privilege and, if there'd been an order to dress to a desired character, Lucy thought it couldn't have been better calculated to fire the curiosity or envy of the uninitiated, better than any sales pitch. Her own and St George's assurance came from different moulds, his from aristocratic insouciance and hers, she assumed too humbly, from years of trained footlight exposure. It didn't seem to matter how acquired, so long as the awful

186

drag of shy and useless diffidence was sloughed away early and the right of progress re-established. At that moment it seemed there was a corollary in impudence.

Giles was in the act of cautiously shaking the hand of a straggle-haired young man in studded black leather, jeans and heavy boots but Epiphany spoke past her, firmly.

'You go hungry tonight, Gonzo. If you read the New Testament, I'm sure you'll find the appropriate parable, about the wedding garment? I'm afraid you are not appropriate.'

'But I don't hold with all this fancy penguin nonsense, Paul, it's all class and stuff.'

'Is it? In America we don't have class so much as respect, so I don't appreciate what you are saying to me. Therefore, get lost, there's a good feller. Anyway, penguins have dignity.'

St George coughed with some embarassment as he handed Lucy a goblet of champagne. 'Pater would have had him thrown in the dungeons,' he said, 'A touch far to the Right, was Pater. They even laid in pink gargle, just for you. I didn't get a peep at the label yet, but do try it anyway. I recommend.' He sniffed his glass with profound suspicion. 'You never said of what this is all in aid, so to speak.'

'So to speak? Gosh, I hope you never have to say anything really complicated, St G . . . Stuart didn't actually tell me, so I don't know. You're still staring at the Giles person, aren't you? Your fidelity is so, so . . .'

'Touching?' The horsey smile was in evidence again.

'Something like that.'

'Hmph, Pater would have had your chauffeur know his place as well. I should be demoted to ostler or even pilloried for my thoughts, regarding yourself. You are too good to look at actually, and your jewel should be famous.'

She fingered it again and looked round for a mirror.

187

Not seeing one, she touched it softly to her lips and decided that Stuart would want her to enjoy the evening, not to be missing him, but she stayed conscious of the ikon against her skin spreading a warm glow inside her, a tingling of exorbitant sensuality. She drank from her glass distractedly before looking at it and recalling her wish with delight.

Epiphany announced over the chatter, 'I'm told there'll be a relay of more medicine up in Anne Boleyn's room which you have to find for yourselves and then dinner is miles away in the Tudor suite. In twenty-eight minutes.'

St George had his nose buried in his goblet and was looking puzzled. For Lucy he sniffed and muttered, 'Ah . . . really, I'm concerned about this. I have never come across such quality in a rosé, it's jolly well not normal, you know.'

'It's delicious anyway before you complain. Maybe they dyed it!'

St George looked at her agape. 'That's it, it must be.' Distractedly he turned and spotted Epiphany moving past them. 'I say,' he ventured, waiting until his target turned with a quizzical eyebrow. 'I'm not sure why you asked me if I was hiding something, but I am.'

'Routine question, I assure you. Confessions later.' Epiphany smiled but St George remained agitated.

'I'm hiding a most profound and hideously expensive knowledge of Champagne and this is a Louis Roederer 1978 with perhaps a grain of cochineal added to the bottle, my opinion.'

'Then I am undone,' Epiphany said aptly, not hiding his astonishment. 'There are two Masters-of-Wine here and I've got a bet with them. Do I have to pay you to keep quiet?'

St George looked affronted and drew himself tall with a long sniff. 'Sir, ordinarily one would call you a bounder, but you are my host and I recognise one of them – Bruno Stafford, he was always a superbly bad loser. My lip is buttoned.'

'Have another glass.'

'I will, thank you. Nothing is what it seems and this whole setting is a myth. And the ladies are quite out of reach. Fortunately. I say, that chap you threw out – does that mean there's a spare bedroom?'

Epiphany shook his head with a sympathetic smile and moved away to rejoin Giles. St George scooped another glass from the tray and they wandered away from the others down quiet corridors.

The dinner was discreetly served, English 'traditional', smoked peppered mackerel or home made soups followed by rack of lamb or rare roast beef. Some forty guests were arranged in a horsehoe in the Tudor Suite dining room, a log fire a blazing comfort in the carved stone fireplace. Across the cleared wooden floor of the intervening room, music played quietly, mostly piano and oboe without insistence. During the main course, Giles came behind Lucy's chair and spoke in her ear.

'Don't eat too much. When they start dancing we can go out and warm up. Is there enough room for you in there?'

The question was jocular but Lucy could see a snag from where she sat. 'The chandelier. It's too low.'

Giles made a moue of laughing surprise. 'I'll check it out.'

A few minutes later, two boiler-suited men came into the next room with a long step-ladder. They lifted the chandelier about two feet on its chain and went out discreetly. The guests who saw it looked at each other in mystified amusement.

On Lucy's right, St George was almost purring with contentment. 'I heard someone say that nobody's married here,' he said, 'But I know different. Bruno over there, he's married. I don't think he recognised me. And there's you too.'

'Yes, but perhaps not to the ones we're with.'

'Ao . . . What's the idea, sort of musical *chaises longues*?'

She chuckled at his phrase. 'I don't know.'

'Well, what would Stuart have, I mean, it's a good thing he's not . . . oh, sorry, you poor thing, maybe we should mount an expedition to find him.'

'You sound like Pooh. Obviously he's not supposed to be found, and anyway who knows where to look? I've had all sorts of people ringing up for him but no one who actually admits to employing him.'

'Maybe they don't.'

'What? Don't be silly.'

'I mean, suppose he's self-employed?'

'Self-employed what? Sort of freelance civil-servant? That's daft!'

He grinned foolishly in agreement. 'I s'pose you're right. But who knows precisely what he does?'

'Quite . . . I once had a notion that you yourself knew something, when you first came to our house, remember? And what about that business thing you had together, what was it? Is there just something you could tell me?'

'Of course not, do you imagine I'd hear anything before you did?'

'No idea. He unloaded five grand on me so I could start a business and I got Decibelle, well that's feasible if he's suddenly on a good salary but this, do you know what this is worth?'

She fingered her pendant under his glance, and decided not to specify. 'Well, an absolute fortune anyway. If it wasn't such a lover's secret I'd be embarrassed by it.'

'Gosh, you mean you weren't joking? Pink is the rarest, the most sought-after, 'bout as common as turkey's teeth.'

'Yes, but he doesn't know that I know what it is. He didn't try to tell me, either, isn't that weird?'

St George chuckled in bewilderment. 'Are you going to tell him?'

'How and when?' she answered with arched bitterness. St George patted her hand in an awkward comfort and saw a wan smile in return.

After the main course, two couples got up to dance and shortly afterwards Lucy followed Giles out to another room. The older girl shut the door and said, 'I'm doing this because Paul thought otherwise you might refuse. Personally, I'm a bit creaky, let's listen.'

She hoisted her right leg and grimaced. 'I need an extended period off my arse, preferably in the sun. How about you?'

'I'm fairly OK. I give gym classes to kids.'

'Great . . . Do you remember a review, a year or two after I left? Two girls did a medley of styles with some ad-libbing. Something like that, yes? OK, whatever you like and I'll be there. We'll talk to Mr Music and there's more instruments coming. Can you hoist that skirt with the belt so you can move? It's a super belt, isn't it?'

'St George brought it. If you want one, just dazzle him.' She smiled to say the remark wasn't cynical and slid up the skirt inside the leather, sinking slowly into a splits. She burped theatrically but after the laughter they worked familiar routines for some time before going back in. More people were dancing by then, the band augmented with a bass, drums, guitar and extra keyboards. The pianist from the dinner interval was now beating time with a gold pencil, and when Giles spoke to him he turned genially, continuing the beat behind his back. They went into a huddle, counting off numbers on their hands, some of the dancers watching curiously. Lucy felt her skirt incongruously hoisted and loosened her belt to let it fall. Then she took off her necklace as well and held it up. St George left his chair in the dining room to come for them, horsily curious and his adam's apple jerking nervously.

191

'Can you keep these for me? We're going to do a turn but you don't have to watch,' she told him gaily. St George retreated, muttering something about trying to stop him.

Giles led Lucy onto the floor and they danced together for a few minutes while the band leader spoke to the musicians. With her only prior association with Giles as the older girl at school, Lucy could not help an old feeling of gratification and pride at being even addressed by her. At the same time she felt a sisterly affinity, one of those vivid chemical sparks that cause crushes in adolescence but only delight in maturity.

There was a pause and the tempo changed abruptly. Renaissance strains from a synthesised harpsichord emerged clearly, an allegretto by William Boyce. The two girls faced each other and Lucy waited, after a slight shake of her head that she wouldn't do the same. while Giles, with practised, fluent hands, twisted her rich mahogany hair into the bun that was always *de rigueur*. The gesture was enough to let people know something was about to happen. In the centre of the little floor they stood with one foot forward, toes pointed and hands joined above heads, curtseying, their necks held high and their brows raised yet with a semblance of timidity in diffident smiles. They began to move towards and away from each other daintily with short steps, making typical Elizabethan half-turns with hands holding non-existent petticoats clear of the floor. Some of the other dancers quietly filtered away, still watching the two girls as their heads arched sideways over shoulders and turned coquettishly. Lucy made a quick pout which Giles favoured with bland disdain and the audience laughed timidly. The remaining diners got up to look through from the other room while the remaining dancers gradually cleared a space for them. Beyond, at the corner of the drawing-room, the bandleader watched and finally made an abrupt gesture.

192

The medley erupted into a vigorous rock rhythm that left the floor otherwise empty. A series of fast kicks sent their shoes flying away and they pulled, swung and rolled each other with what looked like practised ease. Neither seemed to be leading and their intentions mis-matched only once, causing laughter and almost breaking noses; Lucy spoke in that moment and took an anchored stance: Giles leaned back gripping onto her hands, surged up and swung back feet first. There was a small tearing noise as the tacks on Lucy's seams burst all the way to her hips and Giles swung right through wide-spread legs and the double black curtain of Lucy's gown. To a whoosh of approval, Giles slithered and collapsed into a sit-spin on the floor while Lucy turned at once to lift her by the hands.

They spun each other again and again, under and over and weaving arm patterns over rapid hip and foot movements, their feet close together. The sound of a horn accented the finale, infusing extra frenzy to the dancing as they circled in and out of each other's spaces, tight grips and trained balance between them like a centrifuge. With the last horn-blow, Lucy took some distance, letting go hands, pulling away as if gathering herself for the return. Giles read it, dropped down several inches and slapped the front of her thighs, opening her arms and signalling with her head for Lucy to come to her. Lucy gathered and leapt feet first as Giles half-turned, landing sideways on Giles' hips, arms flung upwards and outwards. They both froze in position, mirroring delighted surprise.

There was a burst of applause and Lucy heard Giles blow out her cheeks, feigning defeat.

'You solo now, Rush, I'm puffing.'

The drummer had kept up a soft background pace, barely noticeable after the previous loud rumpus. It was a simple blues rhythm and Lucy nodded, hopping down, covering her legs again with mock-modesty and pretended girlishness. Curiosity seemed to stifle the small laughter as she walked slowly to centre-floor, floating on arched and turned-out feet. The drum picked up volume and she took a relaxed stance, closing her eyes as if to let the music invade her completely, her body primed and warm from the first effort. Enjoying the self was a gift she was delightedly learning.

It seemed to her that energy flowed from Giles standing aside, from the rapt company now filling the dining-room entrance and, remotely, from Stuart, presaging the moment for the real performance. The tune she knew by heart, knew there was no need to think, knew that her body wouldn't fail, feeling it was love that moved her, her special gift that was only given to be shared with others.

Palms upwards she slowly raised her arms and head, her eyes still closed but opening them at the top and bringing everything down again, now glassily aware of her audience as a unit of transfixed attention. The bass began thumping down on the first and third beats, One-and-two-and, then the keyboard came in with the melody she'd chosen. It was the source of her joke with Stuart, *Dance for a Diamond*, which they'd both heard long before he gave her the pendant, keeping its reality to himself at heaven knew what cost. She began a swaying walk-in-place movement to a beat that seemed to resonate through her as the band joined in with the melody. She took a deep breath and began a slow spiral round herself to the left, starting low, her body curved into the circle and feet keeping the rhythm. Her arms floated, tracing the direction of her turn in a circular flow upwards, leaning her weight to the inside of the circle. Reaching up, her fingers fluttering to the top, she started down once more, twisting her body at a counter angle so she seemed to be going left and right at the same time, letting her head fall into a natural rotation, accented at the end by her hair falling sleekly into place.

Alicia would have screamed to see her break the embargo on whiplashing her neck but for several years Lucy had exercised stubbornly in secret to restore its mobility after her fall from the asymmetric bars.

Continuing down to the floor she began to widen her spiral with a series of spins and rolls which melted gradually and bafflingly into each other, the eyes of all the audience except for Giles' unable to follow the intricate tracery, especially in distraction at flashes of brown legs through the sheer black curtain.

Lucy banished the modesty of a sudden as the ballad turned to jazz, twisting back onto her spine on the polished floor. throwing the whole length of her body straight upwards, balanced for a moment on shoulders and neck, rolling down onto her spine again and jack-knifing her legs. The unimpeded energy of the kick lifted her torso clear of the floor and swung her feet beneath her, poising in crouched balance. The trance broken, she snapped into a jazz routine with hitch-kicks and spins, alternating shoulder and pelvic movements sharp and aggressive at first then softly suggestive, executing each step with arms moving in precision, now long and graceful, now taut and tensile, snapping her head into place like a series of exclamation points.

The little band seemed rarely complicit as Lucy came back repeatedly to the up/down spiral, varying it subtly and giving to it a touching quality of entreaty even when speeded up. The ground bass began a cautious change to an insistent pounding on each beat, the rhythm switched in train to blatant disco and Giles's next choice fazed and clarified, a new tune she'd identified by its picturesque adverb in the chorus:

> On the frozen edge of Time we are,
> Is this a planet or a shooting star?
> Who'll be wary?
> Who'll be aware?

Who'll be the one to try the ice?

Who'll tip-toe on the tremble-tight wire?
One fumble means a tumble in a trice,
And never know
How far you can go –
There's no guarantee on wild ice!

Chorus: Dance delightly on the ice of Life,
Take a chance, your slice of Life,
And listen to the bold,
There's never growing old
When you keep on rolling the dice of Life.

(Finale): Dance on the ice,
Stride on the wire,
Dance for delight,
Dance for desire,
Sigh for your siren
Fly to your sire,
High, high,
Higher and higher and
DANCE! . . .

Some of the company started to clap the beat as
Lucy began the walking-in-place movement again but
now almost running, light on tense tip-toe. At each
phrase-end she executed different leaps, going first
straight up and arching fully backwards like a floating
letter-C, her legs trailing deeply behind her. On landing
she put one hand behind her on the floor, kicked up and
did a slow back walk-over, exposing tiny white pants as
the split skirt fell back and front over her head. Standing
for a second she pulled it down in mockery, making them
laugh with her. She ran forward, leapt high as if for a
handspring then suddenly snapped shut into a forward
somersault, straightening from it in a hard, stiff-legged

196

landing on her toes, the skirts flailing. She crouched again and leapt backwards, carving onto her hands for a backspring and then another, the cloth following the aerial curve, accelerating into a twisting straight somersault and landing again rigidly, a double percussion accompanied by the climactic beat of the drum.

There were gusts of appreciative noises everywhere and more clapping but then Lucy sank to her knees in salutation, one foot forward and head down to her genuflection as in a baulked runner's starting position.

Quietly at first and drowned by the applause, the harpsichord began a dactylic excerpt from Schubert's ballet *Rosamunde*. Giles tiptoed back into focus, taking Lucy's hand and leading her up into first position, feet parallel in opposite directions. She kept her hand high as *point d'appui* for Lucy's *relevé* and a single spin, then they exchanged the point and Giles moved her left leg back and right arm forward into a poised arabesque. Relaxing, they linked arms at waist height and moved to a slow *pas de deux* in a circle, then overacted the cygnets' dance from Swan Lake; linking again, they floated their free arms in trained elegance, out and in together, heads poised and high, first in profile and then looking at each other and breaking into natural smiles. Eventually signalling enough, Lucy brought their faces together with a raised hand, then after curtseys to the company and to the band they skipped off the floor together like two little girls. The applause which followed was heady with delight and there were calls for *encore*. Lucy waved an emphatic rearward farewell, feeling the perspiration running and her chest heaving freely. She was not quite as fit as she'd imagined but felt a profound satisfaction at their apparent enjoyment. She had a further mix of emotions in her enthrallment with Giles and a continuing regret for the absence of Stuart. There was something haunting her about it which kept away real resentment and for that she felt strangely grateful.

NINE

The web of our life is of a mingled yarn, good and
ill together; our virtues would be proud if our faults
whipped them not; and our crimes would despair if
they were not cherished by our virtues.

Shakespeare

Outside the suite Lucy slumped against the wall pulling
in breaths, silently amazed at the flow and lack of fault
in her routine. Giles seemed to emit the most gratifying
patronage.

'Thanks,' she said fervently, 'You were quite right, I
wouldn't have liked going in cold on my own.'

Giles patted her hands together. 'It was great! I must
get in shape again. Paul wants to see these as a regular
feature in different venues but when I asked him about it
he only said "Gather-ye-rosebuds". I suspect it's a tax-loss
number. I'd guess about half the people here have done
his seminar, so maybe it's some kind of trap.'

They slipped back in later when the dance floor
was full again, acknowledging smiles and praise. With
a break in the music, the company drifted back into the
dining room and Epiphany stood waiting calmly until the
silence wafted itself.

'Thank you to the dancers,' he said, 'Summed up in a
good word, "delightly" . . . People keep asking what this
is all about, so I'll tell you . . .

'The first batch of invitations were sent to alumni,
all currently single at least at the time of asking. Each

had to specify an ideal partner either by name or by personal inventory. I put some real energy into seeking out such partners for you, even though you may not know who they are, and neither will they yet know your specification. This beautiful building and general dazzlement I'd prefer to describe as a stimulus rather than a lure, even though one or two took a deal of persuading. Now that I have you here, you have yet to find each other.' Epiphany smiled his own delight and there came clapping and murmurs as people tried to scan the room unobtrusively.

'Secret beginnings,' Epiphany went on, 'I met someone recently who was leading a part-secret life, well, we all do that, you may say, but we do it *covertly*, secretly dreaming there's something else to come and we're just making do with this in the meantime. The secret in this case was open, it seemed like building a storehouse of treasures and surprises, all to be shared, sometime. And now the partner has started doing the same thing . . . That was by way of a small digression to distract you from what this is really all about!'

Sinking his head into his shoulders, he looked around furtively and stage-whispered with glee. 'It's a Conspiracy, a worldwide spreading conspiracy, but because that's a word to create suspicion we'll call it a Consensus, the Consensus of Human Intellectual Progress, C.H.I.P. This is a gathering of exceptional people chosen by each other, the kind of people who should recognise in what's happening their responsibility and who can give a lead simply by their enlightened and treasured existence. The Progress we seek is beyond what constrains us now, for which we need people with candour, confidence and influence who do not seek leadership and power but who need to feel part of the ponderous glacier of change – people who understand that political systems are a flawed but necessary evil which must be contained and supervised. I recall Dr Comfort's proposition that politicians should be conscripts, dragged screaming from their beds at four in the morning and forced to sit in the House for a fixed term – because anyone who *wants* to be a politician is *automatically* unsuited for the task.' Epiphany smiled at the deep murmurs of approval. 'As we cannot yet conscript them, we have to watch and guide the ones we have, to nurture them and to keep a steady eye on their inherent and terrible weakness . . .

'Here we are people favoured enough to be well-established in or leading particular fields, though myself I'm just a fad like macro-diets or save-the-redwoods. But I'm also an explorer/inventor. I'm encouraging conscious units to assist in the improvement of our environment over the widest possible range, any one of which can seem like a fad in certain lights. Those lights too are part of the balance because there's a huge vanity in some people – they actually believe they can change society!'

Epiphany looked round the room as if seeking such a culprit. 'And the secret is, they *can* – not by getting other people to change but simply by transforming themselves. Not only is that all it needs, that is all each individual need aspire to. Our alumni mention frequently how often people approach them asking "Why are you so assured, how can I have what you have, what's the secret?" The secret is of course, knowledge, especially the knowledge we already contain. We explore the ways of honesty to our feelings and, by extension, to systems that work properly, gradually influencing social and political trends until they come into line with the truth within. Like the sword of Zorro, the conspiracy will mark you, you'll see it all around you, brightness and eagerness to see a whole colony thriving, not just the individual nest being feathered. And there's an immediate – and humbling – effect, the discovery of how many more people there are to talk to than you ever imagined, because *you* seed a new and open attitude, acknowledging our nothingness and then discovering the transformation is running ahead of us, we are the wind behind the flame. We are proof that it is already happening, do you see? Society is now being transformed, because of and for each evolving individual, micro- to macrocosm, rival countries, whole nations which currently despise or fear each other will come under the same influence. Rivalry shows a trend to betterment, and see even now how the big boys, lacking a fight, begin to vie with peace propaganda. Have I said enough?'

There were some vigorous nods and Epiphany smiled unabashed. 'Oh, you all want to start exploring? OK, let's drink to the here and now. Remember Peggy Lee and the old, sad song: *Is that all there is?* And the answer?'

About half the company seemed bemused while the rest chorused, 'No! this is only the beginning!'

Epiphany sat and Lucy glanced quickly at St George, who seemed to be smiling indulgently to cover a deep concern.

'I hate rallying cries, don't you?' he whispered.

Lucy nodded mockingly. 'Highly suspicious. I suspect there's a deal of rocking and rolling in the Wennersley–Farquhar crypt tonight, if they could see their scion with a bunch of dangerous free-thinkers.'

St George shook his head. 'No, no. They wouldn't understand that bit, they'd just see a revolting display of enthusiasm and head for the nearest drinks cabinet.' He paused and then showed his teeth in suspicion. 'I say, though, you and I, we didn't select one another, did we?'

Lucy shook her head. 'No, that must have been Fate – unless you had something to do with Stuart's missing it?' St George was ill-equipped to brush over this accusation but his incipient look of furtive guilt dissolved with a tap on his shoulder. Giles Raintree stood like a vision behind his chair, her arm held up and palm down like a swan's neck, her green eyes indicating the dance floor. St George swallowed in alarm and followed her without a word, Lucy grinning after them open-mouthed until a hand lighted on her elbow.

'Bearing up?' Epiphany asked her, 'There's too much to this life. Watching you dance was like over-dosing on pleasure.'

Lucy looked up radiant at such a compliment, then it was shadowed by a thought. 'The evening glitters but you twisted the knife about secrets, we'd started doing that, me and my man. He seems to be better at it, though. He's a pro; I keep wanting to be found out, I can't wait for the fun.'

Epiphany looked surprised. 'So you didn't guess who I was talking about?'

Lucy showed only astonishment. 'You've only known us since Heathrow, a few weeks back – and that doesn't seem much excuse to ask us both to a posh scrum like this? Such an exciting idea, except that Stuart and I are married.'

'You were ideal. I was going to let people try to guess who was the one married couple here. Do you think you'd have been spotted?' Epiphany sat in the vacant chair next to her and followed her pointing finger.

Lucy said, 'Not if he's as faithful as St George. Look, she's dazzled him cross-eyed.' For a few moments they watched as Giles led her victim around like an adoring retriever.

'So you still don't know where Stuart is?'

'Not a squeak . . .' Something in his inflection caught her. 'Do you mean that *you do*?'

Epiphany nodded shortly. 'I put some people onto it for you, back in Washington. Remember what I said when you arrived? Your ears only, promise?'

'Sure, but – ' Lucy sent her thoughts back to the introductions. 'Lurking behind the curtain, you said, Oh God, THE Curtain, the iron one? He didn't – is it dangerous?'

Epiphany shuddered his mouth down in denial. 'No, he was just going to see someone, take some papers, that's the official bit. Maybe there was more to it, but we know he's all right because of the calls you get daily. Nobody seems to know what's holding him up.'

'But that man Stayres was asking . . . Are you supposed to know all this, Paul? Where do you come into it?' Lucy felt herself floundering deeper with his bland response.

'Not really. It's espionage on espionage, nothing illegal about it. You could say I've a vested interest in his safe return, which actually means I'd like a word before anybody else gets one. I think we should leave it at that for now. Come and dance.'

Lucy took a deep breath and let it go with a slump of shoulders. She couldn't see within herself whether relief or concern predominated. After a lengthy silence she stood up and allowed him to usher her onto the floor, looking round at the scene for distraction. To a slow number there seemed to be many intense conversations running, which Epiphany appeared to take for granted.

Lucy looked up at him in admiration and was suddenly aware that he neither needed it nor thought of others as lesser beings. She ventured, 'This awareness or encounter thing of yours, this seminar, what does it mean if I don't want to do it?'

Epiphany smiled back in appreciation. 'Nothing and everything. Maybe you're a conspirator already, I suspect you are because you seem secure and unafraid to seem foolish. If your dance had gone wrong would it have worried you?'

Lucy shook her head. 'For me, no. I'd find it a giggle. I'd be sorry to mess up the entertainment, maybe, so I'd continue it by clowning.'

'So relaxing, isn't it? It's what enables you to dance freely. It's realising how foolish and laughable we all are, especially if we invest in a stance or a position. But there's one little corollary, can you see it?' To her puzzled gaze he explained, 'What about the vital part that's doing the realising? There's the transcendence, the Self in action. And that's where we find our compassion . . . To answer: no, nobody needs it, but some people have to do it to find that out, even when I've told them so. It's a good living!'

Lucy smiled back. 'With all the changes coming now, how do we know where we are? Have we reached the Hundredth Monkey, Watson's syndrome, if enough people start doing something, it becomes universal? How to spread security, that's the hard part. Secure people don't need to get belligerent.'

They had found a space on the floor and Epiphany still listened politely. Lucy looked at him and cocked her head.

She said warningly, 'I hope that isn't an indulgent smile? All right. I was going to say that people compete happily in business for example, outsmarting each other whenever necessary or possible, but hopefully without so much insecurity that they have to stab each other in the back. *Mirnie Soryevnovanie.*'

'Hey?'

'It's Russian for Peaceful Competition. Instead of what we have now, this absurdity. But nobody can be easy or secure with big nations quivering in pathetic fear, fingers on the triggers.'

'International Stand-Off,' he nodded at her gravely. 'We'll get there eventually, it stands to reason. It may take a few generations, that's all, so in spite of what the papers say, I can't have Napoleonic ambitions.'

'And you're discounting nuclear war, Paul?'

'Absolutely. I mean, it's possible, so it's vital we guard against it. Meanwhile the swing is beginning, believe me. Doesn't Stuart tell you any secrets at all?'

'No . . . Well, actually, he did once. I do know something quite *amazing.*'

Epiphany seemed uncanny then but he'd already sensed she wasn't going to be drawn on the subject and decided to amuse himself. 'Me too,' he said promptly, dropping his voice to a whisper, 'My tame senator told me that Moscow hears that our Cruise and Pershings weren't armed.'

'Oh, Crikey, so it's true!' Lucy breathed. 'That's the very one I wasn't going to tell you. If it's so secret, why did you – you must have known I'd already heard it?'

'I guessed . . . Did he mention there was another side to it?'

'No, he – sorry, yes, but he didn't say what.'

'Or tell you where he got it?'

'No.'

'He told someone he got it from the next President of the USA.'

'Who's that?' Lucy asked, irritated by an unexpected naïveté in herself.

Epiphany stretched the corners of his mouth into a grossly exaggerated grin, his eyes unfocused. After a moment Lucy chuckled at what seemed an absurdity but Epiphany qualified his non-answer.

'Can't be too many with more than $600 million who really want the job. People that rich prefer to control the Presidency remotely.' Epiphany refrained from mentioning the offer of one of those 600 units for a twenty-four hour lead with some significant marketable information.

Lucy came surprisingly close with her next question. 'If someone who's not in the Clandestine Services is dabbling in this stuff, what about treason and Official Secrets?'

'If the secret is the other side's, not ours, there's no problem, is there?'

'By theirs, you mean Soviet? Is that where he is, then?' she asked, round-eyed and cringing.

Epiphany shook his head without replying.

'It has to be Czechoslovakia then, for his language. Holy Ghost! Thank God for the phone, that's all. But

London's been calling for him, and I know he works for this man called Stayres.'

'Ah, Adrian.' Epiphany nodded thoughtfully.

'Yes,' Lucy confirmed, 'I was getting really rattled, he must know I'll be pining.'

'Aware of you though, and he wouldn't want you to, would he? Instead, why don't you do something he'd like?'

'What do you mean?'

'Something he can do already which you can't, then you could join him, surprise him with it.'

'Plumbing, plastering, wiring, carpentry, carburettors . . .?' Her face was a picture of distaste.

'That doesn't look like it. Something fun, sporty?'

'Ski-ing! I've never done it. He was in the Army team. He was going to teach me.'

'Pretty boring for him. That's the perfect surprise. Giles is almost a beginner, why don't you go with her? You should get on all right.'

Lucy nodded thoughtfully. 'She makes me feel privileged. So do you. I asked her if you were together and she said she wasn't sure.'

He smiled quizzically, giving nothing away. 'Will you do the cabaret for us next time?'

'When Stuart's here? But I won't be – yes, I could wear a mask! I wonder if he'd know?'

'I guess he might do that,' Epiphany answered dryly but Lucy looked doubtful. 'But no Giles, she's too beautiful, he wouldn't notice me at all.'

He didn't bother to flatter by expressing disbelief but he looked down from her eyes. 'You keep holding that pendant. May I see it? It's really pretty . . . Hmm . . . And they say you can't improve on nature.'

'I hope they're right, whoever they are,' she answered gaily.

'I don't get you.' He looked at her face and then back at the pendant; in suspicion of his clairvoyance she

206

covered it modestly with a hand but his expression told nothing. Nor could she ask him for a guess and found she was delighted in not knowing if he knew, the design being somewhat exclusive.

'My mother came closest,' she allowed, 'Said it was like angels' wings. Like your little homily, full of possibilities.'

Throughout the rest of the evening St George made confused endeavours to escort Lucy whilst pursuing Giles earnestly among hordes of other pursuers. The excitement begun with Epiphany's speech seemed to grow to a controlled frenzy as each single male tried to dance or talk to every female whether occupied or not.

For her part Giles was delighted and amused by him though it became clear that she did have a proprietary relationship with Epiphany. St George's expression seemed to crease with growing anxiety and confusion until at last in some kind of deep champagne clarity he looked around and guffawed at his private joke: he was the only male guest who hadn't been taunted with the knowledge that one of these golden apples was labelled specially for him.

'Beware of achieving your desire,' he said ponderously to one young man engrossed with his own dazzling discovery. The bland and helpless returning smile showed his message went undecoded; it occurred to him also that there must be several who had already found their heart's desire but, as in real life, still felt compelled to check the field in case there was another still more desirable. He pronounced in a loud voice that Epiphany must be a very subtle fellow.

St George passed out eventually on one of the sofas, his smile beatified, shoes and tie flung away, his fine nose remaining on alert like a nervous game animal. For her part Lucy left the bedroom door unlocked and, in the morning, he thanked her for this respect, bringing her a pot of tea and later champagne, this time its natural vintage gold.

'Imbibe for both of us,' he ordered firmly, 'I'm flying.'

'Me too,' Lucy said swooningly, basking in his comfort.

The flight back to Oxford was placid and dreamy, heightened by an encounter with a hot-air balloon at 6000 feet over Hertfordshire. St George circled it, intruding on their quiet passage since neither of them could decipher whether the occupants' waving gestures meant them to close or leave. At that height Lucy found herself able to share the wonderful silent suspense they must be feeling, especially when St George cut the power and they whispered in descent themselves. She drove home grateful and sad to solitude and later to the eerie jolting intrusion of the telephone's single trill. It didn't console her now but merely added to her worry and bewilderment. As an antidote she doubled her work-load and after a few days at dusk brought Decibelle to Carsey, throttled back and whispering, low into Horrocks' strip of meadow. After switching off and locking the rotor, she hauled the little machine backwards into the garage and sauntered home down the lane. There was no kind of reaction to show anyone had noticed.

That evening she had two callers, one with an American accent and a very shaly voice, asking after Stuart and leaving a number to call. He gave his name as Riverson and said he worked for U.S. Immigration.

The second caller had a clipped and hectoring tone, roughly demanding to speak to Stuart. He gave no name but was clearly Dutch South African and Lucy was uncertain how to react after her attempts to reason with him met only with abuse. She suggested as calmly as she could that the caller leave his number and Stuart would surely get in touch on his return.

'I wants for you to get 'im beck,' came the harsh, curt reply, 'An' maybe you isn't frighted enough yet, well just wait, you.' He hung up abruptly leaving her tense and furious. After that he began to call twice a day in increasing boorish frustration and then stepped up the frequency to include drunken threats long after midnight. She considered calling the Police in spite of the man's dire warnings but then she had another call, the accent again distinctly Afrikaans but softer and concerned.

'Mevrouw Kody? Soddy I cawn't give you my name, but we were wondering if anyone with a Dutch kind of speaking has been in touch, a man named Cornelius.'

'It seems like you know already,' she answered stiffly.

'You've been getting calls, hey? Did he ever say where he was?'

'No. Why the question, does he do a lot of it?' Lucy's tone remained cold and unfriendly, but she asked, 'Can you stop him?'

'Yiss, with yaw help. What's he after?'

Lucy explained the gist of the calls, that Stuart was to pay a ransom or there were going to be some punctured people about. The voice sounded unsurprised.

'Yiss, I see. Well, I can tell you we're on your side and we wants to catch him, so perhaps if you could tell him where Mr Kody is and let us follow him there, what do you say, hey?'

'My husband's away on business. I can't tell you where.'

'Look Mevrouw, I said we'se on yaw side. We can help you get rrid of this pest, see?'

'No, I don't see. I'm going to call in the Police. It sounds like some underworld gang you're in.'

'Well, I should warn you for yaw husband's sake, if the Police are pulled in and learn the whole story, it might go badly for him, your old man, after that stunt he tried to pull.'

'What on earth are you talking about?'

'He didn't tell you?' the voice exclaimed in some excitement. 'Nothing about diamonds, heh? A great big

209

haul it was, hah hah, but this jackal Cornelius killed a man to get a lump of the action and he's still hot for it. I think you're going to need some protection and we've got the team to do it, see?'

Lucy took a long, deep breath to suppress her swirl of alarm. 'Excuse me, when was this and where, please explain, will you?'

The caller had no need to hide his triumph in dispelling her thoughts of calling the Police. He assumed a chatty, confidential tone but allowed himself to be drawn only slightly, a teasing meanness.

'Couple o' month back. Swaziland border. Bloke called Runyan put him up to it, but it seems he wasn't really muling, only thought he was. Maybe a diversion. Then we catched Runyan and guess who sends bail money, 150,000 rand? Your husband, that's who, yet he was clean on the border and we fair scragged him. And then Runyan jumps his bail, doesn't he, so we figure he collected his parcel after all and got out. But he was seen in the Seychelles by one of our Police doctors on holiday, only last month. Damn slack Customs there only found him clean after we tipped them off. Your husband give you some nice bits of ice, any chance? Well, you wouldn't say, would you, not on the phone, but then you surely would to Mr Trigger-happy Cornelius, heh? The barrel of a gun can make an awful mess of a pretty face, even with the safety on.'

Lucy had nothing to say as her mind faltered in a kind of silent uproar. If Stuart had been in South Africa when supposed to be on a language refresher somewhere in England, then he'd quite simply lied to her and wasn't working for the Government at all. Why then were so many people looking for him, Americans, South Africans, the Foreign Secretary's office, Stayres at the Czech desk – particularly Stayres since Epiphany had clearly intimated that he was on a mission behind the Iron Curtain? And where had all the money come from, especially for the supreme treasure that hung nearly always from her own innocent throat? She fingered it now with a nervous guilt, casting about for some logical angle. The voice broke in again.

'Can I make a suggestion, Mevrouw? The whole thing will be over clean and quick if you do like I suggest, yaw? You listening?'

'Half,' she answered faintly.

'Hey? Right, next time he calls, tell him your old man's due in say, six hours time. Then you can make us a signal, just lean a newspaper against an upstairs window. You can leave the rest to us, see?'

'Us? No, I don't see. I think you have to tell me who you are first.'

'Sorry, Mevrouw . . . Well, look, I can just say we're operating behind the lines, so to speak? You help us now, it'll all be over, we're professionals, quick, sharp and no nonsense. No more voice, no more threats, you can even pretend to your old man that you don't know a thing. Better that way, eh?'

'But where are you, that you'd see the newspaper?'

'We's been watching you for weeks now, and I'd say your old man shouldn't leave you alone, little morsel, me an' my boys have been drooling long enough.'

'Oh, shut up, will you?' Lucy realised she was more upset about the reference to Stuart than about the salacious compliment. She heard a vague apology and the voice resighted her to its prime target.

'Will you do it, then, Mevrouw? Or else tell us when your old man's coming back?'

'I don't know when . . . What are you going to do if you catch the man? If he's a murderer there's a legal process. I think you're asking me to abet something criminal.'

'Don't think it. He'll get justice, don't you worry. We don't want him to get the drop on you, see? Now, what do you say?'

211

'I was going to ask you why you haven't come to the door and spoken properly but I suppose – '

'Suppose nothing,' snapped the voice. She detected impatience with her gender rather than her resistance since the latter was thus far controlled and not hysterical. She interrupted another apology.

'Next time he calls, I'll tell him Stuart will be home at 6 pm. Then I'll put the paper in the window and then I'll split.'

'Thank you. But there's no need to go, he won't hurt you, you should stay there, to lead him in.'

Her decision made, the voice by now irritated her enough that she hung up. A good part of her annoyance was due to puzzlement at Stuart's duplicity. She began to feel acutely depressed and realised that each recent day had been a disappointment in spite of her enthusiasms, like biting into an unripe peach. Now that bafflement and fear were added, she clenched her fists and swore tightly, wishing she were somewhere else and that Stuart would come and explain himself.

It was only her first shock in a new series and she wondered if the watchers had observed her slipping into Horrock's garage. At least he hadn't mentioned it but any good surveillance would surely have marked Decibelle's arrival. The thought of sabotage didn't occur to her.

She was about to go out the next morning when the telephone rang again; she was quite prepared for Cornelius but instead she heard a nervous, bass cough after her cold hello. Its timbre had a distant but sure familiarity.

'Ludmilla? Your father . . . I'm sorry for the intrusion, I'm calling from Belgium.' Hearing no answer he coughed again diffidently and asked, 'Where is your mother, please, her telephone doesn't reply.'

'You don't normally call her, either,' she answered aloofly, 'Why the sudden concern?'

'Well, it's been sometime since I even got a card or anything. She usually keeps in touch, to say how you are.'

'She's joined the Peace Women.' Lucy had a sudden jolt of insight in that moment, perhaps through her detachment as well as her knowledge. Her tone became accusing.

'You're not looking for her at all, you never do! It's Stuart, isn't it? You want to know where he is, just like everybody else. Why? What's it to the KGB? Let me guess, you want to set him up for a blackmail, yes, like you couldn't recruit me so – God, would Mama have told you where he is? Can you you still do that to her? Well, that's tough, because she doesn't know. And neither do I, so forget it!'

There was silence on the line as Lucy took a deep breath and regained her composure. She realised she must have sounded like a slum fishwife; mustering a smile from the thought, she put a little mock sweetness into her voice.

'And how are you, father dear? Still on the trail of seduction and philogyny, in between bouts of espionage? I haven't spoken to you for about eight years, did you know?'

Simonov's deep voice answered softly, 'Yes, I do know. I'm sorry it had to be that way, but I've followed your life with concern and some delight, you may be sure. I've even got some footage of you giving your gym classes.'

'What? How did you get that?'

He chuckled, still nervous of her disapproval. 'Spy satellite . . . No, I'm joking. One of our diplomats got it for me, I treasure it, you give me a great, if distant pride. You were always a natural clowner, I do remember the early days, don't you?'

'Yes,' she answered quietly, her childhood memories still keen and warm with the fun she had from his

213

mischievous nature. She realised the warmth had quelled her outrage.

'Thank you,' he said fervently. 'I know you as naturally truthful so I won't pretend. You were very astute and quite correct. We would like to know where your Stuart is, yes. I have a particular interest in his safe return, if I can help in any particular.'

'He's just *away*, that's all. Everybody's looking for him, if he's hiding I wouldn't blame him. But if I knew where, I couldn't tell you, of all people, could I? Do you know who he works for?'

'Yes, as a matter of fact.'

'Oh . . . well then, don't be silly. Not even they seem to know where he is.'

'Um, does that mean you don't actually know it yourself?'

'Oh, I know, yes. He's in Europe.'

'Thank you.' Simonov did his best to avoid a sarcastic tone, unsuccessfully. 'Could you be more specific, please?'

'No. Last month he was in Washington, the one before in the Seychelles, with me.'

'And before that?'

'I'll be discussing that with him when I see him. Do you guys happen to know?'

'Certainly we do.'

Lucy gulped, floundering. 'So tell me.'

Simonov gave a taut chuckle. 'I will if you will.'

Lucy saw the trap of betrayal and stopped short. She also realised she was enjoying her father's voice and the remote, if romantic, notion of seeing him again. She cancelled the opening abruptly.

'We're all going to have to sit this one out,' she said, 'Sorry I can't help. I'll tell Mama you called, don't know when I'll see her. Bye.'

She didn't give him time to answer or wheedle but as she hung up she had a chill realisation that her smart reply might conceivably locate Stuart for them. Europe in many minds still meant the Continent excluding Britain and his fluency in Czech could point him to his country of origin. At least Alicia had no idea of his whereabouts should they decide to ask her directly. She thought of going down to Newbury once more but found herself hesitant about meeting Nadia again with nothing firm to tell her. She wished she'd asked her father if he knew about Cornelius and the South Africans surrounding her; if not, it would at least have added to his confusion.

Quite suddenly she decided she'd had enough, that her position was precarious and unhappy which was spoiling her classes and that Stuart would not have wished it on her or even known about it. With some initial misgiving, she decided to respond to the invitation made by Epiphany at Hever Castle, making two calls, one to Giles and one to St George; then she packed a small grip, turned everything off and prepared to close down the house once again, resentful that it had ceased to be a scene of tranquillity. Ready to leave, she busied herself with needless items until Cornelius phoned in the afternoon, very aggressive and impatient until she interrupted him.

'You'll be able to ask him yourself,' she said loudly, 'He'll be in for dinner.'

Her last act was to lean a newspaper against an upstairs window. Its effect was almost immediate, for she was locking the door when the telephone rang yet again. The hit squad, as she thought of them now, dispassionately.

'What was said, Mevrouw?'

'I told him Stuart would be in for dinner. I only hope he isn't.'

'It's good, if you're seen to be expecting him.'

'Not me. I'm off where no one'll find me.'

'No, you stay there!'

'Get lost!'

'Listen, we'll prevent you leaving if you try it.'

'You certainly won't. I can't even be sure who's on the side of right, let alone safety. You have to be breaking the law, that's why no Police. You can just get on with it, I'm splitting.'

'We'll have to stop you, Mevrouw. Don't be doing it, please now. Just wait until we've trapped and fixed Cornelius.'

Lucy curled with sarcasm. 'You want me to sit in the battleground, don't you? What will you do with the body?'

'Don't worry, we'll – ' He stopped suddenly but it was enough for Lucy. She left the handset hanging, crackling its vain protest while she clutched her small bag, slipped out of the back door, hurdled the hedge and ran low along the field ditch for Horrock's house. Even so she was spotted at once. To her right on the far side of the road she could see a figure charging to cut her off.

She reached the house before he could intercept but she only had access to the garage and her escape bid would be fruitless if she was found there. She returned resignedly to walk back along the road, trying to regain her breath while a big man with a florid face panted up to her and made to grab her arm. The action itself switched on Lucy's fluid programme of response. In a quick trained instinct she flung her bag at the man's face then spun a full circle on the gravel, taking off at the end of it, sighting as she came horizontal. The sole of her right foot smacked him sharply on the side of his jaw just as he chopped the bag aside. His whole body juddered as it hit the ground already unconscious, an arm trapped beneath at an impossible angle.

Lucy stood like an owl, first her eyes only and then her head turning very slowly. She saw no other movement anywhere; reassured, she picked up her grip. A pocket

216

phone muttered inside the man's clothing as she walked quickly to the garage. Nervously watchful all the time, she pulled Decibelle out onto the grass, removed the blade latches and applied the brakes very firmly. She took one last careful look round and through the garage windows before committing herself, then snapped on the mags and pulled the engine over. It fired on the second pull, a loud betraying clatter and the little machine hopped and trembled in agitation. She engaged the drive to spin up the main rotor, seating herself and strapping in as it began to whup-whup over her head. With her crash helmet fitted and her bag behind one knee, she waited in fraying tension for the build-up to complete. At 180 rpm, her left hand released the brakes and pushed forward the throttle, disconnecting the rotor drive. In still air, Decibelle sprang ahead like an eager pony, airborne in less than 20 metres but she kept deliberately low, just inches above the blur of rippling grass to build up speed and distance from the scene of threatened nastiness. The man on the ground she had dismissed completely, feeling her action both justified and essential. She snatched a quick glance behind her and through the greying propeller-disc cringed to see a running figure slow down in defeat. There was something black and ominous in its lowering stiffened arms but she couldn't know if he had fired. The engine would have drowned any report but it would have been a lunatic and hasty action on his part. She tightened her fury and put more than a mile behind her before she began to climb, turning away to the Southeast. To her right the village was spread out, distant but very familiar to her from the air and she could see at least three figures grouped by Horrocks' house. She felt no more curiosity about them, only a calm disdain from her exalted, supercilious viewpoint. She knew that Stuart would approve of her leaving, would rejoice at it, certainly he would have been up in arms himself to know she was intended as a tethered goat.

For now Lucy determined to be found only if she herself chose it, and when it happened it would be to a full and open mutual confession. She smiled at the thought of attempting to play the grim prosecutor whose feelings are impossibly bound up with the accused.

TEN

What will not woman, gentle woman, dare
When strong emotion stirs her spirits up.
                                        Robert Southey

Haute Savoie and, Epiphany had declared, some of the
finest ski-ing in the world. St George flew them incognito
from Elstree to Geneva and they saw the Alps on their
approach in the late afternoon, a line of stately bergs in a
cotton-wool sea. The descent took them reluctantly into
the grey of deep solid cloud and Lucy sat transfixed in the
co-pilot's seat as St George quietly talked her through
the entire instrument approach sequence. He seemed
still to glow shyly in their company, which made them
actually cautious in their praise in case he should feel he
was being mocked. He'd protested a mild 'I say!' when
Giles said he reminded her of Biggles, surprised too that
she'd ever heard of the fictional war-time ace. St George
declared that he hated snow but still the farewell was
both sad and excited. They kept their destination secret;
he took off for Paris immediately while they needed
another four hours in a coach to rise above the cloud
again, into bright magic starlight and frosty stillness.

Epiphany had lent them his penthouse apartment in
Tignes and arranged for a playback answering machine
at Giles' London address to serve as their relay point for
other callers. Beyond his dark hint at Hever, he had no
further information for Lucy but according to Giles he'd
simply commended them both to a positive approach

and to learn something every day. Each evening Lucy telephoned home in the hopes of catching her mother on a visit but more than a week went by before it rang out correctly, showing the receiver had been replaced. She wondered if Stuart had been puzzled by the constant engaged signal and perhaps reported a fault but at last Alicia answered, querulous about damp and cold water and people calling, threatening her, demanding to know where and when Stuart could be found.

Lucy trembled with a new anxiety. 'Mama, I think you should leave Carsey at once. I really thought the South Africans would have finished their business by now.'

'No-o!' Alicia said dramatically. 'One of them accused me of a trap, in bad English, he said, "hah hah, you tries to catch me!" I said nothing and he said, "See you later, my frau."'

'Mama, please go quickly, he's a real bad biscuit.'

'Ach . . . And your neighbour came, Horrocks . . .'

'Mama!'

Alicia didn't pause. 'He wondered too where you'd gone, he said there was a lot of talk in the village about strangers and there was a bullet-case on his grass would have gone in the mower machine. Hah, I ask him why he wanted to cut grass in December and he acted very suspicious . . . Liouba, do you yourself know where is Stuart?'

'Only vaguely. He's on a mission, somewhere foreign. Did the phone ring at about six, a single tingle?'

'Yes, like before. You left the receiver hanging, why?'

'I was in a hurry. You too, Mama, please get out of there!'

'All right . . . Nadia's sick again but it's, you know, psychic. She's asking for you. Will you speak to her?'

'Yes, all *right*, later. Go at once, d'you hear?' Lucy's imagination took in a local gun-battle, distant automatic fire and mortars down the line but Alicia still hadn't finished.

220

'Liouba, your father rang too and I spoke to him . . .'
She waited vainly for some reaction before going on.
'You see, Nadia overheard a conversation, Stuart talking
to someone called Alexei, does he know any others?
Your father admitted nothing, only that he'd be delighted
to meet or talk to Stuart, as soon as possible. But Nadia
said it sounded like they knew each other and wanted
something from each other . . . Yes, and Stuart had been
given something by the U.S. President, the new one.'

'What new one?'

'I mean the next one.'

'Mama, don't be so daft! And please leave at once, it's
not safe, d'you hear?'

'Yes, yes, all right. But where are you?'

'I'm not going to say, Mama, just in case. You can get
me through this relay.' She gave the London number and
added, 'It's the house of Doctor Raintree, a machine will
answer.'

'Oh? And where is this doctor?'

'With me. I'll speak to you when you're in London.'

Lucy hung up abruptly, knowing where more questions would lead even if she didn't answer. She visualised
the hassle of explaining an answerphone system whilst
trembling with anxiety.

Alicia however couldn't resist another call to Antwerp.
She found herself over-excited and unsure what was safe
to tell.

'Sasha, do you know what is happening? Our Ludmilla
was being threatened, South Africans again— '

'I know. I sent some protection but it was just too late.
She made an unconventional escape.'

'What do you mean?'

Simonov had no intention of supplying Alicia with anything but he was surprised she didn't know about Lucy's
new toy. She missed the hint in any case, moving to cut
him off from his smokescreen.

'Pah, you were looking for him yourself.'

'True, but for reasons different from them. I found out what they want, would you like to hear? A criminal wants something from Stuart and an unofficial South African police party is trying to trap the criminal. If Stuart turns up, keep your head down because my people will eliminate the whole lot of them, he's more important to us, you may not realise. Give me just a hint of his whereabouts and then we can be sure that my masters will let me remove this other threat. He has some vital information, for the world!'

'About the missiles,' Alicia asked with sly conspiracy.

'Ah, he told you. About Cruise and Pershing, yes. But there's more to it, do you know?'

'Sasha, I'm British now, I could be shot for telling you.'

He sighed. 'In that case, you don't know, otherwise you would bait me with it. And they don't shoot people, they're too soft. Now I must locate him, doesn't *anyone* know?'

'Foreign, but a long weekend only. That's weeks ago, I'm so worried, you can imagine what it's like for our *dochka*.'

'Yes, yes. No sentiment, please. Just try to get me a clue, perhaps from her.'

'She would never— ' Alicia started to say, suddenly realising that she had told all she knew. It made her furious and she moved back to the accusative.

'You are too late to give protection to her anyway, Sasha.'

'*What*? Tell me, is she hurt?'

'No. She has left the country. They won't find her.'

'Nonsense . . . can you?'

'Not even I. There's a phone in London, a machine only. But they can call me.'

'They?'

'Yes. She's gone away with a doctor friend.'

Simonov sensibly refused the new bait. 'What's the number of the machine?'

'I won't tell you, Sasha. You've anything to say, you call me first. I'll go back to London.'

'How did they leave England?'

'By air, a special flight.'

'Where from?'

'Too many questions, Sasha.' She didn't actually know but she could sense him biting down his rage for several moments while he no longer gave her the triumphs of hearing him explode in fury. She still knew exactly where to place the needle of non-cooperation, followed if necessary by a retreat into illogic. The explosions used to make her feel righteous but now his control made her uneasy with the guilt of unnecessary sourness. He compounded it with a concerned farewell.

'Call me if you hear anything, Alicia. Meanwhile you'd better stay away from their house yourself, just in case things get nasty.'

'All right, Sasha . . . He's been doing his single call every day, so he must be safe somewhere. Mysteries, always mysteries . . . Sasha, you can have the number, there's no harm . . .'

Maryša Kubin had watched in terror as Miloš Procházka approached the exit barrier, trying with little success to disguise the limp where Stuart's kick had damaged his knee. He'd insisted she stay back in case there was trouble, a precaution tragically justified. Her heart shrivelling inside her breast, she saw the Official's interest steel and brighten. Miloš tried to turn away but heavy hands took him, heaved him through the gate, his feet scrabbling in useless resistance. He began to strain his head towards her but must have realised the give-away and their eyes never met again. As she quietly left the line her head was in screaming turmoil, wanting to tell him pointlessly that he should never haved played it straight, taking the car back after bumping it even so slightly. He'd had difficulty driving with his damaged knee; Miloš had wanted to stay calm and correct and they must have seen the small damage only afterwards. The truth neither of them could have known lay with the missing radio.

Believing the worst, she faded away from the airport and went at once to ground, to a catatonic half-life whose only purpose was the protection of her unborn baby. The BA 111 left without either of them and she felt herself quietly dying of sadness, long before she felt the first stirrings in her womb. Although she had none of the guilt for what her lover had done to Stuart Kody, she had naturally rejoiced in secret that he was fleeing with her and that Stayres had made it possible. Now the action seemed to have found its price for, as she later admitted to herself, she knew from the sound that his second blow on the skull must have wrought some lethal damage.

It was many days before she could bring herself to call the British Embassy, pretending to be the mother of Stuart and enquiring after him. After a series of diversionary talks, they arranged a scrambled link with Stayres in London and she haltingly explained her position. Stayres made no attempt to hide his exasperation.

'Procházka has been swallowed up. No news and I can't show interest without starting an avalanche. What happened to the courier?'

'He was only tied up, to give us time. That's all I know.'

Maryša couldn't take any more and she terminated the call, leaving Stayres with a single piece of information: Kody was still in Czechoslovakia, now illegal with his visa long-expired. It wasn't enough to work on so he kept it to himself. Kody was beyond official help or sanction and had to be written off for they could never acknowledge any involvement.

Meanwhile Breakspeare at the Foreign Office kept roaring at him, apparently under pressure from the PM and the CIA. He did admit that Mrs Kody continued to receive her reassuring call every day and that she must have retained her sanity since there were no more enquiries from that direction.

Just as Stuart's original Cruise information had eventually filtered to Washington via moles in the Kremlin, the news that he was somewhere in the Eastern bloc eventually leaked from Stayres' department back to Moscow. This took some time but the very fact of Stayres' silence was enough to narrow the search. Thus the whole of Czechoslovakia's huge cadre of KGB watchdogs was mobilised into a nationwide hunt, an enormous pressure of manpower. They looked in all the wrong places for the first part of January, largely because they'd been given a fixed notion of a high-echelon jet-pilot spy as their target who would surely be chasing aeronautical secrets or even, unthinkably, hardware. All the latest Migs were withdrawn to the Soviet Union, every airbase was double-guarded and the paranoia fed on itself with consummate greed. Only much later did they begin to check the hospitals and to raid every known dissident faction and underground meeting point. Normally very low-profile because of the long-held feelings of the Czechs that the Russians had betrayed them and their former friendship by the 1968 invasion, the presence of so many Soviet enquiry agents generated an atmosphere of unusual tension throughout Bohemia and Moravia; in particular, the Prague STB became jumpy since they had something to hide. They'd been working on the proven principle that if a man disappears and no one complains, he must be either illegal and therefore automatically disowned by his employers or else he has no kin in which case he is no further problem. Not only was it best forgotten but also no one wanted to be seen currying favour with the KGB who only recognised their failure when someone asked about deaths in detention.

*   *   *

It hadn't taken Simonov more than a few moments to deduce that Lucy and her friend would have used St George's air taxi for their 'special flight' but he left it at that, deciding that he didn't need to know more. Only much later when Czechoslovakia became the hunting-ground did it occur to him that St George might know something himself although he would surely have shared it with Lucy. From records of filed flight plans, his agents soon discovered that the Seneca had taken two people to Geneva and left at once for Paris over two months before, with Lucy's whereabouts still not known.

Simonov considered the guises he might try on St George to find Lucy and, by extension, Stuart, whether as an Antwerp diamantaire or an English Civil Aviation inspector. As he could see neither leading him convincingly to the required answer, he settled for the truth backed with a cudgel, his Russo-Flemish accent being too much of a giveaway.

'Monsieur Far-kew-har?' he enquired, not realising the negative effect this might produce in as dedicated a miso-Franc as St George.

'Airce?' came the questioning reply, deeply suspicious.

'I'm looking for my daughter, Mrs Kody. Do you know where I could find her, or her husband?'

'Which?'

'Well, both, if you please.'

'I do not please,' St George said icily. 'She's in retreat, waiting his return from a business trip.'

'Ah, one of his flying visits, perhaps? Tell me, please, were you ever partners with Mr Kody in one of your ventures?'

'Possibly,' St George answered, puzzled and then deeply alarmed.

'The running of arms, I believe, was your boast. Now with Mr Kody in Czechoslovakia, perhaps I can remain silent on this issue if you would just let me know his

226

exact whereabouts and his mission, presumably to do with aviation – '

St George hung up at once, having been tricked into revelation once before and knowing that a modern inquisition tends to be irresistible. He changed his base immediately and covered his tracks by switching aircraft with a leasing company, logging under the name Bigglesworth, as suggested by Giles. Even so he decided the less he knew the better, abandoning the intention he'd had for a while to make enquiries through his diplomat friend who'd been arranging the Spitfire spares for the museum. Stuart must be lying very low and very effectively, or had succeeded in killing himself; St George decided against the latter since it should have been discovered and the hunt cancelled.

In addition the thought of a husbandless Lucy gave him a confusion of emotions, the base content of which he only managed to smother with an inner appeal to centuries of nobility.

Excitement partially distracting her from worry, Lucy had dutifully signed on with the ski-school in Tignes and spent her first three days in complete misery doing awkward snow-plough turns and exhausting flat traverses while being shouted at by a disgruntled instructor, his perfect Gallic smile having failed to win her on the first morning and quickly faded to a sullen disgust. Giles, having ski-ed once before, was in another class and unable to help; matters came to a head when they clashed with a group of four children being coached by a tall, fair, quiet-spoken Canadian. Lucy had already heard him saying to them, 'Now, kids, you only have to enjoy yourselves. Let me worry about your ski-ing, relax like sacks of potatoes . . . let's do aeroplanes, ready? Follow me, dagga-dagga-dagga!'

Enviously, Lucy watched the group coming down towards them, missing her own pupils and also wishing she could do as well; they were all grinning and making machine-gun noises, their arms horizontal but banking in the turns, their skis miraculously leading through. They stopped above her group just as the instructor shouted at her to pay attention. Lucy ignored him and called out, 'Do you speak French?'

The Canadian looked at her sharply, smiled and answered '*Oui, un peu*' in what seemed like a deliberately execrable accent.

'Well, would you tell this person here, from me, that he's a travesty of a human being and shouldn't be allowed near beginners or even people.'

The Canadian grinned with delight. 'Certainly. *Jacques, la jolie mam'selle dit que vous êtes espèce de con.*' He looked smugly at the victim who promptly threw a most satisfactory tantrum, not hostile, for the Canadian was tall and powerfully built, but flinging off his cap and goggles and gargling out a torrent of unintelligible abuse, stamping his skis.

During the tirade, the Canadian said, 'My name's Gordon. Would you like to tag along with us?'

One of the children, a monkey-faced boy of about ten, said, 'We're on an expedition, we going down the Lost Piste, to find a snoffalump.'

So they finished the Tovière and disappeared behind the hill on an unmarked run, the Piste Perdue, which became narrower and steeper and eventually a less than two metre-wide bumpy chasm winding in violent turns between cliffs. It was much too hard for a beginner but the children crashed and yelled their way down, falling frequently, and Lucy followed in a kind of rigid terror until the hard part was over and they shussed down to the Val d'Isère bus. After that impossible beginning, Gordon took them to some fine, sweeping, easy runs, teaching the children by teaching Lucy. They watched her wide-eyed and she in turn listened gravely, happy there for the first time and now having to try not to clown.

228

By the end of the morning she was doing parallel turns and already learning to carve. Within three more days she was up to Giles' standard so the two of them booked Gordon as often as he was free and gradually became more fanatical. Partly to bury her anxiety, she willed herself to be at ease and to thrill and tingle with the presence of mountains, the vast, high and eerie quiet in the sparkle of rarified air. Remembering their flight to Geneva, she could picture herself on a sunlit peak above the roiling grey morass of cloud which had stretched so depressingly over the whole winter country.

At first the days passed in a marvellous therapy of absorption and exhaustion which would still have been intolerable had she been alone. Her friendship with Giles Raintree was her most precious reality, shielding her from growing alarm as the days formed weeks and there was no word of Stuart nor anything encouraging from England. Alicia had eventually admitted her conversation with Simonov, telling Lucy that there were now more than two factions staking out the house. Lucy realised that with the right catalyst there might be a very nasty scene, the catalyst being either Cornelius or Stuart or both. Whichever it was, she would be no help there and the only constructive thing she could come up with was to call Stayres in Century House.

He asked her with some energy where she was and if she knew how to find Stuart, to which she answered blandly, 'Hiding and Yes.' She asked him straight off to make sure that instructions would be left for Stuart on no account to go home after he came in for debriefing. She refused to elaborate or answer the obvious questions until an inspiration crept in unbidden, after Stayres had given up and tried to sign off with a typical amphigory.

'Let me know if there's anything else I can do.'

'As a matter of fact, there is,' Lucy answered cautiously, 'Strictly between you and me . . . Can you get hold of satellite pictures for a specific area, in Europe?'

The reply was understandably cautious although to Stayres it was an extremely naïve question. But for microfilm and electronic data banks, places like Century House would by now have subsided into the Thames under the sheer weight of unrefined material.

'Such a thing might be retrievable, depending rather on what's being offered.'

'Oh. Naturally I'd have got Stuart to ask for me, if he hadn't been away.' There was no reply to this inconsequence and she realised he was still waiting. On careless impulse, she said, 'I'll be able to tell you where he is.'

'Exactly?'

'Yes, of course.' Lucy had no qualms about whether Czechoslovakia was exact enough for him.

'He's all right, then? You see, I don't mind telling you we've been worried, he went off to do a little job for us, didn't report in but it didn't matter. Now the cousins seem to want him very badly and they think I'm not cooperating. I'd begun to fear the worst, frankly.'

Lucy felt her arm shaking the receiver but managed to betray nothing in her voice. She couldn't help Stuart and was now helpless before a new priority.

'He's fine, he just got delayed. He calls home every day. I'm not there at the moment but as soon as I can speak to him I'll get him to call you.'

'Do that, please. All right, what area are you chasing?'

Her memory was prompt. '50° 25' North, 11° 30' East, say.'

There was a cough at the other end, surprise at her ready response. 'Where is that, precisely?'

'Border of the Germanys. Southwest of Leipzig. Er, a ten mile radius would be enough, five or even less if it's all rural.'

'That's East and West Germany, are you sure? Not Czechoslovakia?'

'Yes, sure.'

There was a lengthy pause and then she heard him say, 'Ah, yes, got it . . . Mrs Kody, not there, don't even think it another moment! You're abetting suicide, you couldn't get a weasel through the wire there, there's mines and I/F sensors, machine guns that train with them on any warm target, laser sights that can't miss, Dobermanns – one tinkle of alarm and he's got a division of heavy tanks and half the Air Force on his neck.'

Lucy gulped silently at the force of his words but willed herself to stay blithe. 'OK, that's man talk. Let's say this is for an article, a story, how about that? Can you help me?'

'Do I get a signed original? The photos you want against Stuart's whereabouts – it stinks, Mrs Kody, they want the goods intact and if you're up to something crazy and I mean it's 100 per cent insane – '

'Who's "they"?'

'Across the water. Seems it's something they really need to know – is he all right?'

'Yes, I told you.'

'And you know where?'

'*Si.*'

'So when's the coming-out party?'

Lucy quailed inside as Stayres kept confirming her fears that Stuart was somewhere on the other side beyond control or official assistance. Setting the fears aside was almost beyond her as she strove to continue her charade. At least, she thought, the problem of Nadia's infant son would absorb her energies to some thorough extent. She heard Stayres cough again and mutter something before speaking properly down the line.

'Not my bailiwick, so I suppose I can take a chance . . . Very well, Sat-shots, yes. Will you come and collect?'

'No, I can't. Can you have – how about the British Embassy in Geneva?'

'Fair enough. Anything else?' The last question seethed with irony.

231

'Well, yes . . . Is there someone who can interpret them accurately, if necessary? You know, for the wire, booby traps, searchlights, radars, what-d'you-call-'ems, goons?'

'I expect so. For the article, authenticity?' Stayres made only the merest attempt to cover outright sarcasm but then corrected himself for the needless disrespect, since she might be playing right into his hands. 'I'm sorry, that's unfair of me. I realise you have far more personal concern for his safety than a faceless department. If it were real, of course, you might ask for some unofficial/official sanction, assistance, diversionary measures and so on – for the story, good guys hearts in the right place and so on, um?'

Um, Lucy thought with detachment, they'd hardly risk a diplomatic incident for a pint-sized, unwitting and helpless Russian defector with no secrets to sell.

'Give me a couple of days, then ask for Peter Hegel at the Embassy.'

'Thank you. Oh, can I be incognito, please, just in case?'

'Ah, yes, the pen-name. Why not call yourself Karen?'

'Roger.'

'Um?' queried Stayres before he understood and rang off with a chuckled 'Wilco'. To Lucy it seemed unfair that he could be light-hearted. She herself had to deal with frequent wakings in the night, the hollow stomach, the clawing through the lowest point of morale to find the certainty of Stuart's life even in his protracted, unexplained and impossibly cruel absence, by the phone calls which continued daily to their house in Carsey. Every few days she plagued the reticent telephone engineer, Fogarty, for confirmation. At least she was clear about her own course, to be absent as promised from a scene of conflict and to wait stoically for his return. She reasoned that how she distracted herself in the meantime was her own affair entirely.

ELEVEN

'Fifty thousand warheads are but the rage of ages
gathering its logic.'

Grivas Bodili

The majority of battlefront casualties are caused by
bullets and shrapnel striking the rib-cage on entry,
splintering and dispersing untraceable bone and also
transmitting the huge impact/shock through the whole
cardio-thoracic area – the kind of injuries the flak
jacket was designed to prevent until its own inventors
discovered the Teflon-coated bullet.

Half a centimetre either way and the armour-piercing
7.62 would have hit Stuart's rib-cage on the way in. He
was not so fortunate with its exit and the group of small
splinters left a jagged hole in his right chest. He would
hardly have survived in the chaos of battlefront, yet his
actual situation was little better.

Technically he died at 10.30 pm on the night he
was shot. An ambulance had come for him after a
lengthy delay and because of his apparent condition he
was summarily tossed onto a rubber-sheeted stretcher,
half face-down and untended instead of on his back and
well-covered. As a result he was not asphyxiated by his
own blood from the punctured right lung which stopped
haemorrhaging on the way to the hospital. Owing to the
clean entry the actual lung damage was slight and closed
rapidly but the bullet's velocity-shock following on his
skull trauma made a perilous combination, unknown to

the receiving staff.

Dr Pintová in Roudnice's emergency unit had enjoyed a quiet evening, the weather keeping people indoors. Instead of road accidents they'd had three cases of domestic burns which had gone to another unit and one minor stabbing with a kitchen knife.

When Stuart was trollied in, one of the officers with him reported a single gunshot wound and Pintová might have been forgiven for assuming he'd been hit fatally in the heart. Routinely, he applied a stethoscope, listened with a dubious expression and was about to fold it away when he sensed more than heard a slight flutter. He glanced at the nurses who were none too happily removing fouled clothing and one of them looked at him questioningly. He listened again intently and after a few seconds there was one more beat, then silence. He hesitated another moment, looked up again and then stabbed the buzzer for the 'crash' team; within thirty seconds the trolley was with him, the team bustling but with precision, the clothes removed and the monitors in place. Pintová could see bone splinters by the grim exit wound and told them not to bounce the chest since it might do more damage. He took the two paddle electrodes, placed them on opposite sides of the chest and called for the hit. The body convulsed and then the cardiogram began to produce a faint and irregular trace. They put a drain into the right lung and respirated him, put in drips, filled him with anti-biotics and cleaned him up. Only then did someone notice the massive contusion over his right ear and considered the added symptoms of concussion.

After X-rays, Pintová removed the splinters and sewed up the wound, then they bound the chest, taking extra precautions against accidental knocking to the cracked skull. Once it was evident that he must have been the victim of robbery with violence and had all his papers stolen, the security Police withdrew their guard, leaving orders for the staff to contact them when, or

234

if, he recovered consciousness. He was still high on the danger list and Pintová admitted when asked that amnesia would possibly follow such a concussive blow and yes, there could certainly be damage because of the technical death. If this had happened in the ambulance then damage was certain but if on the table, hopefully not. There was no chance of the patient absconding on his own, not for several weeks and the ICU was anyway monitored round the clock.

To himself Pintová also admitted both guilt and elation; he might have saved a life, but given a fraction more work-load, a headache, a good book or even the urge for a cup of coffee, he'd have let him go. That was when he looked round and wished to change his thinking, to imagine himself always surrounded by beautiful, adoring assistants, even if it were not so; his old professor had once remarked that there's nothing like a pretty nurse to make a doctor conscientious. Cynically, and *sotto voce,* he added, be kind and respectful to the other ones as well, you may need them to cover up your blunders.

A week later there was an explosion in a paint factory and the unit was overloaded with serious cases. Along with several others Stuart was transferred by ambulance to the Pod Petřínem hospital in Prague but in the jostle of the journey he relapsed and suffered another technical death at the time of arrival. Once more he was put into intensive care and remained there for ten days, drifting away and back and upsetting staff who liked names, numbers and good order.

Sounds began to make slow sense as they filtered through his semi-coma but he felt awkward with them; he couldn't shake off the feeling that he knew an easier and less guttural way to speak. Each day one of several people would talk to him; he understood their questions but could not bring himself to answer. He didn't know

235

why and the frustration sometimes caused the tears to flow, eliciting a brusque sympathy.

He was moved to a ward of rather stark white misery where the four lines contained uncurtained beds like separate stalls of purgatory. When able to begin a shaky walk, at least he was allowed up to relieve himself and the independence of this small function really began the change, plus the cunning required to alleviate a dozen small discomforts. Before he ever answered a single question he had made a conscious decision about survival, after a vivid dream with English dialogue, that he must here speak only Czech.

The dream was all golden light but it was not a projection; he knew for certain that it was part of his experience He had been there and there had been someone with him, whose name was Light, wearing a sheath of honey skin and waving a bright crest of hair the colour of teak and sycamore. The figure moved lightly too, skipped and danced, played, leaped and swam, the water darkening her pastel timber colours . . . Water and tree, the images had swirled and the shock of memory had come with such sweet anguish that he had cried out, 'Wake up, come up here, quickly!'

She had opened a reluctant eye to the hatch and then seen his expression, not resisting his urgency, uncurling from her warm, languid sprawl in the fo'c'sle. His hand found her in the companionway and she had gasped and clutched at him as they stood in the cockpit and gazed around.

The elegant sloop sat in the arms of a deserted bay, the rocks to the West higher than their heads and blocking that part of the horizon. There was no trace of wind and the hull lay on an indigo mirror which they could see through to white sand thirty feet down and seeming only inches below their keel. Tugging her arm again, he led her forward and with some creaking and swaying laughter, they climbed the harsh rope ratlines and finally sat side by side on the crosstrees, their bare legs dangling.

In the space of a few minutes, the whole world went through every shade of gold, the moon sank painlessly over the western horizon now visible from their height and moments later the eastern horizon bulged up a viscous sun, an episcopal skull-cap rising from a reverent genuflection.

Her name meant Light; she'd gripped his arm fiercely but said in hushed invocation, 'Thank you. I think we'd better go home, I can't take any more beauty. I'm saturated . . .'

In the weeks following he returned frequently to the dream for grateful solace, a golden private world where sheets were soft and voices gentle, and food prepared with love was a natural cause of celebration. As the hurt receded, his nature began to reassert itself and he resented the restrictions, the joylessness of the ward and in particular the debility of his body.

He started to plan for the day of departure, vaguely because so little made sense and he had nowhere to go; his watch had gone and there was no idea in his head about dates and the passage of time, only a strong sense of having the answer hidden somewhere but in self-defence his system wasn't ready to divulge it.

Frequently he'd been subjected to bouts of frustrated questioning both by hospital staff and security Police; his only ally was a senior nurse who would produce an X-ray of his skull fracture and talk intensely about other cases of amnesia in her experience. To judge by her tone, few of them recovered but Stuart gained some perverse confidence from her that it was a matter of patience, time and will. She brought him a book entitled *Meditace* meaning meditation but he found its turgid style revolting, a government-sponsored and artless work. He tried to feign an interest but she wasn't deceived and to his delight one day expressed her approval of his

237

judgement. After that when she had any time to spare she would come and hold his hand and give him the gist of various exercises in her own words. Her name was Zdena, a spinster in her late forties with a hardened manner concealing a distant wistfulness.

She found him some wax earplugs and taught him to listen to the sounds emanating naturally from his head. It made him aware of a recurrent tinnitus in his right ear and she taught him to cancel the complaint. She said with some smugness that the most expensive Western research had failed to find a cure for tinnitus but that like other self-generated discomforts the cure lay in the attitude.

To his sceptical response she insisted, 'Suppose an ordinary headache, just a nervous condition, I don't mean from a cold or too much vodka. Most people react by straining against it, wishing they didn't have it. After all the straining and wishing they still have it, but worse because of their frustration. What helps is to accept it, look at it, accommodate it. Puf! Suddenly the headache or discomfort has no power to discomfort any more, even if it stays. Robbed of its power it usually disappears anyway. The same with the singing in your ear – listen to it, see what it has to say. You may find the concentration leads to that space between wake and sleep, the place between armies, what's it called, *mrtvé pásmo?*'

'No man's— ' Stuart couldn't tell if failed memory or caution had prevented the third word in English. She glossed over his mumble, not understanding. In silent solitude he tried her exercises and found himself frequently on a strange, delicious borderland but always trying to stop himself longing for that elusive golden paradise.

The tinnitus actually changed ears sometimes as if proving a non-physiological origin and the deep humming from behind the earplugs seemed to lull him into a wonderful peace of dreams. He was also patient but quite certain they were leading somewhere. The themes were largely of warm firelight, of graceful flight, of sun on blue with backgrounds of white sand, green jungle. They held a charged sensual overtone which remained locked away and elusive for many weeks; he realised at last that his reaching out and straining for this element was impeding its appearance yet it was almost too great an effort to suppress the longing and to accept only the present and the actual.

He must have succeeded unknowingly at some point because it all came back with another semi-waking dream, a frantic and violently erotic fantasy wherein he was shielding her body with his own against a series of marauders who then miraculously disappeared and left him holding his prize, a quicksilver sweetness, the lissom, light dancer from the other dream. He awoke flooded and at peace, her name inside his mouth repeated over and over; he could even sense her fragrance in his nostrils while his hearing seemed to quicken to her sparkling private laughter.

With this buffer against the knowledge of his desperate situation, he began the first of many weeks of planning and surreptitious observation, against the severe risk of being seen to behave normally, sharply or slyly and being branded a malingerer – not that Pod Petřínem was a haven except for someone with no alternative. He realised that it couldn't continue and in all likelihood had only done so because of the initial Police interest in him; as long as he remained amnesiac and unclaimed there would remain the problem of where to send him. The Police had begun to lose that interest and he realised things were turning serious when he heard mutterings about his bed being needed. His clothes had been burned and he saw no chance whatever of simply walking out, especially without money, and the risk of being caught stealing was unthinkable.

Only in stages did his mind finally piece together the events just before the attack, extending cautiously back in time to the farm near Rakovnik, to poor old Louis and his big old barn full of straw and a tractor, other machinery, as well as something mysterious and very frightening.

His brain blocked this fearsome thing completely and he was largely distracted from dwelling on it by his worry and longing for Lucy. It was to cause him awful remorse later that he had forgotten about the danger from a man called Vincent Cornelius, the South African renegade who could be relied upon to seek vengeance.

They sent him down to physiotherapy where he began to exercise and to ease the ache in his damaged rib-cage. The scar of the exit wound was largely concealed under the bulge of pectoral muscle, a small puckered star which Dr Pintová had sewn with unusual care. He worried that Lucy would be furious or repelled by it, yet the lump of bruise tissue over his ear was quite marked and they said it could take six months to go down. After a while he came in for some good-humoured teasing about how hard he worked himself on the weights and soon they found him cheerfully helping others with varying disabilities. He felt that as long as they were pleased to have him around, the more chance he had to formulate some plan of escape, a theme which dominated his entire waking life like a burning ideology.

He sometimes heard older patients talking quietly and sadly about journeys they had made in other days and the virtual impossibility of it now. He saw that for them it was becoming, as for the younger generation, something too painful to imagine any more, so their minds would shut off their dreams in self-defence. Stuart felt almost marked and cautious in his differing attitude, an inexorable determination to get clear. Clothes and money, clothes and money, but one chance only. Caught stealing or even acting suspiciously he knew could lose him his freedom for ever. It was only when he heard, from a new and officious visitor accompanying the regular houseman

240

on his rounds, an ominous name, that he even considered an appeal through official channels. It was a name to chill him to the marrow: Bohnice, the insane asylum, sounding as absolute as a death sentence.

After pondering for a while, he decided he couldn't chance the legitimate channels because he didn't know if Maryša and Procházka had cleared the barrier. If anything had gone wrong for her, he could be arraigned and sentenced for bringing her false papers and Stayres and the diplomats would be forced to disown him.

He kept up his charade of total amnesia, watching the visitor through his guise of vagueness and detachment and seeing a decision forming. Notes were made, there were shrugs and nods and the pair moved on. Stuart lay in a cold, confused terror, strangely fragile and vulnerable, unable to understand why so much still seemed bewildering. No one had told him how close he had been to death or how severe the shock to his system.

That afternoon a casualty was brought in, a young student with a broken leg and severe contusions from a traffic accident. He had no Czech but the Doctor spoke halting English to him. When Stuart heard the words he wanted to rush over and gabble furiously; it was even worse when the student had two boisterous visitors later on. He had to wait until the quiet of midnight before sneaking over and cruelly waking the sedated casualty. He knew he'd be watched by other patients but they would naturally presume it was the national pastime, pursuit of foreign currency.

'Sorry to wake you,' he whispered to the pained eyes struggling from sleep. 'I'm in trouble.' He found himself quivering with the relief of speaking English.

'Me too,' said the youth ruefully, 'What's your prob?'

'How long's your visit?'

'Another week. Why?'

'I need clothes and money. I'll pay ten times for either as soon as I get home. Will you take a gamble?'

'What happened to you?'

'I got clobbered and had all my gear nicked. I can't go to the Embassy because, well, never mind the reasons. How tall are you?'

'Five-ten.'

'Good enough. Feet?'

'Nine, nine and a half.'

'Great. Jeans, sneakers, jersey. Can you do it for me, get your friends to bring them to you?'

'Yeah, OK. You'll need long johns, a coat and a hat, it's brass monkeys out there.'

'Is it? Why?'

'Mid-winter's a good reason, in'it?'

'I suppose . . . I've been putting off this question ever since my memory came back . . . What's the date, roughly.'

'February 25th, I think.'

'Oh my God!' he breathed, closing his eyes.

'Why? How long have you been around?'

Stuart groaned almost silently. 'Nearly three months. I came for the weekend and my wife . . .'

'Boy, she'll be hopping, won't she, rolling-pin time? She'll probably have gone off with – sorry, that's not cheerful for you.'

Stuart shook his head in the faint light. 'Money. How much can you get me?'

'Phew! Not much, say twenty quid, tops.'

'It'll get you two hundred, plus the clothes, if you'll take my word on it. It's all I can give you.'

'Well, it's an even better deal than the touts are offering. Sure, I'll ask my mates to bring them tomorrow, if I don't imagine I dreamt it. My name's Greg. Where do you live?'

Stuart's answer was quick and truthful and he realised that Greg was bright, since with just the knowledge of his village, he'd always be able to find him. 'Don't worry,' he said, 'It's worth far more to me than I'm

242

offering. See you tomorrow. Don't acknowledge me, they think I'm – '

The door opened at the end of the ward and the night nurse stole in on her rounds. Stuart ducked down below the bed, waiting carefully until he glimpsed her bending over to rearrange someone's bedding, then he padded quickly back to his own bed, his heart pounding with an absurd memory of schooldays and ragging. He knew that if they tried to transfer him the next day he would have to stage an accident but in the event he was lucky again because the weekend was just beginning and even in winter people had things they would rather be doing. The ward windows were very high and he hadn't noticed any snow falling.

The next day he spent extra time in the therapy room doing a double work-out and trying to keep a low profile in the ward. Greg's visitors came again with more jocularity which the dour inmates and staff clearly resented. The three went into a huddle of conspiracy and made efforts not to look his way. It made him feel even more conspicuous.

In the night, Greg told him that for those odds they could raise £40 and would have it the following day with the clothes. Stuart's tension increased to an intolerable level and only through physical exhaustion was he able to find sleep. He couldn't plan anything and he had far too much to fear; mostly he thought of Lucy in a jumble of pity, sorrow and longing.

Thoughtfully, one of Greg's friends brought the clothes wrapped in a white pillow-case inside his shoulder-bag. In the small confusion of the visitors' arrival he dumped the pillow-case at the foot of Stuart's bed. Still with no plan to cause him hesitation, he simply put on his hospital robe over the coarse smock, picked up the bag and his towel and went out to the washrooms. They were fortunately empty but because there were no doors on the cubicles, he had to put the robe back on and sit for half an

243

hour with the towel over his knees. The clothes fitted reasonably and in the pocket of the blue anorak there was £20 English and a jumble of Czech crowns, with a piece of paper bearing Greg's address. Shortly before he estimated the visitors' bell would ring, he folded the smock and gown to look unused and went nervously back through the ward. Nobody spoke to him or seemed to notice. He passed Greg's bed and called out quietly, 'Greg, thanks. Come on, guys, let's go.'

He put the linen on a chair and turned to join them. As a sudden afterthought, passing his bed, he took the paper from the progress clipboard and folded it away. It was his only identity. He left between the two friends but through the window in the swing door he saw the ward supervisor and the English-speaking doctor approaching, stern and unanimated. Both had seen him and Stuart knew all about the perils of collusion, how hard it was to draw people into conspiracy since the informer system always led them to fear one another. The matron knew Stuart far better than the doctor, especially since he'd worked long and hard to draw a smile from her; in the end she'd come close to relenting and quietly explained her vow, made in the summer of 1968, that she would never smile again unless the Russians went away. She only knew him as *Nikdo,* nobody, but he realised with the extent of the paranoia that he himself could be a suspect informer.

As she looked at him in affront, Stuart spoke to them both in Czech. 'Visiting time is over and these friends are leaving. I seem to remember them and I'm going to walk with them a while. I was hoping I could jog my memory, do you understand?'

'It's against the rules,' she answered, covering herself and deferring to the doctor. He looked at the faces ranged towards him, the two English youths uncomprehending and unconditioned to everyday fear, Stuart's face open and anxious, the matron's firmly closed.

'You would do well to jog it,' the doctor said finally, 'You would remember the rules and respect the authorities. Go back to your bed and hand over those clothes. At once. Matron, call the Police.'

He reached out to grasp the jacket but Stuart spun away, his reaction blur-fast from his pent-up fear and the unfamiliar grip of the sneakers.

'The way out!' he shouted in English, 'Let's go. Show me!'

One of the students hesitated but the other led off at once, his exuberance untouched by fear. Stuart jinked away from the Doctor's second grab and raced after him. He heard running footsteps behind but otherwise there were no shouts, whistles or alarms. In his terrified state, anything that gained a second was welcome but later he had cause to wonder why no one blocked their exit; he decided charitably that the two may have felt they had done enough to be protected from each other.

They jostled and swerved through the shambles of departing visitors and after more corridors and corners, the three went leaping down the outside steps into a cold clear afternoon.

The Castle bridge was the only near way to cross the deep ravine and they ran towards it like vandals past the two immobile guards and into the courtyard, passing the main door of St Vitus' Cathedral. Stuart was leading now, more confident on familiar ground. Distantly they heard a siren and he blessed the doctor and matron silently for their collusion in allowing him the small headstart before doing their duty. His lungs began to heave but eased slightly as he sped down the immensely long, broad flight of steps which hugs the southern wall. Even long unaccustomed to running, he had the stimulus gradually to outstrip the other two; desperately he wanted to stop and thank them but realised that the gesture could be self-cancelling if he was caught because of it. Without looking back he waved and jabbed an exultant thumbs-up

245

before steadying his pace. It felt vibrantly good to be running and breathing again and to be gratified at his hard-earned fitness.

He took the Mánesův Bridge as his second wind came and only slowed to a walk on the other side when there were enough pedestrians to absorb him, pulling off his anorak and clutching it with only the different, inside colour showing.

He considered at first walking several miles of outskirts to the beginnings of Route 6 to try hitch-hiking but he realised that if he didn't get a lift straight away, he would be far too conspicuous at least for his own nerves; apart from which it was plainly Sunday and the chances against him, especially with the daylight fast fading. He went instead towards the International Hotel and after a few minutes waiting found an incoming taxi. In an attempt to put off any questions or follow-up, he told the driver to leave him at a hotel in Rakovnik and gave him all the English money for the two-hour drive. When the taxi had set off back to Prague he found a small café and had a meal of dumplings and a litre and a half of Prasdroj beer which made him reel deliciously and helped with the ten mile frosty walk to Louis' farm.

The old man was solidly asleep and took about twenty minutes to wake and stumble downstairs, leaning aghast by the kitchen door in a long, russet nightshirt and a greying old woollen cap.

'It was the battle helicopters, I suppose?' he said, thickly, 'I shouldn't have mentioned them. Scared you off.'

Stuart shook his head. 'Not quite. May I come in, I'm freezing.'

'No. Can you imagine my fear? Half my life I live with it and in three months I have as much again.'

'I wasn't free. I'll explain. It's cold out here, Louis, and I've come to do what I have to.'

246

'But you . . .' Slowly he let the door open and Stuart slipped gratefully inside. There was still warmth in the fire but the old man needed some prompting.

'Any of that brandy left, Louis? I feel like it's the end of Lent.'

'It hasn't started yet,' the old man answered seriously, fetching the bottle and two glasses. 'You can't drink alone, it's bad for morale.'

He poured and they clinked together but only Stuart smiled, the Cognac searing deliciously. He poked a blaze into the fire and told Louis about Procházka's attack on him and the reasons for it. Louis felt the still-fibrous lump on his head and was dubiously apologetic, then Stuart remembered the piece of paper, his progress chart from Pod Petřínem. It was the first time he'd looked at it, having avoided a possible belying of his amnesiac detachment; he'd discovered only recently from the nurse Zdena the cause of the star-shaped scar under his right pectoral.

'I had a gunshot wound as well, but the big problem was my head, he fractured my skull. I should have been incinerated afterwards, to kill the evidence.'

'Show me,' Louis said and then quickly negated it. 'I'm sorry, that's what St Thomas demanded. I believe you.' Louis sounded reluctant, his tone holding a bitter sympathy. 'But it has been a terrible time for me. No one to talk with or complain to . . . Somebody once said to me, "Why not imagine that you came far from here, where you made a conscious choice to live the life you have?" Dear God, I would not have chosen this one, would I?'

Stuart shook his head understandingly. 'Maybe he meant you did choose it, perhaps it was better than an alternate choice.'

'But I have been serving that war-machine out there like a golden calf for nearly forty years! My heart and my sanity . . .' Louis smiled then, eschewing self-pity. 'Yes. Anyway, she's still ready. You must prepare tomorrow and leave the next morning before the snow cancels all. It's very late this year, very unusual. I finished the fuel, I did it the very next day, it is full now but I . . . I haven't started it in all that time, I'm afraid. I was so down, disappointed. You understand?'

'Of course I do. You should sleep again now, I trust more peacefully.'

'But I did turn the propeller by hand. She should be all right. Maybe we ought to – '

Stuart shook his head and said, 'That's enough.' He helped him to his feet and urged him towards the stairs. The old man shuffled gratefully, his wizened smile creeping back into place, perhaps only in the comfort of one winter night to be shared.

Stuart lay in the musty room trying too hard to sleep, once more terrified to admit how much he was preventing his thoughts from straying into the barn, as if his physical damage had made him timid. He knew what was there with complete clarity but some over-riding synapse in his mind was refusing to acknowledge it. It felt like a curious half-commitment and made him think of an expression of Lucy's, something about ambivalence, 'like a hitch-hiker too proud to hold out his thumb'. He decided in the end that it was simply a reaction of his survival system to extreme trauma; he tried to tell himself that it would go away once he'd finished a thorough pre-flight and heard the mighty engine once again. He was not fully convinced because he knew he was afraid and had been before, not with an abject fear which he could have conquered but because he was right to be afraid, because you didn't take such an old airframe into the sky without first dismantling it to examine every one of its myriad parts for corrosion or decrepitude; furthermore the only inspection and repair had been made by an untrained Bohemian peasant. Who wasn't about to fly in it himself, he added pettishly, before remembering the light in Louis' eyes when he'd envisioned such an experience.

They both woke soon after dawn, Stuart feeling strung out with tension and too little sleep, Louis all alert and business-like. After a breakfast of oats and coffee, they began to dismantle the Spitfire's huge den of straw, removing the front wall completely. Their hands grew red and their breath steamed in the cold country air.

Stuart asked if the barn had been rebuilt sometime because he was sure the wings wouldn't clear the doors. Louis said it hadn't, and the same problem had occurred all those years ago when he'd hidden it. He described how it had to be jacked onto little trolleys and moved diagonally for a few feet. He produced the trolleys and seemed quite confident. 'We can do a run-up now or this evening,' he said, 'But the workers will be in the Rybnik field today, that's the one with the pond alongside the Berounka here. You must stay out of sight all day.'

'Sure. Is there any chance you can make a phone-call for me?'

'Where to?' he asked with some apprehension, 'I only spoke to one once in my life, it was quite frightening.'

Stuart couldn't help smiling. 'It's to England. Perhaps someone you can trust would do it for you. There's no danger.'

'But international calls are always monitored.'

'I know. Here's the number.' Stuart wrote down St George's office telephone, hoping his memory played no tricks. 'If there's a machine, you wait for it to finish talking, otherwise just say the word.'

'What word?'

'Very simple: just "Scramble".'

'I remember!' Louis said gleefully, 'Jára used to say it. They'd all run out trailing their parachutes and wires. And the other one, Tally-ho! It means "Here we go, after them boys, taka taka-taka!" The hunting cry. "Watch for the Hun in the sun!"' The light was gleaming again in the deep old eyes.

'If you get a chance,' Stuart added earnestly, 'Please just ask one thing: "Is Lucy all right?"'

Louis had to recite the question several times and then went off in a car borrowed from the collective supervisor. He returned shortly before lunch, saying he'd made the call himself, excited and triumphant. A woman had answered and tried to say many things but of course he'd hung up, not understanding the English.

'And the question?' Stuart asked, trying to quell his agitation.

Louis nodded. 'I had to call again,' he said sheepishly, 'I asked it. She said "*Ano*", but in English, Yes, OK . . . Hiding. Is that right?'

Stuart gulped and then found that some of his trepidation of the night before had suddenly dissolved with the outright relief. The remainder he disguised with sheer activity although he was convinced it would return at any moment to give him violent shakes. He spent the whole afternoon in the barn sitting in the cockpit, going over every control and procedure until he was fluent and faultless. He adjusted the rudder-bar star-wheels until the pedals gave him the right reach and he practised fingering everything with his eyes shut. His confidence grew with the familiarity and he tried to ignore the terror that it might suddenly dissolve as soon as the engine roared and even more as the wheels finally lifted off from the winter stubble.

When the workers had all finally gone, Louis had shared some end-of-the-day gossip with the supervisor after he'd put the tractor away in the other barn, then they had a meal of tea and hard scones in almost breathless anticipation. In the early dark, Louis hooked up the external batteries and the two of them went slickly through the starting procedure like honed professionals. When Stuart thumbed the Start and Booster coil buttons, however, the great propeller turned over three times and then abruptly stopped. They tried all the connections in turn but in the end Louis had to admit defeat: the ancient starter motor had finally given up.

He removed and dismantled it but one horrified glance at the brushes was enough; the brush-holders were a tangled mess and would have to be completely replaced. His dismay was unbearable, for with no other means of starting the Merlin he was convinced he'd never see it airborne and all his years of work had come to nothing.

Over the evening, however, he managed a change of heart and left on the bus for Prague in the morning carrying the heavy unit in a bag slung from his shoulder. He got back long after dark, exhausted and defeated. The contact at Kbely was away in Brno and wouldn't be back for two days, and he'd been given brusque refusals in half a dozen repair shops.

'We used to be a land of engineering geniuses,' he said disgustedly while Stuart harboured another terror of being stuck or caught and executed. He thought with regret of poor St George on a nail-biting stand-by but he suppressed, in sheer self-defence, any lingering thoughts of Lucy.

They waited out the two days in gnawing frustration until Louis went back to Prague once more, and once more weary of his massive burden, returned in complete dejection.

'I knew the museum was shut for the winter but he works there, he's allowed in and out freely all the time. The guards know him so well, but now there's a complete shut-down, the STB is doubling up everywhere, snooping behind everything that flies. Some rumour that the West has someone looking to steal a Russian plane. All the new Migs have been pulled back except those in the deep ramp-silos. I begged him of course, to go into the museum section and do an exchange for us but he said he couldn't possibly, not without creating suspicion. I suppose I must believe him.'

'There simply has to be another way to get it going,' Stuart answered in twisted puzzlement. 'There's power all around, electricity, tractors, all sorts. Surely we could . . .'

But like Louis, he came up against the same enigma, how to crank over a massive twenty-seven litre engine with something you could then detach from the propeller. They wrestled with it fruitlessly and more crazily hour after hour but with Stuart insisting on a tractor's power take-off as a basis, the old man finally came up with a solution.

With an acetylene torch he opened up a 150 litre steel barrel, leaving twenty-five centimetres of skin attached to one end and mating the other end-plate to it. In one of the flat heads of what then looked like a huge blackened side-drum he cut a hole the same size as the propeller's boss or spinner and then he welded four curved hooks of metal rod to the same rim. Offered up, each hook fitted behind one of the wooden blades and the spinner in its jagged socket kept the new unit roughly central. When the belt from the power take-off came tight, Louis explained, and the Merlin fired and accelerated, in theory the hooks on the drum would lag from the blades and detach themselves.

Stuart argued that the drum would then be a lethally spinning hazard or more likely be glued immoveably to the propeller by its airstream. Louis shrugged in the full exhaustion of his inventive powers.

'Let us leave something for the Good Lord to take care of,' he said, 'After all, we cannot chance a rehearsal.'

Nevertheless he looked thoughtful for some time before wandering off to the other barn and returning with a huge post-hammer. Stuart prayed that this implement would be an unnecessary solution but they were both too tired to discuss it any further. Louis kept looking doubtfully at the sky, muttering but keeping his thoughts to himself. His worry revealed itself after they'd had a

252

late snack and some tea and had gone outside again; they stopped and looked at each other in utter dismay, unable to bear the thought of further waiting. The sky and temperature had been threatening snow for the past two days but they had both carefully refrained from mentioning the possibility. It began that evening in earnest, big soft flakes presaging a heavy fall. They went back in and poured stiff drinks, sipping in defeated silence.

Stuart spoke first. 'It seems an ill-fated venture, Louis. I just can't believe any of this.'

'You can go anyway,' Louis said, none too firmly because he knew Stuart's answer already.

'No. I can't possibly leave while there's snow, it would point to you here as the origin like a beacon, the tracks in the snow.'

'I could mess it all up with the tractor and a harrow.'

'That would be just as obvious. I thought of going now, so the falling snow would have covered everything by morning, but it wouldn't even be a question of extra risk, it would be absolute suicide in the dark, no radio, no destination, no aids whatever. Not one chance in a million. Our only hope is that it stops snowing and thaws, before I go completely nuts.'

Louis got up and prodded needlessly at the fire, staring into the flames for long minutes before finally voicing his thoughts.

'I remember in the early days, expecting your father all the time, I once decided what to do when the snow came. It was very easy. Now that I am old and lost my adventure, I feel it's perhaps too crazy, and besides I have nothing left really, no means except my pension from the state. Did you say you have plenty of money?'

'I will have soon. Why?'

'Well, I . . . it's making me shake to think of it. How would you like to set me up with a little apartment in Montmartre, say, and enough to live on? I am very cheap and I promise not to last too long.'

253

'Louis, I tell you I would be absolutely delighted but –'

'—I know what you are going to ask. It's very simple. I tried and I know it can be done, only just. I hope the British Royal Air Force doesn't object if I remove the armour plate from behind your seat? Naturally, I am confident that you will not need it for this short flight, and in any case my old bones can still stop a few Russian bullets. You see, I can squeeze in there and crouch above the wires as long as it's not for too long.'

Stuart's mouth had fallen open. 'Can you really? You've tested it for room?'

'Yes, well actually it was almost impossible, I got stuck for half an hour, but age has shrunk me a lot. I'm sure I can do it.'

Stuart was suddenly torn between his delight for a solution and the heavy responsibility of piloting someone else in his increasingly nervous ignorance. Thinking rationally, it was something he once more had to set aside and forget. There was no bearable alternative, and besides Louis was already preparing for his final task. The parachute lay on the floor in its ancient and brittle canvas bag next to the Spitfire's logs and manuals in their dusty brown-paper covers.

'What can I bring?' Louis asked, wringing his hands then suddenly grinning, 'Not my favourite chair, that's for sure!'

'No. Just what you can't do without, small things of sentiment. Everything else is replaceable and we don't need to take the manuals.'

'Good idea, we'll leave them right here, to show them what we've done!' he agreed gleefully. 'I will just bring a picture of Jára and one of Marie and my favourite pipe which I never smoke any more. Oh, thank God I no longer have a dog. That would have been very hard, I've loved too many dogs. Did you notice how few there are in the city? You have to have a licence now which costs a stupendous sum, 150 dollars, so there are almost no dogs except for guarding. Strange capitalist solution, isn't it? In Paris, I can have a poodle, *hein*? I think not.'

He chuckled with the lightness of all care fled away and rubbed his hands repeatedly. 'Apart from when I fell in love, this is the greatest adventure of my life. I am glad for the snow, it forces what my courage failed. I falter still, but we must do it. And Rolls-Royce will not let us down, it's unthinkable!'

Stuart said nothing but poured himself another Slivovitz to cover his anxiety. He made a meal of leek soup and mushroom omelettes while Louis went back to the barn to make his preparations. A car drove up while he was still in there, the first visitor to the farm since Stuart had arrived apart from the farm workers and he realised they had become careless because of it. The Spitfire was no longer concealed behind its wall of bales and any casual visitor looking round the door would see it at once. He froze in a quandary but when a knock came at the back door, he opened it to admit the collective supervisor, a man gaunt yet ruddy with health, his hands not even as task-worn as Louis'.

'So. Who are you and where is Mišek?'

'A nephew. I'll go and get him.'

'There is no need. I am just investigating. When an old man of habit buys extra food and is suddenly going on errands here and there, makes a phone call, the tongues wag. You see, there is a big hunt on in Rakovnik, trouble for all of us, the Cheka – urrgh!'

Stuart hit him solidly just below the heart. There was an exhalation and a two second pause before the man collapsed to the floor, his eyes glassy. Stuart trussed him quickly before going to fetch Louis. At first the old man was horrified but gradually began to nod his approval, ending up with a little staccato chuckle.

'You did right,' he said in the supervisor's hearing. 'He was always a swine and a tattler. That's why he had the job. The only problem is if they come looking for him. We'll put the car in my other barn, well it used to be mine but now only he has the key.'

'Is he married?'

'Only to one who will not complain at sleeping alone.' He went over and looked down at the captive. 'Paláček, only because I consider myself a gentleman I will not kick you in the backside, or even in the front. But that is the only reason.'

He was about to add more abuse but in sudden restraint turned away and ignored him completely. Stuart checked the captive's bindings once again, put a cushion under his head and served up their supper while Louis went out quickly to hide the car.

He needed Stuart's help and a roof hoist to remove the heavy section of armour plate after a long battle to loosen it but the task was finished before midnight. He then checked everything once again, fuel, oil and hydraulic levels, worriedly topping the radiator's enormous 14 gallon capacity with some neat tractor anti-freeze in lieu of ethylene-glycol after discovering a small leak in a hose connection. He apologised that there was no oxygen in the bottle, saying he'd never been able to get it refilled, and he'd also given up on the old valve radio. Stuart shrugged and assured him they wouldn't matter.

They both managed to snatch some sleep being nearly accustomed to repeated periods of tense anticipation. Because of Paláček's interference they couldn't delay any further: in the dawn they'd have to take their chances together in the air or else go on the run, in a country where a fugitive life is almost inconceivable, especially in winter.

Their sleep ended long before dawn, however. In the graveyard depths of it, Stuart was sure he heard something even before the stream of panicked shrieks from Paláček, clear orders to bring the Cheka with guns and a hang-noose. Still fully clothed, Stuart leapt up fumbling for the light switch but it was dead to his touch; out on the landing he saw Louis' torch wavering towards him, uncertain.

'I've got it,' Stuart said firmly taking it for him. 'Must be someone outside.'

'Yes. Have to stop them. Quick, go! I'll bring my trusty!'

Stuart stumbled down into the kitchen seeing Paláček still lying where he'd trussed him, silent now, wide-eyed and cringing. Stuart ignored him and went straight to the back door, seizing a poker from the fire. He opened the door very cautiously, ready to leap aside but the flashlight showed only footprints leading towards and away again. They were not large and had left a small waiting area in front of the door. Tentatively he followed them curving away, round towards the barn, ceasing where the snow-line marked the threshold, where the snow-covered canvas on the Spitfire's cowling canted up towards the sky. To have come to this point and face discovery was too much to bear and to leave at once in darkness remained suicidal. Being so tense he leaped a foot when he heard a sound behind him.

Louis was moving in a crouched stealth, a short firearm in his hands. The muzzle of his piece even flared slightly like a bugle, an hilarious anachronism but no doubt deadly with choppings of scrap iron. Stuart nodded nervously in the snowlight and turned back to the barn, torch at the ready and Louis at his shoulder. They heard another sound from within, a rustling of straw.

'*Nazdar?*' Stuart called softly in Czech, 'Hello? Who's there?'

He sensed the gun-muzzle thrusting past his shoulder, Louis presumably having sense not to fire from behind and deafen him. Something moved in the blackness of the hangar and Stuart stabbed out with the torch. He caught sight of a face and smashed down with his arm at the same moment, never discovering whether his

257

action caused Louis to fire or was merely simultaneous. The noise was thunderous and appalling; Stuart's senses reeled in utter disbelief and disorder as he ran forward to the figure lying on the floor. All his confusions of the last three months flashed in and out like stabs of electric current torturing his brain's every ganglion. His scream was as profoundly terminal as that of the burning pilot, his canopy finally cleared, his body falling free, seeing huge leaves of burning parachute trailing out behind like forfeit possibilities.

The small figure lay slumped against a straw bale, the face distinctly of the dream but smeared and pale, lifeless, the gold sadly faded out to waxen: Lucy.

TWELVE

I love the night, I love the night!
I love the element of danger and the ecstasy of flight!
Chris De Burgh

A few days after her request to Stayres in London, Lucy
went alone down to Geneva in a tour bus. She met Hegel
at the Embassy and found herself markedly impressed
with his contrasts; he was over 6'2" but very quiet
spoken and only faintly accented. He wore studious,
rimless glasses but the eyes behind them gleamed with an
alert intelligence. His clothes were soberly cut to cover a
heavily muscled frame.

He called her Miss Karen and treated her with
unstressed respect but a couple of times as they examined
photoprints he leaned minutely into her personal radius
and Lucy felt the air almost crackle. She wondered if he
noticed, even if her hair rose up to him as to a static
charge; she seethed with confusion and a longing for
physical closeness which then focused on Stuart, leaving
her bewildered yet gratefully relieved.

The area round the map reference she had given
Stayres was extensively forested and Lucy surprised
Hegel with the notion that her would-be escaper favoured
open ground to be able to see over distances in moonlight. From a wide scan they narrowed to an area of what
he was able to verify as pasture on the Northeast side of
the wire, even though the trees to the South extended
right up to it. He was also gratifyingly impressed

with her familiarity with aerial photographs which she didn't explain. For his part, as he pointed out various features, he didn't appreciate how gruesome the reality for her became.

'The wire is between three and four metres high, diamond pattern with holes too small for fingers. Small enough fingers would be cut by it, anyway. It's also buried in the ground so you can't wriggle under. The wires are ten metres apart, and the earth in between is a different colour from being prepared for footprints and mines. This is a concrete strip for patrol vehicles and this is a deep ditch to prevent vehicles crossing. The area you are looking at is not so frequented and doesn't seem to have a dog run but for sure it is mined and armed with SM-70s, short-barrelled shot-guns firing at three different levels, triggered by wires. They were described as a "new socialist accomplishment" when they installed them. They also have a Dobermann or Shepherd for every kilometre, that's more than 1300 just for the DDR. I won't ask you to guess what this little backyard fence cost them. It was more than 6 billion dollars.'

'Gosh . . . tell me about watchtowers,' Lucy said.

'Two kinds, one is closed upon a concrete column, like so, you see? The newer ones have a square tower with brown mirror glass like an ambulance, you can't see what is inside.'

'Um . . . Can you narrow it down to here?'

With quiet efficiency Hegel produced another enlargement for her final choice; she didn't tell him it was based on the largest gap she could see between concrete cylinders.

'The first 500 metres is called "protective strip" then there is a five kilometre "forbidden zone" for which they need special passes. In the protective strip the fields are worked but strictly in daylight only and under guard. For the purpose of all this, I quote the words of Herr Otto Grotewohl who instigated it: "To keep out spies, diversionists, terrorists and smugglers," in fact all those hordes of evil Westerners trying to get in to be parasites upon the munificence of real Socialism.'

Lucy smiled at his soft irony but then he went on to talk of electronic beams and the automatic weapons linked to them. He could see her interest dwindled when he told her that the only way to detect a beam was to look straight down it, which meant you had already broken it, which meant you had already been ventilated like a colander.

'Artistic licence notwithstanding?' Lucy filled in, appreciating his restraint from patronising her literary intentions. She had an urge to kiss the corner of his sympathetic smile. 'When were the pictures taken, do you know?'

'Not exactly,' he answered, 'But plainly late autumn, winter before the snow. The trees there are evergreen but these are all bare, oak and beech, I imagine.'

The photographs had an eerie and astonishing clarity considering they were taken from more than 100 miles out. Hegel said they were relatively primitive, ordinary black and whites taken on a clear day for which only atmospheric dust or damp would impede vision. Clarity from above through a small amount of murk was a minor problem unlike horizontal peering through an extended crust. More sophisticated surveillance cameras could already read car number plates through night-time blizzards, heralding the end of the age of infidelity. Lucy smiled ingenuously and decided to find no nuance in his remark.

Her final chosen print he took away and expanded and then at her request ruled gridlines on it so she could edge-mate the map-references. She needed finally a 1:1000000 aeronautical chart but decided for discretion's sake not to ask him where to find it. The precaution proved a waste of time since Stayres had briefed him to take her seriously. She let him take her out for coffee and he revealed that he was originally from Minsk, a 'white

Russian', and spoke the language fluently. Lucy decided that Karen should not do likewise despite her interest; she found his understatement fascinating and pressed him for more colour and background. Not even a man as controlled as Hegel should be asked to resist this flattery and he let it out that he had 'been over' more than a few times and was fluent in three European languages as well as half a dozen useful dialects. Lucy joked her scepticism that he was too big to be a spy, let alone a mole. Hegel answered that he was just the type to be not the type.

'I almost forgot,' he added. 'You have something to tell me, for Mr Stayres.' He looked at her obliquely when she didn't answer at once. 'Someone's whereabouts, wasn't it?'

Lucy was prepared for some fury at her deceit but evidently Hegel wasn't briefed on this point.

'He's in Czechoslovakia,' she said, cringing prematurely. Hegel merely thanked her but she could imagine Stayres' eruption when her perfidy was relayed to him. Presumably it would confirm any jaundiced feelings he might have about Russians. She had a notion that they were deceiving her on some point but it was nothing definite. She couldn't know it was a lethal omission, so her tone remained lightly jocular.

'And of course, your name isn't even Hegel,' she ventured with a smile of conspiracy.

'And nor are you a Karen.'

'Oh?'

'There's something languid and Scandinavian about the name, for me at any rate. It's a passive name – the loved one. You're not passive, you radiate.'

'Sounds tiring,' Lucy answered with a chuckle, quelling the natural reaction to converse about her original name Ludmilla meaning all-beloved, and her adopted one meaning light. It took some effort, for his interested hazel eyes and long lashes seemed to welcome confidence and indiscretion; she decided firmly that it was safer in the clean and blinding light of the high mountains and left almost hurriedly.

She took a taxi to Cointrin airport and from one of the flying schools she secured the required chart. Another tour bus was waiting bound for Tignes/Val d'Isère and brought her back in time for a late supper. The rest of her scheme sounded terrifyingly simple and all the remaining arrangements could be made by telephone. It would however take several weeks for Nadia to convey the message and instructions to her parents beyond the Wall and to receive their confirmation, so Lucy determined to confine her plan strictly to her subconscious and to resume her ski-ing with gusto. At first she began to devise deceptions to cover her mission, a visit to her father or sickness for Alicia, and even considered persuading Stayres to occupy Stuart for forty-eight hours should he return at the wrong moment. She realised that anyone except Nadia would be sure to try dissuasion or prevention if they knew the truth, yet a continuation of a life full of unexplained absences was unthinkable. For the moment at least it had one poignant advantage, that the longer it continued the better skier she might become, to keep up with him, to race him, even sing together as they flew the valleys, a marvellous ploy Gordon taught to distract from over-concentration on their skis or the immediate terrain.

When not in the confidence of the teaching mode, Gordon was very shy with females and reserved with his questions. It was therefore only after several weeks when he insisted that they stopped hiring and bought their own skis and boots that he heard her surname for the first time. As they left the shop carrying brand-new Dynamics he questioned her tentatively.

'Unusual name, Kody with a K. I knew a guy in the British Army team called Kody. Any relation?'

'Stuart?'

'Yeah, that's the one.'

'My husband.'

'Well, whaddya know! It was my first season, he was too good for me, at least then.'

'Amazing,' Lucy answered, feeling a link and yet more deprived than ever. 'And now?'

'Ah, well I do spend the whole winter here. Does he keep it up?'

'No. Silly man got married, didn't he?'

Gordon laughed shyly. 'So he sent you off to learn so he can get back to it?'

'Not exactly, no. Listen, how long would it take me to reach his standard?'

'Um, well, that depends on your guts, really. He was pretty fearless, very cool if I remember, but not quite enough kill to be a champion. He won some races, though . . . I would say in three months you could stay with him if he was cruising. You're exceptionally co-ordinated for . . .'

'A woman?'

'I . . . no.' Again the shy laugh. 'A girl as poised and good-looking as you, both of you, doesn't often trouble to do anything well. They don't need to bother, usually. I guess the attention we give them makes them idle.'

'And miserable.'

'I suppose . . . but I've met some women who seem to love doing absolutely nothing.'

'For me that's misery, Life's maddeningly short. The sooner they hit us with some longevity pills the better. Now that I'm here I want to learn and learn, to get as perfect and as fluid as possible, I want to surprise him, delight him. I want to do what they're doing.' She pointed with her stick up at the 12,000 foot Grande Motte and away to the right where the powder fiends had made the long trek across the high ridge above the dreaded wall, to go scything their private scours down the near vertical, virgin gullies off La Grande Balme. 'Can you imagine it, learning in secret? He was going to teach me

264

one day, so I can pretend not to know, fall over a few times, be hideously incompetent, then suddenly get it and go Whee-eee!'

Gordon gleamed with delight and they became firm friends, he treating Lucy and Giles like two demi-goddesses and adopting a conscious pride in their company. His brotherly easiness with them became a solid, reliable barrier against the more troublesome of the local males who outnumbered women by about ten to one, but one day of blizzard in January, he walked into their apartment as they were doing aerobics together on the floor, dressed in tights and zany leotards. The tape-player was quite loud and they were both deeply involved in their exercises although more in grace than aggression. He sat down quietly and watched unseen, utterly spellbound and when Lucy finally saw him, she crumpled into tears and fled to her room.

Allaying his concern, Giles went to her and returned shortly. 'Stuart's actually missing, we don't know where,' she explained, 'Something about the look in your eyes probably triggered her off, something that he does, maybe a cross between adoration and idolatry.'

She spoke with a kindly voice and patted his shoulder. Gordon smiled wanly, but the next day his stupefaction had changed back to brisk professionalism and they began to learn again, losing their confidence first on some severe mogul fields and later after a good snowfall in some heavy powder which required mastery of another technique. The better they became, the more mercilessly he drove them but, being used to disciplines, they thrived on it.

If he had no fixed schedule, Gordon delighted in taking them the furthest distances and guiding them off-piste in difficult conditions. One memorable day they went way beyond Val d'Isère up to the top of the drag-line and trekked from there over the glacier, the source of the river. They went with another instructor, a brilliant skier but a wild and fiery Spaniard called Pepe, his girlfriend and a suave middle-aged Italian. Pepe made noise all the time and Giles and Lucy debated whether he did it to get attention or to prevent anyone else from getting it. They were ascending in a six-seat cabin up the Iseran when Gordon asked Pepe the impossible question.

'Pepe, listen, supposing one day God said to you, "Pepe, you are no good, you are too noisy and I have decided to punish you. You can have a choice: you give up ski-ing or you give up sex. Which is to be?"'

For Pepe it was no choice. 'I give up sex,' he said promptly. 'How about you, *cariño?*' he asked, prodding his girl-friend sharply. Quiet and demure, she answered that she would unquestionably give up ski-ing. With much laughter the question circulated to include the Italian who was tanned and handsome; he was the only one to hesitate. Lucy too found no difficulty in the choice but Giles was thoughtful at the clear outcome: none of the girls would forgo their loving, none of the men their ski-ing.

'Priorities,' she said ruefully, 'Interesting, isn't it?'

About this time, they discovered the sparkling thrill of ski-ing with a personal stereo, carving their flights down vast white emptiness with swooping rhythms seeming to occur in the middle of the brain. It became the day's biggest decision which tapes to encumber pockets, the anticipation over-riding all discomfort.

As time passed in a steadily growing alarm, Giles used her skill to keep Lucy sanguine and, because her resources and Stuart's bank had both dried up, lent her money and firmly refused to let her skimp; she urged her to buy cheerful clothes and most important as the real deep cold set in, a pale pink, all-weather ski suit which was light and soft and blissful to wear. It was hideously expensive and Giles found its counterpart in her favourite lime green. Enchanted, Gordon christened them Limey and the Pink Panter.

Every day they rang the London answering machine and piped the code to make it replay any messages. There was nothing for Lucy except a few regular words of chat and sympathy from her mother and there were some unkept assurances from Epiphany that he would visit them soon. Later, through the local pub, Alicia had herself managed to get hold of the telephone engineer, who was able to confirm a single daily call coming through with complete regularity. Intensely serious, he gave them an anxious twenty-four hours when he called the machine to say the call hadn't come through on a forlorn Sunday, but he kindly confirmed its renewal the next evening. He also told of the abiding rumours about the strangers in the village. Prodigious busybodies themselves, the local drinkers were all convinced there were two rival groups pretending not to be watching each other, although outwardly showing the trappings of land-surveyors and badger-watchers. Terrain-masking snow and badgers' hibernation had confirmed their scepticism without deterring the vigilantes. Mr Horrocks sent his regards and seasonal greetings, glad to know she was safe. Lucy concluded that the renegade soldier Cornelius hadn't appeared to her first lure or else was waiting separately, smarter than the others. Her unrelieved dread was that Stuart might go home to her without debriefing or warning but there was nothing more she could do about it. She cowered from any acrimonious contact with Stayres. With Giles she contrived a routine of maximum distraction, learning French, ski-ing all the best days, otherwise exercising and reading all the classics they could find or persuade Epiphany to send them.

The call from Nadia interrupted this idyll like a collapsing deck-chair, panicking Lucy at first because of her lack of practice with the autogyro. Nadia's father had somehow secured the necessary pass into the 'forbidden zone' and had made a couple of runs already, testing for informers. For Lucy it was clearly 'Go'; she couldn't disguise her pale reaction from her friend because Giles had become extremely close and she gave in eventually to her concerned queries. Giles was naturally disbelieving and then utterly horrified, realising finally that since Lucy was both determined and committed, she might as well be as supportive as possible.

Hegel had decided there was no need to follow Lucy back to her hideout since any venture near her chosen spot on the wire would take her via Frankfurt, where in fact one of his colleagues picked them up from a standing airline watch. From there they hired a car and arrived in the small village of Bergheim, which had a tiny no-star hotel. The agent housed himself in a pension across the street.

That same evening, a large closed rental truck pulled into the little car park. An exhausted, strained Nadia stepped frailly from it accompanied by an elderly, stocky little man, with an endless grumbling repertoire of humorous, stoic complaints. In the back of the truck was tethered the autogyro, Decibelle, its temporary import papers allowing entry into France and Germany for sales display purposes. Hegel's man couldn't see inside the truck and could only report the meeting. According to the landlord's wife they made several calls to the airport weather centre which seemed to afford them a recurrent lifting of anxiety. Checking for himself, the agent was given a twenty-four hour forecast of scattered cloud and light winds, the night temperature just below freezing; the waning moon had lost one quarter. Hegel relayed the information to Stayres in London and was ordered at once to join the party. Evidently Stayres was eager to curry favour with the Americans by producing Stuart Kody. He told Hegel to take some heavy, silenced weapons in case of hazardous pursuit, yet both understood that a breach of the wire in anything lighter than a battle tank was out of the question.

The following day Hegel and his colleague monitored the couple staying in their rooms all morning while the girls from Tignes went off in their car with some boxed equipment and a spade. They walked fields and woodland consulting a chart but were very careful not to be seen anywhere near the wire nor even looking towards the frontier. They returned with a lightened carton and ate in the hotel so the box hadn't contained a picnic. In the afternoon only the stocky old man appeared, getting into the truck and staying there more than three hours.

Except in the factory, Decibelle would never have been given such a thorough pre-flight inspection but Allcock, once he had learned Lucy's real intentions, became abusively terrified for her. He disguised it with endless complaints about foreigners and German beer 'like 'orse-piddle', and was relentlessly painful about things like *wurst*-ever sausages. Lucy called him an imperial hangover which he chose to take as a compliment.

Darkness came and they submitted to a rural early supper. Afterwards they sat around nervously looking at watches and muttering quietly. Before nine o'clock the tension seemed to rise with the moon and at last they heard, from the small lounge, the telephone jangle in the hall. Nadia got up at once and went to the desk. The hotelier's wife held the instrument and looked at her in surprise, handing it over without a word when she said *'Ich bin Nadia.'*

Into the receiver her voice trembled. *'Ja . . . In ungefähr zwei stunden . . . Ich werde vor mitternacht anrufen . . . Gott segne.'*

She handed it back and turned abruptly. Lucy was already standing in the doorway, still and pale. Nadia jerked her head down once but then her hand flew to her mouth and she bolted for the washroom. Lucy and Giles went silently upstairs to don their warm ski-suits. Allcock zipped his greasy anorak, sniffed rheumily and shuffled out to the truck.

269

Within five minutes they were gone, Giles going east in the car, the other three southwards in the truck. After ten minutes, Allcock found his already chosen site, a quarter-mile drive to a house with closed shutters. He parked behind a mammoth rhododendron and then let down the tail-gate from the inside, where it was warm with kerosene fumes from a little heater. Lucy helped him ease the Bensen down the ramp and they turned it and pulled it out onto the gravel drive. The grass was long and tufty and the drive needed weeding. Allcock complained about it but Lucy couldn't respond. She had thought she knew fear from anticipating her first dance appearance before a large audience. It now seemed laughingly trivial; she was beyond shaking, beyond feeling cold, beyond feeling. She was left with only her preset routine and her own discipline. Her mouth was dry and her upper stomach seemed full of acid and sawdust.

Allcock slid the aerial out of a Blaupunkt walkie-talkie. 'Decibelle to Limey,' he said and repeated it.

In a moment, Giles' strained voice came back, 'Limey, Spot One.'

'Ignition. Call Spot Two.'

'Right.'

Nadia stood watching with her body cramped into a nervous S-shape. She was clenching a canvas holder, a child's breast-harness which Lucy took from her with a few words of encouragement. Lucy put it on and then fitted her crash helmet. She checked her watch again with a blink of torch and said 'Bollocks!' sharply when Allcock muttered something to her, then she eased herself into the single seat and strapped in with deliberate, resigned care. Distantly they heard a car, the noise receding and dying away. Again by torchlight, Lucy adjusted her altimeter, nodded to Allcock and tightened the brakes. Allcock turned the drive propeller once and said sharply, 'Contact!' Lucy thumbed up the magneto switches and cracked the word back at him. Allcock flicked the blade

270

expertly and the clear bright silence was shattered as a hundred Rolls horses jostled smokily and then settled to their striding rhythm. The rotor coupler fought for parity and the blade began to swing lazily overhead, gathering its purpose.

Allcock ducked and moved away, waiting for another hand-signal from Lucy before crouching to his transceiver. He spoke again and listened with his ear pressed flat, then he turned towards the frantically vibrating machine. The rotor-wing was now only a pale blur of reflected moon but he could see Lucy's hands taut on the brakes and stick. He gave three rapid stabs of torchlight and the engine noise surged as her hand slid forward on cue.

At full power the brakes began to slip so Lucy released them and felt the fine gravel crunching under the tiny wheels. She kept her heading with rudder towards the pale grey silhouette of the house and allowed the speed to build up longer than usual to increase her safety margin. She hadn't told Allcock it was her first night flight, even when he queried her lack of instrument lighting. She felt her inexperience with a new keenness and wished insanely that she'd had a large Scotch to allay some of her tension.

At nearly twenty-five knots, Decibelle seemed to will her into the air, the trim set slightly back to compensate for a light fuel load. The climb was rapid and she cleared the house with fifty feet to spare. All around, the countryside was dark with trees or gleamed a pale mystery, a mere scattering of lights except for the village, one or two distant cars and off to starboard the first of Giles' two yellow flashing markers, sunk into the earth so as to be visible only from above. Keeping a peripheral watch on them, Lucy banked away to continue her maximum-rate climb, spiralling for height to begin her approach from a pre-calculated distance, three thousand feet and two miles from the wire. As a stab of shrouded torch reflected the altimeter creeping to the mark, her

271

nerves began to scream at her since she knew even the small and spindly frame of the Bensen could be sending alarms already to scurrying radar operators. Her hearing filled with imaginary klaxons and a rattling of breech mechanisms. Still at full power she eased off the climb, levelled out and ran in down the line of yellow lights. She had a moment's fright thinking she could be going the wrong way until the moon on her right reassured her.

She crossed the second light at the autogyro's near-maximum of ninety knots, just over 100 mph, imagining a silent prayer and wave from Giles below. It was hard to keep the belief that the high engine noise didn't reach far ahead until closer than a mile though it was a vital factor since the whole distance didn't thus demand a complete power-off approach with the resultant greater height and conspicuousness. Her eyes now well-adjusted, she was just able to see the opaque airspeed needle in the four o'clock position; keeping it there, she eased the stick forward and steadily reduced power, maintaining her ninety knots in a shallow but steepening dive, aiming to cross the wire in one and a half minutes, at thirty-five feet, flat out and in dead silence. The altimeter unwound palely like the timer in Death Row and over the toes of her fat winter boots she could now see the dark edge of woodland ending abruptly in a line. Immediately beyond it was another line, the second row of wire and then a wide expanse of colourless blank surface bordered with a stand of dark spruce. The parallax of her approach made unfamiliar but eventually unmistakeable the overhead satellite picture she had studied in such apprehensive detail, except there was one lethal exception, an additional feature which would have turned her back in a rotor-breaking turn had her passenger not been waiting helplessly.

The gaunt silhouette of a watch-tower appeared on her left like a message of doom, jolting her with an electric spasm of terror. She was quite certain it had not been on

Hegel's satellite picture, so either she was in the wrong place or the photograph was out of date. Lucy clenched in the helplessness of fury mixed with immutable decision, since it had to be the latter. Committed, her rapid descent continued, the angle steepening towards the wire as all the while the throttle slid back under her thin-gloved hand. At last it ran out of travel and she promptly starved the engine of fuel by leaning and snapped off the magnetos without even any terrified relief. The strip of pared earth and the obscene razor wire were already below and then rapidly, tormentingly behind her. Before seeing the tower most of her cringeing was caused by the engine noise; now she was rigidified in contrast by the tremendous hiss of airflow through the tubular framework and the whupping of the spinning rotor. Her teeth vibrated at high speed while icy air invaded her collar, yet inside her suit she could feel unwelcome perspiration dripping from her armpits. Her forward pressure on the stick continued as the speed started to fall away, forcing it as if to confirm her calculations. She still had perhaps a third of a mile to cover by dwindling impetus alone, all of it over zones that were protective, prohibited or forbidden. She forced her eyes to keep steady on the spruce copse and to resist the sideways pull of the watchtower or any desperate, pointless search for sentries. Her options were now reduced to a virtual nil, to complete the mission or to land anywhere, re-start and make a frenzied retreat. The child would be picked up next morning if there was no confirmatory call and only Nadia would have been racked for nothing. Lucy understood in a new sense the meaning of commitment, wondering starkly if insanity is a pre-requisite for a life worth living.

Still pell-mell, the Bensen now dropped towards the cold earth and Lucy touched her right rudder and stick, easing back slowly all the time. The dark exaggerated the speed as she skimmed only feet above the ground, her glide rate falling off rapidly, the blur of spruce filling the visor frame of her helmet. Level now and back, back on the stick as she watched the earth decelerating just beneath the little nosewheel. The diminishing rate needed only its own judgement; it would run out when the rotor head exhausted its stick-back travel, at which point the machine would cease to fly and must settle like a leaf from a few inches. From too high it would crumple like an old chair, slamming a cell door somewhere for ever.

It happened thus almost by itself and Lucy emerged from her intense bout of concentration in a whimper of bewilderment. The rotor swished lazily overhead and Decibelle sat in frozen stubble twenty feet from the nearest evergreen. Just beyond it she could see the tiny flutter of a luminescent burgee but for a long minute she sat listening rigidly for sounds of alarm behind her. Very cautiously she took off her helmet and looked round. Two hundred yards away the wire stretched blackly in frosty moonlight, the fearsome watch-tower looming only half a mile distant. She took a deep breath of cold, dry air and gingerly removed her straps. At first there was no sound beyond the quiet purposeful swish of the slowing rotor and she forced herself to stand on the hard earth, to believe that no harvested stubble could be sown with mines. From the direction of her approach a dog barked, harsh and sporadic, and panic seemed to lurk like a sadistic escort hoping his prisoner will go for the break.

Expecting a lengthy, troublesome search she was almost amazed to find, just five feet in from the little burgee and without the aid of a torch, a mound of dark clothing. It concealed a large wicker basket and Lucy rummaged layers of blankets until she found warmth. The infant didn't stir as she lifted him out and wrestled the inert form into her breast harness, guiding floppy legs into the slots and then wrapping him doubly with a small

274

comforter. She realised then she had misjudged the size of a two-year-old and that he could certainly restrict the back-travel of the Bensen's control stick.

Tentative with her new imbalance, she crept out of the trees and threw away the burgee flat among the scrub. Decibelle sat in terrible exposure, the rotor almost stopped as she ducked ponderously beneath it. Cradling the child's head she heaved at the nosewheel to face the dark line of the border. Then she crouched and looked carefully all around, her eyes wide and seeking every facet of reflected moonlight.

There was a host of bright stars but no other lights visible and no sound except the constant irritant of the barking animal, a large hound to judge by its bass resonance. It came distinctly from the direction of the watchtower and, as she looked, a light flared briefly. It was enough to show the post manned, predictably enough, yet it filled her with an extra wave of fear. The child seemed to weigh double in a new responsibility and once again she had to force aside any thoughts that were less than useful. With the exhaust towards the trees and their background to shroud a silhouette, she decided that her best bet was not to flee obliquely for the border but to aim initially for the tower until she had speed enough to bank for the getaway. The stubble cracked and whispered loudly round her feet, the whole night eerie with a tremulous fear she thought would stay with her forever. Her shoulders ached more with tension than her burden as she willed herself to move, to begin the fateful sequence. Just the idea of making any noise seemed completely unthinkable and it was as though someone else's hand clicked on the mags, tightened the brakes, engaged the rotor-coupler and eased on a quarter-inch of throttle. She wanted absurdly to squeeze her eyes shut against this other person's deliberate racket as its hand pulled the propeller slowly into a compression stroke, stood away, gathered the child's head tightly, took a

275

deep breath and wrenched the blade downwards. The engine clunked over, bouncing the prop against the next compression but with no sound of ignition. She repeated the action once, twice, three times and the feeling of sickness rose sharply to the back of her throat, almost unhingeing her. She didn't understand engines and had no feel for the tinkering of knowing mechanics. She wondered crazily if the unconscious child could sense her panic as she struggled to think rationally.

Going forwards past the left mainwheel she squeezed the throttle open a little further, certain from its position to expect a roaring over-reaction which she could quell quickly provided the brakes held, unlikely without her weight on the wheels. The feeling of the whole operation getting away from her kept bringing back the nausea. With another taut effort she went back, drew herself together, compressed and flicked the blade down again. In the stillness the effect was far worse than even she expected.

The machine seemed to leap and then slide across the ground against locked wheels. Lucy grabbed at the fluttering rudder and dug in her heels until the movement stopped. She had to let go again to dart quickly forward round the propeller and snatch the throttle back to idle. Relief and a new terror mingled as she clenched for composure and wrestled her encumbered body into the seat and straps. The rotor spun up lazily overhead as she fumbled with the harness and flicked her eyes constantly towards the watchtower. The barking had ceased for her because of the engine noise but she could still see a light and the moon's reflection on some hard surface. At last strapped in, she tested the stick-back range and found she had to shift the child sideways to allow full movement. She realised it shouldn't be necessary except as a desperate last measure.

Still peering ahead, rigid and intent, she gave no thought to anything behind or beside her, knowing that if she looked and found something there she would die before they shot her. She wound on some throttle to hasten the rotor's wind-up and by now she felt enough practised judgement to know roughly when it had reached potential flight speed. When the feeling came she shoved the power full on and slipped off the brakes.

For a moment nothing seemed to happen as the wheels lifted out of a slight furrow, then the Bensen strained forward, the roar of the drive-engine an excruciating, cowering embarrassment. It also caught her unawares as it bucked and leaped over the hard uneven ground, a condition not announced by the almost static touch-down. The stick tugged wildly in her hand as the bouncing chassis struggled against the rotor's inertia, increasing its violence and her fright at the same time. Her hands full, she tried to steady the child's lolling head but only dislodged her helmet against his thick wool covering. There came a vicious thump and suddenly Lucy realised they were airborne before she intended. It was too soon but such a relief that she held back tentatively and just managed to hold it in the air instead of crunching down again. Somewhere ahead a searchlight came on, pointing at first away but then knifing lethally across towards the spruce. Lucy banked carefully left keeping as low as she dared and headed for the dark line of trees marking the far edge of the wire. To her right the glaring white beam rapidly traversed the field and the edge of the copse, although it didn't catch her until she had the actual wire in sight and her speed really building.

The beam pinned her squarely as she rose for the final bid, lost her briefly and then trapped her again. She kept her eyes away from it which saved her from the numbing sight of approaching tracer arcing towards her in lazy parabolas, each phosphorescent blip bracketing another four unmarked but lethal projectiles. The light was bright on her instruments showing her at nearly eighty knots and the drive engine's RPM edging on the red maximum.

277

With everything lost she became calm suddenly, jinking to the right and throwing off the beam for a moment just as the dreaded double wire slipped underneath and was replaced by the dark carpet of the tree tops. Only then did she see further ahead the stream of apparently friendly fireflies leading her way home until with a new spasm of terror she recognised what they were, Russian-made and Russian-fired heavy machine-gun rounds seeking unprotected flesh and a perilously frail machine. From the frame beneath came a double thump, a loud bang as a tyre exploded followed by the high banshee scream of a ricochet. She pulled up sharply and jinked again and then saw a merciful pale opening in the trees, a patch of moonlit grassland leading away. To her dismay the lethal tracer seemed to pour into it but then ceased abruptly. She had a moment's quandary about actually going for it to get her bright-lit profile below tree-level and she jinked left as a kind of test manoeuvre. Immediately she saw more tracer to her right and then heard the rasping tail of fire as an anti-tank rocket scythed past into the darkness, still climbing.

Almost jibbering, Lucy dived for the trees' cover as the tracer stopped quite abruptly. She throttled back at once, certain that her heart was pounding in deadly overspeed just like the engine. The pale and distant horizon seemed to waver and then lost itself in a flash as the armour-piercing rocket connected with something solid near the skyline. Very cautiously she eased up and saw respite and sanity, the two flashing yellow markers manned by a surely terrified Giles in the field below. She wanted to land between them, anything to curtail her torture but realised in time that it was the wrong way to secure their unhindered escape. Tautly she held her line towards her starting point, at last seeing the house, crossing over it and dipping towards the gravel drive, suppressing speed rapidly with power off and a high angle of attack.

In a state of such alarm that his muttering had ceased, Allcock switched on the truck's headlights to give a pale reflection off the chipped stones. Aware that she'd lost at least one tyre, Lucy tried to set up again for a static touch down but it required judgement born of extended practice which she knew she hadn't fully acquired. Her landing on the other side had been particularly lucky but now after the immediate past terror she felt an offhand carelessness about it. In the end she was left with some residual forward motion and the ruined tyre dragged the machine round in a half loop, dipping so the rotor's tips thumped the grass several times before she could cant it away with the stick. She leaned the mixture and cancelled the magnetos at once, expecting sudden silence but instead she heard a car engine starting somewhere beyond their circle of vision. Allcock doused the truck lights and came running with Nadia and the two of them were suddenly pinpointed by another vehicle's headlights. Allcock stopped dead in his tracks but Nadia's priority was absolute.

Lucy called to her and spoke clearly in Russian. 'Yes, I have him. He's sleeping. Who else is here?'

'Oo the bloody 'ell's that, turn yer fooking lights off!' Allcock shouted into the darkness, then he ducked under the still swirling rotor and engaged the spin-up gear to brake it. Caught in the lights Lucy was unbuckling and trying to disengage herself so that Nadia could glimpse her sedated child. A third figure strode into the lighted circle followed by another. Seeing the reflected rimless glasses and the heavy frame, Lucy suddenly recognised the first one with some embarrassment. It took a while to turn into cold fury.

'It's Hegel from Geneva.'

'That's right – Miss Karen. What have you done, something truly crazy! Where is he?'

Lucy's voice cracked as she patted and began to undo her bundle. 'He's here.'

279

'No! Kody, your husband.'

'I told you, far as I know, Czechoslovakia.'

'Don't start it again! We thought you were getting him out, some good reason for the furore you will have made over there . . . What is this, please?'

She answered slowly, her voice peculiar. 'This is Feodor Defector Junior.' With Nadia's silent and almost frantic help, she lifted the child from the harness and handed him to her. The mother was overcome and had nothing to utter but a low continuous keening of the child's name. Unburdened, Lucy turned on Hegel, her fury dampened by exhaustion.

'What the hell was a tower doing there, hey? *Hey*? Your stupendous bloody photograph didn't show any tower there, you must have found me an *antique*!'

Hegel shook his head, mystified. 'They were the ones London sent me, that's all I know. It was all for a baby?'

'As some of us were never?' Lucy controlled herself with an effort, sure that he was telling the truth. 'They fired at me, tracers and rockets, they even hit something. Barney, did you see they were actually shooting, lighted bullets! Peter, will you give us a hand to get her in the truck?'

'Karen,' he said with quiet impatience, 'Come, Mrs Kody, about your husband, Stayres wants him badly, for the Americans, can you – '

'I don't know anything!' Lucy almost screeched, 'I thought he worked for Stayres, maybe it's for someone else. Is it?'

'No, it's true. He was on a small mission, but he's disappeared.'

'You don't bloody say!' she swore back, straining at the leading strut unassisted. 'He phones, right? Every bloody day. That's all I know. I presume from Czecho. Try tracing the calls.'

'So all this, and the photographs, they were nothing to do with him?'

280

'Right. A-and the one without the tower, was Stayres trying to get us killed or was it just carelessness?'

'I could have said, I did really, they *were* old, you could see from the quality. I'm sure it wasn't deliberate – he wants your husband, don't you see?'

'God, I don't know . . . please help anyway, we're illegal in either Germany, we should get the hell away from here, miles away. Find a pub, talk all you like. Yes? Oh, cripes, my knees!'

Lucy collapsed suddenly on the frozen grass, her arms flailing until she jammed them between her thighs. Allcock stood up from his stooping lift at the damaged wheel and the three of them leaned over her in concern.

Lucy moaned quietly. 'Oh Barney, help! I've gone soggy and wet myself. I've sort of run out – literally. Excuse me, gents, I – no, not you!'

Her protest wasn't wholehearted enough to stop Hegel. He bent and lifted her without effort and headed for his car.

'No!' she cried out vehemently, 'The van! And we have to wait at the crossing for Gilesey. Please, put me down and get Decibelle inside, quickly!'

Hegel dithered for a moment and then decisively changed course, lifting her into the truck's cab. Nadia was preoccupied with Feodor and anxiously searching for a pulse. Hegel settled Lucy and went back to where Allcock was heaving at the autogyro unassisted.

'You are all bloody insane,' Hegel muttered savagely, making his great strength tell as Decibelle slid up the ramp. Allcock didn't voice any approval. 'Listen over there and pull a bit 'arder,' he muttered, 'Turbines and heavy rotors, geddit?'

Hegel stopped and listened. '*Scheise!* You're right. Look!'

In the distance, from the sound's direction they could see a powerful rotating beacon and down-pointing

281

searchlight. It dipped out of sight and in the lessened beat they could hear a klaxon wailing.

'Better 'ope that woman has her flashers switched orf,' Allcock said, thinking of Giles' exposure nearer the wire.

Hegel was suddenly galvanised. 'Be quick here, they could follow over and cut loose. It's been done before. They say sorry afterwards. Carl!'

The urgency of his shout brought his colleague running and the three of them hefted the Bensen inside. Allcock quickly bracketed the rotor and hobbled out, slamming up the tail-gate.

'Where to?' Hegel shouted but Allcock was already scurrying round to the cab, swearing furiously. The hunting Mil-24, a huge twin-engine gunship, was checking the wire in sections, pulsating loudly just out of sight. The two vehicles crept away under a half-clouded moon, their lights extinguished. They picked up a white faced Giles at the crossroads with the briefest word for her relief. Hegel shook his head and thumped his wheel in frustration while in the truck Feodor whimpered and tried sleepily to wail.

'You shut up!' Allcock said with such nervous force that Lucy began to giggle, but his expression didn't crack until several miles separated them from the dreaded border and some instant radar-guided nemesis.

'Strewth!' he muttered eventually as they approached a small township and slowed by an inn. '*Bier*. Wot they carry bodies away on, right? Four biers, *bitte*. Strewth!'

There was a huge fire glowing off ruddy faces, frothing *steins* of pale beer and a murderous foreground of oompah-oompah marching brass. Nadia's quivering fright was slowly turning to a shining joy, interrupted by short confusions of tears. Giles clinked her huge glass with Allcock and told of her terror at the threat of the searching helicopter. Waiting for his colleague to fetch their drinks, Hegel took Lucy aside and spoke earnestly, his broad face full of concern.

'. . . simply that they're bound to find out it was you,' he tried to force through her puzzlement.

'How?'

'I shouldn't have to explain after what you saw in Geneva. I told you that stuff was virtually obsolete. They have things up there which can compare junior footprints! You didn't even take the British markings off that – that *thing*, whatever it is, for heaven's sake! It's a terrible affront, they'll have to take revenge. You know what that means?'

His expression had a desperate quality and she suddenly understood. Wide-eyed in a scared question, she drew her finger across her throat. Hegel confirmed with such regret and dismay that she moved to him and seized his lapels.

'My old man's with the KGB,' she said quietly, 'He'll take care of it, don't worry. Are you married?'

'Yes, but – '

'Happy and faithful?'

'Yes.'

'Thank God. This evening you have to resist for both of us.'

'Don't please.'

'All right . . . When you picked me up, I thought I'd sorry – I'm sorry, you're a bit overpowering. Just allow me this.'

Lucy reached her hands behind his hard, broad neck and pulled his face down. She kissed the corners of his mouth in turn and then laid her cheek against his day's growth of beard. His frighteningly solid arms came round her again and lifted as if she were just a bundle of weighty velvet. A heavy Bavarian cheered and thumped him hugely on the shoulder, registering surprise and apology when Hegel stood unmoved and dangerous. Lucy felt like a fragile doll in his hold though with some relief that he was too big and solid for her complete attraction, but as man of the moment he was perfect. Only his worry spoilt it, yet intensified its fleeting nature.

'You're hiding out already, aren't you?' Hegel said.

'Yes. How did you know?'

'Stayres. But he doesn't seem to know where. Does anyone else?'

'No.'

'So get back there quickly and do nothing to expose yourself. I suppose you could try to negotiate, but not yet. Give me a call in a few days. I'll find out if they had a snoop satellite anywhere near at the time, or if I hear anything. If there's no chance of a deal, there might be a call or two I can make. I can't be sure. But do believe me, they'll mean business. What you did was unpardonable.'

'No,' Lucy said in his ear, 'What Nadia's so-called husband did was unpardonable.'

'I don't know about that, but it's beside the point. I know about your father but his position isn't steady. The Border Guards Directorate will be mad for your blood. Look how many lost their lives for a minor infringement of airspace, a whole 747-full. I'm sorry, but your daring was also utter stupidity. Stayres will be furious, with me as well. And me? Well, thank you, I now have to worry myself to sickness and try not to think about you at the same time. Kindly don't think of me, in case I sense it. We should go now, to be seen with you would be our bullet as well.'

He kissed her lengthily inside the collar of her ski-suit while she still held on to his neck. He breathed in and then eased away slowly, setting her down.

'It will take a long soak to wash away the fear,' he said.

'Oh, ugh! Can you tell? And more to come?'

He nodded solemnly. 'For certain. Work fast, before they find you. And let me know, yes?'

She agreed and he withdrew from her abruptly as his colleague joined them. The two drank quickly and disappeared, leaving Lucy on the fringe of her friends, her exploit and her own new fear keeping her a little distant, the memory of Hegel's massive care supporting her tenuous self-possession.

Allcock was highly relieved when as an afterthought Lucy suggested finding a lock-up in Germany for the time being, to avoid any frontier exposure with the autogyro. None of them could have envisaged the full force of the hazard she'd created, for in reaction whole squadrons of jet-fighters were redeployed to front-line continuous readiness, guards were trebled everywhere and the surveillance and chase helicopters were stepped-up in their affronted, unceasing vigilance. Not even a fox or a weasel should change sides of its own free volition.

THIRTEEN

Whoso loves
Believes the impossible.

Elizabeth Barrett Browning

Lucy and Giles resumed their routine with a studied bravado which was partially cheered by a later call to Hegel. He was able to confirm that there hadn't been a Russian planet satellite over their position at the time of the wire-jump and the geostatic early-warning eyes didn't yet fully cover their section. He emphasised ruefully that it was only pure luck and that the KGB could still work out the kind of machine used and sift through the very small number of owners. He found it difficult to be ominous against the tone of Lucy's blithe relief and warned her strenuously to stay in hiding.

Not long afterwards Alicia left a message and Epiphany phoned to relay a news item about a bizarre shoot-out in Carsey, Gloucestershire. Two men had died and the bodies were left with all identification removed. Through Alicia, the telephone engineer confirmed that the 'land-surveyors and badger-watchers' had all gone and the investigations and rumours were crisply snowballing, aided by the Kodys' continuing absence.

Epiphany apologised that he was still tied up in London and asked them to come home for a while. Giles had to answer stiffly that there was yet another reason for them to stay undercover. At first he saw it as a subterfuge and grilled her about *'une affaire de la piste'* and Lucy had to take over the call in support. She accused him of doing something similar in England and he repeated his assurance to join them soon. Lucy's response was as sweetly sarcastic as Giles'.

Alicia was brimming to tell Lucy about the miracle of Nadia's baby, how her parents had smuggled him away and through the border, diverting suspicion from themselves with a great show of hysteria and accusations of cradle-theft. She expected a more satisfied response from Lucy whose main concern was the continuation of Stuart's daily call. Her other piece of news was that a man with a limp had turned up in Carsey and obtained Alicia's number from someone in the pub. His name was Rollo Runyan and he was waiting very anxiously in London for them to return. He had an earnest question about one of the *cocos-de-mer* they had brought back, but Lucy didn't understand. She only reminded Alicia that they'd given one to St George after she had herself had refused it on the grounds of 'indecency'. They were all reservedly mystified that Lucy could still get some reassurance from Stuart's wordless calls but she would shake her head dolefully and explain that it was all she had and that she must somehow keep the faith. Without Giles' support she declared she would long since have become an embittered alcoholic.

In Florida, Texas and Virginia, the *rezidenturas*, agents-in-place, had moved with instructed caution to steal the Americans' AWACS evidence. Not having their own satellite in position was only a temporal drawback for the Soviets and made no difference if the situation stayed short of urgent and in this case the Chief Border Guards Directorate could move with deliberate certainty. It was easier than expected, for after the aircraft type and registration had been relayed to London, it took less than half an hour to trace the owner of the experimental autogyro. She was not at home; Simonov was informed because his team had been keeping watch on the Kodys' house until the South African business was settled. The connection that the owner was also his daughter took marginally longer to make but gave him just enough time to call Alicia with a warning. He was fully aware that it could have been a trap to test his own loyalty.

The message was garbled by the time it reached Lucy because Simonov had given her no details, simply the briefest possible word that she should stay in deep hiding whatever the cost. Lucy couldn't clarify for her mother without adding to her anxiety but she was more than half-full of remorse. What had been no more than a very daring response to a cry from the heart and then a personal challenge had turned sickeningly serious. All she could do was to give Alicia some reassuring patter every day and silently apologise to the absent Stuart for her jeopardy.

For herself she kept up the active distractions and her bold front and the eventual exposure was both unexpected and cruelly undeserved.

On Giles' birthday, Lucy and Gordon took her to dinner at Le Refuge in Tignes Le Lac, a feast of oysters, Muscadet and steak *au poivre*. It was a joyful meal slightly marred by the stares and muttering of two heavy-set Aryan types at a nearby table. Their stares were a marked change from those of the intense white sunlight, under which the resort people exchanged closed looks caused by impersonal black shades or by the suspicious-looking gimlets of tightly-shrunk pupils. These men were open-eyed and deliberate in the gloom and made Gordon quietly furious. He was soon to regret allowing the girls to prevent him making a scene.

After the meal he had to meet some next-day clients in the Bar-2100 so Giles and Lucy decided to walk back to Val Claret across the frozen and snow-covered lake. Half-way over they strayed off the hard path and began to flounder in deep snow which muffled their laughter as well as any sounds of pursuit. Lucy was alerted by a panting just behind her but as she turned she was seized in a powerful grip, crying out and stumbling.

'Run, Gi, get away, quick! I can manage,' she gasped, her first thought being of the KGB's *mokrie dela* terminators. But surely, she thought, they'd have used some lethal silent weapon and not exposed themselves. As a test she spoke quickly, hoarsely in Russian, that he should wait, she had something to tell.

'*Stoi! Vam novosti skazhu . . .*'

'*Hein? Liebchen, nicht verstehn,*' came the leering incomprehension.

With a sigh of relief that it was nothing more than basic assault, Lucy went limp in the man's arms in seeming compliance. Surprised, he relaxed his grip enough to slide a hand inside her jacket. His breath was foetid with beer and there was enough reflected light to see his face. He looked over her shoulder with satisfaction to see his friend catch Giles in a powdery tackle, hearing her cry as the two of them almost disappeared in the snow. Lucy put her gloved hands gently on the man's cheeks and looked at him, watching him relax and begin a triumphant smile, bending for a kiss. He murmured some endearment and reached his hands further, seeking her breasts; very smoothly she withdrew her right hand, bunched the fingers and jabbed him in the throat, in out twice, like a piston. At the same moment she brought her knee sharply into his groin. He exhaled his full capacity of foul breath right in her face and sat down with a defeated grunt. Lucy turned at once and floundered to where she could see the other dark shape wrestling in the snow. For a moment she was at a loss, having never been faced with a prone antagonist and fearful of his reaction against Giles who was completely buried under his striving form.

'Get up. NOW!' she ordered, trying to keep her voice tight and level. His face appeared, the eyes bulging as he turned to look up at her.

'Ernst!' he shouted, looking round wildly.

'He's dead and you're next. Get up!' she almost shrieked but he lunged for her leg, just missing it as she stepped back and sank to her knees again. Suddenly she had time to be afraid; she had no purchase to use any speed and agility, the deep snow reduced her to a clumsy sack and in the full grip of either man she knew she could be overpowered and helpless. She took two paces away and sank deeper but then she heard Giles give a massive gasp with a cry at the end of it; the big form lunged at her and must have used Giles' prone body as a springboard. Lucy was already rolling onto her back, her senses telling what had happened before she could think it out. Whipping her legs up, she lashed out blindly and one of her boot-heels made a solid connection with the oncoming jaw, tearing it right open. Her other leg almost dislocated itself with its unabsorbed momentum.

There was no movement, just the ghostly cold stillness and a rasp of tortured breath some distance away. Lucy felt herself shaking violently.

'You all right, Gi?' she called eventually.

There was a muttered oath from out of sight then Giles' head appeared, hands trying to brush the snow away. 'You did them *both*? How?' she exclaimed in bewilderment. 'Oh God, look!'

The second attacker had a big spread of blood under his head but Lucy rolled away from him.

'I am not interested in his personal problems,' she said, trying to be facetious but her voice was cold. 'The other one's conscious, they can sort themselves out. Let's find that path and get the hell away from here. You all right? I heard a monster grunt.'

'I think so. I thought he'd crushed my ribs. He jumped *off* me!' She vomited with sudden violence and after a moment Lucy followed suit, looking round quickly to see if they were still vulnerable. The two shapes remained where they were, unmoving. Her trained calmness in

290

action dissolved slowly back to character and her fury suddenly welled over.

'Make me leave, Gi,' she said, her voice husky. 'I want to go back and kick their foul faces in, I want to hurt them more, I'm so livid!'

'I know, me too,' Giles coughed. 'The path's to the right somewhere, come on, let's go!'

They floundered quickly away and eventually crossed the even surface cut by the Sno-Cat. Ten minutes later they were back in the apartment sipping brandy and observing each other with pale sympathy, feeling strongly the urge to discuss it all with someone else. Lucy called the 2100 but Gordon had already left; she paced restlessly, put on a tape, changed it for the television, switched it off, ran a hot bath and finally announced, 'Gi, I've got to go back.'

'Back where, England?'

'No, out there.'

'What? Why?'

'If they can't move, they'll die. They're quite certain to freeze to death within hours. They were both heavy, neither would be able to carry the other, not in that snow. So what happens? And if one of them gets off the lake maybe, is he going to start making admissions or is he going to hide?'

'I don't know. We ought to call the Police.'

'We *must* try not to, we'd have to guide them. I should check.'

'I don't see why the hell you should!'

'I know, but it's manslaughter, equals Police and/or jail, anyway enquiries, publicity, discovery. In short.'

Giles accepted the logic and sighed. 'All right, let's go.'

'No, you stay here.'

Giles looked at her solemnly. 'You did it all. I couldn't help you. Where did you learn all that stuff?'

Lucy gave her a pale smile, some of her spirit returning with the decision. 'All Russian children learn to roll in the snow and kick each other half to death. Didn't you know?'

'Hm . . . I'm still coming with you.'

'All right. But keep to the path and be ready to run.'

They found the second attacker without difficulty for he was still unconscious, his head on the same dark stain. The other had gone weaving off in the dark but after a hurried discussion they decided it wasn't sensible to follow, nor so urgent. They went back to Le Lac for reinforcements, finally locating Gordon who had to quell his rage to organise a search party. The walking man was found half-delirious with cold and exhaustion so they had to radio for two 'blood-wagons', stretcher-sledges for retrieving injured skiers. In spite of the girls' pleas to be allowed home, a gendarme had been notified and then prevented by his superior in Val d'Isère from letting them go without a statement, for which an interpreter was required. At first they said vaguely that there'd been a fight, hoping the implications would be obvious and the matter closed but the walking man was brought in and pointed at them with violent gesticulations. He was unable to speak, his hand on a badly swollen throat and he walked round his groin damage with painful caution. The gendarme refused to believe at first that the man could be serious yet he insisted on making a statement, in German, which then had to be translated into two languages. Predictably he accused them of soliciting and having their pimps ready to attack and rob two innocent holiday-makers. After all that, Lucy and Giles were interrogated separately, facing considerable scepticism until the inspector arrived, fortunately with a knowledge of karate and able to vouch for her stances and reflexes. In spite of it all, the outraged assailant insisted on pressing charges which involved counter-charges and more statements, dragging on for hours in mounting tension.

They got to bed very late but still Lucy slept fitfully, fearful of everything and getting up several times. Giles heard her from the other bedroom and called out to ask if she wanted a sleeping pill. Grateful, Lucy went in and sat on her bed, whispering.

'I just want him back, to hold him, just a word or two. Everything's suddenly out of hand, yet up here it's so hard to take a warning seriously. Stuart's really calm, he'd know what to do, I suppose, but it would mean I'd have to tell him, about the border. He'd – oh God, I was going to say kill me, but I think that's what someone else has in mind already . . . what the HELL can he be doing all this time?'

Giles covered her hand. 'Well at least you know he's thinking about you.'

'The calls! It's ridiculous that he couldn't just say a few words – I almost want him to stop doing it, it's like he's pandering to me, fearful little woman waiting by the fireside . . . a bloody single trill isn't much use when you're being set on by some rabid Prussian humanoid, let alone having bloodhounds baying in the Urals.'

Giles didn't answer but held her hand quietly in the dark. Eventually she said, 'You can sleep here, if you like.'

'Thanks . . . I'd like to but I'm full of need. I think I'd find it confusing because of my loneliness. I wanted to assault that man Hegel, you understand?'

'Of course, that's my job, remember? I mean, I'm here if you need me, not some latent predator. Anyway, you're not an undiscovered deviant, so stop worrying.'

Lucy paused a moment and then quickly slipped under the duvet, holding Giles' hand in both of hers, close between her breasts. 'Thanks. That worry dissolved the moment you voiced it. I've grown to love you with such a right, good feeling, but it was beginning to concern . . .'

'I know. "The things that spoil a relationship are the things left unsaid".'

'Who said?'

'I dunno, the wretched Epiphany, probably. It's only sense, though. When you have a real friendship you can only get hurt by misunderstanding. A friend can do no wrong except to be less than truthful. Score yourself ten.'

Lucy said shyly, 'Stuart helped, he's so straight forward. The secrets, well, they're different, they should stay in the games category. I can't really understand him getting into a devious business, may be I just don't know anything of what's going on. Were you Paul's lover before you did his seminar?'

'No, I was a student shrink and wanted to investigate him. Possible thesis. I was really antagonistic, especially after looking into some of the other head-banging cults. He talked me into doing the weekend properly and making me pay, otherwise he said you don't bother to go for the value. I was a bit mortified to find it magical, though I became convinced you have to be stable and intelligent first, to handle it properly. You can imagine my tutors went berserk; any enthusiasm about encounter groups sounds pitifully silly if you're not involved, even pernicious, and they wanted me to state the bald facts of what happened. It's too personal for that, it belongs only to the participants.'

Lucy didn't say any more, overcome by exhaustion and then the contrast of gentle contact. Giles kept almost still as she sensed her sleeping, reaching lips softly to kiss her forehead and smooth her hair, feeling her own need for tenderness.

By the following evening, the men had been persuaded by the Gendarmes that they had no chance with their charges but by that time it had become public knowledge and a news item worth putting on the wires. Rare is the newshound amenable to persuasion by the rabbit-victim who keeps him fed, and in France such a rarity would quickly starve.

Epiphany called two mornings, after the incident, while Giles was out buying fresh bread. 'What the hell?' he shouted, 'I thought you were in hiding and there's your name and whereabouts in several papers. You OK? It says you claim to have fought them off, hell, couldn't you do something quiet?'

'I'm afraid that's done it,' Lucy answered, trembling but still ironical. 'I suppose we should have been raped or just let them die.'

'Sure . . . who's after you, tell me!'

'Paul, I'm sorry. It's the KGB, Border Guards. I pulled a stunt and it's not forgiveable.'

'What sort – never mind. Look, we can't protect you there, this has just broken, we should be OK for twelve hours at least. We'd better shift you across the water . . . I'll get clear here and meet you in Paris. Order a car for after dark.'

He rang off and Lucy saw her hands were trembling where she'd been mechanically fitting recharged batteries into her personal stereo. She wondered if Alicia had also seen the article and been trying to get in touch with them. She called the answering machine, voiced the code and after the windback she heard her mother speaking in Russian which had become unusual between them.

In agitation she waited out the message. '*Liouba*, knowing your feelings I wouldn't normally allow this but he insisted absolutely on speaking to you. Please call your father at this number in Antwerp. Then tell me what's happening.'

Lucy assumed that her father wanted to tell her to run but just possibly he might have some solution or escape clause to offer. In fact the Soviets had not yet reacted to a clue as obvious as a newspaper article.

As she looked up the code she heard Giles step out of the lift and open the door, a long baguette under her arm and holding a slab of fresh farm butter. She nodded to her distractedly and heard her go into the bathroom, the water running loudly.

The voice answering growled hello and added, '*Qui parle?*'

'I want to talk to Mr Simonov, please.'

'*Un moment, s'il vous plaît.*'

She waited fidgeting and puzzled, urgent for relief, then her father came on the line, the resonant voice missed and well-remembered. He knew better than to attempt a soft preamble.

'Ludmilla, I asked you to call because I didn't want to relay it through your mother, it would be worse, if that's possible. I have tragic news for you, I'm afraid. I'm very sorry.'

As she slowly absorbed this slight buffer and realised it could only mean one thing, Lucy sank to the floor, her eyes glassing over like a mortally wounded animal. When she tried to clear her throat only a strangled sound issued and it was half a minute before she could speak properly. Simonov waited in his own agony.

'Wh, why do we always want to know when, where, how?' she asked distantly, 'What does it matter? Oh, *Papochka*, if you knew how I loved him . . . I suppose you'd better tell me.'

Almost choking himself, Simonov answered, 'Prague, Czechoslovakia. It was . . . more than three months ago, we were looking for him all that time but without much of a clue, and then— '

'Who killed him?' Lucy almost screamed, 'Who was it, TELL me!'

'No one. It was reported suicide – while in custody.'

'NO! He would *never* do such a thing, don't tell me that!'

'I agree it doesn't sound in character. I've only got the Prague STB report to go on, relayed through Moscow. I would like to be with you now, just to be there.'

'I . . . thank you. Did they bury him in Prague?'

'No, he was cremated.'

To a moan of profound despair, Lucy's hand released the receiver and left it dangling from the hall table. In a daze of not knowing whether to run or hide, she turned and grabbed her skis, slipped out into the waiting lift and was gone.

Moments later, in response to the raised voice, Giles came out of the bathroom and called to her, seeing the receiver swinging and the open door. Cracklings still issued from the telephone so she picked it up and listened, puzzled by the accented but accurate English.

'. . . no enquiries so they didn't bother to inform anybody. If only he'd told someone where he was going . . . They said he was limping, there was something wrong with his right knee, might have affected his driving because he bumped the car, did a bit of damage. What's so stupid is that all he had to do was hand it in and say sorry but apparently the radio was missing. He tried to get on the plane without telling anyone. The word was out and they stopped him at the airport. He went crazy there, they told me, so they put him inside too cool off, but without taking his belt. And . . . well, I won't go into it. It's mystery, not the sort of thing for a trained jet pilot to fly off the handle like that . . . I'm just chattering to keep with you, *galoupka*, you don't mind?'

Giles interrupted, 'I'm sorry, this isn't Lucy. She seems to have gone out. Do I gather . . . yes, I do, I take it you were telling her some very bad news?'

'Who is that speaking?' Simonov asked in pained surprise.

'Giles Raintree. I'm her sort-of flatmate.'

'Oh, the doctor. It's yours then the answering service? Where are you calling from?'

'Who am I talking to?'

'Her father.'

'What? In Russia?'

'No. Listen, if she ran out you'd better go after her, she's going to be very distraught. I want to know where she is, I want to come to her.'

'I'm sorry,' Giles said chokingly, 'She's been in danger, I can't tell you.'

'I know. She still is. Find her and ask her one thing more, in his memory if you like: did he ever tell her his other information, perhaps it could save her. Ask her for me, about the missiles, he had something else, could be worth more than a life, if she knows.'

'Eh? Oh hell, you sound like another of those filthy tricks outfits. Can't you leave that stuff out of it?'

'No, I'm afraid not. If I get that from her, I might be able to call off the dogs.'

'Well, she's probably past caring. I'll see if I can find her. Does she know where to call you?'

'Yes, she just did. Her mother doesn't know yet, tell her that, will you?'

'OK . . . why . . . never mind, you must be hurting too, I guess. I'll catch her. Goodbye.'

Seeing Lucy's skis gone, she hurriedly donned her own kit, finding things with difficulty because her eyes were full of tears. Her feeling for Lucy had grown so strongly of late, a mixture of motherly, sisterly and something else which she'd avoided defining beyond a vague idea of empathy. The feeling surfaced of a sudden that she could, although a very different character, put herself in Lucy's mind and know what she would probably do. She would go and find the most treacherous off-piste challenge and hurl herself full-speed into it with a surge or a scream of raw defiance, willing the mountains to take her life if they chose and thus her misery along with it.

But which way? Two choices, she decided quickly, either the nearest chair to the Tovière, flat out down the red run through the Picheru basin and down to the Piste Perdue or . . . the Wall where two people had died only a week before . . . think, think, she wrestled with herself, finally snapping on her boots.

Rushing out, she crashed into Gordon in the doorway, pulling him into the elevator with a rapid explanation and her surmise.

'Which do you think?'

'She wouldn't hurt anyone else,' he said at once, 'so she wouldn't take the Perdue, she'd be sure to hit a slow-poke with no room to pass . . . but since the deaths, they've fenced the top of the wall and she'd see it on her way up.'

'But she wouldn't just go off it, Gordon!'

'I dunno . . . I reckon she'll go up the Motte, over the ridge and take one of those vertical gullies. Snow's thick, and they've started detonating the avalanches, but only the east side so far. She wearing her pink outfit?'

Giles nodded and hurried after him in awkward strides. When they reached the lifts only one cabin line was running and the queues already stretching to at least fifteen minutes. Gordon barged through the ski-school priority lane, winked at the huge lady inspecting passes, stopped a whole family and dumped the two pairs of skis in the side boxes. They were on their way almost abruptly.

The parallel lift started up then and after a few more pylons their own stopped in the shadow of the hill. It was very cold and their intermittent stamping seemed to heighten their frantic impatience.

Gordon voiced for them both. 'If she's on the other line she's way ahead. If she even went this way.' He strained his eyes upwards, vainly trying to penetrate the prior cabins. 'So what happened?'

Giles repeated Simonov's words and Gordon scowled heavily.

'Seems out of character, too sneaky, trying to sidle off just because of a shunt. He was bluff and open.'

'You knew him well enough to say?'

'Well, maybe not, but I'd guess so, yeah.'

'Trouble is, it doesn't make him any less dead, whatever your opinion.'

'Right. I guess the main thing's to find her, keep her steady till she can work through it.'

'Too damn precious,' Giles said, her eyes brimming again.

Gordon nodded with his firmly shut, willing the wretched lift to get started again. They swayed in cold silence over the trap of a fifty foot drop but at last the car started, moving so gently it was like teasing. Gordon growled his frustration that there was no means of accelerating the climb. As they left the half-way point where the cabins transfer onto the second cable, Giles pointed to a distant figure making the long trudge over the Wall, towards the top of the Grande Balme. It was too far to see colours and Gordon shrugged nervously, pointing to several others at intervals behind it, the early deep-snow enthusiasts looking for steep and maybe lethal unblemished acres. He drummed his feet, grimacing.

'Well, we know she can handle it, but that's when she's been relaxed and not pressing. And it's early: by ten o'clock there'll be instability there . . . You get evaporation underneath and the new fall can sit almost on a rising air-cushion, ready to slide away.'

'Please don't,' Giles said quietly. 'I wonder if they've got some binoculars at the top?'

He nodded. 'But if they make us wait, forget it. I think that's where she'll be.'

At the top they scrambled from the cabin and ran clumsily up the steps, their skis clashing in the tunnel. Gordon managed to get some binoculars and trained them away to their left. Giles fastened her own and laid out his skis for him, guiding his boots into the bindings.

He clicked down, handed the glasses back to an incurious lift-man, grasped his sticks and said 'I think so. Let's go.'

As they poled themselves half-running across the initial flat, he added, 'She must have gone like hell down there, to be that far ahead.'

He had no time for more as the ground fell away and they barrelled off the Côte at reckless speed. Gordon was intent and primed with purpose but Giles' less honed instinct quickly let her down and she took a long, crashing fall. By the time she'd recovered he was half a mile ahead, punishing the first part of the *Face* piste, hunched down and frequently airborne. Giles followed more slowly, staying in control, reminding herself how useless would be another casualty and then tensing in deep alarm to have used such an expression.

Lucy wanted solitude or oblivion, she couldn't have said which in her confusion, just anything to ease the grief that had become a sickening physical pain, an organism in disarray. There were three people ahead of her, however, already trudging the high ridge and one or two others behind. She resolved to go on further, to lose sight of everybody, feeling the wound working at her spirit like a blunt saw. In one attempt to overcome it, she switched on her stereo and heard enormous, sombre, over-bearing bass sounds in a minor key, the end of a number she vaguely recognised. She panted harshly in the thin air but her eyes were dry behind the goggles and she was overheating from her relentless efforts. The next track was fast and frivolous so she turned the volume right down, looking impatiently ahead for the three in front to choose their take-off point, to leave her with the mountain and her growing sense of madness. Thoughts of her mother and of Giles, the hurt she might do them, kept trying to intrude but she willed them away, sadly mindful of her former brave and perhaps glib attitudes, the acceptance of life's changes without fear or regret, and finding them crumbling away to nothing.

'How do you deal with this one, blithe Epiphany?' she thought with bitterness, realising they had only been words spoken to herself in ignorance, she had never really calculated with the possibility of losing her love. 'No, I don't pity myself,' she muttered out loud, 'But I don't care for any moralising. I'm gone, stunned, out of it . . .'

The leaders rounded an outcrop and waited on the edge of a broad defile, their breath steaming, checking their pockets, glasses and boot clamps. As Lucy passed them they called out to her in French, whether compliments or teasing she didn't hear. She went on and on punishing her super-fit legs until the climb became too steep to avoid pointless backsliding and too slow to sidestep any higher. Looking to the right she caught her laboured breath for a moment, seeing the sickening drop of more than seventy-five degrees, hundreds of feet down a perilously narrow *couloir*. It looked no more than about twenty feet wide and would also need an accurate traverse in the middle to clear a jumble of rocks which blocked the fall-line.

For several minutes she looked at it as her personal Eiger, as though offering herself and the whole of her store of courage to the fates and leaving all the rest to their devious whims. The snow was very thick and overhung the higher ridges like rough cake-icing. She didn't think about an avalanche and wouldn't have cared, feeling now almost exultant in her new-found skill that such a dramatic exit was available. She looked back and saw that her afterguard had already gone, zig-zagging their swings in joyous parallel down into the great white bowl. The sun was well over the Eastern ridge, its heat in her face as a warning but still she waited, her body cooling quickly in the dry sub-zero air. Distantly another figure trudged in rapid steps, sticks waving and she fancied that it was also moving to some private music.

Abruptly she turned up her little stereo, gripped her stick handles and dropped over the edge, no fear, no glee, no feeling, only the automatic balance, weight even on both skis, shumf-shumf-shumf, edge to edge on the absolute brink of control and with such a sudden clear detachment she hear the words of the song, Dire Straits' *Love over Gold*.

With a shriek of refusal at the line 'Throw your love to all the strangers' but committed to the fall, her thigh muscles strained to the limit, Lucy arrowed past the jagged rock obstacle, turned, forced out her heels and cranked her knees into the mountain. She stopped in a deep flurry and wavered in precarious balance, clairvoyante, jubilant and yet still baffled.

'He's not DEAD!' she screamed and the bare rock walls above echoed the last word in mockery 'dead, dead.' Typically she changed it and won, shouting louder, 'He's NOT!' The Not-Not reply seemed to satisfy her, to vindicate her feelings so tortured that she could believe without evidence and suppress her own certainty, backed up by his daily calls. It wasn't as if the calls had recently ceased with his dying because that was stated a three months before and the immediacy of the news had confused her.

She heard a long shout from above; looking up she recognised the hurrying figure from before, Gordon's white sleeveless anorak and his woolly deerstalker. He was gesticulating furiously with one stick, indicating movement. Not understanding, she waved to him in a huge relief, feeling a strange giddiness, a kind of ethereal unreality which almost sluggishly turned to terror as the near-vertical surface suddenly accelerated in admission of its mischief. Lucy thrust and pointed her skis straight down and tried to fly the moving surface but it seemed to vapourise and she disappeared under what felt like a flurry of body blows, tumbling weightless, disorientated. She felt this ultimate irony like a pitiless flaying. Stuart

303

is alive and I'm dying, is alive, is alive, she said over and over, the frantic bare seconds of white drowning seeming to last for hours.

When the avalanche stopped Gordon saw no sign of her and wavered in a small quandary of going to find helpers or searching at once on his own. He launched decisively off the ridge and scythed into the gully, deciding to prod his own path down from where she'd been standing, blessing the rocks for a marker. He was saved from hours of desperation by a tiny red triangle barely showing about two hundred yards down where the slope's angle decreased slightly. It disappeared as he watched but crunching his turns he followed the spot un-blinking, knowing the near-impossibility of climbing back if his hunch was wrong. Then he saw it again, just the tip of one ski and he knew he could save her. His relief was so great he almost fell on it, scrabbling the loose snow aside, shaking the ski to show he was there.

It took him two or three frantic clawing minutes just to free her legs but her other ski-tip had to be buried deep beyond her head. She was hanging downwards with one leg bent behind her, the ski parallel to her body. Her mouth and nose were full of snow and her breathing stifled. Her first and correct reaction when the tumbling stopped was to draw in her arms so she could clear a breathing space in front of her mouth but then she found she was too winded to use it. She became aware of which way was down only slowly as the blood pressure built up in her head, while her legs were over-stretched in a wrenching fore-and-aft splits which she couldn't alleviate because of the snow jamming her skis. She remembered you were supposed to make swimming motions during the slide but by now it was far too late. There was no light, no air and no respite until she felt the blessed relief of someone's tugging.

Gordon worked in alternating frenzy and care, hoping the deeper ski hadn't damaged her eyes or face, while his own position was awkward and precarious, the snow deep and soft, at an acute and still dangerous angle. Finally he was able to burrow a hand down in front of her face, clearing an open passage for air. He checked it for bloodstains before removing her skis and then levering her upright. Normally a calm professional he understood then why surgeons mostly refuse to operate on their loved ones.

He heard Giles arrive, stopping cautiously off their fall-line and approaching with a series of steps and sideslips. She called out anxiously.

'Yes, breathing,' he answered, taking off his glove and clearing Lucy's face. Her goggles and hat were missing, her hair soaked and every fold of clothing jammed with snow. 'Keep your skis on,' he said to Giles, 'It's tough to get started again in this. Soft and loose.'

Lucy made a sound somewhere between a sob and a sneeze and quickly tried to sit up. Opening her eyes she was blinded by the brightness and threw up an arm.

'You're supposed to be singing, come on, choirs of angels!' she spluttered, brushing heaps of snow away and then raising her arms to conduct. '"Bring me my bow of burning—"'

She coughed to a stop when she saw the deep concern on their unsmiling faces. 'Sorry . . . It's just I realised I don't believe it. Gi, the phone calls, Mother said they were still going on, but anyway . . .'

Giles didn't want to repeat Simonov's suggestion that Stuart might have had a stand-in but she couldn't help looking doubtful. 'Well, maybe he— '

'Got someone else to do it? You mean if he was out of touch somewhere? That's it! But then he'd have had a reason, wouldn't he? He'd have arranged it, knowing he wouldn't be able to call himself.'

To Giles the flawed logic was obvious. 'But Lucy, your father said they'd— '

'I know, suicide. That's the lie, do you see? They're

trying to trap me, probably without telling Papa, they'll have fed him a lie. But anyway, the main thing is that I don't believe it, I just don't feel it, I just realised my sadness was, well a kind of projection, like I can feel a real sadness at the thought of, say, Alicia one day not being here. But she is. And so is he! It's funny, it was the Dire Straits made me think of it, they had another song about Romeo and Juliet. One of the lovers doing something drastic thinking the other was – I've just thought of something.'

Gordon interrupted. 'Pinkie, you'll stiffen and freeze. We ought to be getting you down.'

'Yes, all right, but listen: what's it called when someone tells you a lie and you don't know it, or rather you ignore the feeling and later, when you find out the lie, you get a funny sensation that you knew at the time there was an untruth, something in the air, I don't know, call it retro-sussing. St George too, he was avoiding something when he flew us out here . . . I think St George knew what Stuart was up to, he's probably in on a secret and can't tell. Epiphany too, he knows something different.'

'Then how— ?'

'Hah!' Lucy said, reaching for a ski, 'You can deal with Paul. I am St George's arch-wheedler, you can just leave him to me. Gordie, I lost both my sticks and the stereo, should we dig around or do they scatter?'

'Offering to the mountain,' he said shortly, 'Forget 'em. Take my sticks. Let's just get off this hill before it decides to have another go. Luckily you were near the top. If you hadn't stopped when you did, you'd . . . You feel OK now?'

She nodded vigorously and shook out her hair, then struggled awkwardly with her bindings on sinking skis; but their descent was almost joyous in carved and synchronous short swings until they could rejoin the fresh piste and pour on the speed again.

*   *   *

St George was in a fever of anxiety, impatience and excitement. Five days previously, his secretary had received the call he'd been hoping for during a baffling three months. It wasn't Stuart's voice, however, but a defined guttural male accent which asked for confirmation of his name and then said one single word: 'Scramble.' A few moments later, the same caller had enquired about Lucy and been reassured.

St George cancelled all his charters and readied both himself and Barney Allcock for a flight to an airfield as yet unspecified whence the second code call was promised. He made his secretary and Allcock so jumpy when it failed to come that they finally insisted that he went back to work, still under his alias. As a result, Lucy took more than half a day to find him, interrupting a quick turn-round in the Hebrides.

'Hair?'

'Biggles, it's Lucy. Where did Stuart go, you have to tell me. Was it Prague?'

'God . . . Listen, I can't tell you, it was, you know, hush.'

'St G., I was told this morning that he died there three months ago, so don't mess around. I'm stretched right out.'

'He can't have . . . who told you that?'

'Indirectly, the KGB. They say he committed suicide, last November or December.'

'God. That's not possible, I assure you, unless— '

Lucy forced her voice down but couldn't contain its vehemence.

'I KNEW it! Just tell me why not, by all that's decent, *please*!'

St George had a horrified speculation which was to plague him for days after, that Stuart had been tortured for the code-word and that for some obscure purpose someone alien had sent it. Then had come a second message denying him encouragement for Lucy.

307

'Poor thing, most frightfully sorry . . . Listen, actually, I'm in a bit of a stewmer myself. I got a message he was coming out but that was ages ago. I should have heard a second message shortly after, same day really. Nothing happened, it was awful, then much later another call, foreign accent again, something about a technical problem but the call was cut off.' Over Lucy's shrill protests he said, 'Where can I call you as soon as I hear?'

'France.' She gave him the Tignes number, no longer caring about security. 'St G., you have to tell me exactly where he is, what's going on, what could have gone wrong. You HAVE to!'

St George cleared his throat for a long as he could make it last, giving in inevitably. 'All right, now you know I know, I suppose . . . Listen, we had this plan, we were going to pick up an aeroplane but he's been gone three months instead of days, I mean his papers must be way out of date and so now he can't get out any other way, d'you see? It's a bit of a nail-biter, frankly.'

'Just stop gabbling and tell me how to find him.'

'I can't, well, only indirectly. I have one name, Louis Mišek, and one phone number. There's a museum in Kbely, that's just outside Prague . . .'

Lucy listened and jotted carefully, still without being given the full picture. When St George had finished she said coolly, forcefully, 'Can you put me on to Allcock now, please?' St George made an abrupt, affronted sound but after a long pause she heard Barney Allcock's tentative ''Ullo', clearly suspicious of the instrument.

'Barney? Bensen used to make an overhead control column instead of a stick, remember? Do you think you could rig Decibelle like that for me?'

'Wur, yus Miss, take a bit of time and the machine's not 'ere, it's still in Krautland. Wot for?'

'Space. I may need more room.'

There was a pause and Allcock spoke with deep suspicion. "Ow much more room, Miss Lucy, you mean like another bod?'

'Yes, Barney, but bigger than last time. Full sized.'

'Gawd, Miss, you can't be doing that, there's yer weight an' balance schedules, be all over the shop.'

'Can't we lean backwards or something? We'd be three hundred pounds maximum, that's like one fatty, I know she can lift that, we can lighten up on everything and may be get a long run up.'

'Strewf, Miss, you'd 'ave to be bloody desp'rate. Better I widen the seat, keep that weight back, and extend the rudder bar. Fookin' dodgy, beg pardon. 'Aven't you chanced enough?'

'No, not quite. And can you hush the engine down, make it really whisper?'

'Shouldn't, see, silencers cut the efficiency. 'Sides, it's the prop makes the racket.'

'I know, I'll keep the revs down for that, don't worry.'

'Don't worry?' Barney almost squealed at this absurdity. 'Where you going this time?'

'I'm not sure, I'm going to recce first and find out. Can I employ you again, Barney, ask you to go to Germany and get things ready? . . . Thanks, OK, call me when you've fixed somewhere to stay and I'll be right over.'

When she called Hegel at the Geneva Embassy, the soft heavy voice stirred her again. She explained her wish to go to Prague and after he'd referred to London and called back he seemed almost suspiciously co-operative. He assured her she'd have papers and visa and a flight booked the following day and that he'd meet her at Cointrin airport himself. Lucy didn't even hint as to how she'd get Stuart out when she found him, little knowing that London's priority was not the confirmation of Stuart's death so much as the continued existence of Miloš Procházka.

309

Fascinated, Giles observed the clarity and determination of a high-spirited and bright young woman researching the possibilities of something entirely insane, calling for courage or carelessness of a preposterous order. She knew that Lucy, after her too recent tilt at death, must be skirting the very borders of sanity; she showed no signs of blundering, however, and was calmly fixed on going into Czechoslovakia, finding Stuart, getting him to a place where she could then come back and ferry him out. With the KGB Border Guards already seeking her for the previous infringement, Lucy shrugged away the notion that she could make things any worse. It was beside the point.

That night she slept again sharing Giles' bed but in the graveyard hours woke her friend with a series of terrified whimpers. In a small quandary, Giles reached a comforting hand but elected not to wake her, thinking Lucy might benefit in catharsis of her particular torment. To wake and find the horrors imaginary, distorted and then dispersed can be wonderfully relieving; she didn't know that Lucy's nightmare was all of the future, all unfulfilled and ending in watery disaster as winter came late to Central Europe.

For Lucy they were lined in a frozen field all silently imploring or accusing, Alicia, Hegel, Stayres, St George, Giles and even gentle Gordon. They stood as if at a wake while Allcock ran his checks and then flicked the drive propeller on a whispered 'Contact!'

The silenced Rolls swished in the conspiring night and Decibelle took to the dream's frosty air like a sinister gadfly, skimming the evil wire unheard and unseen, lower than a Cruise missile, turning and quartering back and forth in the prohibited zone waiting for the signal, a smooth place to set down with cover for the machine. At last a clearing next to a dark forest, crisp bright in a half-moon and new-fallen snow. Set up for landing, the power reduced to an owl's hushed passing, terror

310

mounting but a perfect touchdown . . . something wrong! A check on the harness with no forward movement, the nose-wheel settling, and still settling, a cracking all around, seeing and hearing the reason at the same ghastly moment, an ominous crushing round the tiny wheels as they subside into the pale surface of a huge, barely-frozen tarn. She tore off the harness and slithered clear, hoping the machine might survive without her weight, herself disappearing at once into black and gasping cold, surfacing in dead shock to the violent hissing of the engine's death throe. Barney's anguished face was superimposed on the image as the still-spinning rotor clashed with broken ice and steaming water, swirled like a dying reptile and was abruptly stilled.

She whimpered her despairing way in cold gripping tight as a vise towards too-distant trees, sheets of ice collapsing beneath her progress, combined with her dark clothes to impede her movement, looking back over the pond's surface to see only a broken hole and the trail of her desperation. Forward again and the bank lined with soldiers dressed in green, their rifles raised and the Officer giving the order, Take Aim! But his voice is Czech, '*Zamiřit!*' and she had a violent final contraction, understanding words never known to her.

She is seized by an *ex machina* hand, a saviour who turns out to be the beloved Giles, sweet, warm and fragrant, clutching her shivering form and gentle with platitudes. Lucy never even woke and not till the morning did Giles remind her of her only words: 'They can't shoot me, I don't speak the language. Tell them!'

Lucy had looked at her in bewilderment, snatches of the dream returning and then she smiled.

'*V Rossii, tolshchina l'da nadezhnaya.*'

'Now what does that mean?' Giles asked wearily.

'It means, in Russia there's no doubt about the thickness of the ice.'

FOURTEEN

'With luck we will never find out how the Apache shapes up against the Hind.'

Flight International, 10 Sept '83

A dog barked, timid and distant, a hesitant response to the night-sundering echo from Louis' blunderbuss. At first almost paralysed with terror, Stuart had forced himself forward and ducked late under the wing, almost braining himself. Whimpering to his knees he used both arms to lift her inert form, expecting to expose multiple wounds, though his hands stayed dry. He felt her stirring and then try violently to wrestle away.

'No! Where is – Let GO of me, I'll kill you, give him to me, NOW!'

Unspeakably relieved and suddenly fearing damage to either of them he let go of her and she scampered back, trying to tuck herself between two straw bales. Stuart moved forward and knelt in front of her, his heart pumping in a shredded mix of emotion.

'Lucy, Lucy!' he kept calling to her and repeating his own name but she kept her arms up in defence, as if warding off dark forces. Her fright must have caused shock, primed as it was by the unintelligible screeching of the imprisoned Palaček. She whimpered another protest when he spoke to Louis so he quickly translated for her.

'I asked him to shine the torch on my face. There, look! Can you see me, Lucy?'

312

Peering cautiously over her arms she cried, 'Oh God! Stuart . . . here please, hold me, I'm so sorry . . .'

As Stuart folded her to him he heard Louis ask, 'Who is this woman, Stuart? Not your wife?'

Stuart nodded solemnly to the old man stopping his anxiety. He almost whimpered to her, speaking rapidly, realising then that Lucy didn't understand. 'Please tell her I'm sorry about the gun. I – '

Stuart nodded quickly and translated; after a long pause Lucy said, 'I had a dream I was being shot by Czechs. And Stuart, it didn't smell like you at first, you know, please forgive me.'

Stuart was long accustomed to the different scent of the student's anorak, realising at the same moment that Lucy was also unrecognisable to his own nostrils. He held her and soothed her gently, finally attempting a light remark.

'Frankly, it's not your scent either. You smell a bit like the Horse and Groom in Carsey on a Friday night.'

'Thanks.' She nodded in the torchlight, sadly and slowly. 'What an identification! So we never go on Fridays. Who's holding the light, is it Mišek?'

'Yes, how did you know?'

'It's how I came here. Was that him screeching inside the house?'

'No, that was Palaček, trying to give us away. So how did you find me, and WHY? Lucy, what the hell *is* this?'

'Oh, don't be cross,' she said with complete exhaustion. 'I . . . missed you. I was going to come and get you out. First, my beloved ex-father told me you were dead, said you hanged yourself in a cell in Prague. Then St George got your messages . . . Listen! We have to get away from here, quickly. I met the Kbely man and he told me there was a big alert on, he hadn't been able to help you, he was really scared. Later he sent a boy to my room to tell me I was being followed, then I discovered my papers had all been nicked. I left everything and got out through the building works, see, I wasn't going to come here till tomorrow. A cabby took all my pounds and smoked like a tramp steamer. He kept pointing in the mirror and saying "Cheka", I don't know if he just wanted more money. Anyway, he took about thirty quid and I jumped out in a place called Kladno. He did a lot of shouting after me.'

'Kladno, that's only about twelve kilometers away! When? when was this?'

'Only twelve?' Lucy said with affront. 'I ran most of it. I'm pooped. I suppose about an hour ago.'

'Here, help you up. Come in the house – mind your head here.' He tapped the underside of the wing of the almost invisible Spitfire, realising from her lack of remark that she hadn't seen it, probably crawling into the barn in great fear. He walked her carefully to the house in both arms, Louis lighting the way with a dimming torch. Stuart explained there was a power cut as the old man got busy lighting candles, Lucy startled to see Palaček's eyes reflecting from down on the floor, narrow with disappointment. Louis had a strange defeated expression and started undoing his jacket with gloomy finality.

In the continuing tension Lucy asked, 'Please someone tell me what's going on? Why is that man lying there tied up, was he the shouter?'

Stuart put his hand on her arm and looked at Louis. 'I'll tell you in a moment, lovey, please hang on.' He moved to the old man's side and said quietly, 'Louis, there's no change. We don't have a weight problem with the guns out, only space. She's small and extremely flexible. It's been done before, two in the front.'

'It has?' Louis didn't hide a knowing sarcasm.

'Yes, I read about it. A pilot landed in the desert next to his shot-down buddy, picked him up. One pushed the stick and rudder, the other the throttle and trim.'

'Both pilots, and they'd never have closed the hood.

314

Jára told me of another, that's why I was going in the back. A pilot and his friend in England, they took off all right but they didn't come back. It was after a party.'

Lucy said quietly from her isolation, 'You know I don't understand?'

Stuart nodded but continued in Czech. 'Louis, we all go. There's no choice. They're looking for her as well.'

'Three's impossible.'

'Louis, if I have to truss you up like Paláček, I'll do it! You're coming or they'll execute you. You *wanted* to come, remember?'

Louis nodded slowly, heavily, and then refastened a token button. 'Please tell her I'm sorry she was shocked by the gun. I hope I missed the aeroplane as well. Ask her if she'd like some tea.' His tone changed to a feigned bitterness. 'And ask her too, why is she not at home making babies for you like a proper woman.'

With only a hint of a smile Stuart translated, watching Lucy look round and bend to the fire. She found the poker and began stirring up a small blaze.

'Then remind him,' she said. 'That it takes two? Look, please, what is actually going on here? I think we must get away, they'll be combing the countryside. You were both fully dressed, were you just going out, you and Mišek? He looks a bit formal – have I wrecked anything?'

The old man glanced up at his name and Stuart saw he was wearing a black jacket turning green with age, a frayed dress shirt with an old silk tie bearing a bold *Croix de Lorraine*. Paláček watched them balefully from the floor but Louis didn't even glance in his direction.

'Nothing formal, Lu. We were hoping to leave at dawn, and it's the bottom line for all of us. Let's eat something first and I'll fill you in.'

She nodded and adjusted the kettle on the fire where it soon began popping its complaints. Watching her, Stuart

315

felt a terrible surge of emotion, so much love and fear for her it must affect his vision and judgement. Quietly he added, 'There's a biggish risk, Lucy. I was going to take it for a reasonable reason but now there's no choice, for any of us.'

Lucy shrugged. 'That fine with me, if you just come home.'

'Dear God, if you knew how I've been longing. You kept me alive, I think you must *be* my life.'

She looked up at him stilly from her crouch by the fire; there was mud on her jeans and she was draped hip-length with a thick dark jersey. The scarf had fallen round her neck and her tawny hair shone in the candle-light like a mirage. He knew she was about to speak or rush to him and fear came back in a rogue swell. He nodded abruptly to break the moment, glancing at the clock.

'We should eat and move out,' he said, 'Details later.'

'Oh Stuart, you're not saying enough to me . . . St George muttered something about an aeroplane.'

'I know, I'm sorry, Lu. We've almost had to bar discussions ourselves, Louis and I. It's been very bad on the nerves . . . Anyway.' He nodded reassuringly and pointed to the table. With a shrug of trust, Lucy sat and began slicing at a loaf of hardening bread while Stuart crossed the room to the pile of manuals, picking out the well-thumbed Pilot's notes, flicking till he found the drawing of the starboard cockpit-side. He laid it on the table in front of her and slid a candle over.

'Can you see to read the key and numbers?' he asked her.

There was enough of the panel showing for Lucy to recognise the engine instruments. She leaned forward suddenly in alarm, for the drawing and its quality were far from up-to-date.

Before she could remark on it, Stuart said, 'It's true, it's an aeroplane, but an old single seater. I think we

316

can do it if you sit on my right hip with your left thigh up across my stomach, has to be clear of the stick.'

Lucy's exhaustion and now concern had stifled all her usual playfulness and she peered closely at the drawing and legend as Stuart continued. 'Your other leg can stretch out on mine, down on the right. Behind your back'll be these two important controls I won't be able to reach, flaps and undercarriage . . .'

She didn't look up at him or play any games of disbelief and when he'd finished she repeated it all accurately. Her tone was still far from playful when she added her ironical contribution.

'Piece of cake,' she said, shaking her head in contrast. 'And what will you be doing all this time, pray?'

Stuart grimaced palely. 'Getting orders from the back, I expect. The old boy's incredible, even if slightly bonkers. Understandably. He says he'll be happy to go and live in Paris if we set him up. I really hope so, he's a half century behind . . . Anyway, no choice now, not with Paláček alive . . .' Stuart closed his eyes and groaned. 'To think you might have arrived just after . . . Lucy, I— '

On pure instinct she raised her hand to interrupt him, her bright hair swishing to the shake of head. 'I think you're about to apologise, um? Please don't. Let's get it over and go home. I'll believe it all in a week, all right? How many hours have you got?'

'Flying?' He shrugged, 'You're not supposed to know about it.'

'Oh . . .' She frowned and then asked innocently, 'Will you let me have a go?'

'Certainly not, it's— ' Stuart managed to stop himself adding anything about the Spitfire's age and possible frailty, let alone his own appalling ignorance. 'You're still very brown, Lu, where've you been?'

'It's a secret,' she said quickly, 'And you so pale?'

Stuart acknowledged ruefully as Louis passed them

mugs of steaming tea. The old man pointed at the kitchen clock.

'First light in less than an hour,' he said, 'We must go then. We must pray the tractor starts and then our system. Your wife, will she be all right or hysterical?'

Stuart waved away the notion and looked at her proudly. '*Krciti rameny,*' he said, explaining at once. 'See, she shrugs her shoulders. She's calm.'

As they finished their tea in silence, Louis watched her in a way both enquiring and admiring. Stuart however began to feel too much the knot of scarified solar plexus, his task compounded by anxiety. The feeling strongly evoked a patrol in Ireland's County Derry, apprehension not only for himself but also for his responsibility, the pre-dawn full of fear and guilty whispers, soldiers joking furtively to cover their own nervousness.

They stood up almost together and Stuart made sure once again of Palaček's bindings. He carefully avoided the presumption of a snide goodbye and Louis ushered them outside, tense and silent, their breath steaming white and stealthy.

The quiet was shattered by the generator as Louis switched on the barn lights. At the threshold they could see more than a foot of snow but it had stopped falling. There was no wind at all, mercifully removing any awkward decision about take-off direction. Even this thought carried *hubris* in the assumption that the engine would start after its hibernation and neglect. The Spitfire sat grey and mute in the sudden brightness, paint-stripped as though a mummified discovery, no life or potency lurking within. Lucy stopped dead before the reality and looked in silent awe, only her eyes moving from the machine to one man and the other, trying to form and answer her own questions. She wanted to tell herself she'd caught two boy scallywags in the act of some nocturnal prank but it was plainly all too grave. They had the set expressions of grown-ups in a last act of guilty desperation and it

318

crossed her mind as an absurdity that two Westerners were fleeing from where they need not have been when two real prisoners of repression might have gone in their stead. Gone to what? rose the next question and Lucy stopped this mental sequence abruptly.

She watched as in rehearsed sequence they disconnected the twelve exhaust tubes and trollied the aircraft half sideways through the door, jacking it down on the smooth and cracked-looking balloon tyres. They pushed the tail round to align it and then Louis with a grim expression went off to get the tractor. They heard it start after a hesitant cranking.

Stuart folded Lucy to him and asked, 'Have you had any sleep?'

'None, not even a snatch in the car. I'm all wobbly . . . How about you? I've got too many questions all at once, you know . . .'

'Yes. Let's wait till . . .' His voice tailed off uneasily.

The tractor puttered round the corner and Louis slung off a broad canvas belt; he positioned the tractor to one side and together they fitted the belt over the propeller-boss formed by his welded drum.

'Find something to block the tail-wheel,' Louis said, gasping with effort, 'Otherwise it will pull round when I tighten up. And don't look so, is it the cold? It has to work, believe me! See, dawn is near. Ask your wife to wait aside, I will help her in afterwards. Most unusual, so quiet and watching. Is she American?'

Stuart shook his head and restrained the words, fearful of Louis' reaction to all things Russian. He kept every other expression out of his face as well, having imagined this moment of the engine's truth too much in recent days, his fear now greatly increased by Lucy's presence. Even with the lights' reflections he could see the sky was greying. He turned away abruptly and fetched an iron weight to block the tail and placed their two makeshift chocks in front of the main gear. With a feeling of parchment in his throat, he palmed Lucy's shoulder, hefted the parachute and climbed onto the port wing, lowering himself gingerly into the cockpit. He saw Lucy rigidly monitoring every move as the excitement and tension climbed to frenzy, Louis' jerky movements seeming like spasms, his own facial muscles in a rictus of apprehension.

After Louis's efforts with the armour-plate, he found the seat had been left disturbingly loose but he decided not to mention it, fearing further delay, somehow suppressing the care of his training that this could be fatal negligence. Not harnessing the parachute was an unseen, deliberate act, certainly unremarked by Louis who stood in front of the wing waiting for his signal, his eyes as bright as a working Collie. In the crackling cold and silent tension Stuart finally nodded to him, his hands replaying practised movements . . . Fuel – ON . . . Throttle – Half-inch open . . . Propeller pitch – Full/Fine . . . Prime KI-Gass to resistance . . . Ignition switches – ON. Two thumbs up to Louis.

'Contact!'

The tractor started up again with its nervous rattle and inched away to the right, its power-drum spinning inside the loose drooping belt which kept trying to slide off. Like a jousting knight, Louis kept prodding it back with a pitchfork before it could fall. It tightened slowly, juddering under the increasing friction but the huge propeller stayed immobile. The Spitfire started vibrating and bouncing and Stuart realised with crushing dismay that the tyres would only hop sideways and never allow the belt to tighten fully. Louis overcame the problem at once with heavy-handed viciousness, letting the tractor's clutch out with such a full jerk that the propeller lashed over with sudden violence. It stopped against compression just as suddenly and the aircraft bounced again, the belt slackening abjectly. Stuart took his poised finger off the booster-coil button and stared narrowly at the blades jutting in defiance. Louis moved the tractor forward again to re-tension but by now the tractor's drum was steaming inside the belt while its engine roared fractiously. Once again Louis jerked it hard for the last inches and like a torrent of release the blades turned again, stiff and stubborn, once, twice, three times while the airframe bucked and Stuart pumped frantically at the primer and flattened his finger against the coil-button. With a mind-shocking roar which echoed back from the barn into a blasting of grey-black smoke, the Merlin thundered into life, the canvas belt slapping between unequal forces until Louis turned his wheel hard left and pulled away obliquely. With straw swirling about her, Lucy covered her ears, quailing as the aircraft jumped away again in reaction but then the belt slipped off the propeller-drum and fell harmlessly to the ground without being struck by the blades. The home-made drum stayed firmly in place however, even when Stuart had blipped the throttle several times. It was also slightly off-centre and causing an unhealthy vibration, adding to the decrepit rattling and ferocious cacophony.

Louis stared grimly at the drum as he moved the tractor out of the way, realising that such a heavy engine lacked the flexibility to speed ahead of the grasping metal hooks. He switched off the tractor and climbed down, careful of his brittle limbs. By the door of the barn he bent and hefted the great mawl, walking lop-sided and lethally close in front of the thrashing propeller. Like a solemn, fearless executioner he lifted, swung and smote. For such a frail looking old man it was a huge solid blow and the vibration lessened at once. Stuart couldn't see the immediate result but the spinning drum slid off the hub with its four hooks flailing as Louis tried to leap aside, parrying with the shaft of the mawl which it tore from his hands. Barely missing him, it ripped across the snow-covered yard, struck the tractor's main wheel and bounced crazily upwards, clawing at the air.

Louis watched it fall back, his expression impassive as he wiped his nose on his sleeve, but then Stuart saw his face appear along the cowling, clothes and hair rippling in the slipstream, grinning over a gnarled thumb-gesture. Inexplicably, his ancient figure then hurried away into the house, now clearer in the growing light and bright reflection of snow. When he emerged again in a few moments he had something flapping in each hand, scurrying beneath the wing and shortly reappearing behind the cockpit. He took Lucy in tow, her arm held protectively.

'*Pojd honem*, come quickly. Up!' he shrieked unnecessarily; Lucy was on the wing root in a moment, turning to help the old man clamber up behind her.

'Chocks are awayed!' Louis roared and then slipped into his native tongue, his voice quavering, shouting over the terrible engine noise, his hair whipping thinly in the buffeting air. 'You'll have to lean right forward to let me in. Keep the brakes on!'

Stuart squeezed hard up against the panel as Louis clambered stiffly over him, clutching Jára's ancient leather flying helmet and small cloth bag for his only cared-for possessions. After a struggle the seat was roughly replaced but the stick bucked suddenly in Stuart's hand as Louis slipped and trod on one of the elevator wires in the lower fuselage, swearing and apologising at once in anguish. Stuart nodded and cycled the stick, looking back past Lucy's anxious face to check the tail surfaces. The elevator's movements betrayed no after-effects but under any normal regimen there would have been alarm and insistence on full inspection. Now he could only shrug and reach out for Lucy, helping her in on top of him, the sheer awkwardness terrifying in such unfamiliarity. He was glad there'd been no time for rehearsal yet Lucy, so supple and compact, was calmly adjusting herself to favour him, fingering her two controls and trying to seem smaller still.

He kissed her temple quickly and felt her lean to it, then he half-turned his head to see how Louis was positioned. He saw the old man crouched and grimacing, pulling on his son's leather helmet, its useless earphone wires still connected. It was entirely comical but there was no humour left in the desperate circumstances. The Merlin coughed missed beats, shaking the airframe menacingly.

His mouth just behind Stuart's ear, Louis shouted out the long-memorised check list. 'Primer locked down! Throttle up to plus four pounds! Supercharger stage two, test, note RPM drop. Brakes hold, Open up to 3000 RPM!'

The noise grew to hideous, hellish proportions while the brakes began to slip and the aircraft lurched slewing to the left.

'Enough!' Louis shouted in real alarm, 'Back to plus nine pounds. Test magnetos, one, two, Good. Brake pressure and pneumatic I can't see. Should be eighty and two-twenty, yes? You ready?'

Stuart nodded and trimmed the elevator the regular half-division nose down and then added another in compensation for Louis' weight aft and the absence of machine guns and ammunition. He trimmed the rudder fully right and then went into adrenalin overflow, seeing movement in the corner of his eye. Palaček was standing by the kitchen door, his hands concealed behind his back. Louis followed Stuart's shocked pointing.

'Ach . . . I told him to stay inside,' he shouted, 'But it's all right. I only cut his feet loose. I didn't want him to die there, no-one would know. Forget about him! Propeller full fine! Fuel main tank and full. Flaps UP!'

Lucy's body jerked in response and then she protested. 'They ARE up!'

'Check!' Stuart shouted back amazed. 'Well done.'

Louis' scream overrode him. 'That's it, let's go! Tally-ho!'

323

Stuart actually found relief in being caught up completely in the moment and he eased the throttle steadily forward, the stick-ring held vertical with real difficulty because his arm was hard against Lucy's chest. He released the foot brakes and the Spitfire began to move, creeping at first, crunching down the new snow and then trundling a bit quicker past the house where he knew the meadow smoothed out. Palaček stood there agape, immobile and for Louis quite satisfyingly flabbergasted. The old man cackled insanely as he pulled up the little hinged door on the left and slid the canopy closed, his hand pressing down on Lucy's head to clear it. The hood was well-oiled and moved smoothly; half the noise was muted out at once. Stuart eased open more throttle and countered the huge growing torque with full right rudder. At plus seven pounds boost, the vibration and surge of power were almost unnerving but the snow was still a big hindrance, an emphatic no-go under the disciplines of flight. He had to apply yet more power to accelerate and with no visibility forward over the canted cowling, he tried keeping his line by a distant tree to his right, partially obscured by the top of Lucy's head. Lest the torque should veer and destroy them on the ground, he increased throttle with what seemed too much caution, certainly too much tension, and the run seemed to be taking forever. Of a sudden he began to feel a subtle difference, some feedback through the pedals, a small tendency to the right showing the rudder beginning to sense not just the twisting propeller stream but a growing laminar flow. He had to see more to the right.

'Head back!' he called urgently to Lucy, unable to spare a hand for the gesture. She tilted onto his shoulder, her head bouncing once against the canopy. The stick began to judder in Stuart's hand and now icily, feeling the dream becoming starkly real, he eased it tentatively forward. The tail lifted at once, too quickly and the propeller whipped up snow even as he corrected. At least now he could see forward, that they were accelerating very fast across the untouched white surface of the field the snow seeming to deaden their rapid trundling. Black smoke issued from one exhaust port but it seemed a minor worry. The airframe still fought to canter left but the rudder was becoming fully effective and its counteraction definite.

With no question left of commitment, Stuart opened up to a massive plus twelve pounds and after a small bounce eased the stick carefully back. The bucking rattle suddenly ceased, the earth made its miraculous, heart-stopping swoon away and Louis began gabbling behind him. Stuart craned to listen in case he'd missed something important but Louis had his eyes firmly shut and was reciting fervently both credo and disbelief in a quavering Lord's Prayer.

They'd been unsuccessful in testing on the ground so it was a misplaced hope that any of the flight instruments would be working. To Stuart's dismay, even as the speed built strongly, there was no response from the ASI, depriving him of the most essential information. The manuals cautioned that climb-out should not be attempted before 140 mph indicated so he had to keep his novice guesswork well over limits. The ancient fighter seemed to be accelerating with great ferocity, alarmingly light and tremulous in his hands, the whole airframe simply an adjunct to the monstrous pride of power in the nose.

'Wheels up!' Louis commanded, somehow recovered from his terrified supplication. Lucy braced in response as she rummaged behind her for the undercarriage control.

'Yes?' she asked Stuart for confirmation, craning to look at him. Their eyes met in too-close focus and he nodded quickly. Craning beneath her own right arm she rotated the black handle; there was a short pause before they sensed and heard the gear cycling, then Stuart remembered to touch the brakes so the wheels wouldn't continue spinning in the housings. The cycle seemed to take a long time and the indicator showed a failure to complete, threatening the vital airflow underneath to the radiator and air/oil coolers.

'Not up!' Louis shouted peremptorily, 'Cycle them again.'

Lucy's face strained as if the failure might be hers. She repeated the cycle with similar result; Stuart checked the panel and saw to his vast relief that the airspeed indicator had decided to function, the yellowing faded numerals showing 170 mph. He brought the throttle back to plus five pounds and then said to Lucy, 'Mind your head, I'm going to try to jerk them, hold on to me.' To Louis he had to shout in Czech what he was planning and the old man squeezed his encouragement.

Stuart prodded the stick forward sharply twice and then again, lifting their bodies stressingly upwards, the control almost too lively and rapid.

'That's it!' Louis shrieked. 'It worked, well done, expert! Now go fast and low, due West by the compass. Look, you can see the mountains, beyond is the Black Forest, and the border. My God, can this be true, Marie would never believe! Listen to the song of my Merlin, hey? Go, boy, go for home!'

Lucy gasped out, 'Please tell me what's the matter, what is he saying?'

'It worked, the gear's up. He's cheering. He's allowed to.'

The white countryside flashed beneath them while the buildings and factories of Rakovnik and the Zlutice disappeared rapidly to their left quarter. The sheer speed in relation to the ground was quite alarming especially at such low altitude. The trembling machine was constantly trying to climb and Stuart had to counter with more and more forward trim as his longing streamed ahead for the border; with such speed and minimal height, if

326

the engine didn't falter, they'd cross undetected inside fourteen minutes. Testing his own confidence he moved the hand-grip a nudge or two each way, getting a thoroughbred's willing response but there was a clutch of alarm from behind.

'Please, remember it's my first time!' came Louis' shouted protest, adding 'And my last!' Stuart nodded his understanding though the old man's triumph was infectious, his excitement peaking. The white carpet below rose up and fell away again and he tried to follow its contours without too much sharp control input. They were so low that the shock came without warning, after crossing a wet, black road standing out sharply against the white surroundings – hangars and aircraft snouts, a huge snow-blower clearing a runway, radar aerials barely glimpsed rotating on a green-glassed control tower.

With a crawl of gun-point horror, Stuart knew their clandestine run was finished, that no military airfield would leave such a buzz unquestioned for a second. Saying nothing he pushed the throttle further forward, watching the ASI creep round to 340 mph, worrying for the engine's stamina as well as the alert, his palms sweaty on the stick and throttle but the rest of his body stiffening with tension and the intense cold of the poorly sealed cockpit. Louis had covered the old bullet hole with tape but it stripped away and set up a mournful wailing. He tried vainly to block it with his elbow while Lucy stayed coiled and still, trying to minimise herself.

The land began to rise ahead, ominous mountains looming in the clearer dawn light, bisected by the dark Strela river and thickening with snow-laden trees. All Stuart's confidence had rested in the certainty of staying well below 240 feet, the downward reach of terrain-based radar, but their dash across the airfield would surely have betrayed their heading to some forward interceptor control. After a short decision he shifted course about fifteen degrees to port, a deviation which could in five minutes put them several miles from a predicted point without much altering their length of run to the wire. Lucy observed the course change against the land ahead but he doubted if she'd seen the airfield from her neck-cramping position.

'How long to go?' she called, her voice strangely calm.

'Nine, ten minutes. Sixty miles.'

'Stay away from watch-towers if you see one. They've got machine guns and rockets called SAMs.'

Stuart nodded against her head wondering how she knew about Surface/Air defences. To allay his own fears as well, he said, 'The SAMs should be aimed for things going in, not out.'

'Don't believe it!' came her emphatic answer, 'The towers are manned.'

Stuart felt jolted by the conviction in her voice, telling himself all the same that their scything low altitude wouldn't give a gunner time or target. He was much more worried about the Air-to-Air missiles and the terrible unseen speed of their delivery, always from behind, both radar and heat-sensing trackers hounding on the ancient Merlin.

Owing to increased border activity since the last observed break-out as well as the intensified vigilance noted in Czechoslovakia and East Germany, a USAF Boeing 135 AWACS, airborne warning, was patrolling west of the border and currently over Bavaria. At 30,000 feet its electronic eyes had a vast all-round scan which covered the alerted base as well as the forward sentinels while multi-scanning listeners had at once picked up the emergency dialogue.

In the path of the fugitive, infra-red sensors picked up new exhaust transmissions from two pairs of heavy turbines in the position where they'd settled and cooled four hours earlier. These were the only two aircraft on the sinister side which computed, in the predicted time-slot, as possible interceptors for the West-bound blip, which the hastily translated dialogue failed to identify. The two aircraft were both far more than adequately equipped to deal with anything subsonic in their vicinity for they were Mil Mi–24 helicopters, designated Hind in the Nato catalogue, a nastily benign-sounding name for one of the most fearful platforms of modern battlefield death-dealing, a tank-smasher and troop exterminator of revolting aspect and ferocious weaponry.

The AWACS had already brought forward, also four hours earlier, two of the first newly-deployed McDonnell Douglas AH–64 Apaches. It had been a simple gesture to say 'We're watching,' even from a forest clearing east of Bayreuth. On signal, two more pairs of turbines whined into life, these almost invisible to infra-red with their latest 'black-box' exhaust shrouding.

The first assessment made in the AWACS was of a runaway Cruise-type missile, comparatively slow and terrain-hugging, about to be given some fail-safe treatment by the two Hinds. A general alarm filled the wires and airwaves of West Germany, both fixed and mobile Tomahawk missiles were primed and two squadrons of F–16 and F–18, Falcon and Hornet fighters, scrambled. Westbound and lower than a drunken dare came Juliet Bravo, still armed with a pair of virgin Hispano cannon, a fighter which had never seen battle but had just once, long ago, amidst a myriad other forgotten tragedies been stricken by a solid ball from an ancient muzzle-loader.

The smoking cylinder mercifully cleared itself and the Merlin thundered its martial growl so familiar to earlier generations of war-nurtured and mutilated Europe. It was the sound which brought a small comfort to the beleaguered British as they heard it daily in their skies for years or weekly in their strident newsreels, accompanied by the clipped accents of the mannered BBC sangfroid, or sometimes, like a privilege in measured and emotional

doses, the eerie, formidable, lion-hearted defiance of
Winston Churchill's sombre oratory.

In the lead of the two Hind gunships, Lt Vassily
Bakunin flicked his radar to a higher definition as the
Spitfire forged towards him. His orders were brief and
unequivocal: divert to force-land or destroy, unidentified
aircraft westbound, surface level, speed 300 knots plus.
His face twisted in puzzlement for he and his gunner/ob-
server in the front cockpit were not flying an interceptor
so much as an airborne anti-tank weapon converted
from a troop carrier. The fastest service helicopter in
the world, the record proudly set by two Russian lady
pilots, it had clocked over 330 kph, only a little short
of 200 knots, and until recent final production of the
Apache, the *Gorbach* or hunchback as it was known to
the crews had been the latest development in battle-tactic
mobility, built to charge over forest or hill like a deadly
buffalo, nose-down and fast, to align laser, infra-red or
low-light TV sights for AT–2C 'Swatter' missiles, 57mm
rockets or 12.7 mm rounds from its terrible, four-barrel
rotating gun, to fire the selected weapon and veer away
at the same elusive speed.

Although trained for lethal action and in command of
such a powerful weapon, Vassily had often wondered if
he was an oddity or merely an adult, that he had no
actual desire to destroy or terrorise. The target exercises
were all good fun and academic and he projected the
reality with the same detachment. Quiet confidence,
he'd noticed, elicited far greater respect than displays
of power, especially to oneself. He would admit that
his only consuming passion was aviation, his knowledge
encyclopaedic.

Given no more information as to type, Vassily was
mystified by the speed of the target on his screen. A
fleeing jet or a runaway missile would be close to Mach
1 even at surface level, a light aircraft on the other

hand capable of no more than 130 knots. He couldn't think of anything that flew at around 300 knots except a lumbering turbo-prop transport and the alert had specified something small. The conundrum fascinated him as they computed the approaching reflex; he voiced his thoughts to his gunner – pointlessly, since Igor Pavlovich was an automaton who spoke little and almost never before midday and was in effect just an extension of his weapon panel.

The on-board computer displayed the intercept course once the target was confirmed and radar-pinpointed. Vassily called his wingman immediately.

'M.2, vector 355, all-round survey, radar West priority, fly on me.'

As the two gunships thrashed across the snow-draped forest on unshakeable interception, Vassily noted Igor arm the fire-control panel and settle himself more comfortably. He was about to countermand the premature action but checked himself. Igor was simply getting in the slot for the ranges where he was invaluable, since as a team they were top-scorers time after time.

Stuart and Louis saw them at the same moment, long, dark, purposeful shapes on a northerly converging course.

'There, look!' Louis exclaimed, pointing with his left hand past Stuart's head. Lucy stiffened in response, searching with her head strained over. It was all she could do not to unfold her from her contortion, feeling her muscular control beginning to flutter. In contrast to Louis's shriek she spoke just loud enough for Stuart to hear.

'What is it, can you tell me?'

'Choppers, big ones.'

'Where?'

'Ten o'clock, level.' He wanted to reassure her but couldn't find any words. Poor Louis had also pushed against the seat and Stuart's own restrictions, his state

331

of excitement still peaking. Stuart was now in a cold quandary of inexperience, knowing only that as long as the Merlin roared he could outrun and outclimb any helicopter, even draw a huge circle round them, but anything costing time would be fatal and they'd fall with pathetic ease to fighter reinforcements surely already scrambled. His mind teemed with a list of worries, low octane fuel, the state of the airframe and controls, but above all Lucy, so desperately missed for so long and now at last with him, but in terminal circumstances. He also knew that if he simply kept going fast and low for the border and took no initiative, either of the Hinds could pick them off in passing with an ample choice of weapon. He could climb out of range of its cannon which would also give him a very slight chance of seeing a missile launched and taking violent evasive action but the climb would absorb precious minutes and allow the faster interceptors to assemble. Once they came on the scene all the options would vanish.

'Arm the cannon!' Louis shouted breathlessly, plainly with no other thought than to blaze through the gauntlet and hope for the best. Stuart shook his head once, adamantly. He'd considered such a possibility before and saw no reason why someone else should die purely as a result of his adventure; it would anyway serve no other purpose than a meagre gesture. Defence of Lucy would have added a desperate complication only if there'd been any question about the final outcome against the firepower and accuracy of a modern gun-platform.

'Why not? Where are your guts?' came Louis' shrill protest, terrifying to Lucy's incomprehension.

'NO! And stop screaming in my ear, Louis. We're going up, hold on.' To Lucy he added, 'Climbing, Lu, tuck in.'

Stuart eased back on the stick tentatively at first, secretly distrusting the entire state of the mainframe and feeling his mental tightrope starting to quiver too fast for control. By climbing he'd settled logically on a compromise, using the vertical dimension to distance the Hinds for there was no longer any hope in trying to beat radar; height at least would give them later speed and greater scope for manoeuvre.

The two Hind crews saw the alteration at once, their computers instantly reassessing the target's reduced speed but also notifying their inability to match the climb. In the lead helicopter, Vassily gaped suddenly at the under-profile of the zooming fighter, almost refusing to believe his eyes. The unique, legendary Mitchell wing, the sweet tapering elipse, had decorated his bedroom wall since childhood but at that distance he could see no other identification. As a pilot he saw the logic of Stuart's move at once and promptly called up his wingman.

'M.2., climb and shadow. I think he's going for speed in the dive. Tease him to me, I'll wait for him down and West. Go!'

The wingman acknowledged calmly, cranking in the power from his twin Isotov turbines for a maximum-rate climb. Himself disbelieving but confident of his leader's recognition, he called back and asked, 'What is it, Vassily?'

'It's a Spitfire! Incredible, eh?'

Mocking him, the prepared answer came back patiently, 'I know it's a Spitfire, but which Mark?'

Vassily grinned ruefully to himself but made no reply, his concentration firmly on the screen and his instruments. The Spitfire was on the same heading as before but now climbing at tremendous speed, something like 5000 feet a minute from initial zoom. He felt his excitement mounting as in a training war-game and he even thought with a measure of dismay of the programmed, mechanical killer in front of him, grim, efficient and joyless.

* * *

333

Stuart flattened his climb at 11,000 feet, his ears popping repeatedly from the pressure change. Lucy's jaw moved against his shoulder, working for equilibrium in her own ear ducts.

'Go on, higher,' Louis called, pummelling his shoulder with long-pent enthusiasm. 'Go up! I want to see if the second stage supercharger works. Eighteen thousand, that will show them!'

Stuart shook his head firmly again without trying to explain. Without oxygen they were already approaching a height that would begin to impair brain function. Levelling out, though, he kept the throttle just short of maximum boost, still fearful of taxing the Merlin to destruction. The airframe shook and screamed and the cold was only bearable because of the furious pace of his bloodflow. Lucy was finally compelled to remove her arm from behind his neck to help suspend her quivering left leg. Behind her, Louis was crouched and now silent, a bony hand still gripping his shoulder. The second gunship was climbing hard on intercept while the other was still far below, just a dark speck against the whitened forest. A mere dozen miles to the West, way beyond the spa town of Marienbad, they could even see the broad cut between the trees, the double fences of razor chain-link and barbed wire, where the watch-towers, scanners and anti-personnel devices marked the Iron Curtain's self-accusing obscenity.

Stuart could see clearly that the lower of the two helicopters was streaking for the border like a long-block while the other still grew in size as it climbed. The urge to flee was irresistible and almost gratefully he gave in to it, seeing no possible alternative. He eased the Spitfire's long grey snout into a shallow dive and trimmed forward, watching the speed build rapidly. The climbing Mi–24 began turning at once to match the increase but it was quickly overhauled. It added to its threat by being invisible in their blind spot despite being unable to keep up. The slip-stream howled like a terror banshee as the ASI reeled up to 430 mph and he began easing the throttle back to avoid engine overspeed. A little late he remembered to coarsen propeller pitch to get more bite on the air, deepening the Merlin's arrogant growl; the steel-lined swathe between the trees loomed ever nearer but somewhere behind and below, the unseen wingman's height might soon match their own and death overtake them without an approaching whisper. Unless . . . Stuart realised that the wingman might not fire if there was any risk of hitting his Number One ahead and below, yet it felt like gripping a loom-full of nerve-wires to keep the Spitfire heading straight towards the leader, steepening the dive still further to do so. In the end he might sacrifice some of his headlong speed in evasive twists and turns, his last attempt to beat the inevitable fire. His whole system was ablaze with adrenalin, his mind fighting for coolness while Louis still gripped his shoulder painfully. Lucy gave only a silent nod to his query for her.

Suddenly she tensed even further and Louis' grip dug deeper for they'd all seen them at once.

'Look, look there!' Louis' voice quavered with distress into the screaming of the wind as he pointed ahead. As if from nowhere, two new giant black-flies appeared in echelon over the white land, low from the Western side. The border was just four or five miles distant, less than a minute away, three thousand feet below. The trailing Hind must have slipped out of cannon range but would still be well in the hunt with its Swatters and some 30 rockets, its gunner surely grimacing with frustration.

Border activity of any kind being under intense scrutiny by both sides, situations could always arise which required fine judgement, restraint and educated command. It was an area where the Russians had a massive advantage in their proven ruthlessness, based on the fact that they had no public opinion to fear, no peace or protest movements at home and their ever-growing might giving the West plenty of reason to fear their intentions.

Vassily Bakunin realised the lone Spitfire was not only heading into an unavoidable double jeopardy but could also be the cause of a tragic flare-up of massively escalating proportions. He himself had no intention of backing down before the Americans and his orders were not ambivalent. No field commander dared give less, facing penalties only for underkill and weakness, a policy which had destroyed a KAL Jumbo and earned formal congratulation for combat readiness. Vassily now thought he could see a way to avoid a firefight or a killing and still obey the spirit of his orders: if he didn't shoot down the runaway, his own presence would lead the Americans to treat it as a hostile and they would quickly destroy it themselves.

In the screaming blur of their speed, Stuart understood his predicament almost simultaneously. With no markings or radio Friend/Foe Ident, the runaway could only be seen as hostile to the NATO patrol coming from Germany, although they were fractionally more likely to give him the benefit of any doubt. Nose-on however, it would simply be a fast-moving blip on a screen while in plan to the naked eye, the shape should be unmistakeable and no possible threat to a modern air force. But there was only one way to show the plan-profile of the Spitfire against the dawn sky, to pull up or turn and thus extend by excruciating seconds their flight for freedom. Just in time he realised there was no longer choice nor time to agonise. He turned the ring firmly over to port and hauled back hard, again clenching in hope that the airframe hadn't lost any of its essential strength. At their great speed the stick resisted fiercely and the G–force of the turn was very severe. Louis moaned loudly as his crouch was forced too deeply for his old and half-frozen joints. Then Stuart realised that his right arm, cramped

336

against Lucy's rib-cage, wouldn't return to the right, a matter of terrible urgency for the turn completed would take them straight back to the cannon's mouth.

'Lu! Can you pull my hand, we have to bank right, can you – '

To his astonishment she'd completed the action before his words were out, taking hold above his hand. She rolled the Spitfire sharply to starboard and incredibly she even eased off the back pressure at the same time. Back on their original heading, taking them straight towards the oncoming Apaches, they had about 1000 feet advantage over the lead Russian. Bakunin couldn't mark the manoeuvre on his forward-looking radar and therefore took several moments to understand the reason when his wingman reported the fugitive's evasive action. By then it was just too late: the Spitfire roared overhead into his direct view, its height advantage dwindled and presenting an easy target for Igor's murderous gun, just one mile short of the border but now protected by a lethal backstop of two AH–64s. They approached the border in a swirling high hover, lean and jutting with evil.

'Do not fire!' he barked decisively but received no answer. He repeated the command shrilly and Igor finally allowed him a reluctant grunt. His eyes were narrowed on the two Apaches; he knew their specifications to the last rivet and a curious dusty coating seemed to have dried his throat.

Seconds later, Juliet Bravo hurtled across the cut in the last feet of dive to maintain the frantic speed of the dash for cover. In the lead Apache, an astonished Captain Chuck Zweiker had made an instant assessment on seeing the Spitfire that it posed no obvious threat and could anyway be picked off at leisure. His only puzzlement was why the Reds had let it go but beyond a quick sight of its unmarked fuselage and underwings he had more than enough to occupy him.

Albee, his co-pilot/gunner operating the TADS, target acquisition and designation sight, followed it out of Zweiker's vision, but the latter was able to link in his own helmet monocular and actually follow it through the gunner's eye-view whilst keeping his own left eye firmly on the leading Russian. He was seeing an airborne Hind close-to for the first time and it seemed truly horrible, bug-like, huge, solid, forbidding, no less revolting or deadly than an Apache except for less sophistication in its electronics. Underneath his own fuselage, the obscene black proboscis of the 30mm Chain Gun moved up, down and sideways, instantly synchronous with the gunner's eye wherever he looked. A touch of the button and you hit what you saw. The fire control panel was also armed for the laser-guides of the 16 Hellfire anti-armour missiles and pods of multiple 2.75 inch rockets. The TADS swept left and right, up and down in a constant survey for other hostiles including on the ground; zooming the camera, they could see clearly on the video display the two helmeted Russians in their camouflaged giant gremlin a quarter mile away, creeping unsteadily to the border limits, gazing back intently on their own screens, their four-barrel guns also swivelling *en garde*.

Calling the AWACS, Zweiker coldly reported his situation and was informed that he had two squadrons of strike/combat aircraft climbing for high cover with an attack capability two and a half minutes from call. He saw the second Russian catch his leader and adopt his protective position. The AWACS also reported the fugitive had now slowed up a clear three miles astern, shortly to pick up an armed escort of two AV–8 Harriers.

'Holy cow!' Lucy breathed in disbelief, 'Did we really get through?'

Stuart was still shuddering in the cold and aftermath of tension, hardly believing himself that they'd made it and now concerned over setting off a terrible incident.

He throttled back in hesitant relief and as the speed-noise subsided, he gently banked the Spitfire and craned his head to see what had happened behind them.

'Oh my God!' he said, pointing in consternation, his left hand shaking for a moment until he replaced it on the throttle lever. The four killer helicopters hung over the trees with barely the width of the border between them, their hovers varying individually like a sinister, morbid ritual of giant horror-film insects. Both pairs held the same battle formation, making a rough diamond pattern between them, each wingman to the left and slightly behind his leader. All four had their dread arsenals fully armed and unsafe and four thumbs stayed in fractional touch with their gunbuttons.

It was hair-trigger deadlock and the Russian commander was the first to break it, thinking on the premise that the first to fire would have an instant victory but a mere instant to enjoy it, assuming he made a killing shot. However, he knew that one of the specifications of the purpose-designed Apache was survivability of a hit from 23mm cannon as carried by the latest Hind E, a hit even on the rotor-head or the cunningly separated engine intakes. His own engines were vulnerably adjacent and in spite of his nose-gun's monstrous capacity of over 4000 rounds a minute, the kind of fire rate which could demolish a house or a battalion of infantry in seconds, he couldn't be sure of penetrating any of the Apache's armour before taking a lethal hit himself. The Hughes Chain Gun fired a heavy shell and its eyesight link didn't miss. A contest of missiles or rockets was equally unthinkable, the split second pause between launch and strike being quite enough for retaliation. The *Gorbach's* biggest safety factor was its sheer speed but in the hover and nap-of-the-earth flying it was cumbersome and very taxing for the pilot. Deciding to negate all advantage, he touched his left yaw pedal and despite a snarled protest from Igor, Vassily turned the huge stationary Hind until its snout was pointing not at the American wingman in front of him but across at his leader. Crisply he ordered his own wingman to make the opposite diagonal, so if either American fired straight ahead he'd fall at once to retaliatory cover from the survivor.

It was a perfect stalemate which Chuck Zweiker understood at once. 'Well, now we got ourselves a Czechsican stand-off,' he said dryly to his own co-pilot, 'Reckon their only problem might be breakin' off without losing face . . . I don't see no reason not to oblige 'em, do you?'

The AWACS called up before Albee could answer. 'Purple One, be advised you have thirty-plus Bogeys One-Sixer, assume Czech Mig–21s, inbound twelve miles Southeast, ETA overhead one minute twentee and, er, you have two-four small friends coverin' Eastbound and roarin' three-six miles One-two and climbing, plus two V.TOLs eight miles astern joining low. We have full Red Alert, oblige you cool, can do, confirm?'

Without taking eyes or aim from his opposite number, Zweiker included his wingman in the same transmission.

'Purple One to Bald Eagle, affirmatory . . . Purple Two, *vamos* and *auf wiedersehen*. Heading as now, backin' off. If you see 'em so much as toss a match out the window, let 'em have it, the whole damn battery . . . Real gentle, jus' keep your bead right on him and slide away. Follow me through and do it re-eal slow. I figure me there's an itchy finger or two round here including mine and they must have been hot for a killing.'

It was the wrong rôle for both of them, Zweiker knew, since the Apache's terrible destructive capability was mainly for ground attack, its forte being to zoom onto a battlefield area, film it on video and retreat at once behind hill or clearing. At leisure then, as practised countless times, he and his co-pilot/gunner would replay the tape, select and compute their targets, climb out of their hide like an express hoist, fire, monitor the split-second trajectory and disappear as quickly, every part of the machine designed to withstand most weaponry except a direct hit from anti-armour. There was the sinister admission too that with the Apache up, most enemy gunners would rather have their heads down. Zweiker had fully accepted that here they had a no-win situation and no purpose whatsoever in a show-down.

Watched by four unblinking pairs of Russian eyes, the Apaches tilted slightly aft, their Chain Guns lowering in instant response to the gunner's helmet sights, computers reading gazes with cold and total accuracy.

High above, four acolyte squadrons positioned rapidly but warily to see the solemnities followed. In microcosm it showed the effectiveness of deterrents, provided that those participating had progressed beyond actually wanting to fire their weapons, but were otherwise fully prepared to use them. As the two Apaches reversed slowly away as though from some grotesque rite, the entire performance was monitored tensely in the AWACS Boeing six miles above, seeing also the fleeing intruder breaking off its orbit and settling on a Westerly heading again, two Harriers streaking up behind it, then at last the two gunships turning and accelerating rapidly away from their razor-edge border confrontation.

In the leading Hind, Igor thumbed his panel disgustedly back to *Safe* and broke his robotic silence. 'Why did you do it, Vassily? We had him cold as a rabbit. I think you must have gone limp in your stick.'

His pilot/commander banked viciously to starboard and swung away to the Northeast. Peremptorily he said, 'Arm your dragon again, Igor, you can sow some teeth. Fire a two-second burst.'

'What for?' queried Igor, strictly a target-man.

'Do it, imbecile!'

Almost at once the big gun made an obscene bopple and some hundred and forty shells smashed harmlessly

341

into a snow-covered hillside. Vassily felt a rare and secret satisfaction that the little Spitfire still lived, especially in his imagination.

'It was your rotten shooting, Igor. As you say, we had him cold, your gun was fired, but amazingly, you missed. You can blame the turbulent air.'

After a few moments, Igor grinned in defeat for on his level at least they were old friends. 'Communism does not admit of sentiment, Vassily Petrovich.'

'Marksman, that is true. It may be the only thing wrong with it.'

FIFTEEN

'. . . love is a constant interrogation. In fact I don't
know a better definition of love.'
Milan Kundera, *The Book of Laughter and Forgetting*

The relief in the tiny cramped cockpit was almost
explosive, their thoughts still wild with speculations.
They all stared ahead, each silently mesmerised but
then Lucy turned to nuzzle Stuart's neck at the precise
moment when an evil black snout appeared just off their
port wing. Suppressing a scream into a scarified indrawn
breath was so difficult and instant that the feat filled
her with sudden pride, especially that it might be her last
conscious act. Stuart caught her spasm and focus in the
same moment but was luckily unable to jink to starboard
owing to the press of her body; he saw another black
snout on the other side an instant later. He knew
he'd never been so close to being overwhelmed, as
ragged, drained and primed for dying as when the
execution squad raises its rifles. The helmeted and
masked head in the alien cockpit was but an impersonal
programmed extension of distant death's command – yet
there was a familiar roundel on the fuselage beneath it! A
dark-gloved hand appeared in the canopy with a jerked,
congratulatory thumbs-up before turning over into a
fingers-down on top of the helmet, the silent military
command: 'Form on me'.

With such a blessed relief it was a few moments
before he realised the bony hand was no longer gripping

his shoulder and then he heard Louis mutter something unintelligible.

'You all right, Louis? What did you say?'

Faintly the voice repeated, 'Well done, Pilot, Jára would be proud, Karel too.'

Stuart nodded only the briefest thanks for with the Harriers so hazardously close he couldn't chance a look round or risk his concentration. Close formation flying needs great skills and confidence and he couldn't tell them he was a complete beginner and to keep away. Although the speed was now down to a moderate 230 mph it was still frighteningly high for his daylight experience; the ground slipped rapidly below even though the altitude had crept back to nearly 3000 feet. The Harriers instigated a long, slow turn and, after about ten minutes when the land had fallen away to below the snowline, one of them broke off, forged ahead and began a rapid, measured descent. Stuart followed with the other still dogging close alongside and presently saw a narrow strip bordered with green, a big orange windsock at one end. There was no sign of aircraft or control tower.

'Louis, we're going down now, can you hear? Can you hold on?'

With no reply he said to Lucy, 'Can you see him, is he OK?'

Lucy craned her head and said, 'He's in trouble, I think. He's all grey and his eyes are closed.'

Stuart had no option but to give his whole petrified attention to the landing, something he'd only practised in his head, having never flown a tail-wheel aircraft let alone one with such a perilously narrow undercarriage. His one remaining prayer was that the gear would lock down and let him at least attempt a normal landing, knowing that the good three-pointer used to be more exceptional than normal.

The lead Harrier completed a tight and rapid left-hand circuit for the Westbound, upwind runway, landing and halting in an absurd few yards and quickly clearing the threshold. Nervously he began to position for the down-wind leg and began a shaky check sequence, reducing airspeed to 150 mph before the most vital action.

'Undercarriage now, Lu, crank the lever back through a full half-turn.'

She reached behind her, fiddled and said, 'Got it.'

It still seemed like some kind of miracle when the trim altered jerkily and the indicator on the left panel haltingly admitted, after a cycle that seemed to last for eternity, that the wheels were down and locked.

'Well done! Now flaps, the other one.'

'Check,' Lucy managed to say, obviating possible condescension.

The flaps hesitated for a long time, for the shared and ancient hydraulic system had insufficient pressure left to operate them. Dreading a fast landing without them, Stuart extended the downwind leg in face of the Harrier pilot's signals on his right. At last he saw the flaps go full down and he turned gratefully base and finals with a surfeit of height. Without foreknowledge of the next awful seconds he saw it only as a fault to be corrected, not as a saving grace, and this time Lucy helped straighten them out of the turn without being asked. The approach settled towards the dangerous lower limit of flight speed as Stuart reached up and slid back the canopy, then there came an explosion from behind, covering Louis' scream. The seat collapsed backwards and Stuart found himself dragged after it with sudden force and nothing in his hands but the stick and throttle, a pull-back on either at such a stage being certainly lethal. He could only bless enough trained instinct to relinquish both as his left arm too was pulled by his anorak, snagged on something unseen. Louis wrestled despairingly with his neck while Lucy blocked his view of everything as she slithered across him. Even if Louis let go he knew he would not be able to pull himself into any active position for she no

345

longer sat sideways but square on his pelvis, bolt upright and looking forward past the cowling, the wind tearing at her hair. Stuart had no idea what to shout in time, certain the ground must be only a hundred feet away.

'Lucy!' he croaked, still pinned from behind.

'Got it!' she called tightly, then the more formal co-pilot's acknowledgement: 'I have control.'

Stuart stared upwards helplessly, his disbelief too reluctant to give way before the facts. He tried again but her voice gathered his sense with a certainty, even in her shout.

'It looks all right! Tell me the figures.'

'WHAT?' With a violent effort he recalled the manual and yelled up, '2650 RPM, airspeed 130 mph.' Lucy simply repeated the figures but Stuart wanted to scream that he'd never landed a tail-wheeler, it was different technique, much harder. For Lucy, harder than what, different from what? To expect hopeless forward vision near the ground, but to someone mushing in it makes no difference. Nobody walks away after a sudden halt from 130 mph, though sometimes they run a few steps blazing with high octane gasoline. Through all the desperate sequence of thoughts he tried to wrestle himself upright but every movement jarred the wires in the fuselage. Lucy called out once and then again.

'Try and keep still, you're jolting the stick, and the rudder too!'

Stuart realised then that her feet now covered his on the pedals and there was a distinct pressure on both of them.

'Lucy!' he croaked again, 'Flare when the ground comes up!'

He saw her head nodding and then her jaw moved, the words carried away.

'What?' he gargled back.

'Old tyres – it looks like chain strip! Were you going for the grass?'

'He hadn't thought of it and it was a much safer idea, minimising sparks in the certainty of a thunderous pile-up. He felt such a conviction of it that he tried for a last second revision.

'Lucy, push the throttle forward and pull the stick back to climb. We'll go round and try— '

Her head shook clearly against the sky and suddenly he saw a tree-top sail past above the cockpit's edge. At the same moment he felt a distinct press of left rudder yet the aircraft banked to the right, yawning slightly before correction. Lucy had actually come in through a gap in the trees, sideslipped and then straightened out again.

The first bump and her weight on his stomach jarred his spine and a piteous moan came from beneath him just as Lucy's left hand brought the throttle back to idle. The Spitfire seemed to drop, mush, climb and then thump onto the mainwheels, bounce twice heavily and then settle on its tail, oscillating between the two. Then there was a trundling sound and a horrible judder from the rear-wheel castor doing its traditional crazy spin.

'Brakes!' he heard her calling, 'Where— ?'

Still prone and in acute distress, Stuart thrust out with both feet but felt the tail begin slewing violently to port. He corrected a swerve he could only imagine, pushing harder with his left foot even as Lucy yelled to confirm it, forcing her own foot on top of his. The yaw reversed itself with some violence, forecasting the accident most common to Spitfires because of their peculiarly narrow wheel base. There was a sudden clinking of chain mail beneath them as they careered across the strip, slewing back again to starboard, skidding on the damp metal and finally completing the ground-loop with a wheel lifting, lifting. There was a last-second reprieve as it fell back, the port wingtip making merest contact with the ground, then the aircraft slewed suddenly round to face the approach. Movement seemed to hang, as in that moment of gazing about on the cliff-edge when balance fails, but nothing

347

else happened. They were left with just the Merlin ticking over in comparative quiet, the sight of the landed Harrier blocked by the canted cowling. Louis gave another groan and Lucy's body seemed to slump, doubling her weight.

Stuart called his name, pleading release, but there was no answer and the old man's grip didn't slacken on his throat.

'How do I switch it off?' Lucy asked, 'Or should I taxi back? Can you stand it?' Plainly she could see his predicament.

Stuart considered the options and croaked, 'Sure. You have to zig-zag, and very careful with the power.' He was about to instruct further when a smile broke across his half-strangled face. He felt an overflow of admiration and gratitude and rasped in stiff formality: 'You have control.'

This time instead of the equally formal reply Lucy gave a shaky chuckle and answered, 'Thank you, dear.' After a series of downwind tacks they stopped by the parked Harrier. Stuart felt her feet pressing on his for both brakes and assumed the agony was finally over.

'Slow-running cut-out, on the left panel. You pull it.'

There was a lengthy pause before Lucy muttered, 'Got it.'

Like a blessing the racket ceased and the huge propeller whickered to a decisive stop. 'Mags off, top left, two switches.'

After the double click her weight came mercifully off him, then she was leaning in from the side to help him. They had to wrestle Louis' arm from his throat and shoulder before he could heave himself upright then her eagerness changed to real concern when she caught sight of Louis' crumpled form. He was hunched and unmoving, his legs apparently locked against the framework to keep his body off the control wires. Stuart got out and started to grapple with the seatback, getting

348

only the faintest response when he tried lifting. Then the old head came up, eyes distant and glassy and a small crinkled smile was enough to light the grey and weathered face. It had the pride of a runner who has shattered his body with a marathon. A hand trembled against his own and he heard the old fierce spirit even in the deathly whisper.

'We Czechs say "it",' Louis got out with great difficulty, 'But Jára called her a lady. She was good, Jára, – and she was *ready*. That's all, Jára.'

With one foot on the parachute, Stuart reached in and heaved at the crumpling form, getting stuck half-way until another helping hand appeared on the other wing. He glanced up quickly to see a round but serious face of a young man in a padded and slotted G-suit.

'Doesn't look too well, I'd say,' the other ventured as they hauled together. Louis was no longer conscious when they laid him on the grass and his skin was like cold parchment. Stuart attempted the kiss of life while the pilot worked on Louis' chest and Lucy swept her hands inwards on his limbs. They kept it up for some time after each was sure he had gone, but then at last Stuart closed the old eyes and felt a welling in his own. He sat down on the damp grass and looked over at Lucy who still held one of the wrinkled, work-worn hands. Stuart's head dropped between his knees in a complete overwhelm of sadness and exhaustion.

'Sorry about that,' the Harrier pilot said awkwardly, 'Relative of yours?'

'No . . . He was about to become one, an honorary member.' Stuart felt Lucy's hand on his arm in purest sympathy. He covered it with his own and looked up at the young man's eager face, then spoke with real affection.

'He was completely crazy. He kept that machine in his

349

barn since 1945. Maintained it without any training and actually expected it to fly.'

The young man shook his head with a muttered 'Requiescat' and then beckoned at the trees. A single camouflaged soldier appeared and ran over in an eccentric waggling of foliage.

'Get on the blower, sunshine,' the pilot said, 'We need a hearse.'

The soldier bobbed and hurried off. 'You're English,' the pilot observed, 'All of you?'

Stuart shook his head and plucked at a blade of grass, gazing at it intently as a sudden harmonious distraction from his current state, relief and disbelief, exhaustion and sorrow.

'Hope it's got anti-freeze in it,' he heard the pilot say, patting the cowling. Stuart looked up to see that special sardonic grin of the unflappable, the face turning to ask, 'You had much time on Spits, um?'

Stuart fingered back his sleeve but had no wristwatch. He gave a wry shrug and guessed, 'About thirty-five minutes, minus the last one.'

He was peripherally aware of Lucy's stare and the pilot's eyebrows lifting very faintly. On that face it registered real surprise and laconic amusement. 'Mark IX, um, four blade CSU?'

He spoke as if he didn't need an answer and walked round it with his hands behind his back, on inspection. Stuart turned to straighten Louis' clothing, laying the old leather helmet across his face.

'Do with a lick o' paint, what?' said another voice from behind the fuselage as the second Harrier pilot joined the tour. The groundsman hurried back from some hidden OP in the trees.

'Is your name Kody, sir? Ah, fear of further embarrassment, they want you to fly on to Switzerland, about 150 miles or so, if you wouldn't mind, sir?'

With such an option ruled out, Stuart shook his head

almost gaily. 'No can do, sorry. No starter motor.' With a sudden vision of some bright young spark suggesting a bump-start from a Harrier's jet blast he added, 'We need a full inspection of the controls as well. It's like a flying pram at the moment.'

'Oh. Well, I dunno. I said there was a lady and a body and they said they'd send a chopper, won't be long coming. Sir, I'd be personally obliged not to have a rain of Russky bombs on my pitch, it's a bit early in the day, frankly.'

Stuart nodded, his grin showing no such care. 'I'll stay and hold your hand, soldier, until we can get an engineer along – and a proper pilot with a proper licence.'

'Beg pardon, sir, but the HQ tone did not leave me with the impression that any further *hex*change of pleasantries would be in the best interests of— '

'All right, sunshine,' interrupted the first Harrier pilot, 'I think he got the gist. Anything for us?'

'Yes, sir. You stays 'ere.' Comically the groundsman waved his greenery in disguise of hurt pride.

Lucy spoke then for both of them. 'Have you got a regular telephone in there, or just a radio?'

'The real McCoy, miss,' he answered brightly, 'Free too, I call me mum in Auster-alia. Come and I'll show you.'

Seeing her holding Stuart's hand the soldier managed not to leer and led off through the trees to a small concrete blockhouse.

As they followed Stuart said, 'You want to call Alicia – isn't she still at the camp?'

'No, Mama's busy mothering. She's been forced to adopt a grandchild since you decided to shirk your marital obligations. I want to get hold of Allcock, he's waiting to hear from me, then St George.'

'Good, I must speak to him to, he's been expecting me.'

Lucy grimaced at this understatement. 'Oh, and while we're at it, you can tell his secretary not to bother with any more proxy calls. I found out.'

'How?'

'Allcock blurted.'

They stopped to enter a musty cavern and the groundsman pointed to the telephone.

'Have you got a directory, Major?' Lucy asked.

'Corporal, ma'am. For whereabouts?'

'Hereabouts, I think. A *gasthaus* in Neustadt called the Aalen.'

Happy to oblige her, the soldier found the number without difficulty and called it, but Allcock took an age to be summoned. He sounded thick enough to have been well-plastered.

'Barney? It's Lucy. Listen, I've got my maniac husband back, Plan D is cancelled.'

After a long pause, Allcock croaked, 'Oh thank the Good Lord for that, miss.'

'Yes . . . Barney, I think you are not well.'

'No, miss. I keeps mistakin' litres fer pints . . . Shall I be taking Decibelle 'ome then?'

'Not yet, little job for you here, if you would. We've got a Spitfire which won't start, motor's burst, it's— ' she turned to Stuart, 'Mark what?'

'Nine. Merlin 61.'

Lucy relayed this and listened, nodding, then she turned to the groundsman. 'Where are we, Captain?'

'Corporal, Ma'am and as such I'm not at liberty to say. They just roll it up like a moveable feast. Forward tactical base, Code Wooster One, Regensburt north area, NATO Strike Command authority only.'

Lucy explained this to Allcock and added, 'Don't worry, Barney, I shall speak to this strike commander and get him to spill the beans . . . Barney, don't hold your hangover against me . . . Is he? Alright, we'll phone him now. Bye Barney.'

She turned to Stuart. 'D'you know St George's number, darling, Barney says to call him, he's frantic about something else.'

Stuart nodded and began dialling the long sequence.

'I can tell him, if you like,' Lucy said, 'But Barney said there's a spare starter in the lock-up in Melton Mowbray. He'll know how to get it.'

'OK. What's Allcock doing in Germany? And Plan D?'

'Nothing much, a private matter.' Lucy smiled ingenuously, anticipating a maze of counter-conspiracies, to even the score for her own barrage of unanswered questions.

It being still very early, St George's number rang four times only before a machine came on with the usual preamble but was then interrupted by the secretary, her voice panting.

'I'm sorry, I just got in, specially early . . . Who's calling?' She shrieked when Stuart gave his name. 'I was doing your call every day, until she found out, then I stopped. I hope it's all right?'

Stuart reassured her and then relayed Allcock's message and her voice trembled down the line. 'Oh, I shouldn't ask if you made it with the, you know . . . But you'd have said "Tally-Ho", wouldn't you?'

'Tally-Ho,' Stuart intoned looking slightly embarrassed.

'Oh, the Hon will be *thrilled* – and wait till you hear what's happened, that dreadful thing on his desk, I'd love to tell you but the Hon would kill me!'

Stuart sighed and suppressed his exasperation. 'Where is he?'

'Aber – oh, I'm not allowed to tell that either. He'll be phoning in soon, any minute.'

'All right. I'll call you back with the location. Ask him to get hold of his friend, Tuffy something, I think it was—'

'Beecham, spelt Beauchamp,' Lucy filled in, causing Stuart to glance in surprise.

'Thanks. Tuffy Beauchamp. Tell him to get over here pronto with the new starter, Allcock's here to fit it. Tell him I'll wait but not to hang around in case some Ministry high-hat gets proprietary notions. And by the way—'

'Yes?'

'Thank you, very much. From us both.' As he hung up he gave Lucy a long look with a half-smile in it but then a new sound entered the shelter, the heavy whirring of an inbound helicopter. The corporal looked darkly out of the shelter and confirmed its arrival with some importance.

Lucy nodded to him and turned back to ask gravely, 'Stuart, the Spitfire, whose is it in fact?'

'Well, it did belong to poor old Louis, squatter's rights or somesuch. He was going to give it to me and I was going to find him a pad in Paris.'

Lucy looked puzzled 'How and where are you going to keep it?'

'I'm not, Beauchamp's going to buy it, pay off my debts. I—'

'You had this planned all along, didn't you, like suicide?'

He shook his head and eased her outside. 'Not exactly.' Seeing a reaction heating up he added, 'I think I have a few questions for you as well, yes?' The glint in her eye was unmistakeable. 'My love, I thank you most sincerely for what you just did, your landing.'

Lucy bowed and chuckled. 'Wasn't very good, was it? Still, for a first time . . . They say any landing you walk away from is a good landing, but then I thought of your old friend. It's so sad, how he would have rejoiced!'

'I think he did . . . We'll bury him in Paris anyway, that's what he'd have . . . Lu, I really should stay until St George gets here, otherwise we might get pre-empted, you know? Would you mind going with Louis?'

'No, but I'm not leaving without you, it's quite clear you're—'

Stuart snaffled her words with a kiss but Lucy resisted and said,

'That won't answer all the questions, all those people looking for you.'

'Such as?'

Lucy began checking off on her fingers. 'Oh, Stayres at some Czech desk, Breakspeare at the Foreign Office, an American called Riverson . . . Let's see, Rollo Runyan, Paul Epiphany, Cornelius . . .' Lucy watched his face as she reeled off the names, unsure if she only imagined changes of expression. Stuart felt a missed beat at the mention of Cornelius but managed to cover it with a different query.

'What did Rollo want, the bastard?'

'I don't know, I've been on his boat twice and still never met him. Mama said he was really frantic, wanted the key to our house but she wouldn't let him have it. He got shirty with her so she told him about all the men waiting. He's chewing his cuticles in London somewhere.'

'Good.' Stuart found himself enjoying the prospect of a nasty, heavy showdown with his one-time friend. Rollo had started the whole chain of trouble, danger and despair. They could see a large black shape in the pale sky, growing steadily.

Lucy surprised him then, venturing with some hesitation. 'I want to apologise.'

'You? What on earth for?'

'I confess I'd begun to have my doubts about what you were up to.'

Stuart coughed, a small puff of steam in the cold air. 'How's that?'

'Well, one or two things. The pendant you gave me, I, er, had it valued.'

When Stuart showed no reaction she grinned and added, 'You remember Nadia Feodorovna?'

Stuart nodded questionably. 'Um . . . the Russian girl with Alicia, lost her baby?'

'Yes. Oh, she got it back by the way, I mean "him". But the point is, she overheard you talking to someone on the telephone, someone called Alexei. Do I take it we know the same gentleman, if that's the word?'

'Lives in Antwerp?'

Lucy puffed an exhalation. 'You admitting it is half the worry gone. I wondered if they were trying to get a hold on you, using me? They tried that with Grady, my er, my ex. They're completely unscrupulous, you know.'

'I know, yes. And not only they. It'll be all right now.'

'That's what was I wondering. Anyway, when Hegel told me you were on a real mission for Stayres, naturally I felt a lot better – ' Lucy stopped when she saw a vicious look on his face. 'What is it?'

'Who's Hegel?'

Lucy by-passed her flicker of guilt, sure that the question wasn't loaded, a conviction of her innocence surfacing in a tease. 'Oh, he's rather a knock-out. He's Stayres' man in the Geneva Embassy.'

'Oh . . . Well, I have a serious message for Mr Stayres. He should change his name and start running.'

'Why, what did he do?'

Stuart shook his head to discourage her, certain that Stayres had sent him to get killed for Procházka's defection and equally certain of his revenge. Without any physical assault, the threatened might and secrecy of the one-man watchdog section could drive that desk-bound murderer to obscurity or worse, without hope of appeal to a section that didn't actually exist, that not even the Foreign Secretary therefore could control. He dismissed Stayres abruptly from his mind.

'Did Rollo try to give any explanation for what he did?'

'No idea. What did he do?'

'Well, he ruined us, essentially. I had to hock the house to pay his bail and he jumped it. The Spitfire should pay it off, but not all the risk and missing you.'

'Stuart . . . Have I got all the logic straight? I mean, why would someone pinch my passport and papers, is that a regular trick? Were they trying to stop me getting out or did they just want the things themselves?'

Stuart didn't know the answer and wondered distantly about Maryša Kubin, who was originally planned to exit as Mrs Kody, but with her own papers. She didn't much resemble Lucy.

'What do *you* think, love?' he asked intently.

'It's, it's as if someone had something on me. My ex-father said they were sending me your effects, passports, wallet, cards and so on. I asked Giles to collect them for me. Weird, isn't it, neither of us with papers?'

A sudden thought hit Stuart like a sunburst. 'Was there anything else?'

'Well, it all rather choked me, they burnt your clothes . . . There was a present for me presumably, a cassette of Bohemian dances, it was sweet of you . . . Oh God, what's the matter?'

Stuart realised his face must have gone if not beatific, then certainly distant, a beacon announcing wild speculations.

'Who did you say was collecting them?'

'My Doctor friend and confidante, Giles. We've been in France together for three whole months.'

Stuart felt as though he'd been kicked high in the stomach. 'Three . . . Why?'

'I had to get away, I was trying to tell you, dammit. There was a South African who wanted to twist your appendages off, something to do with diamonds, then there were some other South Africans who were going to stop him. The telephone engineer says they succeeded, watched by teams of all sorts of suspicious types. Mama said papa had sent some Russians to protect me, there were Americans to protect you and I gather the British were there to see fair play. The British failed, the South Africans did something unspeakable and the

357

others went home. I just hope they haven't trodden all over my garden.'

'Lucy. This Giles chap, where is he, and where's the tape?'

Lucy struggled tiredly with this delicious misunderstanding, torn between pity for Stuart and a remnant of pity for herself for all the injustice and terror she'd suffered. She allotted the remnant a temporary victory.

'Giles and I have a rendezvous in Geneva.'

Stuart screwed his face up in perplexity and indecision, finally asking humbly, 'Lucy please go with the helicopter, we'll meet up later. Get the cassette and guard it, I was going to say with your life but it's not worth that much, anything like. Take no more risks.'

Lucy brightened quizzically. 'Oh? How much is it worth then?'

'The tape? It's beyond price, completely.' Her head bowed to the compliment but Stuart continued, 'Maybe they'll take you to Switzerland in the chopper. It's what they wanted. I must wait for St George, it's only fair. Without passports only the Military can shift us around anyway. Where can I call you later?'

'Epiphany. I'll give you his number. He'll know where we are.'

'You and this Giles?'

'That's right,' she fluttered innocently. She beckoned to the groundsman for a pencil, pulling a scrumpled piece of paper from her pocket. Further words were drowned as with a great threatening rush a big Sikorsky swung in over the trees and settled ponderously, its downdraught shaking the Spitfire and even giving the Harriers some irritation. Two men ducked and ran on a signal from the corporal, a stretcher between them on which they loaded Louis' body like front-line veterans. Lucy's scribbling took far longer than seemed necessary as the huge rotors kept the anxiety churning, but at last she folded the paper and passed it to him, kissing him quickly on the corner of his mouth and passing critical fingers across his stubble.

Stuart grinned, feeling a late-spreading, nervous triumph. 'Catch you later, kid. Utmost care, now.'

Lucy nodded and scuttled away to the waiting helicopter, clowning hands over her head and ducking almost double, the two men grinning from the hatchway. They closed it before she had time to wave and Stuart watched heart-in-throat as the huge beast gathered itself and lumbered away.

A cassette of Bohemian dances . . . This message seemed to have disappeared like a fish-bomb into the whirlpool of his thoughts, a delayed action fuse to ignite a chain of possibilities. Handled correctly it could confound everyone who'd tried to put pressure on him, thanks to Procházka for whom he had little remorse since he'd forcibly taken what Stuart had been about to offer. It had cost him a star-shaped hole in the chest and a still-tangible lump on his skull, not to mention three months total limbo while Lucy had waited, fretting – no, she'd been driven away and to what? Giles . . . what sort of a name was that anyway, he half-growled, hoping the fellow had a real gender problem before guiltily repressing the thought in respect of Lucy's friendship. He shivered against the cold wind and zipped up the anorak though it was becoming ever more alien and unpleasant. The two Harrier pilots were both huddled in their cockpits and running their auxiliary power units. He wondered if they'd been ordered away and how long his bleak vigil might last. At least he had a few interesting calls to make, the first of them to Antwerp.

The groundsman was noticeably less affable with Lucy gone, granting use of the telephone but retreating at once to his bunk, boots and greenery included.

The Russalmaz number answered with a typical gruff

359

"Allo' and there were two minutes of searching silence before Simonov's double-bass came down the line, a highly tentative enquiry.

'*Vraiment*, is that Stuart? I'm terribly sorry, I – where are you, Prague?'

'West of the line, Alexei.'

'Thank God! But listen, have you seen Ludmilla, she's on the run, I – *merde*, this line is monitored, well, too bad, you have to know about it. There's a directive out for her, full sanction, she was too clever, she ran the other way, *East*! She went to Prague to go to— '

Stuart gulped and broke in. 'Alexei – listen! I might know where to find her, what's the problem?'

'*Problem*? Just violation of international boundaries, kidnap, airspace intrusion, just unspeakable insolence to her mother country! When they catch her . . .'

Stuart caught the sarcasm in his tone, although he knew that Simonov was deadly serious about the sanction. Implicit too was that he should somehow get her away from Department V's reach which was one of the longest on the globe.

'Alexei, does she know about this?'

'Of course she does. That's why she ran – but *Prague*, why? Was she looking for you?'

'I expect so. Who told her I was there?'

'I do not know that. All I can say is there are dark forces on both sides and both sides knew, eventually, where you were yourself.'

'You did?' Stuart ladled on the sarcasm. 'Why no flowers and grapes then?'

'We were too late for that. A fraction more efficiency and they'd have had you both, on home ground too. Where are you now – and where is my daughter?'

'Alexei, don't be silly. Please listen. Yes, I was hospitalised but also got what I was sent to get. Any chance I can trade and get these sanctions lifted?'

'Hell, yes! I mean, maybe. We were already trading

with you, you may not remember with your amnesia? I'll remind you perhaps if I say your parcel of Siberian rough is now complete, all you have to do is tell us,' the voice growled, 'Tell us *convincingly*, why they haven't armed the Cruise and Pershing systems although they're deployed as planned.

'Stuart realised he had to tread very carefully. Riverson had forbidden him to reveal this reason because it was preposterous, invented by Stuart; if the KGB discovered its fiction he would lose his credibility and therefore usefulness as a misinformation conduit, not to mention his life.

Did the fact that Procházka's cassette should, if valid, prove his invention correct remove the basis of Langley's objection, and what action would the CIA. take when apprised of the truth? And who was there who could tell Stuart if his first surmise was accurate, that the Americans had merely followed suit on some prior intelligence about the less than lethal SS 20's in Eastern Europe, a fact denied by Riverson, who asserted that the Sov-bloc was armed to the crannies with fissile megadeath. A distant analogy rang a tiny bell, two small boys in a gas-filled garage – Paul Epiphany. If any one held the over-view it was surely this mysteriously influential American.

Cautiously, he ventured, 'Alexei, I have to be very careful here. I couldn't afford to give you less than the truth and for its value I also have to find out who else knows it. I told you before that it was only hearsay, surmise even, but now I have the proof. Do you have authority to deal?'

'Yes! Well . . . Look, I can get it, but only if the subject is really promising. Except for this delay you would have been in full favour as a source for what you gave us before, in fact you should have your diamonds back already, I feel very bad about it. We found the thief but the wretched man's heart gave out before he could tell us where he'd put the stash. This business with Ludmilla is horribly complicating and really you've been much too long. And it's a sanction order proper, I warn you, execute on sight – wherever! Getting it withdrawn depends on every operative calling in and getting the countermand. In the meantime she's a walking target anywhere in the world, d'you understand? If you tell me where she is, maybe we can get a quick stop flashed in there. The general one could take many days.'

'Alexei, I'm sure I could trust you on this one, but the *Vlasti*? I don't think so. If they feel affronted for whatever she's done they might just – ' Stuart left the act unspoken, 'and say sorry afterwards. What has she done, anyway?'

'Oh, nothing! Just took a light aircraft over our rabbit-proof border into West Germany, that's all!'

Stuart sweated with the phone pressed to his ear. Where were these people if they'd known already, they must have a transmission device somewhere on Lucy's person, yet only an hour ago – did they now know where to wait for the military to release her?

'Alexei, are you listening?'

Simonov's tone was now more formal and he explained the reason at once. 'Yes. Stuart Kody, this call is now patched in to Dzershinsky Square. Speak to me and allow me time to translate, all right? They understand the position so far, but not what you have to offer.'

'This is for Lucy's pardon, you confirm?'

Pause . . . 'It depends on the material.' The distant alien voice was guttural and flat. Stuart restrained useless anger and a mounting panic. 'All right. It concerns the disposition of nuclear MIRV warheads in your European tactical, er, defences, if that's the correct misnomer.'

There was another pause for rapid translation and reply. 'You have full and provable details, provable source?'

'I do.'

'Where?

'On tape.'

'With you?'

'No, with a friend.'

There was another pause but with no words relayed, just an impatient query from Moscow. When Simonov spoke again it was as though his lips were in a torturer's vice.

'Bohemian dances, Stuart?'

'Yes.'

'Blessed Boris, I had it sent with your effects!' With a great effort Simonov seemed to recover his composure. The distant query came again presumably asking for explanation. Simonov gave it and then said to Stuart, 'I told him you have the proof in a safe place. There is now granted authority for cancellation of sanction as well as the payment of our debt to you, provided that you undertake to let us have a copy.'

'Don't you want the original, no copy?'

Stuart's puzzlement grew with the length of the pause before Simonov came back. 'No, that is the point and this is where you prove your mettle. They want you to pass it on as a singular, fantastic coup. See, we allow you your triumph. The only stipulations are these, First that you do NOT inform ANYONE that you have told us about it or are sending us a copy, all right?'

'Sure.'

'Easy enough. The second is not so easy. If the story of Ludmilla's excursion over the wire is ever broadcast, the sanction will be re-imposed. All those involved must be sworn to secrecy, even the infant Feodor. Best if he is never told.'

'What – what the hell's he got to do with it?'

'Stuart – you mean you're— ' Suddenly Simonov gave a lively chuckle and said, 'If she hasn't told you, then you'll never know, will you? Heh heh, I mean, it's really serious, that embargo. She must tell no one. Especially not the Sunday papers . . . How long till you get a copy of the tape to me?'

'Oh. Obviously at least as long as it takes to lift the sanction, so all the weasels know about it. So, for how long will I have to make sure she can't be found?'

'A week, outside. I'll be able to confirm it.'

Stuart puffed in profound relief. 'OK.'

'Good. And well done, incredible.' His tone became slightly plaintive. 'When you come to collect, or exchange rather, will you bring her with you?'

Stuart felt some sympathy but had to add, 'I'm not sure, Alexei, about how she feels now, and she doesn't know anything about our dealings.'

'That's crazy. Don't you live together any more?'

'I'm not . . .' Stuart refused to be led on this point but had a sudden idea. 'Alexei, what was the jeweller's name, the one I first met?'

'Grobelaar.'

'That's it. He's keeping a blue stone for me. Ask him to set it in something nice, a dancer's headband maybe, I don't know.'

'He showed it to me. Truly it should stay in a vault forever. Priceless. I'll talk to him and his cutter, don't worry. Although his man Hector always fantasises about houris and bellybuttons.'

'Well, I'll be in touch, Alexei.'

When he rang off Stuart found himself still sweating unreasonably in the damp shelter. He rummaged for the piece of paper Lucy had given him, unfolded it and quickly reeled off the number. Behind him the groundsman began to snore under his camouflage of leaves. As the call rang out in England, Stuart glanced again at the piece of paper, seeing the additional pencil scrawl behind the last fold, Lucy's writing but barely legible. 'I want a divorce like dry 2.'

Before he could even stifle the pain and panic this caused, he heard the mid-atlantic tones of the suave voluble character he'd met just off the Concorde from Washington.

'Stuart! You missed a good party. How was the trip?'

'Mixed. Listen. Please, Lucy's going to liaise with you, perhaps after some rendezvous in Geneva. She's in big trouble with the Soviets.'

'Yeah, I know. I had—'

'You *know*? Then does Lucy know, knew all the time?'

'Well, I had it all set up to shift her but she got defiant and went looking for you instead.'

Stuart fought away his irrelevant questions and continued, 'The thing is, I've done a deal for her safety but it takes them time to get the word around. She may even be bugged as well, I don't know. I'm confused.'

'I follow. I'll have her checked over. How did you deal?'

'What? Oh, I got a lucky break in Prague.' Stuart stopped dead, remembering he wasn't supposed to tell the Americans that he'd told Moscow.

Epiphany wasn't fazed in the least. 'Fantastic! You remember what I told you, about my senator?'

'The next president? Not really. What was it?' Stuart sounded a dullard, even to himself.

'Holy catatonia, how could you forget such an offer? You get something for Langley, right? But you let us have it twenty-four hours earlier. Then everyone's happy, right?'

'Yes, I remember . . . Can you ensure Lucy's safety, Paul, I mean watertight? She went off in an army helicopter somewhere, left here about half an hour ago. She should still be in the air. I'm in Bavaria. Just make sure—'

'Don't doubt it, please. I'll know where she's landed or headed within two minutes of your hanging up.'

Stuart groaned. 'Then who the hell else will know?'

'I've got ways and means, believe me. But listen, what did you get, you going to tell me?'

Stuart's cautious confusion returned with the question, whom could he tell without telling others that he'd told? Even though this one seemed clear enough he had to ensure there'd be no bounce-back assumption.

'OK. They don't know exactly what I've got, by the way, but there is a danger they could deduce it . . . You remember your little analogy about the garage and the boys, and also the princely quality? It's almost as if you knew . . . Well, there's another lot of dud matches over there, behind the— '

'Got it! What's the percentage?'

Stuart was momentarily flummoxed by the speed of Epiphany's uptake. 'Percentage? Oh, live to dud matches? I can't tell you exactly until my data gets analysed but I believe it's less than 10 per cent.'

Epiphany's jubilation was undisguised, a long sound like 'Ha-aar! . . . You might have succeeded where Canute failed, turning the tide. Let me have the proof and you gotta new bank account. Where d'you want it?'

'Sorry, Paul, I'm not with you, I'm too worried. I want you to hire some bodyguards, dozens of them, for at least a week or more.'

'You relax, right? I'll get her a new name and she and Giles'll be off where no one even gets close. You remember my secret vice?'

'No . . . I forget some things still. I can't leave here till, well never mind.'

'All right, you sound a bit ragged. I'll just give a clue – goosefeathers! That ring a bell?'

'No, sorry. I'll ponder it.'

'OK . . . I'll be at the Georges Cinq tonight and then we'll vaporise. Giles can take care of things in the meantime, be sure.'

There was still the problem of his own location and Stuart had no wish to wake the suffering groundsman. He rummaged around and eventually found an ordnance map and on it a bright chinagraph circle ringing a bare rectangle amidst sectioned or mutilated forest. He measured off the map reference very carefully and then rang St George's office number again to pass it on. 'The Hon.' still hadn't called in and was still expected any minute.

Suddenly there was nothing left to be done so he lay on a groundsheet near the kerosene heater, his mind in too much ferment for his physical energy. He thought of a new way to 'clear the screen', staring out through imagined plexiglass into thick cloud while someone else flew on instruments. Someone skilful and utterly trustworthy, someone who never changed . . . What the hell was 'dry 2' and divorce, and she'd kissed his stubbly face so sweetly, and who was this damned fairy Giles and so why had Lucy risked her life to come looking for him? The puppy questions chased their tails for half an hour before they tangled and tripped and at last the screen turned opaque, at least his consciousness freed from conundrum.

The dreams unfolded darkly as if following Ariadne's thread through the labyrinth, the Great Bull's roaring voices synchronised down two tunnels in approaching crescendo and then silence, footsteps and finally absurdity.

'Hair? 'Chew doing down there, Kody, leaving your fahking helmet out on the old sward, um?'

The voice almost squealed with indignation and Stuart opened his eyes to see the groundsman leaning through the opening with his now-moribund foliage and the eager, chiselled querulity of St George behind him, regarding Jaroslav's leather helmet in his outstretched fingers. Stuart hadn't seen it discarded when they stretchered away Louis' body under a black cover.

'Gawd, you look all-in,' St George added, 'But I should say, well done and all that. Anyone take a pot at you or was it, you know?'

Stuart grimaced. 'A piece of— '

367

'Quite. Well, that's what I expected frankly. Take 'em by surprise. Prob'ly never glimpsed you with that paint job. Terrible neglect. Allcock says it's OK otherwise, had to prop the seat up, mind, and some of the wires've gone floppy. Tuffy says he's seen worse, mind you, quite happy to take her home like that, mad buggah, I wouldn't, that's why I've got Allcock for life, ferreting through every tube. Such a comfort to have someone to blame when you get killed, don't you think, um? Can we talk alone, Corporal?'

The groundsman nodded just as the telephone rang and he crossed the room to answer it, listened and cupped the mouthpiece.

'Sir, there's a General Perlmutter who wishes to know how, in the name of sanctified er, copulation, if you get my meaning, sir, you found this airfield and who in the copulating inferno gave you permission to land here. He sounds American, sir.'

'I see,' St George said with some menace, his nose quivering at the affront. 'Kindly inform this General Perlmother that I have an uncle in the Confederate Air Force!'

The groundsman relayed cautiously, listened with some exaggerated flinching and hung up almost respectfully.

'The General opines that you should depart forthwith, sirs, and that you should be copulating somewhat strenuously while you are so engaged.'

''Straordinary fellow,' St George muttered, 'Now, be a good chap, um?'

The corporal ducked out of the OP and Stuart sat up fully, rubbing his eyes with bemusement. With St George's arrival he realised he must have slept a good six hours and pointed to his wrist with a query. St George obliged impatiently.

'2.45 p.m. I must say congrats again, Stuart. Now listen a minute, this is rather important. You awake?'

'Sort of.'

'*Coco-de-mer*. You had two, right?'

'What? No, three. We got one on our first trip a year ago.'

'I mean this time, two. Listen, if I suggested you'd given me the wrong one, would you know what I was driving at, hey?'

A second charge went off in the whirlpool as Stuart cast his mind back over this nearly-forgotten peculiarity, the second Praslin nut. Lucy carrying it on board in Mahé, so familiar in the hand that they didn't put it on the X-ray conveyor but – did they in Nairobi, he remembered the laughter over something? The guess mounted to a certainty as he looked at St George's eager face; Rollo's presence in Mahé, Rollo trying to find him, wanting the keys to their house – for sure Rollo had used them as mules to carry his contraband, all unknowing. The *coco-de-mer* has a concealed and very private entrance more or less where one might expect to find it, and still would not without foreknowledge. For a few seconds, even Cornelius had possessed it in his grip in a Heathrow carpark, but had he really known?

'Opened it up, did you, or just shook it?' Stuart asked mildly.

St George contrived to look guilty and eager at the same time. 'I was going to sort of cut out two of the arse-cheeks and turn it into something useful, like a fruitbowl. Which I started to do. I mean, I didn't think you'd mind, and it was taunting me dreadfully.'

Stuart feigned reproof and said, 'I'll avoid any freudian deductions, St G. At least the contents were in safe hands *pro-tem*. Unfortunately they aren't all ours but I'm sure I can negotiate a nice finder's-keeper's fee.'

'Splendid. 10 per cent?'

Two hundred thousand . . . Figures were suddenly irrelevant forever, dissolving into fragments of meaningless relativity.

'Done,' he said blithely, knowing he could command anything from Rollo at this stage.

'Splendid,' St George said again with finality, opening his hand. In his palm nestled a small pile of pale uncut pebbles which moved silkily as he made small waves with his fingers. His horsey smile overflowed with beatific mischief. 'Ten by weight, honest injun. Now, shall we go and see how Allcock's getting on? Tuffy was trying to talk himself into a spin in a single-seat Harrier but I don't think they'll let him, somehow. Rather fun, though, um? Sort of stop in mid-air and rush backwards as if you'd forgotten your hat. Reminds me, you want this?'

Stuart nodded and took the old leather helmet, such a strange item of gear and so evocative of perilous times.

'Listen,' St George said as they emerged from the trees, 'I sort of let Tuffy know you were only selling because you were a bit short of readies. He said fine, he'll buy it but he'll let you have a go whenever you like. Man of his word, too. Dogfights!' The equine teeth gleamed in the dappled winter light then St George sniffed the air again like pointer.

'Snow's a possibility. Allcock says he should be ready in half an hour and I brought some extra jump leads just in case. Handle well, does she?'

With nothing in his experience for fair comparison Stuart could only smile. 'Like a dream,' he said.

'Splendid. Soon as they've gorn we'll get off ourselves. Where did you want to gair, find the Missus?'

'Damn. I won't know till tonight. Epiphany's going to be in Paris. You met him?'

'Rather. Gave a splendid thrash. My Godfathers, you should have seen your Lucy dancing with old Giles, sublime, absolute organ-stopper. So to speak.'

Stuart seethed suddenly and resolved that the next person to mention Lucy and this Giles in the same breath would eat some teeth. With bitter distaste he refrained from comment and they came into the open and saw

370

Allcock with the Spitfire's cowling open, a high close van next to it; St George's Seneca stood beyond and then the two Harriers, still squatting in a deceptively normal tableau.

Stuart felt some diffidence as a kind of outsider, having met neither Allcock nor Beauchamp before. Allcock nodded briefly and held up oily palms but his appraisal of Stuart was strangely penetrating. The lanky Beauchamp who'd been peering over his shoulder did shake hands but both their concentration was entirely on the relic. Beauchamp muttered a haughty 'jolly good' with perhaps envious reluctance, and Stuart thought of the silent indispensables, the fitters who had to receive aircraft battered and sieved from a mission, groaning at the damage done to their charge by some irresponsible and over-privileged twit.

To St George Stuart remarked, 'Lucy didn't say why your Mr Allcock was already in Germany. What's in the big van?'

'Didn't say?' St George repeated in some surprise. 'Oh. Ahem. Better let her tell you herself. In the van? Oh, tools I expect, spares. You know what these chaps are like, damn jackdaws, doesn't do to enquire too closely. Getting on a bit, Tuffs,' he raised his voice and looked at his watch pointedly. Allcock gave him a swift look of practised disdain and a tolerance of pomposity which were becoming jointly extinct even though the Allcocks might deny thriving on it. The old cockney wiped his hands thoroughly, picked up a long, silvery torque wrench like a hallowed sceptre, rechecked the setting and ritually clicked off on several hidden studs. He closed the cowling and ended the ceremony with a brief nod, surly, dependable and fully practised in the art of disguising inner joy.

Stuart brimmed with nervous pride for himself as well as Louis when Beauchamp strapped in nonchalantly and went through the remaining rituals. As the Merlin fired readily to a joint thumbs-up and Contact!, the two escorts' turbines began to wind up in unison, all three rigorously checking their control surfaces prior to line-up.

'Be seeing you back in blighty, Guv'nor,' Allcock shouted, touching his cap to St George and stowing his tools in the front of the truck. Stuart noticed he didn't go near the big rear doors but simply got in and drove away. He stopped before the exit track, however, watching in his side-mirror as the old Spitfire took cleanly to the air, its wheels folding hesitant and separately.

Stuart tried the Georges Cinq once before they left but Epiphany hadn't yet checked in. He thanked the groundsman and asked if there was anything he could send him but the reply lacked both subtlety and likelihood. They took off themselves and flew just North of West, settling down nearly three hours later at Chalons-sur-Marne, St George explaining that he liked the smaller places, they were more '*sympa*' and the landing fees sometimes negotiable. The fact that it was deep in champagne country and everyone there seemed to know him he treated as perfectly normal and when the pair of them were driven off in the late dusk to a crumbling chateau by an unpronounceable count with a burst of straggly white hair, Stuart's impatience to call Epiphany and rejoin Lucy was stretched unbearably.

The count had prepared them to meet his new lady Marie-Celestine, who did not disappoint them. A demure enchantress of twenty-two, otter-sleek with a high black pony-tail, she must surely have gained her English accent from caricature. In dark princely surroundings and served by the most ancient of retainers, Stuart had to endure several early toasts of a marque of champagne aloof to hangover. Only then was it revealed that the telephone had not 'marched' for several weeks and that Count Arnaud de – would drive him to the village after dinner. Under other circumstances the visit would have been enchanting but at least St George helped with explanations. Lucy's presence was demanded for another occasion and he was shown to a huge high room with a creaking four-poster which would have wound her up impossibly, the thought accenting his longing. As a gentle pointer to his scruffiness, Marie-Celestine brought him two new razors and apologised that they had no clothes to fit him.

When he finally got through to Paris from the village kiosk, Epiphany reported that Lucy was safely asleep in her room with three private detectives outside as well as Giles within. It was all he could do to refrain from the Giles question, even though Epiphany invited him to join them. St George had to point out, as gently as he could, that the Paris airports would be closed for the sleeping hours and that anyway both he and Stuart were in no condition for precise piloting, night-time or otherwise.

Only partly reassured Stuart woke in the early dawn full of torments and guilt. It took a tortuous hour to rouse St George and then the old butler who drove them shakily back to the airfield in a soft drizzle. St George was furious at having to climb the fence and risk his aging bespoke trousers even when Stuart reminded him gruffly of what was in the pocket and how many pairs those diamonds represented.

From the payphone outside the club-house Stuart called Paris again and got Epiphany immediately, his voice tight with urgency.

'We're just leaving! Helluva fight, one of the guards taken out. Can you get to Roissy before eight? . . . How are you coming? . . . Right, I'll get you a clearance, what's the call-sign?'

Stuart barked out the Seneca's lettering and ran to the aircraft where St George was performing laboured checks.

'How long to Roissy, St G, flat out?'

St George's expression left no doubt of his distaste for hurry. 'Ao . . . under the hour. Look, must you pant?'

Stuart grinned as far as he could and nodded. St George gave a great sigh and began to hurry; Stuart felt a huge affection for him and surprise that for all his foibles he was not in the least an irritating person. This opinion received a temporary set-back when Stuart began a question casually.

'St G., this Giles person with Lucy, do you – '

'Ah me! Unrequited again, my life is ever so. I believe I am blinded with romance, can you imagine, seeing the two of them together?' He shook his head and let go a long heaving sigh like an over-fed mare, adding nothing.

Stuart followed him into the cockpit and felt like chewing rawhide; the question clearly wasn't worth raising again, there'd just have to be a show-down for which he felt ill-dressed, unprepared, untanned and three months overdue.

Once established at cruising height, St George changed to the Roissy approach frequency but with a diffident shrug.

'One can but try,' he said, 'But getting a slow-bird in among the breakfast trans-Atlantics – and you know how snotty these Frogs get at any reg. not starting with an F, practically blow garlic raspberries through the VHF.'

He listened carefully for a pause and relayed his call-sign. Instead of having it repeated back with a disdainful question the controller was heard snapping crisply.

'Foxtrot Lima squawk 6212, you are cleared straight in finals Runway Two-eight, two wide-bodies ahead, we keep you clear of turbul-once.' St George's expression was ripe for a cartoon, every facial muscle combining for maximum astonishment.

Even as they landed the taxiing instructions were precise and eager, positioning them behind a speeding Follow-me truck straight to the Air France terminal. Three 747s waited like great cruise liners, dwarfing the pencil thin runabout with delta wings which yet focussed most of the ground activity. A marshall clearly signalled No-Stop for the engines as St George braked, pointed to a beckoning figure and unlatched the door behind Stuart's head.

''Swhat you call "pull", eh? Off you go, good luck. Give 'em both one from me.'

With a grateful nod, Stuart scrambled out into the slipstream and dashed for the building. The waiting figure was listening to his personal radio and shaking his head despairingly. He held a door open and shrieked '*Allez vite, vite!*' in Stuart's ear in passing, the dispairing cry of a gentle soul forced to care about others' manic scurryings. He even took out a whistle and cleared their way through the press of travellers on the next level. He lead at a sprint into the Concorde lounge and cast about him in despair to find it deserted. Beckoning in a final burst, the man led through a far door and clattered down the ramp, skidding up against shiny white paintwork. Stuart had time to puff the briefest thanks and glance at the face as he ducked through the door. It closed behind him at once and the floor shifted simultaneously as the push-truck engaged. Two svelte flight attendants eyed his dishevelment with professional tolerance carried no further than the subsidy demands.

As he stood gathering breath he was spot-lit by many expensive faces gratefully hostile to sight the disorganised and ill-dressed cause of their delay. He saw Epiphany first because he was half-standing, passing something to a strikingly lovely woman sitting next to him, her auburn hair tied severely back into a Grecian twist. Only as he sat did Stuart catch sight of Lucy in the seat behind, looking straight at him, grave and expressionless.

Stuart stopped where he was, his chest heaving and watching her from a distance of about ten feet, searching her face for some sign, something indefinable. When it came he couldn't have described it for there was no apparent change, simply somewhere behind the mask a thought or an emotion triggered an imperceptible difference, perhaps the merest softening of her left eyebrow line.

Jealousy and unreason evaporated and a terrified delight flooded through him, although to Lucy it looked pitiably like desperation or anguish. In response her eyes glowed with her feelings and then with the humour she was hiding; she patted the empty seat beside her with the no-nonsense gesture of a schoolmistress, glancing around as if to claim some aloofness. Hesitantly Stuart approached with dozens of eyes following in curiosity or annoyance.

Aware of them, Lucy stage-whispered typically. 'Do sit down at once and stop drawing attention to yourself. Look at you! This plane is full of frightfully smart people, ze peeck of ze chic.'

The announcements began in French as soon as the push-truck disconnected and the Concorde began to taxi forward under its own subdued power. Lucy looked rested and a picture of groomed perfection. She wore a mother-of-pearl blouse with a deep neck over a white silk skirt, and her hair shone, swirling its reminders of summer. He didn't see Epiphany's hand held out to him and then quickly withdrawn; so as not to fall on her like a starving orang-utang he sat down and stared ahead stiffly without touching her, gathering his breath.

'What's DRY 2?' he asked eventually.

'I've no idea, why? Is it code?'

'Lucy, you *wrote* it. I want a divorce –'

Her mouth opened in silent surprise. 'Oh . . . Oh, Stuart. It was *Day* 2. The day after we got married, remember? I said I wanted a divorce, I was so happy to be with you. In the note I was just saying it again. And my teasing, how cruel!' She pointed to the seat in front of her at the auburn hair.

'That's Giles, my chum. She's a shrink-doctor, she's

376

with that Epiphany rogue whose party you missed.'

Giles turned and gave him a worried smile while Stuart sent his thoughts back shakily to Day 2 and its aura of delirium, Lucy declaring that without the certificate every moment together was an affirmation of willingness, a sigh of contentment. And in the Muslim manner he'd pronounced 'I divorce thee', three times and she had snuggled closer with each in joyous defiance.

He was given only a moment to recall before she brought him back to their predicament. She said quietly, 'Paul had the aircraft passenger list checked out, that is everyone who signed on after us. He says you did some sort of deal for me, is that right?'

'Yes. What happened in the hotel?'

'I think they tried a full frontal, there were shots and one of the guards was wounded. They got away. Did you speak to the twerp in Antwerp?'

'Yes, he sends his love, naturally. However, your crimes against the motherland have to remain secret for ever. Even, he said, from little Feodor.'

'What? That's crazy.'

'Even from me,' Stuart added heavily. 'I have no idea what Feodor has to do with it – yet.'

She looked at him in slow disbelief, her broadening smile uncertain. 'Even from you? For life? That's ridiculous, impossible. How – ?'

'They really mean it, Lu. You must have cocked an over-heavy snook, whatever it was. And I'm not even sure I want to know, not now. The question of flying, for instance . . .'

Lucy put in with a quick, smug smile. 'Don't be silly. You didn't answer that when I asked you the same.'

She waited for him to shrug resignedly before she asked, 'Paul said it was OK to copy the tape, is that right?'

'Yes . . . So you got it.'

Lucy nodded blandly and said, 'Good, 'cos we already did. The original's here, with your passport. Paul put something in an envelope for you, he wouldn't say what it was. Here.' She slipped it out of her purse and gave it to him. It was sealed and Stuart merely flipped it, handing it back casually.

'Aren't you going to open it?'

'No.'

'Why – do you know what's in it?'

'Might be a cheque for a million dollars.'

'Oh, do stop it!' she smiled happily, 'If only . . . Is Tuffy really going to pay for the plane?'

'Sure.' Stuart patted an inside pocket where Beauchamp's cheque resided. St George had been so casual he'd almost forgotten to pass it on, and Stuart felt insanely blasé with abundance. His head swam with impossible calculations, perhaps £250,000 sterling for the Spitfire, less St George's 10 per cent, $1 million from Epiphany's senator, did Epiphany deduct 10 per cent? Then there was $2 million for Rollo's diamonds finally delivered via *coco-de-mer*, less 10 per cent finder's fee, a similar amount fo Simonov's Siberians, (less 10 per cent for Simonov?) and finally $600,000 for his aerial salvage claim which Washington would have to honour in exchange for the tape. The low-budget British had provided merely travel expenses for a one-way delivery and a cheap Procházka so they got nothing for nothing. He felt sickened by the merchants of intelligence and would happily have abandoned any deal with Langley except that they'd be sure to pursue him endlessly.

At the thought of the Czech's demise he felt the hairs rippling in the back of his scalp as another unproveable occurred to him: Had Procházka been a Soviet plant all along, prepared even in league with Stayres' department? If so, then Downing Street had been irresponsible in not actually founding the special watchdog section. And Procházka may have turned genuine defector under the compulsion of love, that most frequent upsetter of life's applecarts.

Wrestling himself back to actualities, he wondered how to begin passing it on to Lucy. He supposed she'd enjoy it most in measured doses but even as he tried to anticipate a schedule, Rollo's grinning face appeared in warning, 'Don't tell her a scrap, sport, it'll change everything, you mark me!' And besides, she had something to keep from him as a permanence, at least until old age.

'Am I allowed to ask how much Tuffy agreed on?' Lucy asked sweetly.

Stuart coughed with some embarrassment since he hadn't actually looked yet and didn't expect her to believe it. He favoured her with a wide, exaggerated smile. 'I'm going to get 20 per cent for you, for saving the day. That seems to be the going rate for aerial salvage.'

Lucy mouthed a huge delighted O. Clasping her hands with delirious relish. 'Oh *please*, don't tell me how much!' she begged, as plans made kaleidoscopic projections inside her head. 'But I do owe Giles and Paul a small fortune, and we'll have to get you something to wear. You'll need some equipment as well, I hope this'll cover it.'

She put the envelope away and lifted out her pendant, turning away for him to fasten the clasp behind her. His hands shook surprisingly and Lucy turned with an anxious look.

'Emotion or palsy?' she asked, touching his cheek.

'I can't tell any more. Where are going, anyway?'

Lucy fastened the clasp herself and looked at him smokily. 'New York first to see a friend of Paul's, very important, I hear, then you're wanted in Washington D.C., then we're all going up to the Bugga – sorry, Gomorrah-boos, where we shall hound the powder, or fly on goosefeathers, apparently.'

Stuart snorted, 'Don't be daft, it takes years to be – '

Lucy waved airily at his objection. 'Don't give me that stuff, it looks easy to me. I saw a video, and you can bone me up on the basics. Are you fit?' She prodded his thigh approvingly and growled. 'I hear everyone sleeps in the same big room and it's amazing what you can achieve if people leave you alone. Mind, it's also a bit annoying what you can't.' Her expression turned arch. 'Paul was briefing us on Concorde etiquette and he says he has it on test-pilot's authority that no one has yet joined the 11-Mile High Club, since the Concorde loos are much to small for such a clubhouse.' She paused, her eyes in a teasing smoulder. 'Unless one of you happens to be a contortionist. He says the Captain will give us a certificate.'

In self defence Stuart kept silent and held her strong slim hands, watching her eyes and feeling himself begin to drown all the same. He realised it was own attempt at self-control which was producing his trembles since fatigue and tension seemed to have fallen away. He made sure to be as light as a mantis when he took her head between his hands. Lucy lifted her pendant to his lips and their eyes quested each other in profoundest intimacy.

On dancing tails of afterburner fire, the eerie-flighted delta reared up from the tarmac and gravelled its majestic climb towards the West. Lucy watched from her tiny window until low cloud obscured the view; she let out a breath and then asked a question.

'Any chance of resuming a normal life now, do you think? There's my poor garden, all my clients, *and* my new business, all gone to ruin because of you. You haven't even said what you were doing all that time anyway?'

'Nothing much,' Stuart said, suddenly realising the truth of this remark. 'In bed, mostly. It was pretty boring. I hardly remember.'

Lucy returned an exaggerated snort. 'Is that all? St

George told me about this fellow who used to go home and tell his wife the absolute truth, a real blow-by-blow of all his infidelities, in such disgusting and squalid detail that she never believed a word of it.'

Stuart chuckled. 'All right. Details later.'

'I don't want to know, thank you. I wanted to go second class but Paul wouldn't hear of it, says we've to change price brackets. Ugh . . . Look around you, on this plane everyone's First-Plus, we had bubbly even in the lounge. I was thinking if we sold this,' she held up her pendant again, 'you could resign, settle in, sort of.'

Stuart said cautiously, 'I hear there's a bit of a problem about resigning. I think Mossad are the only ones who allow their people to actually resign.'

'You just split an infinitive, you should say "actually to".'

'Thanks. It was a sweet offer but I was going to get you another one anyway.' Although the blue stone had been earmarked for Rollo, Stuart had no reservations left about costing his troubles, in spite of the sneaky loading of the *coco-de-mer*.

'*What*?' she exclaimed, reminding him that extravagance could distress her. 'The same?'

'Well, same stuff, different colour. Blue. Blue for a boy.'

Lucy's mind refused any more surprises. 'That's nice,' she answered demurely.

The stewardess approached with a 1970 vintage Heidsiek, carefully remembering her charges' names. 'M'sieu' Epiphany-e, Mam'zelle Rhine-tray . . . M'sieu' Koddy-e, et . . . Madame Procházka!'

Stuart spilled from his glass in a cascade of alarm and embarrassment, yet another cause for the stewardess to tolerate him. He could hardly stand the wait as she mopped at his scruffy jeans, his mind clamouring.

'Where did you get that name?' he gasped eventually.

'What's the matter? I am Maryša Procházka, it's

Czech,' Lucy answered glibly. 'It'll really fool them, Paul says, Paul got it for me, he's got a contact in the Foreign Office, I think – among other places. Terrifically quick and helpful, used my own photo and everything. Hey, I wonder who's got mine, she might be in a spot of bother.'

Stuart nodded, his chest constricting. 'Yes,' he agreed, heavily. 'She just might.'

THE END

DANCE FOR A DIAMOND
by Christopher Murphy

Stuart Kody agrees to help out a friend – if only as a means of getting some of his own money back. But when he discovers that the 'favour' involves removing a large number of diamonds from South Africa without observing the normal courtesies of informing the police, customs authorities or the Diamond Commission, he begins to think he may have made a mistake. After all, it's all very well to irritate the authorities, but it's not such a good idea to cross swords with the world's richest monopoly.

Stuart finds himself pursued across the red-dirt roads of Africa and into the jetstream above America by a ruthless opposition. And when the grimy fingers of competing espionage teams seem to be pulling all the strings, the pursuit accelerates to an electrifying degree . . .

For sheer excitement of pace and authentic background, Christopher Murphy emerges as an author to rival Bagley and MacLean at their best. Watch out for more novels of adventure from this inventive new writer.

'Another winner . . . a book with authentic background to help bind together an ingenious ploy'
Financial Times

0552 13047 8

A SELECTED LIST OF FINE NOVELS
AVAILABLE FROM CORGI BOOKS.

THE PRICES SHOWN BELOW WERE CORRECT AT THE TIME OF GOING TO PRESS.
HOWEVER TRANSWORLD PUBLISHERS RESERVE THE RIGHT TO SHOW NEW
RETAIL PRICES ON COVERS WHICH MAY DIFFER FROM THOSE PREVIOUSLY
ADVERTISED IN THE TEXT OR ELSEWHERE.

☐ 12504 0	THE SMOKE		Tom Barling	£3.99
☐ 13253 5	SMOKE DRAGON		Tom Barling	£3.99
☐ 12639 X	ONE POLICE PLAZA		William J.Caunitz	£2.50
☐ 13081 8	CROWS' PARLIAMENT		Jack Curtis	£2.95
☐ 12550 4	LIE DOWN WITH LIONS		Ken Follett	£3.50
☐ 12610 1	ON WINGS OF EAGLES		Ken Follett	£3.50
☐ 12180 0	THE MAN FROM ST PETERSBURG		Ken Follett	£2.95
☐ 11810 9	THE KEY TO REBECCA		Ken Follett	£2.99
☐ 09121 9	THE DAY OF THE JACKAL		Fredrick Forsyth	£2.95
☐ 11500 2	THE DEVIL'S ALTERNATIVE		Fredrick Forsyth	£3.50
☐ 10050 1	THE DOGS OF WAR		Fredrick Forsyth	£3.50
☐ 12569 5	THE FOURTH PROTOCOL		Fredrick Forsyth	£3.95
☐ 12140 1	NO COMEBACKS		Fredrick Forsyth	£2.99
☐ 09436 6	THE ODESSA FILE		Fredrick Forsyth	£2.99
☐ 10244 X	THE SHEPHERD		Fredrick Forsyth	£2.50
☐ 13047 8	DANCE FOR A DIAMOND		Christopher Murphy	£3.50
☐ 13269 1	OPERATION FAUST		Fridrikh Neznansky	£2.99
☐ 12307 2	RED SQUARE	Fridrikh Neznansky & Edward Topol	£2.50
☐ 12541 5	DAI-SHO		Marc Olden	£2.99
☐ 12662 4	GAIJIN		Marc Olden	£2.95
☐ 12357 9	GIRI		Marc Olden	£2.99
☐ 12800 7	ONI		Marc Olden	£2.99

All Corgi/Bantam Books are available at your bookshop or newsagent, or can be ordered from the
following address:

Corgi/Bantam Books,
Cash Sales Department,
P.O. Box 11, Falmouth, Cornwall TR10 9EN

Please send a cheque or postal order (no currency) and allow 60p for postage and packing for the
first book plus 25p for the second book and 15p for each additional book ordered up to a maximum
charge of £1.90 in UK.

B.F.P.O customers please allow 60p for the first book, 25p for the second book plus 15p per copy
for the next 7 books, thereafter 9p per book.

Overseas customers, including Eire, please allow £1.25 for postage and packing for the first book,
75p for the second book, and 28p for each subsequent title ordered.